20172852R

20172852R

D1428548

ime

... Dublin with her

Love Comes Tumbling

DENISE DEEGAN

PENGUIN
IRELAND

PENGUIN IRELAND

Published by the Penguin Group
Penguin Ireland, 25 St Stephen's Green, Dublin 2, Ireland
(a division of Penguin Books Ltd)
Penguin Books Ltd, 80 Strand, London WC2R ORL, England
Penguin Group (USA) Inc., 375 Hudson Street, New York, New York 10014, USA
Penguin Group (Australia), 250 Camberwell Road,
Camberwell, Victoria 3124, Australia (a division of Pearson Australia Group Pty Ltd)
Penguin Group (Canada), 90 Eglinton Avenue East, Suite 700, Toronto, Ontario, Canada M4P 2Y3
(a division of Pearson Penguin Canada Inc.)
Penguin Books India Pvt Ltd, 11 Community Centre,
Panchsheel Park, New Delhi – 110 017, India
Penguin Group (NZ), cnr Airborne and Rosedale Roads, Albany,
Auckland 1310, New Zealand (a division of Pearson New Zealand Ltd)
Penguin Books (South Africa) (Pty) Ltd, 24 Sturdee Avenue,
Rosebank, Johannesburg 2196, South Africa

Penguin Books Ltd, Registered Offices: 80 Strand, London WC2R ORL, England

www.penguin.com

First published 2006
2

Copyright © Denise Deegan, 2006

The moral right of the author has been asserted

Set in 12/14.75 pt Monotype Dante
Typeset by Rowland Phototypesetting Ltd, Bury St Edmunds, Suffolk
Printed in Great Britain by Clays Ltd, St Ives plc

A CIP catalogue record for this book is available from the British Library

ISBN-13 978-1-844-88094-X
ISBN-10 1-844-88094-X

To Jan and Zoë, with love

I

A bird has just flown into my car – a moving car, a moving bird, heading in different directions yet somehow magically intersecting. I thought, at first, that it had simply flown close to my open window, passing by on its way somewhere else, but a manic flapping behind my head has made me realize otherwise.

'It's a blackbird,' says Fint, beside me.

'I don't care what it is, just get rid of it.' If he hadn't been smoking, we wouldn't be in this mess. I put on my hazard lights and swerve my VW Beetle on to the hard shoulder. We hop out, Fint leaving his door wide open. It's the first time I've regretted driving a two-door. Fint runs to the back and bangs at the window. The bird flies up front, and out. In a blur, it's free.

'Now that's what I call spooky,' he says.

'I know. *Weird*.'

We stand looking at each other.

'An omen,' says Fint, eyes wide in an effort to look menacing.

I laugh. Fint is about as menacing as a sandwich.

We get back in. He looks over his seat. 'By the way, he shat on your upholstery.'

'Thanks, Fint.'

He smiles, pulls out his laptop and opens it up. I start the engine. We're off again. And late. I'm keeping just under the speed limit in the fast lane, when I realize we have company. At my bumper is a black Mercedes Sports Convertible. I'm wondering what kind of idiot drives with his top down on a bleak March day in Dublin when said idiot swerves to overtake me on the inside. *He didn't even give me time to pull in.*

'Unbelievable,' I say.

'What?' asks Fint, looking up from the laptop.

'People like that cause accidents.'

'People like what?'

I nod at the culprit up ahead. 'That guy just passed on the inside.'

'Oh,' he says, and goes back to work.

'Is that it? "Oh!" Fintan, he could *kill* someone the way he's driving.'

Fint's head turns slowly in my direction, his eyes suddenly knowing.

'Stop looking at me like that,' I snap.

'Like what?'

'Like you know what's going on in my head. Like you think I'm overreacting because of what happened to Brendan. Like you *pity* me.'

He looks like he's thinking before speaking. 'I don't pity you, Lucy. I just feel that you shouldn't let every careless driver you see remind you of what happened. It's been eighteen months.' He pauses. Then slowly says, 'Maybe it's time to let Brendan go.'

My head swivels in his direction. 'Brendan was my *life*, my future –'

'You still have a future, Lucy. Just a different one.'

'I don't want a different one. We'd be married. I might even be pregnant . . .' I feel tears on the way.

'Lucy, stop.'

'Did a dangerous driver cheat you out of your future?'

He looks guilty.

'Well, then, you don't know what you're talking about.'

2

He sighs and looks out his window. 'You're right, I don't. I'm sorry.'

'He'd have been thirty today, Fint. Thirty.' Fint reaches across and puts a hand on my shoulder.

We drive in silence for a while, then pull up at lights. I glance to my left.

'Ha! Didn't get far, did he, for all his rushing?'

Fint looks across at him.

'Roll down the window,' I say.

'What? Why?'

'Someone should tell people like him –'

'Lucy, you are not a vigilante. You don't know him. This is how road-rage incidents start.'

I roll it down myself. Stretch over. 'Excuse me?' I call.

He glances over. Good-looking guy, around the forty mark. Tight hair cut, almost shaven. Dark eyes. Black cashmere sweater with soft collar. He turns down his radio.

'Are you planning on *killing* someone today?' I ask.

His eyes widen. I prepare for anger. He studies me a moment, then smiles. 'It wasn't on my agenda, no.' He pauses, then adds, 'Wine gum?'

'I'm *sorry*?'

He holds out a packet of sweets.

I shake an irritated head. 'I suppose it never *occurred* to you that driving like that could cause an accident?'

His smile only widens. 'I'm touched by your concern,' he says, his tone flirtatious. Which makes me angrier than ever.

'Yes, well, if you continue to drive like that, you'll be touched by something with a lot more impact.'

'*Lucy,*' says Fint under his breath.

'Anyone ever tell you, you look lovely when you're angry?' he calls across.

'That old chestnut!' I roll up the window and glance straight ahead. 'Gobshite,' I mutter.

'*Cute* gobshite,' corrects Fint.

'Fintan, do you have to look on *every* man as a potential conquest?'

'*Potential* conquest. My dear, you underestimate me.'

I shake my head. The lights go green, and we move off. The Merc stays level with us, like a shadow. 'Oh, *great*,' I groan. 'Now, look what I've started. Shouldn't have opened my bloody mouth.'

Fint looks across at him. 'Oh, I wouldn't say that,' he says. 'This is just beginning to get interesting.'

Deciding to lose him, I speed up.

So does he.

'Jesus, what are you doing?' Fint's pinned to the back of his seat.

The Merc catches us but has to slow again behind a tangerine Nissan Micra doing, I don't know, thirty?

I slap the steering wheel. 'Ha! We got him!'

'Lucy, what's got into you?'

'Nothing.' My voice is light, innocent. I check the rear-view mirror. He's passed the Micra and is behind us again. He whips into the inside lane. I accelerate. As does he. When we're neck and neck, I peer across. He's like an ad for tooth whitener. I raise an eyebrow, turn back to the road.

'You're taking on a Mercedes. D'you think that's wise?'

Almost by way of an answer, it eases ahead of us, heading for the horizon.

'Show off,' I say.

We round a bend. There he is, up ahead, stuck behind a slow car in the fast lane. There is a line of traffic inside him, so no lane-hopping this time. I join the end of the line. And look dead ahead as we overtake him.

'You absolute hypocrite!' says Fint. 'Overtaking on the inside.'

That wakes me up. I slow down, wonder at myself.

Fint looks across at me. 'What was that about?'

I've no idea.

'That was *so* not like you, babe . . .'

What was I doing? I just told the guy he was driving dangerously, only to race him and do the same myself. How could I do that – forget Brendan and how he died? Disloyal. Stupid. I indicate and turn off for the industrial estate where the client we are on our way to see is based. Within minutes we pull up outside the offices of Copperplate Press, one of Ireland's leading publishers, located way out here on the fringes of Dublin city, because they are also, unfortunately, a book distributor and require enormous premises. One meeting takes up a half-day, by the time you've got there and back. Still, I shouldn't complain. They're not a bad crowd, dynamic by industry standards, with good titles. And I love the work we do for them: designing their book jackets and promotional material.

Fint and I run a graphic design firm, Get Smart Designs, named after the comic secret agent Maxwell Smart of 1970s fame, whom Fint has always resembled, even as a boy. It was my father who drew attention to the likeness, the show being before our time. When we checked it out on the Internet, the similarity was uncanny. And hilarious. We're both twenty-nine and have been in business together for five years, having first cut our teeth with some of the bigger firms. Eventually we teamed up to do it our way. Things have gone well. A staff of six, besides ourselves, might sound small but is pretty respectable as design houses go. I'm the creative one, Fint the business brain.

We met at art college. Though I was doing Fine Art and he

5

Graphics, we shared one important thing: college was the first place either of us had fitted in – Fint because his sexuality had always made him feel different, me because I consistently fell short of my mother's expectations. We became inseparable and have stayed that way. Fint seeks my advice on his (complicated) relationships and I try to avoid his interference in mine – at the moment, that involves convincing him that I don't want another. Currently, Fint is seeing a dentist he met on an Internet dating site called Gaydar.

He leans forward in his seat now. 'Isn't that . . . ?'

There is a black Mercedes Sports Convertible parked at the front door, its hood coming up. It's him.

'Don't look over,' I say, pulling up the handbrake. 'Wait till he goes in.'

Fint jumps out. Legs it over to the car. The driver emerges. He's tallish, though I've never been great on height. Fit. I'm surprised to see denims and wonder what he's doing here. He and Fint talk for a minute or two, then look in my direction. They begin to walk towards me. Before I can decide on the best course of action, they're on the path in front of my car. Fint's new friend stoops suddenly to peer through my windscreen. I pretend I've dropped something.

'Michael Schumacher not coming out?' he calls to Fint.

'I think she's shy,' offers my business partner. Helpful as ever.

Right. That's it. I step out, chin high. 'Ready, Fintan? Or are you just going to stand around *chatting* all day?'

'Oooh.'

I walk through them, heading for the door.

'Hello,' he says with that smile.

I nod, keep going.

He runs ahead of me. Holds the door. Joins us in the lobby.

'*Exhilarating*,' he says.

'Sorry?'

'The race. Exhilarating!'

I raise an eyebrow. 'I'd have described it as dangerous.'

He doesn't blink. 'So why did you do it, then? If it was so *dangerous*?'

He's got me there.

Fint heads for reception, leaving me alone with him.

'Better tell them you're here,' I say, nodding to the desk, arms folded.

'Time enough,' he replies, not budging.

I shrug. Walk away. Over to the black leather couch.

He follows. Sits at the other end. Unfortunately it's a two-seater.

I pick up a paper.

'Look,' he says, 'I'm sorry if my driving offended or annoyed you or whatever the problem is.'

'There's no problem.' *Now just go away.*

'It's just the way you took off back there . . . I thought you were challenging me. No. To tell you the truth, I thought you were *flirting*.'

'Well, you were wrong. I was definitely *not* flirting.' *The nerve of the guy.*

'Sorry . . . My mistake. It's the car, you see. People are always trying to race –'

'Not me.'

'You know,' he says, leaning forward for a close-up, 'you have a remarkable face.'

'*Look*. That might work for –'

I'm interrupted by Matt O'Hagan, MD of Copperplate Press, who's practically sprinting across reception, shouting, 'Greg, Greg,' at the top of his already loud voice. Matt: small

7

man with the presence of a low-flying aircraft. Think Danny DeVito. 'Greg' stands. Matt reaches him, extends his hand. They shake. I'm waiting for my 'hello'. But it doesn't come. I'm invisible. 'Greg' is gushed over by Matt, who, I realize, was aware that he'd arrived without his presence even being announced. If you knew Matt, you'd appreciate how unusual that is.

'You found us easy enough?' asks Matt. 'We'd have sent a car –'

I've never known Matt to send a car anywhere for anyone. Tight ship, Copperplate Press.

'Actually, I enjoyed the drive.' This is directed at me.

I look ahead.

'I was just introducing myself to –'

Matt finally remembers I'm not a mannequin. 'Oh, Lucy, Lucy, hello, hello.'

'Hello, Matt.' I stand, smile, shake his meaty hand. 'We're here for a meeting with Orla. There's Fintan behind you –'

'I see, I see.' He doesn't look around. 'So, you've met Greg Millar, then . . .'

Greg Millar. Greg Millar? Not Greg Millar, the international bestselling author? *I knew he looked familiar. It's the hair. So short. It threw me. Makes him younger.* I call to mind my impression of his jacket photograph and give it a haircut. Inside, I groan. It is him. And, knowing my luck, Copperplate has probably just signed him or something.

'Lucy, here' – Matt bangs me on the back – 'designs our book jackets, does a bloody good job too, don't you, Luce?'

He has never, until now, called me Luce.

I produce a smile from somewhere. 'Well, I'd better get going, meeting at two. Nice to meet you . . .' I've a problem saying his name.

'Greg.' He holds out his hand.

'Greg,' I confirm, shaking it, trying to ignore the look of amusement that's spreading across his face.

I can't get away fast enough.

That night I lie awake and wonder if a person like Greg Millar could really have found something remarkable in my face or if he was, in fact, just amusing himself. Compliments have always been the exclusive property of my elder sister. And when you grow up in the shadow of extreme beauty, you quickly learn how unremarkable you are. If it wasn't Grace's hair, it was her smile, her eyes, her anything. People didn't seem to be able to control themselves with the compliments. Then they'd see Lucy, standing there looking up, and rush some sort of sympathetic you-too-dear comment, which only served to make things worse. I'm not unattractive, but remarkable, no, with my black hair and brown eyes, definitely not remarkable. My clothes? Yes. They're 'unusual', 'colourful', 'different'. Lefty. Funky. Often commented on. My face? Fine, satisfactory, but nothing that warrants compliments from best-selling authors. So I dismiss Greg Millar and his compliments. Quite easily. Then fall asleep in a lighter than usual mood.

2

Next day I'm at my desk, working on a corporate logo for a financial institution and trying not to nod off, when Matt rings. I move the receiver an inch from my ear – always a good idea with Matt.

'I want to set up a brainstorming session,' he announces. Something's up. Matt getting involved in day-to-day business is not what you'd call the norm. 'We've signed Greg Millar.'

Aha!

'I want all heads together for the marketing campaign for his new title. Millar himself will be sitting in, so I want a good show. Yourself and Fintan from Get Smart.'

'When were you thinking?'

'Next Monday. Give Glenda a call to firm up a time. I've asked her to get a copy of the manuscript over to you. Remind her about it when you're talking to her, would you? Oh, and it might be wise to get cracking on some ideas before the meeting.' He hangs up.

This is the first time I've heard of an author being included in a Copperplate Press brainstorm. But then Greg Millar is not any old author. He's Greg Millar, international bestseller, whose books hit number one before they even reach the shops. Pre-orders, apparently. Matt has been in the business long enough to know that golden-egg-laying geese don't often walk in off the street. When they do, you build a nice warm nest to keep them there. Greg Millar is getting the keep-goose treatment. Which would be fine by me, if I didn't have to brainstorm in front of him. I'll catch a mystery bug.

But no, five days later, here I am, Ms Professional, following her business partner like a shadow into the meeting room at Copperplate Press. This is business. And business I can handle. Just let Fint do the talking. The boardroom has undergone a transformation. Decorating its walls are blown-up covers of Millar's published titles. Running up the centre of the table, like a line dividing a road, are his hardback editions. 'Media folders', containing newspaper and magazine clippings of reviews and articles, form a mini-skyline at the top end of the table. On the sideboard, refreshment with a French theme – pain au chocolat, coffee, even croissants, though it's afternoon. They've done their homework. Millar spends his summers in the South of France, as I discovered when I did mine.

Oh, God. There he is, the man himself, looking my way. Smiling. Of course. My plan *was* to sit beside Fint with my chair back just a little. Low profile. OK, hidden. But, as Fint settles himself beside Millar, I see that the only remaining chair is directly opposite the author, who's now standing in our honour. I offer a businesslike nod, then sit and busy myself with my briefcase. I look up to find him studying me. He beams over. There's something innocent about his smile. It seems to say, 'Great to see you again.' That's all. I half smile back. Then look away. Concentrate on business.

'So,' says Matt, standing, his bald pate catching a beam of afternoon sunlight, 'thank you all for coming at such short notice.' Blah, blah, blah. I tune out. And in, occasionally, to make sure I don't miss anything '. . . a *personal* thrill . . . one of the world's leading crime writers . . . decision to move to an indigenous Irish publisher in the home market . . . every support available . . . you will all by now have read the manuscript. So, *Lucy*, any thoughts on covers?'

He always does that, Matt, lulls you into thinking he'll waffle on for ever, then *boom*, he'll spring. And, though he's done it time and again, he still manages to catch me out. I look at my spiky-haired, dark-suited partner. This is where he is supposed to step in.

'You can stay sitting, if you like, Lucy,' says Matt.

Fint nods for me to go ahead, as it's clear that's what Matt wants.

'Thanks, Matt,' I say, glued to my chair. 'First, I'd like to say that I really enjoyed *A River Too Wide*.' Millar's new book. I feel the author's eyes on me. '*Fintan* and I' – I look at my partner, hoping everyone else will – 'had our own mini-brainstorm back at the office. After a lot of thought, and some argument,' I say, smiling at Fint, 'we feel that, while the jacket should complement the traditional look of ' – what should I call him – 'Greg's' – *cringe* – 'previous titles, we think that perhaps this time round, we might move towards a cover that focuses more on the main character than on the plot. Cooper is such a great protagonist –'

'*Great* idea,' Millar interrupts. 'Why hasn't anyone thought of that before?'

'Well,' I say, 'it made sense in the beginning to have the jackets primarily indicate the genre, because you were establishing your reader base. And we think that the covers should continue to do that, just shift focus a little to Cooper. He has such a loyal following. He's another Morse, really, isn't he?' I stop. *I haven't given away the fact that I'm a fan, have I?*

'Do you have anything for us to look at, at this stage?' asks Matt, pushing it as usual.

'Only roughs. I need to source some images before showing you anything.'

'Hmm.' He looks at the author.

'I'd love to see your roughs, Lucy,' Millar says, with what seems like genuine enthusiasm rather than the double entendre I initially suspect.

Matt's nodding furiously.

I decide there and then to bill him extra for the job. I pull my work from a folder and hand it across to Millar, excusing it with 'They're just concepts at this stage.'

He takes a moment. Then: 'Wow. These are incredible.' He passes them to Matt.

'*Yes*,' he enthuses. Anything to keep Millar happy.

It's decided that Get Smart should start work using the planned jacket concepts. The brainstorm moves to other areas of marketing – in-store display, author tours, signings, talks, PR, advertising. Orla, in marketing, is a natural performer. Jim, the sales manager, equally enthusiastic. PR woman, Debbie, suggests a list of possible 'angles'. The only person who doesn't say much is Emma, the managing editor. And it makes sense. How much editing would a person like Greg Millar need? As we're leaving the boardroom, the author suggests we 'celebrate'. Matt comes up with just the pub. I start to make my excuses but get a warning look from him. It's settled. I'm going.

We get to the pub just before the after-work rush. Matt spots that the snug is free and makes a dash for it. Dutiful as ever, we file in behind his short round body. Fint, behind me, remembers an urgent call he has to make and disappears rather than sliding in beside me. When I see that Millar's next up, I realize what Fint is at. My self-appointed personal Cupid is popping out to refill his quiver. With friends like Fint – well, you know the saying.

Snug is right. We're packed like cosy sardine buddies. Matt dominates the conversation but, in fairness to him, knows how to keep it lively and sharp. Everyone chips in. Except me. At first I enjoy listening, but soon become aware that Millar, beside me, has gone equally quiet, speaking only when asked a direct question. He's making me edgy. I feel he wants to turn to me and say something. I avoid looking at him, yet notice his every movement, word, breath. Our legs are touching, something I wasn't initially aware of when we sat down but that I'm intensely conscious of now. I consider shifting position but am afraid to draw attention to what's happening. In any case, there isn't anywhere to shift to. A tension is growing between us, made worse by our silence. It builds in intensity, until it gets to a point where I want to reach out, draw him to me, kiss him. And not stop. *What the hell is wrong with me? I want sex with a virtual stranger.* I'm shocked. Horrified. Disgusted with myself. I am mourning Brendan. This should *not* be happening. I don't even like the guy. It doesn't make any sense at all. My face is burning. I hope no one notices. I have to get out. Cool down. Get a grip. I stand and excuse myself. People have to file out to let me pass. What is going on?

The cool air in the toilets is a relief. Piped music, something light from the charts, makes everything seem more normal. I look around. Nothing like porcelain lavatories to bring you back to earth. For want of something to do, I tap open the door of a cubicle. *Might as well use it while I'm here.* I read the graffiti – BEWARE LIMBO DANCERS. Arrows point to the bottom of the door. I hear high heels make quick uneven steps. Their owner slams the door next to me and takes a long noisy leak. She sighs with the simple, uncomplicated pleasure of relief. I remember why I'm here and begin to tense. *Maybe I could slip away. Would anyone notice?* I think of Matt. *I should stay . . . I could sit in a different place, though. It wouldn't be rude. It'd be fine, thoughtful even – no one would have to get up to let me back in. Great. Sorted.* I wash my hands, hum to the music, look in the mirror. One last deep breath. I walk out.

Wham. I crash straight into him.

'Oh, God, sorry,' I say, stepping back.

He puts his hands on my upper arms to steady me. 'Are you OK?'

'Yeah, yeah, fine.'

Three seconds of silence, then 'Have dinner with me, Lucy.'

I wait for his smile but it doesn't come, leaving nothing to hide behind.

'I can't . . . I'm sorry.'

'Why not?' he asks with childlike simplicity.

'I'm . . . with someone . . . Sorry. But thanks. Really.' Brendan is private.

'Is it serious?'

'*Sorry?*'

'Your relationship . . . Is it serious?'

'Yes, it is.'

'Well, that's *no* good.' His smile is back. 'That's the last thing it should be. Whatever happened to fun?'

It died.

'Come out with me. And forget about *serious* . . .'

'I can't.' I can hear the finality in my voice.

So, apparently, can he. 'I'm sorry,' he says. 'Of course, you can't.' He shakes his head as if he was stupid to ask.

'I better go back,' I say.

'Of course.'

He disappears for a while before rejoining the group. Not long after that he leaves.

At work the next day he rings to discuss the cover of *A River Too Wide*. But not over the phone. We have to meet, apparently. I briefly wonder if this really is business, but then remember the way he backed off the day before. I tell myself to relax. Of course it's business. He wants the best for his book. Still, no other author has ever contacted me directly.

'You know, publishers don't really like their authors to deal directly with the designers they use,' I explain. 'They kinda like to control the design themselves, you know?'

He has his answer ready. 'It was Matt who gave me your number.' Then he suggests lunch.

'Tricky,' I lie. 'Busy for lunch all week. It'd have to be at our offices, I'm afraid.'

'Fine. How about tomorrow?'

Probably better to get it over with. 'Ten?'

'Ten.'

Tomorrow comes. And with it the deadline for the bank logo. By ten I've put in three hours. I'm manipulating a computer-generated design on screen when Sebastian, one of our trainee designers who doubles as a receptionist of sorts, struts into my office like a peacock, wearing a flamboyant mix of pastels – pink, lemon and white, reminding me of Neapolitan ice cream. Movement behind him attracts my eyes, still adjusting to middle distance. Millar has followed him into the room. That irks me. How does he always manage to elicit special treatment? Sebastian never shows visitors in, just buzzes us when they arrive at 'reception' (his desk). And yet there he is, offering to take Millar's classy, navy jacket. The author declines. I start to shut down my computer. Sebastian offers tea and coffee, something that he is usually too busy to do. Again Millar refuses. With nothing more to offer, Sebastian reluctantly leaves. I come from behind the desk to shake the author's hand. He beams, making my planned gesture seem way too formal. I cancel it, which leaves me at a loss – what am I supposed to do with myself out here between him and the desk?

'So,' he says, checking a chunky, expensive-looking, diving watch, 'how much time have we got?'

There's something about the way he says it that makes me suspicious. 'An hour should do it, I think.'

'Great, grab your coat, we're going out.'

My eyes widen. 'I'm sorry. I can't . . . I – '

'Oh, come on. Nice spring walk on Stephen's Green . . . we'll talk business, get some air, feed the ducks. Think how creative we'll be.'

I look at my desk, then back at him. 'All right, but I've got to be back here at eleven.' I tap *my* watch to make the point.

We do talk business. Then just talk, not difficult when you share a passion for books. It's strange how unsure he seems about his novels. He asks what I think he could have done better, what characters I feel he got wrong. As if (a) I'd know and (b) I'd tell him. I do say what I liked, what worked for me. At twelve – *is it really twelve?* – like Cinderella, he has to go. To collect his children from school. Greg Millar is a dad. A dad who always picks his kids up from school, though they've a nanny. Seeing him in this context changes my view of him. To someone safer, more human, somehow. After two hours that seem to have run on fast-forward, we walk to his car. He unlocks it but doesn't get in.

'So,' he says, smiling.

'So,' I echo with false bravado, as my arms fold, my feet shift, my glance is lowered.

'Now you know,' he says. 'I'm just a regular guy, not a jumped-up prat in a fast car.'

I'm embarrassed that he has seen through me.

'Have dinner with me.'

I think of Brendan. Visualize his face. And I can't do it.

'It's just food,' he says.

'I know, Greg. It's just that – '

'Nothing *serious*. I swear.' He criss-crosses his heart.

I haven't seen that done since I was a child. It makes me smile.

'Tomorrow,' he says. 'I'll pick you up from work.'

I enjoyed his company today. He lifted my spirits. He *is* a nice guy. I wonder if we could be 'just friends'.

'I'll take your stunned silence as a yes.'

It's just dinner.

'I'll call you at work,' he says. 'Tomorrow.'

I give in with two tiny nods.

He punches the air. 'Yes!'

And I'm smiling again.

'Can I drop you back at the office?'

'No, thanks. I feel like a walk.' I picture my desk covered in pink Post-it notes from Sebastian. I remember the unfinished logo. It can wait.

That night, in bed, I change my mind. Seeing Greg Millar, even for one meal, would be a mistake. It feels like an act of infidelity but, quite apart from that, it goes against the failsafe security system I've installed in my life: work hard, keep it at that. It's an effective formula for feeling numb. And feeling numb is how I survive.

The following day, when he calls, I try to pick a suitable moment to tell him. It is impossible. He talks like it's a given. He has booked the restaurant. Sounds so enthusiastic. 'No' just won't come out. The call ends. We are going. By six I have adopted a philosophical approach. It's only dinner. I'll leave at eleven. Ten thirty. I'll keep it superficial. Impersonal. I'll enjoy getting out of the apartment and that'll be it.

He wanted to pick me up at six. I opted for seven. At that exact time I get a call to say that he's in the lobby. I delay going down, not wanting him to assume there is anything special in my having dinner with him. I am not dressed up. I look respectable – that's it. I take the stairs, like I always do. Rounding the last corner, I see him: perched on the edge of the red leather two-seater in the lobby we share with an architectural firm and PR agency. He's leaning forward, forearms resting on legs, absorbed in the *Irish Times*, frowning. First time I've seen him without him seeing me. He looks freshly showered, cleanly shaven. Crisp white shirt. Denim discarded in favour of linen. That he has made an effort softens something inside me. He glances up. Catches me – *oh, God* – smiling at him. Why am I smiling? He beams like a hero from a Western. He stands, folds the paper, lands it on the glass-topped table and starts towards me, and I swear it's in slow motion. I swear too that I hear spurs whirr and click.

I laugh. Don't know why.

Closer.

He's had a shaving accident. A tiny nick near his ear makes him vulnerable, human. I want to touch it. What's wrong with me? Together now, he stoops to kiss my cheek. Then the other. A gentle scent of aftershave fills the intimate space between us. I stop breathing. Avoid his eyes. Think of Brendan. He takes my hand and we walk, in sync, out into the crisp air. He is humming a song I have always liked. When he gets to the 'Knock me over stone cold sober' bit, he sings it. I look at his profile. And I know I should have said no.

3

It's already dark, but Greg suggests a stroll to the restaurant. Being a walker and having a head fuzzy from a day's work, that suits me. Our offices overlook the canal. A walk to the hub will take us past my favourite building – the Pepper Canister Church – and through a little of Georgian Dublin.

Conversation is easy. All too soon we're at the restaurant, a two-star Michelin, off Merrion Square. I've brought some of our bigger clients here for lunch, occasionally, but have never splurged on dinner in my off time. The maître d' greets me like a regular but Greg like a personal friend. He stays with us for a complimentary pre-dinner drink, then shows us to our table – one of the finest. A reverse snob by nature, I've never been able to fault this place. The art is the real thing – Louis le Brocquy, Roderic O'Conor – the ceiling high, the space open, the walls white to better show the paintings. The waiters, who at first appear stuffy, are gentlemen. Dining tonight, I recognize three prominent businessmen, a celebrity dancer and her husband, and a TV anchorwoman. Those I don't recognize have an air of confident, anonymous wealth.

I am true to the promise I made myself, keeping things light, superficial. This works until we're waiting for our main course to arrive, when there is a lull.

'Lucy,' says Greg, clearing his throat, 'there's something I've been meaning to tell you. It's a little awkward. Well, I'll just say it.' He pauses. 'I know what happened. With your fiancé. Fintan told me.'

I can't believe he did that. 'He had no right –'

'The only reason he did was to protect you. He'd seen us talking that time in the pub. He didn't want you hurt.'

'Someone should tell him I already have a mother. *Jesus*. When did this *conversation* take place?'

'You make it sound subversive. It wasn't. After you and I . . . spoke, I went out for a smoke. Fint came and set me straight. That's it.'

I shake my head. 'Unbelievable.'

We're quiet. I imagine he's regretting his honesty.

'I'm glad Fintan told me,' he says. 'When you said there was someone else, I was going to leave it.'

'Might have been better if you had,' I say flatly.

For the first time since we've met, I watch his face fall.

'I shouldn't be out – with anyone,' I try to explain.

He seems to consider that, running a thumb along his lower lip. When he speaks, his voice is gentle. 'For a long time I felt like that – after my wife died.' I want him to go on but instead he says, 'Listen, we don't have to talk about this. It just didn't feel right, my knowing, and your not knowing I knew . . . God, there's English for you!'

I smile.

'I guess, all I want to say is that I understand. That's it.'

'What was your wife's name?'

'Catherine.' He looks past me. 'Hard to believe it's been five years,' he says, almost to himself.

Absently, I pick up my dessertspoon, run it along the table-cloth, make circles with it. Eventually I look up. 'Does it get any better?'

His mouth smiles but not his eyes. 'A bit.'

'Only a *bit*?'

He cups his chin in his hand. 'For a long time, I didn't want it to. That would have meant forgetting.'

Oh, my God. 'That's how I feel.'

His eyes hold mine. 'Of course you do.'

I've never told anyone that. I didn't think they'd understand. We're silent as the meal arrives, and the waiters lift our dishes in fluid, synchronized motion. I pick at my food, appetite gone. All I want to do is talk.

'How did Catherine die?' I eventually raise the courage to ask. I want to know if it was as unfair as the way I lost Brendan.

His voice is hoarse when he answers in one word, 'Childbirth.'

I didn't expect that, not in this day and age. 'You don't have to tell me . . .'

Rotating the saltcellar and without looking up, he starts to talk. 'We'd been warned not to have another baby. The first was very difficult on Catherine. She wanted to risk going again. I didn't. When Rachel was four, it came to a head. Catherine was heading for forty and wanted a brother or sister for Rachel before it was too late. She'd been an only child herself and didn't want that for Rachel.'

'So you agreed to go ahead.'

He looks up. 'No. She stopped . . . taking . . . precautions. She only told me *after* she got pregnant.'

God. 'Must have been hell going through that pregnancy.'

His eyes meet mine. 'I was worried, very worried, and angry, but I really never thought . . . I'd lose her.' The last three words are almost a whisper.

Silence.

I reach across and place my hand on his.

The more we talk, the more I appreciate that mine is not the worst story. How much harder to lose someone you've shared children with. So many practicalities I've never had to deal with, like trying to cope with a heartbroken five-year-old who blames her baby brother for taking her mother away, like being woken during the night to feed a tiny boy you are finding it hard not to resent, like having two very dependent people relying on you to keep their world spinning.

'Didn't you have *any* time to grieve?'

He laughs at that concept.

'But how did you manage?'

'I got help.'

'A psychologist?'

He laughs again. 'A nanny, someone to look after Toby while I tried to cope with Rachel.'

'What about your family? Didn't they help?'

'Well, there's only my mother and my younger brother, Rob. It's not in me to rely on people. Rob was pretty stubborn, though, about bringing Rachel out a lot. It was good – it got her away from the war zone for a while.'

'How are they now, your children?'

'Great, thank God. Hilary – the nanny I hired – is still with us. She loves them as if they were her own.'

'You were lucky to find her.'

'Don't know what we'd have done without her.'

In one evening I learn so much about him. How much he loves his children, his writing. And how both have kept him going. I open up about Brendan, how he died in that insane car crash. I talk about the guilt, anger, grief, loneliness and, yes, how the work I've been throwing myself into, in the year and a half since his death, has never been so productive. I admit that my job has become the only focus in my life. I talk of my lost future, and of my inability and refusal to see another. He surprises me by saying that he saw all this in my eyes the day we met. It was what had made me 'remarkable'.

The tables around us have emptied, one by one. We are the last. But there is so much left to say. It little matters where, but my apartment is close and neither of us feels like being in anonymous company in some noisy, packed venue. It isn't as if we fall into each other's arms the minute we get through the door. We're just talking. Some small memory brings me close to tears, which usually only happens when I'm alone at night. We have shared so much in the last few hours that it seems natural when he clears my tears. When I look up, his face is incredibly close, his eyes, lips. Then I am kissing him as much as he is me. The attraction I felt in the pub erupts again, though stronger now. This time, I don't fight it. Comfort, passion and understanding consume the past. Our shared melancholy ignites us. This is different to anything I have known. And afterwards, when Greg starts making five-year plans that include me, I laugh, though I know he is serious.

Quickly we become inseparable. Well, as inseparable as work and his children allow. We speak over the phone enough times a day for Sebastian to start calling him 'Lover Boy'. We meet for brunch whenever we can and go out most evenings. It feels like an orange disc of effervescent Vitamin C has been dropped into the still water that was my life. I have never met anyone so alive. On any given night, you never know where you'll end up: bowling, shopping, art gallery openings. Bars, bingo, clubs. The airport. Church. He is up for anything as long as there is adventure and fun to be had. In fact, he's making me see that adventure and fun are to be had pretty much anywhere. He seems to know everyone. And if he doesn't, he gets to. He is so vibrant; you can almost feel his heart pumping. He lives life like it might be snatched from him at any moment. To me, that makes so much sense.

I begin to do the same. When Greg does crazy things like chase me around a video store pretending to be a stranger who wants to be taken home, I am not embarrassed. I don't care what anyone thinks. I laugh out loud when he carries me from the store. For the last year and a half I have been 'Poor Lucy' to my friends. The more time I spend with Greg, the fainter my prefix becomes and the more I realize that hanging out with people who see you as a delicate piece of china makes you feel like one. Lucy Arigho, handle with care. Goodbye to that. Through Greg, I am learning that it is possible to live again. It is possible to enjoy myself without guilt, because I know I haven't forgotten Brendan.

I can be happy.

Sometimes I wonder if we are seeing too much of each other. But when Greg's not there, everything is flatter, buzz-less, slower. At weekends, when he is with his children, I see friends, shop, visit art galleries. But whatever I do without him seems like filling time. I don't expect to be included in his family life. I've seen enough TV to know that many lone parents are careful about introducing new partners to their children, and I respect that. In any case, meeting Greg's children would bring our relationship to a level I don't want to think about.

I haven't told anyone. Fint knows, of course. And Sebastian, sleuth that he is, has worked it out for himself. Outside of that, no one. I'm still getting used to the adjustment myself. I don't want to jinx it, just live it. But then Greg asks me to the book launch of a friend, and we get snapped for a social column. I imagine my dad opening his Saturday paper and clocking his daughter smiling out, a stranger's arm around her. He wouldn't say anything, but I know he'd be hurt I hadn't told him. We're supposed to be a team, Dad and I, partners in imperfection. I have always been good enough for Dad, the person who encouraged my quirky sketches, the person who convinced my mother I could make a career out of my talent. And so I need to talk to him before Saturday, when the paper comes out. Unfortunately, my mother is Information Control. She'll want, *expect*, the news first. And I've learned to avoid upsetting her whenever I can.

Always one for the practical gift, my mother, so I arrive armed with smoked salmon. I'm smuggling in a giant bar of Fruit and Nut for Dad, who is, as usual, on strict rations. Mum answers the door in her Alpen apron, wearing the standard uniform of camel round-neck pullover, tweed calf-length skirt. No jewellery. Sensible shoes. The haircut of a woman twenty years older. It would be unkind to say that she looks like a priest's housekeeper. But she does.

We've never been easy with each other, Mum and I. A 'cup-a-tea' gives us something to do. She does the kettle bit. Me, the cups and saucers. Always saucers in our house. We make the usual small talk, Grace and family featuring strongly. When she offers the recipe for the apple tart she has heating in the oven, I know we're running out of topics.

So I come out with it. 'I'm seeing someone.'

'Oh.' She looks surprised. 'Who?' she asks, setting her cup back at the centre of its saucer. 'Someone from college?'

'No, Mum. Greg's a writer. Greg Millar.'

'Greg Millar.' She squints, trying to place him. The oven timer pings. She ignores it. At last she looks at me. 'No, doesn't ring a bell. What kind of books does he write?'

'Crime novels. He's pretty popular.'

'I'm sure he is, dear. So. How long have you been . . .' She roots around for the appropriate phrase. '. . . "seeing" him?'

'A few weeks.' I picture his face in my mind and want to smile.

'Early days, then,' she says, bursting my bubble.

'It's not serious. It's just . . . I thought you should know . . .

in case . . . I don't know . . . you hear it from someone else, or something.'

'Sure, who would we hear it from?' She looks over at Dad as if to say 'We never get out.'

He doesn't see her, sitting as he is in his armchair, behind the paper. His favourite spot.

'D'you want me to get the tart?' I ask.

'Oh. Yes, Lucy, please. And cut a slice for yourself and your father.'

'Did someone say apple tart?' His head pops up.

I smile at him.

He rolls the paper and drops it on the chair, stretches and makes his way to the table. He's quiet until I hand him his slice. 'So, it's not serious, is it?'

Knew he'd be listening. 'Nah,' I say, unable to stop smiling.

'This looks good, Mum,' he says, scooping up two quick dessertspoons of whipped cream and landing them on the tart, then flattening the heap with the back of the spoon.

She watches him and frowns.

'D'you know, Lucy,' he says, 'that people have a habit of saying that things aren't serious when that's exactly what they are?'

I give a one-shouldered shrug, lift my eyebrows innocently. 'Well, it's not, Dad.'

'Don't ever commit a crime, love, you'd never get away with it.'

I make a face at him.

'How did you meet him?' asks my mother.

'Work,' I say, deciding to skip the exact chronological detail.

'I'm not surprised. You do little else.'

I've had a lifetime of learning when to keep my mouth shut. And this is what I do now.

'Is he good to you?' she asks.

'Yes. He is.'

'Does he make you laugh?' asks Dad in a tone that implies *more importantly*.

I nod and start to smile, thinking of the way Greg mimics Matt. He squats down, comes right up to me, then looks up and asks me to dance. He gets the voice, the mannerisms just right.

'Oh, dear,' says Dad. 'I think we've lost her.'

'I hardly know him, Dad.'

'I believe you,' he says, looking like he doesn't. 'So, how often d'you see each other?'

'A good bit.'

'Every day?'

'Pretty much.'

He has a way of getting information out of me. The good cop approach.

'Ah,' he says, in a case-dismissed tone.

We're silent. The monotonous ticking of the kitchen clock reminds me of afternoons spent at this table trying to interest myself in the life cycle of the earthworm.

Suddenly he points his fork at me. 'Didn't he write *A Time to Die*?'

I sit up straighter. Beam at him. 'Yes, yes, he did.' *Good man, Dad*.

'Is *that* him?' asks my mother. 'His books are *filthy*. He's divorced. Or separated or something. Oh, *Lucy*.'

'He is not divorced. His wife died, Mum. Hardly his fault.'

'Yes, well, just be careful. Men like that are complicated –'

'OK, look, I'm going.' I stand, trying to do it slowly, trying to keep my voice upbeat, stay calm. 'Thanks for the tea, Mum.' I kiss her cheek, grab my bag.

'There's no need to go –' she starts to say.

'I'm late. Gotta go.' My standard excuse.

Dad follows me into the hall. 'She didn't mean it, love. She's just worried about you.'

'Yeah, right.'

'She means well, Lucy.'

'Sure.'

'It's like the apple tart.'

What is he on about?

'Did you see how I got that cross look of hers when I loaded on the cream?'

'You noticed?'

'Of course I noticed. Anyway, why d'you think she made it, if she didn't want me to have any?'

'Beats me.'

'She thinks that by giving out, she shows that she cares.'

'Oh, come on.' This is what happens when your father retires early to take up psychology.

'And d'you know why she's like that?'

'Enlighten me.'

'Her mother was the opposite – airy-fairy, never around, no discipline whatsoever, let them run wild. That's why Mum has always come down hard on you. Both of you. She thinks that's what good mothers do.'

'I don't know, Dad.'

'Trust me, Lucy. She only wants what's best –'

'But that's the problem. She always does. Nothing else is good enough. Nothing will ever be. I knew she'd have a problem with Greg. She had to. I don't know why I came. I really don't.'

'She's just a worrier. Wait till I go back in there. She'll be all upset. Guarantee you.'

I'm quiet.

'How's the work going?'

'Fine.'

29

'Good. Good. Look, the main thing is that you're happy. And you are, aren't you?'

I nod.

'Well, then.' He lowers his voice. 'Let it all wash over you. Like I do.'

4

I'm cooking vegetarian curry. Curry, because it's his favourite. Vegetarian, because I am one. Stupidly, I decided to impress him and have gone all out, dry-frying the cumin from scratch and grinding the garlic and ginger in a stone mortar I bought especially in the Asian market. No simple curry paste tonight. Which, of course, means I'm way behind and hassled when he arrives. I haven't even changed. He kisses me, lands a bottle of Bollinger down on the worktop. I smile and turn back to the cooker, expecting him to open the champagne, a not unusual thing for him to bring. But he doesn't. Instead he reaches for the back pocket of his jeans and asks if I'd like to read the Acknowledgements for *A River Too Wide*. He hands them to me.

'Oh, OK, great!' I say, putting them aside for the moment. 'Let me just get this under control first.'

'Here, let me do that,' he says, making to take the ladle from me.

'It's OK. I'm nearly there.'

'Nope. You read. I cook.' He picks up the Acknowledgements, curled up from being in his pocket, and hands them to me. He begins to stir the sauce. *I'll fly through it. Take more time with it later*. But, as I begin to read, I grow to appreciate the situation. Beside me is one of the writers I most admire, handing me his work for an opinion, even if it is just the Acknowledgements. It is, after all, the most personal part of a book.

'There's another page when you've finished that,' he says, looking over his shoulder.

'OK.'

'You know what? Why don't you skip to the second page?'

'Why?'

'It's the Dedication.'

There's something about the way he says it. Could he have dedicated it to me? No, we've only been together two months. Still, I hold my breath as I turn the page.

On it are three words: *Marry me, Lucy*.

I freeze. *Oh, God. Oh, no.* He's taking my hand and pressing into it a small, navy, velvet box he has pulled from his jeans. *It's too much. Too soon.* I keep my eyes fixed on the box – so I don't have to meet his.

'Open it,' he says softly.

I'm stuck. If I do as he asks, he'll assume . . . If I don't, I'll have to tell him. But he's waiting. I have to do something. So I lift the tiny, resistant lid. Inside is a solitaire, in the shape of a triangle. So simple. So special. It couldn't be more perfect. That he went out on his own and selected this for me and instinctively got it so right is gut-wrenching, considering what I am about to do. I look up at him. I don't want to hurt him. I love him, I realize.

'What is it?' he asks.

'Nothing,' I croak.

Silence. I can smell the curry starting to burn.

'You don't want to,' he says quietly.

I look down at the ring to avoid answering but watch in horror as a tear falls as if in slow motion, landing with a splat on the diamond. I worry that the shop won't take it back.

'You don't love me,' he says.

'I do, Greg. I do love you.' I make my eyes say it too. 'But it's just too soon.'

'Not for me.'

I drop my head and shake it. 'I can't.' It would be like moving on, neatly slotting someone else into Brendan's place. And I can't do that. Not now. Maybe not ever. 'Marriage is such a big step,' I manage.

'It's Brendan, isn't it?'

I nod. 'I'm sorry.' I close the box, place it on the worktop and push it towards him, hating myself for hurting him. That I'm crying doesn't make me feel any better. He takes my hands in his, kisses my forehead, pulls me into a hug. 'Shh,' he says, rubbing my back. Then, with a 'Shit, the dinner,' he lets me go, striding to the cooker, lifting the pan and carrying it to the sink. He opens the windows. I feel like laughing. And crying. And vomiting.

'So much for that!' he says. He doesn't seem in a hurry to get back to me.

'Greg. I'm really sorry.'

He shakes his head.

'Maybe in time –'

'No. Let's forget it.' He looks down, shoving his hands into his pockets, leaning against the sink. 'I was wrong to ask so soon.' He sighs. 'I guess I just wanted to show you how committed I am to you.'

I go to him. 'And I'm committed to you. But we don't need grand gestures, Greg –'

'It wasn't a gesture. And it's not a whim. I've thought this through. It'd make so much sense, our getting married. As it is, I've two separate lives – you and my family. It's like you're not fully part of my life, you know?'

I nod. I feel that too.

'But you're right. I have to stop rushing things for fear they'll end.'

I put my arms around him. Into his chest, I say, 'This won't end.' But I, of all people, know that it can, in one split second.

He pulls back. Smiles. 'Let's pretend I never asked. OK? Let's forget the whole thing.'

I try to think of ways I might have said no without hurting him.

He reaches for a nearby roll of kitchen paper. 'Here,' he says, ripping a sheet off and putting it to my nose. 'Blow.'

I half laugh.

'Come on. Blow.'

I do.

He squeezes it over my nose. 'You love me,' he says. 'That's a start.'

Maybe, but it doesn't feel enough.

First thing next morning, I make my way to Fint's office, bleary-eyed from lack of sleep. He is juggling, something he only does when trying to come up with ideas. I turn to leave.

'Where you going?' he asks, letting the balls flop, one by one, into his hands.

'You're busy.'

'Nah, nothing coming.' He returns the colourful, authentic juggling balls to their shiny metal box. 'So how are you?'

'I'll just close the door.'

He raises an eyebrow.

Door secured, I slump into the chair on the opposite side of his desk, reach forward and help myself to one of his juggling balls. I drop it from hand to hand. He waits.

'Greg's asked me to marry him,' I say, my voice flat.

He eyes me carefully. 'You don't seem too happy.'

'No.'

He says nothing.

'It's too soon,' I explain.

34

He thinks for a moment. 'How many weeks is it now?'

'No. Not that. Too soon . . . after Brendan.'

'Oh.' He nods. 'I see.'

'I can't do it to him.'

Fint stands, comes from behind his desk. Takes the ball from me. Sits on the desk. 'Brendan's dead, Lucy.'

'Don't say that. He's not gone. I feel him all the time. He sees everything I do. I can't just marry someone else. I can't do it to him.'

He eyeballs me. 'So say no,' he says, calling my bluff.

'I did.'

'Well, then. What's the problem?'

I hesitate but then give in. 'I love him.'

'That *is* allowed, Lucy.'

'When we're apart, Fint, I feel flat, like something's missing. I know he has to be with his kids. I do. It's just that if we were married we could share our lives completely. We wouldn't have to keep splitting up and going our separate ways. At the end of the day he always has to "get back".' I wait for him to say something, but he doesn't. 'I'm afraid. What if something happens to him before –'

'Hang on. Whoa. Slow down.'

'What?'

'Nothing's going to happen to Greg.'

'How do you know?'

'Because lightning doesn't strike twice.'

'Not true. A guy in the States, a park ranger, was struck by lightning seven times. It's in the *Guinness Book of World Records*.'

He smiles. 'Remind me to include you in the next pub quiz.'

'I'm serious. If Brendan and I had known how little time we had, we wouldn't have hung around for all the practical things to be in place – apartment, furniture, whatever. We'd have married straight away. We'd have had a child. And I'd have a part of him to hold to me now. I don't want that to happen again.'

'Lucy, it won't.'

'I couldn't bear it. He makes me so happy. I love him so much.' I'm crying. Again.

'Come here.' He gives me a Fintan Special – a great big bear hug. And lets me cry. When I've moved to the intermittent sobbing stage, he pulls back, hands on my shoulders. 'OK. Here's what Uncle Fint thinks. One: you love Greg. Two: I don't blame you; he's a great guy. Three: you're lucky to get another chance. And four: you should enjoy it. That's it.'

'But what about Brendan?'

He removes his hands, looks past me, eyes unfocused. After a few moments he is back in the present, his expression sad. 'You know how close I was to Brendan. I miss him too. And I miss him for you. I miss your being together. But do you think, for one second, that he'd want you to be miserable for the rest of your life because of him? Really, do you? Because you know the way he loved you. And he wouldn't want that. He'd want this – happiness, a future. I know he would. I feel it, Lucy.'

I want to believe him. So badly.

He takes on his logical, in-control voice. 'When you met Greg, you were in pretty shitty form, weren't you?'

I remember back. 'Yeah.'

'Why?'

'You know why. It was Brendan's birthday.'

'Have you ever thought that Greg might have been Brendan's present to you?'

I squint at him. Fint is not a religious person. 'Come *on*.'

'Were you supposed to be at that meeting with Orla?'

'No.' One of our designers, Jake, had rung in sick.

'And what a coincidence you and Greg meeting like that – in traffic, on your way to the same place.'

'Life is full of coincidences.'

'Why did you even talk to him in the first place?'

'You know why. He was driving like a maniac.'

'Which upset you because of Brendan. So, really, it was fate, something set in motion in another world.'

'You don't believe that. Fintan, you of all people.' The world's greatest cynic.

'So how did I think of it, then?'

I can't work. I leave the office and walk. Though about as religious as Fint, I find myself lighting candles in the Pepper Canister Church. I try to talk to Brendan but find I'm talking to myself. Not even the tiniest flicker of a candle flame. Nothing. I walk some more. Then drive. I pull up outside my sister's house. If I'm not going to hear a spiritual voice, at least I'll hear a sensible one.

5

I don't make a habit of asking Grace's advice. It's hard to listen to people who never make mistakes. But today I've asked. And I'm waiting for an answer, watching her carefully, from the other side of the ironing board. She is ironing and beautiful. Like an ad for it: You too could look like this, if you had an iron. Who needs a gym when you can pump iron? Hard to believe we're from the same gene pool. Why have I come? Do I really need the Voice of Reason?

'They're not easy, you know, children,' she says.

Is that it? I tell her I'm thinking of getting engaged to a man I met two months ago and this is what she says? I wouldn't mind, but Grace is the world's greatest mum. She loves her kids. Gave up her career as a doctor because she wanted to be there for them round the clock. I just don't get it.

'But Shane and Jason are great,' I say. Her kids.

'Not twenty-four hours a day they're not,' she says, iron suspended mid air. 'What we're having here is a rare moment of peace.' Jason's asleep and Shane's at Montessori. The iron goes down again.

'I know it's hard, but they're young,' I argue. 'They get easier. Don't they?'

'They'd better,' she laughs, lifting the iron. Jets of steam shoot out and up into her honey-blonde hair. It won't frizz. 'Look, Luce, you're my little sis, I'm going to be straight – as long as you don't tell Mum . . .'

I look at her as if she's just insulted me – I only ever tell Mum things I think she'll eventually find out.

'Parenting is the hardest, most thankless thing I've ever done. I'm not complaining, it was our decision – they're our kids and we love them. But his wouldn't be yours. You'd get all the hassle – probably more – but none of the good things that come with a child being part of you. Have you thought that they mightn't accept you?'

'Maybe not at first,' I try. 'But *in time –*'

'They might drive you apart. It happened to Colette.' Her best friend.

'She had to put up with manipulative teenagers – that's different.'

'All children manipulate their parents. They've developed it into an art form. Trust me. Even babies manipulate their parents.'

They can't be that bad. Jason was up a lot during the night. Grace is tired. That's all it is. Exhaustion talking.

'What about discipline?' she continues, lifting the iron and this time drawing her head back to avoid the steam. 'If you *do* get married, who'll discipline them? Have you thought of that?'

In a word, no. I've been so focused on the dead I've forgotten the living. 'Greg. Greg will discipline them.'

'Well, he should – if Colette's experience is anything to go by. And when he's not there?'

'I don't know . . . I'd have to, I suppose.'

'And what if they turn around and say, "You're not my mother"?'

I don't want to hear this. 'They've a nanny,' I suddenly remember. 'Hilary. She'll do the discipline.' *Thank God.* 'And I'm good with kids. You know how good I am with Shane and Jase.'

'You spoil them. And that's fine. An aunt should spoil her nephews. But a parent can't afford to. They'd turn into tyrants.

Another thing – parents can't switch off. You hand them back to me at the end of the day and off you go to your peaceful apartment. Parenting is full time. They don't go away. Just think about it, OK? It wouldn't be easy, that's all I'm saying.' She puts a folded pillowcase on a pile and takes a shirt from another. 'Jesus, I hate ironing.'

'Grace. I'm not sure why we're talking about children, here.' What about the simple fact that it's too soon?

She looks straight at me. Puts down the iron. 'Because he has two . . . I take it they know, the children?'

'I haven't said yes.' My way of saying, 'This kind of landed on me.'

'But they know you're seeing each other?'

'I don't know. I don't think so.'

'Haven't you met them?'

'Not yet.'

She throws me a don't-you-think-that-would-be-an-idea look.

'There's no point unless I'm going to be in their lives, is there?'

She comes from behind the ironing board to sit with me at the kitchen island. Her voice is gentle when she says, 'Lucy, I just mentioned the children to make you appreciate the practicalities of this . . . I know you've been through a tough time, and more than anyone you deserve happiness, but do you really need to say yes now?' She pauses, then adds, 'I mean, how well can you know someone after eight weeks?'

'I know Greg.'

'But how? How can you know it's love after just eight weeks?'

'I feel it.' I touch my heart.

'I'm just worried,' she says. 'Worried that it's too soon after Brendan.'

I let my head drop. 'I died with Brendan, Grace.' When I lift my chin, my face is alight. 'Greg has brought me back to life, given me reason to live. He is offering me another future.'

She says nothing.

'He understands, Grace.' Slowly, I repeat, 'He *understands* . . . He lost his wife.'

'Oh,' she says, as if she is just beginning to understand herself.

'It's not just that. I love him. He's made me happy again. I never thought I could be.'

'I just wish you wouldn't rush. There are so many reasons not to – his fame –'

'He's a *writer*, Grace, not a movie star. People either don't recognize him or don't care.'

'The age gap. Eleven years, think about it, Luce . . .'

'Age doesn't matter when you're with the right person. And anyway, he's so young in his outlook. Sometimes I feel *I'm* the older one.'

'You've got the rest of your lives to be together.'

I look at her. 'I will never' – pause – 'make the mistake of assuming that again.'

She stops, her eyes moist.

But I don't want her pity; I want her approval. I want her to say, 'Do it.' Because suddenly I want to. The more hurdles she puts in my way, the more I want to jump them. Every one. I don't want anything to stop us. I love Greg and want to be with him. Be part of his life, his family. And, out of nowhere, I have the strongest feeling that Brendan wants this for me too. 'It's right, Grace. I know it is.'

She takes my hands in hers. 'Then don't listen to me. Always the cynic, always looking beyond what people say, never trusting. And still I didn't know the man I married until after

I married him. Don't listen to me . . . Sure, you never do anyway, do you?' She smiles.

'No,' I say, smiling back. It *is* hard to listen to the person I've been compared to and fallen short of all my life, the person who got a degree that pleased our mother, the person who married young to a guy with no complications – not too old, not widowed, not a father and not famous. Kevin, Grace's husband, shares the top percentile with her in looks, intelligence and all the things that matter to society. They are a Mary Poppins couple: practically perfect in every way. There have been times I've caught Kevin looking at me as though thinking *Thank God I bagged the right sister*. Which only makes me glad he did. Imagine being married to someone with such high expectations. Not that that would be a problem for my sister. The only thing that keeps me on the same side as Grace is our mother. Even the perfect daughter isn't quite good enough.

Greg sweeps me up into his arms, kissing me over and over, telling me I've made the right decision. 'You won't regret it,' he says. And I'm laughing. 'We'll be so happy. The kids will love you.'

I know it won't be that easy but smile anyway.

'You'll have to meet them.' He thinks for a second. 'I know – we'll have a barbecue. Invite Rob.'

I wait for him to suggest his mother too, but he doesn't. Instead he says that barbecues aren't 'her thing'.

He asks, 'What day is today, Thursday?'

'Mm-hmm.'

'Well, then, how about Saturday?'

'Saturday?' *Only two days*. I'm suddenly nervous. After all that Grace has said . . .

'Saturday. My place.'

I take a breath. 'All right,' I say with false jollity.

Greg starts planning vegetarian options while I try to remember everything my sister said about stepchildren.

Greg comes to bring me to his home, which will become my home, to meet his children, who will become my stepchildren. If I hadn't spoken to Grace, would I be as nervous? I feel like I'm going for an audition. If I bring presents, will they think I'm trying to win them over? If not, will they think me tight? Greg has told me not to worry about gifts, just to bring myself. Did he check with the children, though? And what should I wear? I don't want to look too young and highlight the age difference. Nor do I want to look as if I'm dressing like a wannabe mother. Although Greg has told me a lot about Rachel and Toby, all the way there I bombard him with questions. What do they like, dislike? Is there anything I should or shouldn't say? He tells me I'll be fine. We're driving along one of the most salubrious roads on the celebrity belt of Dalkey, sea on our left, when he indicates and swings into a driveway. Up ahead looms something more than a house. It's the kind of place that might be chosen for celebrity weddings. It has turrets. And grounds. It doesn't just overlook the sea, it's right on it. A blue, blue sea with little white caps.

'My God, Greg!'

He dismisses it with 'It's just bricks and mortar.'

'A *lot* of bricks and mortar.'

'Could all be gone in the morning, Lucy. Nothing's certain in life.'

One thing's certain to me. Given the Dublin property market, Greg's home has to be worth millions. This is life on a different scale. While I'm trying to digest that, he jumps from the car, comes round and opens my door. He takes my hand, and we crunch gravel till we get to the steps. He slips a key in the lock.

But there is no grand tour.

'They were out back when I left. Let's go see.'

I catch a fleeting glimpse of old and new – original features combined with stripped wooden floors, oak blinds and architectural furniture. I want to stop and admire the art – paintings and sculpture – all modern, all wonderful. Oh, and he has a library . . . He drags me on. We reach the patio. On a newly cut lawn, bordered by swings, a climbing frame, a trampoline and a basketball hoop, two children are playing football with two adults. They are so absorbed that at first they don't see us. It's not a challenge to work out who's who. The slight, dark-haired boy with the khaki combats and light blue top featuring multicoloured skulls looks about five: Toby. The equally dark and slender but much taller girl in three-quarter-length denims and cerise top has to be Rachel. Greg's brother, Rob, has the trademark family colouring and build, his face more boyish than his elder brother's. You can tell there's six years between them. Only Hilary, the nanny, stands out as different, fair and sturdy, her hair pulled back into a tight ponytail. She is wearing a loose, white, long-sleeved T-shirt over dark, stretch denims. I'd imagined an older woman, someone middle aged.

Rachel tackles Rob.

Hilary shouts, 'Go, Rachel.'

Toby calls to his uncle, 'Over here, I'm open.'

I smile. At five, he already has the lingo?

Rachel gets the ball. Rob retreats to the goal. He dives as she kicks hard. Toby groans and holds his head, while Hilary and Rachel cheer and high-five each other.

'Guys,' Greg calls, 'come meet Lucy.'

44

Four heads turn in our direction. Rob's sudden smile is wide and welcoming. He starts towards us. Hilary has to say something to the children to get them to move. I feel guilty for interrupting their game.

Rob reaches us first and extends a hand. 'Welcome to the family,' he says, his shake firm and honest.

I return his smile. 'Thank you.'

'I see he hasn't offered you a drink.' He tut-tuts at his brother. 'Can I get you a beer?'

'That'd be great, thanks.'

Hilary arrives with the children. She looks even younger close up. More my age. A year or two older maybe. The heaviness of her body in the distance must have added years.

Greg introduces us all.

'Hello,' I say, smiling from one to the other.

'Hi,' says Toby, yanking up his trousers from behind like a little man.

Hilary says, 'Nice top.'

'Oh, thanks.' I look down to remind myself what I'm wearing. 'Oh, it's from BT2. Greg got it for me.'

As I watch Rachel's face cloud over, I realize my mistake. *How stupid to say Greg got it.*

'Rachel, say hello to Lucy,' prompts Greg.

'Hello,' she mumbles, looking at the ground.

'That was a good goal,' I say.

She shrugs without looking up.

'*I'm* a good kicker,' declares Toby. 'Did you see *me*?'

'Yes, I did. You were great out there on the pitch.'

He looks to where they were playing, then back at me as if I have visual problems. 'It's just the garden.'

'True enough,' I say, feeling stupid.

'Can we have our Coke now?' Rachel asks Hilary.

The nanny looks at Greg.

45

'Yep,' he says.

She takes the children inside.

'OK. Let's get this show on the road,' says Greg, rubbing his hands together and heading for the barbecue.

'D'you want a hand?' I offer.

'You're grand. Sit down and get to know your future brother-in-law.'

'You sure?'

'Yeah. There's a knack to this thing.'

Rob and I sit at the long wooden patio table that reminds me of Italian family get-togethers. He's so easy to talk to. A teacher who writes music in his spare time, he is also keen on questions. After finding out where I live and went to school and what I do for a living, he asks how Greg and I met.

'You're not serious,' he says, looking over at his brother. 'Greg Millar flirting in traffic.' He starts laughing. 'Wonders will never cease. As for getting engaged after two months? I don't know what you've done to him.'

'What *I've* done! It's completely the other way around. It's what he's done to me.'

'Now, now, don't get smutty!'

I laugh. 'I'm serious. Greg has changed my whole outlook on life. He has such a great philosophy – '

'Greg? A philosophy?' He looks dubious.

'He lives for the moment. Embraces life.'

'*Greg?*'

'Yes, Greg.' *What's his problem?*

'Well, I don't know what your secret is,' he says, 'but I've never seen him so . . . so *zesty*.' We look over at him. He's singing an old Eartha Kitt song, complete with hand gestures, in between flipping burgers.

'But he's always like that,' I say.

'Maybe with you.'

'Not just with me, with everyone. He's so, so . . . well, as you say, zesty.'

He cringes. 'Did I say that?' Then adds, 'Must be love.'

'What are you two talking about over there?' Greg calls.

'You,' I say, going to him and slipping my arm around his waist. I look over at Rob and rationalize. Lots of people are different with their families, more responsible, serious. I am, with my mother. Must be the same for Greg and his brother.

Hilary and the children come through the patio doors.

I drop my arm.

Rachel is carrying a fishing rod, Toby a pair of binoculars, Hilary what looks like a picnic basket.

'Where're ye off to?' asks Rob.

'Picnic,' calls Toby excitedly. 'Wanna come?'

'No, thanks, buddy, someone has to eat the barbecue.' He makes it sound like it's a chore.

They head for the gate at the end of the garden, and I wonder why they aren't eating with us.

Later, when Greg's upstairs reading Toby a bedtime story, and Rachel and Hilary are in another room watching a movie Rachel has apparently been 'dying to see', Rob and I get talking again. After a few beers we've mellowed. He has started reminiscing. I feel guilty, wondering if I should stop him – Greg's childhood is the one thing he's reluctant to talk to me about.

'Don't know why,' he says when I'm straight with him. 'If I were Greg, I'd be telling everyone. How many people can say they brought up their kid brother?'

'What d'you mean?'

'Didn't he tell you? Our da died when I was four. Greg was ten.'

I'm stunned. 'I knew your dad had died. I just assumed it was relatively recently.'

'I have two memories of my father. One was wrapping me up in a warm towel after a bath. The other was letting me blow my nose into his hand when he didn't have a hankie. That's all I know of him outside of a few photos. Greg and my mother don't like to talk about him.'

'You said *Greg* brought you up – what about your mum? Didn't she look after you?'

'She'd to go out to work – two jobs, both paying shite, a supermarket and a dive that called itself a hotel. She was always gone. Greg did everything. Got me to school, fed me, helped with homework, put me to bed, never complained. Every night he read – *Sinbad*, *Biggles*, *Superman*, *Spiderman*, *The Hobbit* . . . Our heroes came from the library.'

'I can't imagine how hard it must have been, becoming a father at ten.'

'You know, I never felt he was doing it because he had to. He never treated me like some stupid kid he was stuck with. He spoke to me man to man. I fucking worshipped the guy. Trailed around after him. Copied everything he did. Wanted to be just like him. He wasn't like a father. And he was better than a brother. He was my hero, you know?'

I imagine them, Little and Large, side by side, but *never* holding hands. Large looking out for Little. But why hasn't Greg told me any of this? He's so open about everything else. Why would he hide this from me?

'I was tough work, though,' Rob continues. 'Always first to put up the fists. I'd lose it, like that.' He snaps his fingers. 'Greg was the one who stopped me hanging out with the troublemakers. He taught me to fight through hard work, getting somewhere, not lashing out. He kept my eye on the ball, until I learned to myself. He put me through college while he worked, in a printer's first, then bookshops, until his own books started to get published. I was so fucking proud of him when they did. If there was one person who deserved it, it was Greg.'

'Wow.' It strikes me that I'm engaged to a man I don't really know at all.

'They're lovely kids,' I say to Greg later. We're sitting on the sofa in his enormous, bay-windowed living room, giant table lamps casting warm and cosy light, waiting for a taxi to take me home. 'So well-behaved and really beautiful.'

'It's the genes,' he jokes.

I throw a cushion at him.

'I didn't see much of them, though,' I say.

'Probably best not to rush these things.'

'Why didn't they stick around for the barbecue?'

'You know kids. They love picnics. And they're so happy down by the sea. You and Rob seemed to hit it off,' he says, changing the subject. 'What was that long chat all about?'

'A lot of things,' I say, 'including your childhood.' I eye him closely.

He stares into coffee.

'I bet you were such a cute kid,' I say, to ease him in. 'I can just imagine you. Curly hair, shorts, long socks, a cut on your knee . . .'

He smiles. 'Sounds a bit Little Lord Fauntleroy. We were more like the scruffy kids from a *Beano* comic.'

'I wish I'd lived next door.'

'So do I. Think of what we could have got up to.' He looks suggestive.

'Not with *my* mother around.'

'Dead right too. Look how lovely and innocent she's kept you.'

I make a face.

'It's funny,' I say, 'how your parents had two boys, while mine had two girls . . . Who did you get on better with – your mum or your dad?'

He looks at his watch. 'This taxi's taking ages. I think I'll give them another buzz.' He gets up to make the call. 'It's on its way,' he says, alighting on the sofa opposite.

'Your father died so young,' I say, thinking I should be honest about what I know.

'Hmm.'

'Must have been tough.'

'It was no big deal. We were fine.' His tone is flat.

'Rob said it was a heart attack.'

'You know what? I'm tired, Lucy. Can we talk about this another time?'

'Of course. I was just concerned. I mean, if your father died so young from a heart attack, you should be careful. You should have regular check-ups.'

'Lucy. I said I was tired.'

'Sorry.'

6

Greg is keen to rush ahead with a wedding. I worry about the children. Surely we should get to *know* each other first. We compromise and leave the date open until we see how things are going. When I ask Greg how Rachel and Toby are feeling about everything, he says that they are still getting used to the idea. I think he is being polite.

I am so careful around them. Friendly without forcing conversation, extra sensitive to anything they say or do, and quick to react accordingly. I never refer to Greg and I as a couple and *never* touch him or let him touch me in their company. I buy all the step-parenting handbooks I can find.

Toby and Rachel seem sweet and well-mannered, though not in a hurry to engage in conversation. They prefer the company of their nanny. Which is totally understandable. I know this must be very hard for them and that much of the effort will be down to me. But I also feel that if I'm patient and sensitive to their needs, if I give them space, just concentrate on being their friend, and carefully build a relationship with them, then eventually we might all fit together.

My father takes Greg for the customary game of golf that occurs any time there is a hint of a boyfriend getting serious. It's a family joke by now – Dad is the least judgemental person I know. He ends up loving everyone. He won't have a problem with Greg. Can't say the same for my mother.

Mum can spot a charmer at ten paces. She has no time for

them. Yet she is melting under Greg's charm. There is a very simple reason why. It is genuine. Greg has an unusual quality that endears him to, well, pretty much everyone. He takes a genuine and intense interest in things other people fail to notice. I have seen this again and again: on Grafton Street, with the man with the black eye selling poetry; in Dún Laoghaire, with the woman selling fish on the side of the road. It's always the same. He becomes fascinated with some aspect of their work or lives, and involves them in animated conversations that can go on for up to ten minutes, and that would probably last longer if I wasn't beside him making moves to go.

With Mum, I don't think Greg even understands that he's cracking a hard nut. He simply spots her patchwork, neatly cast aside in the kitchen, and becomes obsessed. How did she choose such colours? Did she ever think of depicting a narrative on a quilt? Does she know any men who do patchwork? Maybe she could teach him? Or maybe he could come up with a story for one of her wall hangings? At home, nobody appreciates Mum's patchwork. She has her sewing cronies who recognize the painstaking hours of effort that go into her work. Not us. We just don't get it. Boyfriends have always complimented her cooking, never her patchwork. Big mistake, I realize now.

I'm nervous about meeting Greg's mother, Phyllis, but hopeful that we will get on. On the day we are to visit her, I dress with conservative care and hurry Greg to get there at the time we said we'd call. Eleven. At five-to, we drive through two imposing redbrick pillars, and on to the grounds of a beautiful old building, also redbrick, that looks more like a sanctuary for war veterans than like the type of nursing home I had envisaged. In a bright, leafy reception area we are told that

Phyllis isn't feeling up to two visitors today and will see only her son.

Greg looks apologetic.

'I hope she's OK,' I say.

'I'm sure she's just tired.'

'You go ahead.'

'You sure?'

'Yeah. I'll go for a walk in the gardens.'

'I won't be long.'

'Take your time.'

The lawns are beautifully manicured, the shrubs trimmed, in keeping with the type of superior establishment she seems to occupy. After twenty minutes my mobile rings. Greg is on his way out. We meet at the door and walk to the car.

'Well? Was she OK?'

'Fine. Just tired.'

'She's not ill, though, is she?'

'No, thank God. She's fine. A tough old bird,' he says, with love in his voice.

'Why is she in a home, Greg?'

'Her choice.'

I look at him, not understanding why anyone would want to go into a home, even one as plush as this.

'I know it's odd. I've tried to get her to come live with us. It'd be good for her to be so close to her grandchildren. But she's very independent.'

'But being in a home isn't being independent. Is it?'

'In there it is. You should see the set-up. She's in a section for active residents. She lives in a suite. It's like a top-class, one-bedroom apartment, en suite, the lot. She comes and goes as she pleases. She has one or two good friends whom she likes to fuss over, look after. She has the chapel, her flat-screen TV. She has every modern convenience without having to cook or wash for herself. Rob brings her out shopping, once a week. And she comes to us for lunch every Sunday – under her own steam – takes a taxi, there and back.'

'She sounds like a character.'

'Oh, she's a character all right.'

As we drive out the gates, I say, 'I didn't know places like this existed. Must cost a fortune.'

'Doesn't come cheap. But I'm glad to be able to do it for her. She's had a tough life.'

We drive in silence for a while.

'D'you think she just didn't want to see me?' I ask, finally saying what's been bothering me.

'No, Lucy. She was tired. That's all.'

When he doesn't look me in the eye, instinct tells me to worry. Is this one more person who doesn't want someone new in Greg's life?

Ben and Ruth are Greg's in-laws. As their daughter's replacement, I'm uncomfortable with the idea of meeting them. But Greg reassures me that they won't look on it like that.

'Their focus is on their grandchildren, Lucy, not on me. You're going to be Rachel and Toby's step-mum. I think it'd be good for you to meet at this stage. I think they'd appreciate it.' As we're driving to meet them, though, he surprises me by saying, 'I should warn you. You might find them a little cold.'

'Oh?'

'It's nothing to do with you, you understand.'

'What, then?' I'm sceptical after the Phyllis incident.

'It's to do with me.'

'In what way?'

'It's no big deal. I'm just not their favourite person in the world. I'm not worried about it. You shouldn't be.'

'But they're your in-laws.'

'Didn't you know? You're not supposed to get on with your in-laws,' he jokes. When I don't react, he says, 'Look. They adore the kids. Rachel and Toby are their last link to Catherine, who was their pride and joy. They absolutely dote on my children. And they're polite to me. That'll more than do. I'm just telling you, because I don't want you to think that their chilliness has anything to do with you. OK?'

'OK.' I lean over and kiss him to show that whatever they think, they're wrong.

We arrive at the Four Seasons, where we've arranged to meet them for drinks. Our car is valet parked, and the hotel doors are opened by smiling uniformed men. The central flower arrangement in the lobby is bigger than I am. A piano tinkles in the background. When Greg spots them, sharing an antique sofa in a distant corner of the lounge, he takes my hand, squeezes reassurance and leads the way.

They stand when they see us, their smiles reserved. Ben is tall and noticeably lean, with an air of success that has me imagining him as chairperson of a string of companies. A man used to getting his own way. His wife, by contrast, seems timid, slightly plump and about six inches shorter than he is. She has an auburn rinse in her hair, which could benefit from being a shade lighter, and a pleasant, gentle face. It's easy to see who is boss. Greg introduces us. We sit. The conversation is formal, stilted and about the world at large. I expect it to turn personal at any moment, with a 'So how did you two meet?' or a 'So what do you do, Lucy?' but that never happens. Nor does Greg encourage it. I feel real tension between them. Everybody knows what's happening here. We are doing our duty – we are letting them know. And they are doing theirs. They are listening.

In the car, afterwards, I share my surprise with Greg. 'They didn't ask anything about me.'

He looks at me and smiles. 'Don't take it personally.'

'They didn't even ask how we met.'

'It's not you. It's me.'

'What's the problem between you, anyway?'

He sighs, long and loud. 'I wasn't exactly what they'd planned for their only daughter. Didn't go to the right schools. Wasn't from the right part of town. Wouldn't know an old boys' network if it came up and bit me on the arse.'

'He's a snob, basically,' I say, guessing that Ruth just follows his lead.

He smiles. 'Ben thinks that writing books should be a hobby.'

'Arsehole.'

He shrugs. 'Doesn't bother me. It's his problem.'

'Well, I think you're great,' I say, squeezing his thigh. 'Although, I don't know.' I take my hand away. 'What school did you say you went to again?'

He makes a face at me.

Greg wants me to join the family in the South of France for the summer. Much as I'd like to, I can't do that. I am a partner in a business. I have responsibilities.

'Doesn't that make you more flexible?' asks the man who fails to see obstacles.

'Not really.'

'You could design from there. The villa's set up with everything – e-mail, ISDN. And we could buy anything else you need. Think of the work environment: sun, sea, sand, stars.'

'My clients, Greg. They need to see me.'

'You could pop back for meetings. I'm sure Fint would be open.'

'I don't know. It'd be asking a lot.' I think of options. 'Maybe

I could take a two- or three-week holiday and after that pop over for weekends.' The idea of any holiday at all is a novelty.

'Why not run the idea by him, at least?'

'Greg, even if he was happy with me working from there and my clients were OK with it, and everything was fine on the work front, what about the children?'

'What about them?'

'Would they really want me there?'

'Lucy, this would give you a chance to spend more time with them, get to know each other better.'

I see the merit in that. As it is, every time we meet, it is to sit down to a meal, which makes everything seem formal, stilted. Maybe if we were all on holiday . . . Then again . . . 'Where would I stay, though? I couldn't stay with you. Imagine how they'd feel. Me suddenly moving in.'

He reflects – for a split second. 'You could stay near by. It wouldn't be a problem. I could look into it . . .'

I run it by Fint, still not totally convinced it's what I want. When I see his face, I realize that this is the first time that his joint roles as Cupid and business partner have opposed each other. He tries to camouflage his initial surprise, then asks a series of logistical questions, the replies to which inform him that the villa is fully equipped, that I can be on a plane and home in two hours for brainstorms, meetings, etc., and that Greg will cover the cost of flights.

'It'd just be for the summer, right?'

'I won't stay that long.'

He sucks a thumbnail. 'It *is* our quietest time.'

I let him mull it over.

His face is brightening. 'You know, it's not a bad idea', he finally says, 'for one of us to cover base while the other takes a proper break. Maybe next year I could finally get in that trip to South Africa I keep talking about. Stay a decent amount of time . . .'

'Of course. But I'm not sure I want to spend the whole summer there. I was thinking of just playing it by ear for a week or two. Work but view it as a bit of a holiday, then see how it goes.'

'My God,' he says, clapping his hands to his face. 'Stop the presses. Lucy Arigho finally takes a holiday.'

I smile for his benefit. 'If it's not working out, I'll just come home,' I say to myself as much as to him. 'And I'll be over and back all the time.'

'Let's try it, then. See how it goes.'

Before heading to France, a night out is organized so that Greg can meet Grace and Kevin. We go for a meal in a hip Italian in town. Greg is in amazing form. He even brings Kevin to life, which is an achievement. But then I wonder. My brother-in-law's laughter sounds false, as if he's more impressed by who Greg is than by what he's actually saying. Or am I wronging the guy?

Leaving the restaurant, Greg suggests going on to a casino on Merrion Square. Grace, who hasn't been getting out much lately, is game. Kevin isn't. Which makes me question my judgement. If he *was* impressed by Greg, he'd be hanging around. Then he explains, one alpha male to another, that he is *Medical Director* of a start-up pharmaceutical company. It's at a 'very vulnerable stage', and they need him there. He has an early start and really should get home. Greg understands. I think, *Must be great to be so needed.* When he says goodbye to Grace, he reminds her that Jason wakes at six. I can't imagine she'd forgotten.

From the outside the casino looks like any other three-storey, Georgian redbrick on the square. Inside, it's like a gentlemen's club. Grace and I are slow to part with our chips, expecting to lose. And that is exactly what we do. Greg piles his chips high and barely looks as the wheel spins. And he wins. Consistently. He gives away chips to the dealers – for 'luck'. Grace and I retire to the bar.

'Is Greg OK?' she asks.

I'm surprised. 'Yeah, he's fine. Why?'

'Oh, nothing, I was just wondering. Is he always so energetic?'

I laugh. 'Always.'

'He never seems to stop, though. Does he?'

'He's just one of those people who's always on the go.'

'Must be exhausting.'

I eye her. *What's she getting at?*

'Dad was shattered after playing golf with him.'

'Did Dad *talk* to you about Greg?' It feels like a deception, somehow.

'He just mentioned the game, that's all. Greg wanted to go for another eighteen holes.'

'He was probably *joking*. He does have a sense of humour.' I can't believe Dad talked to her about Greg behind my back. 'Grace, are you trying to tell me something here?'

'I'm just wondering why he's so highly charged . . .'

Suddenly I'm defensive. 'Greg lives life. He *experiences* it. And d'you know why? Because he knows it could be snatched from him at any moment. Maybe if you'd lost someone you loved you'd be more *highly charged*. Greg is alive. And he's making the most of it.'

She bites her lip. After a moment's silence, and with regret in her voice, she says, 'Maybe more of us should be doing that.'

And I'm sorry, then, for snapping. 'The boys are young. And Kevin's snowed under. Start-ups are always like that.

Remember when Fint and I set up Get Smart. I don't think anybody ever saw us from one end of the day to the next, unless of course they were working for us. It'll get better, Grace.'

'Might help if he'd a sense of humour.'

'Who? *Kevin?*'

'Who else?' *Where has this come from? I've never heard Grace complain about Kevin – ever.* 'He's so serious,' she continues, moving her swizzle stick around the glass with a finger. 'He never laughs.'

'He was laughing tonight.'

She gives me a look that cuts right through me. 'That wasn't laughter.'

Oh. 'Is a sense of humour so important?' I try.

'When times are tough, it is. It binds you together.'

'Kevin has other qualities.'

'Name one.'

'Grace! What's got into you? You're perfectly happy with Kevin.'

Her 'Yeah' sounds tired. She reaches for her bag and stands. 'Come on, let's go.'

I follow her, trying to work out what's upset her. We find Greg, and I tell him it's time to go. He suggests a nightclub. Grace cries off. We catch a cab and drop her home first. By the time we get to my apartment, I'm tired, looking forward to my pillow. Fired up by his victories, Greg has other ideas.

7

Greg, Hilary and the children go on ahead to France, while I finish up a job at the office. A week later Greg collects me at Nice Airport, looking tanned and fit. He lifts me up and swirls me round. I laugh, embarrassed by the looks the gesture generates. But it feels good. It's only been a week, but I've missed him. He grabs my case and takes off. It's an effort to keep up. We leave the cool, air-conditioned Arrivals Hall and walk into a wall of heat. I root around for my shades. We reach his illegally parked Range Rover in minutes. He throws my case in the back and makes for the front. I follow, thinking he's opening my door for me, like he always does. When he jumps inside, I realize my mistake. Left-hand drive. I go round to the other side. The engine's running when I climb in. The car's an oven. 'Jilted John', a punk favourite of Greg's, is blaring. Two months ago I'd never heard of it. And, though it's fun, I ask him to turn it down and the air-conditioning up. He looks surprised but obliges immediately.

We follow a royal blue sign for Marseilles, Cannes, Antibes. The grey and lush green of Ireland has changed to hazy blue and faded olive. We hit a motorway. Sea on our left, mountains on our distant right. We really are on the Côte d'Azur. Greg's *flying*. Hitting 150 kilometres an hour. The limit is 130. Even that seems high. I ask him to slow down, and he does, apologizing. We turn off at the exit for Antibes and make our way through the outskirts.

'Nearly there,' he says, resting a hand on my leg.

At a roundabout we take a smaller road. Then a smaller one again. We begin to climb.

'There it is,' he says, pointing up the hill. Surrounded by pine and eucalyptus trees, I catch a glimpse of a large two-storey villa. It has a terracotta roof and walls of a lighter shade, hidden in places by bright purple bougainvillaea. Its shutters are a friendly light blue. It looks wonderful, I tell him. He has found me an apartment near by, and I ask if it's far. A quarter of a mile further on, he says.

'I thought we could dump my stuff there now.'

'Ah, come say hi to the kids first.'

As we pull up outside, I tense. My future family is inside. We'll be seeing a lot of each other. I'll have to fit in. Can I? He gives my hand a squeeze, then swings open the heavy wooden door. It's cooler than outside but not much. Overhead fans slowly rotate. Ceramic tiles, terracotta in colour, flag the floor. The walls are a warm yellow, and every so often there are floor-to-ceiling pillars that remind me of Ancient Rome. I wonder how old the place is and whether it was, in fact, built by the French at all. In the living room three large sofas flank an incredible fireplace. I've never seen anything like it. It's in the shape of the sun's face, its wide-open mouth housing the hearth. Around it, the sofas are strewn with children's clothes, sunscreen tubes, books, a bottle of Evian and an inflatable bright green turtle. A large, very dark mahogany chest acts as a coffee table. On it is a pottery vase filled with eucalyptus and bougainvillaea. A woman's touch. Hilary, no doubt.

As Greg leads me on, I suddenly stop at one whole wall lined with books, wanting to explore. There'll be time later, he says, taking my hand. From outside comes an echoey distant scream, followed by a splash.

'Come on, they're in the pool,' he says.

Walking out on to a terrace, I'm blinded by white light.

Everything seems overexposed. I shade my eyes, then lower my sunglasses. To my left, beyond a low stone wall, is the view down to the bay, and it is spectacular. Straight ahead, a table, made from a long slab of ancient wood placed on trestles, is charming in its simplicity. Multicoloured towels hide the chairs that surround it. On the ground are flip-flops and sandals, scattered as though abandoned in a hurry. Small wet footprints lead to and from a large rectangle of blue in the near distance. And there they are: Toby being hurled into the air by Hilary, and Rachel swimming towards them. Toby reminds me of Mowgli from *The Jungle Book*: slight and sallow, with his longish, dark hair and little red triangle of togs. His goggles are huge compared to the size of his face, which makes him look half alien, half fighter pilot. He's laughing. Rachel is a streak of dark hair and splashing arms and legs. Hilary, robust in a black one-piece costume, catches Toby and spins him around in the water.

'Hi, guys,' calls Greg as we reach the pool. They turn.

'Dad!' shouts Toby. 'Did you see that?'

'Sure did. You should be in the circus, Tobes.'

'I know. Yeah.'

I smile at his unaffected honesty.

'Do you want us to come out?' asks Hilary.

'No, Hilary, we're coming in.'

I look at Greg. My bikini's packed at the bottom of my case. I'm visualizing it when he grabs my hand and jumps, taking me with him.

'Wee,' he calls.

I'm going in.

The sudden drop in temperature adds to the shock. I find myself under water, face up, legs higher than the rest of me. I pull them under me and feel for the bottom. How can the centre of the pool be this deep? His hand is gone. I can't see him. I kick and swim to the surface, breaking through into dazzling light, gasping for air but ending up coughing. I make it to the side, where I cling, head down, trying to restore normal breathing. When I have, I look up. He's already out of the pool, shaking himself like a dog. I open my mouth to say 'You big eejit' but close it again. What would the children think? I look round. They're laughing. Yep, I'm the entertainment. I give a little chuckle to show I'm a good sport, then put my palms flat on the hot slabs lining the pool and push myself up and out. Greg comes to me with a towel. I could strangle him with it.

'That's mine,' says Rachel, who has stopped laughing.

'It's an emergency,' says Greg, handing it to me.

'It's *mine*.' Her voice is louder now. Definite. 'I don't want her to have it.'

Mortified, I hand it back to him.

'I'll get you another,' he says, disappearing into the villa.

I stand alone, feeling conspicuous, stupid and *wet*.

'Your legs are bleeding,' Toby calls.

I look down. The dye from my red leather sandals is running in little streams down my feet. It looks like a scene from the Old Testament. I want to disappear. Vanish. I make for the villa, dripping red.

'Here you go,' Greg says, when I get inside. He wraps a large white towel around me.

I stare at him. 'Why did you do that?'

He stops, as if considering for the first time what he's done. 'I don't know. I thought it'd be fun?'

'I am trying so hard to make an impression with Rachel and Toby.'

'But they thought it was hilarious.'

'No, Greg. They thought *I* was hilarious. I want them to like me, not think I'm a joke. I felt like such a fool out there.'

'I'm sorry.'

'How can they respect me if you don't?'

He looks hurt. 'But I do.'

'Well, that's not how it seemed. It was such a stupid thing to do.'

'I'm sorry. I was just trying to break the ice. Everyone's just so nervous. But you're right, it was dumb. And I'm sorry.'

We drive in silence to the apartment. It is in a small, upmarket block. On the second floor, Greg opens No. 26, then hands me one of two keys. My first impression is of a bright, airy space. Very modern, with clean lines and white walls. Most importantly, it is air-conditioned. Greg, carrying my case, shows me to the master bedroom. While he heaves the Samsonite on to the bed and opens it, I go to shower.

Red dye swirls down the plughole, taking my anger with it. I reach for a white towelling bathrobe. It still has its sales tag on. That he has thought to go out and buy this for me reminds me of what's important – Greg is a good person who means well. Usually, I love his childlike approach to life. *Usually*, it's refreshing. Maybe if I hadn't been so tense, trying so hard to make a good impression on his children. I wrap my hair in a towel and go in search of him. He's sitting on the bed, looking guilty. And suddenly I wish it were just the two of us, no children, no complications, no one to impress or to win over. I shake my hair free from the towel and the thoughts from my head. I go sit beside him, wrap my arms around him.

'I'm sorry,' he says again. 'I should have given it more thought.'

'Forget it.' I smile when I say, 'It cooled me down.'

He kisses me, then gets up. 'Come see the view from the balcony.'

Outside, the air is hot and dry and carries the fragrance of,

I'm not sure, herbs – rosemary, maybe? The cicadas sound as if they're on overdrive. Off in the distance, a glittering sea merges with a clear, blue sky. No wonder it's called the 'Côte d'Azur'. Pine trees near by are heavy with cones, like eco-friendly Christmas decorations. A eucalyptus is so close I can almost touch it, with drooping silver-green leaves that look cool and unruffled in the heat. Its bark is peeling off in thin strips, like flesh-coloured stockings, revealing smooth white skin underneath. I turn to tell Greg how magical it all is and how happy I am to be here with him, only to discover that he has sneaked back inside. I find him sitting up in bed, bare-chested and beaming, clothes abandoned on the floor. A leg is draped over the sheet in exaggerated seductiveness. He raises and lowers his eyebrows. I laugh, let my robe drop and join him. And soon I have forgotten everything, except how much I adore him.

When we eventually return to the villa, Hilary has made dinner. A tuna pasta dish. The children's favourite, I'm told. Greg must have forgotten to mention I'm vegetarian. Still, I can't afford to be any more different than I already am. So I tuck in with what I hope looks like enthusiasm. *At least it's not steak*.

I wear a friendly face, say little and listen, hoping to learn as much as I can about this pre-prepared family I've promised to become part of. Toby chats about sharks, in particular about the fact that they have to keep moving to stay alive, which means they have to swim in their sleep.

'Imagine that!' he concludes.

That he seems oblivious to me is reassuring. Maybe I'm not such a big deal to him. Rachel, on the other hand, I frequently catch peeping out at me from behind a curtain of hair she's let fall between us. When I smile, she looks away. When dinner's over, I start to collect the dishes. Hilary stands quickly, taking the plates from me.

'It's fine,' she says. 'I'll do it.'

'No, no. I'd like to help, Hilary.' If I'm going to be eating here, I don't expect to be waited on.

'It's OK,' she says, looking down at the plates in her hand. 'I know where everything goes.'

'At least let me carry things to the kitchen.'

'I'm fine. Honestly. Thanks,' she says firmly.

I look at Greg. He shakes his head as if to say, 'Don't-worry-about-it.' The children excuse themselves and leave the table. I offer to make coffee. Greg seems to understand that I need to contribute and takes me up on the offer. I get to the kitchen. And stop. It's beautiful, large and spacious with an old-fashioned sink and simple wooden cupboards painted pale green. Shelves carry ceramic crockery and baskets. The work surfaces are oak, as is the chunky, basic furniture. Overhead are large wooden beams. Really, really pretty. I wonder if Catherine designed it, or if they did it together, or if it was like that when they bought the villa. I bring myself back to the present – coffee. I start to search the obvious places.

'What are you looking for?' comes a voice behind me. Hilary.

Instinctively, I feel I've walked into her territory. I don't want to upset her, so I turn and offer an apologetic smile. 'Coffee.'

'I'll do it,' she says.

'Hilary, look. I don't want you to feel that you have to do anything for me. I'm going to be around a bit, and I'd like to pull my weight.'

Her face is blank; I can't read it.

'It *would* be great, though,' I say, 'if you could show me where the coffee is.'

Without a word, she opens various cupboard doors and pulls out an original steel coffee percolator (so romantic!) and the paraphernalia that goes with it.

'Thanks,' I say and set to work.

'Sorry, but could you *move* please,' she says after two seconds. 'I have to use the dishwasher.'

'Sorry.' I shift along. Feeling like a buffalo. Maybe I should stay out of the kitchen for a while.

'Hilary, aren't you having coffee?' offers Greg.

'No, thanks. I've got to get Toby ready for bed.'

'We're on holiday,' he says. 'There's no rush.'

'I'd prefer to stick to routine, Greg, if that's OK?' I wonder if that's supposed to imply that I've upset it.

'Sure. Whatever you think,' Greg says.

She coaxes Toby away from the DVD he's watching.

Rachel gets up.

'Going up already, Rache?' Greg asks.

'I'm tired,' she says, looking directly at me.

Greg doesn't seem to get it. 'OK,' he says. 'Say goodnight to Lucy.'

''Night, Lucy,' says Toby.

'Rachel?'

She looks at me, eyes dark, then turns to go.

'Rachel,' says her father, in a warning tone.

'It doesn't matter, Greg,' I say quietly. I smile at her.

She glares back.

'Rachel doesn't like Lucy,' offers Toby matter-of-factly.

I can feel myself redden.

'She doesn't want her to be on holidays with us. She doesn't want her to be in our family. She hates her, ackshilly.'

Oh, God. For the second time today, I want to disappear.

'Enough, Toby,' says Greg. 'Rachel, I told you to say goodnight to Lucy, now say it.'

68

I don't want him to make her. 'Greg, please, it doesn't matter. Really.'

'Goodnight,' she says, as if the word means I-hate-you. She races to the stairs and thunders up them. Hilary follows, looking calm and unruffled by the exchange.

'You can't force her to like me, Greg,' I say, quietly.

'I know. But the least she can do is have manners.'

'*I* have manners,' says Toby.

'And a big mouth,' retorts his father, tickling him. 'Bristle attack,' he says, grabbing two little bare feet and rubbing them against his evening stubble. Toby screams. And they both laugh. I sit watching, feeling like an outsider, wanting to be somewhere else.

A while later Hilary comes back down. Though she returns the smile I give her, it's without any great warmth. I have upset Rachel, why should she be warm?

'Is she all right?' Greg asks her.

'She's a bit upset. The change, an' all,' she says, lifting Toby from Greg's lap. 'Maybe you could have a word with her when you go up. Come on, squirt,' she says to the boy.

'Do I have to?'

'Yes. You have to.'

Off they go, him twisting her hair in his fingers.

Greg winks at me. If it's to cheer me up, it doesn't work. He offers me a drink, and I join him in a beer. We've just settled outside on the terrace, when Toby comes out, squeaky clean and dressed for bed. Hilary kisses the top of his head and says goodnight to him, then to us.

'My God,' Greg exclaims. 'It's a mass exodus tonight.'

'Tired,' she says.

Greg brings Toby upstairs for story-time. Watching them disappear, I feel guilty: by just being here I've upset everyone's routine. That's when the true implication of what I've done hits me. I haven't just promised to marry a man, but a man, two children and a nanny. I listen to the sounds of them moving about inside, and try to come to terms with that. Theoretical children are so much easier than real ones who come with personalities, opinions, objections. *Can Rachel really hate me? Already? She doesn't even know me. Then again, that's the problem*, I reassure myself. *Rachel doesn't know that I'm on her side, that I want what's best for her, that I want us to get on. If only I could make her see that. Not that she'd listen to me. She probably wouldn't listen to Greg either – he's the one who brought me here. She'd listen to Hilary, though. It's so obvious she loves her. But would Hilary help? She seemed touchy earlier, but I was getting under her feet. She has always seemed pleasant until now. Maybe I just need to try to get close to her.*

'Let's go,' I say, when Greg arrives back down.

'Where?'

'To the apartment.'

'Why?'

'So we can be alone for a while.'

'We're alone now.'

'I know but really alone. Just the two of us.'

He looks hurt. 'This is home. The apartment's for appearances, for you to sleep in, that's all.'

I have to get out of the villa. I go to him, kiss him softly on the mouth and whisper, 'It could be for other things too.'

He smiles. 'I know somewhere closer.' He takes my hand and leads me to his bedroom. 'See, much quicker,' he beams, tugging at his clothes. I tell myself it doesn't matter that we're technically still in the same building as everyone else. We're alone. I close my eyes and think of nothing but what's happening in this room. I forget it all until the bed begins to groan and protest with a telling rhythm. I tense. *What if someone hears? How thick are the walls? Hilary is probably still awake. Next door. Can she hear? Oh, God.* My embarrassment amuses but doesn't stop him. I hit him with a pillow. He laughs. And keeps going. Which, I decide, is actually fine by me.

Afterwards we lie in silence, a film of sweat covering our bodies, the air so heavy, it's hard to breathe. I ask why he doesn't have air-conditioning.

'I like to live like the locals.'

'I'm sure plenty of them have air-conditioning.'

'Not the traditionalists.' He turns on his side to face me. 'I might be a foreigner. But I don't have to act like one. This villa's designed for the heat. The Millars are a tough breed. Don't want us becoming too soft.'

'How about a few electric fans, then?'

'Wimp,' he says with a smile. But I can tell he's given in.

'Greg?'

'Mm-hmm.'

'Do you really think Rachel hates me?'

He tucks a stray strand of hair behind my ear. 'No. She doesn't hate you, just the idea of sharing her life with you. She'll come round once she gets to know you. Don't worry. It'll be fine.'

I trace parallel lines on the sheet with my finger. 'I thought that maybe Hilary might put in a good word for me with her.'

'There's an idea. If she listens to anyone, it's Hilary.'

'I don't know, though. Might be unfair to ask. Sometimes I get the feeling that Hilary doesn't like me.'

'Hilary?' he says, propping himself up on an elbow. 'Hilary's a dote. She'd do anything for us. Want me to ask her?'

'Eh, no, not for the moment. Just let me get to know her a bit better first, OK?'

'OK.'

We're quiet for a while.

'Greg?'

71

'Uh-huh?'

'Could you drop me at the airport tomorrow?'

'Leaving already?' he asks, carrying on a joke he thinks I've started.

'I want to rent a car.'

'A car? *Why?*'

'Just to get around.'

'Sure, I'll bring you wherever you want to go.'

I smile. 'I know. And thanks. But you've the kids. What if I've to go back to Dublin for work and you need to bring them somewhere?'

'I'll work something out.'

'I don't want you to have to. My being here is putting them out enough. The last thing I want to do is impact on their plans.' I pause. 'And, Greg, I really think that, for the moment, we should try to remain a bit separate, you know?'

'What do you mean separate?'

'Well, I don't think it's a good idea for me to be a constant presence at the villa.'

He scratches his head and takes a long breath before speaking. 'Lucy, I know that Rachel's behaviour was upsetting, but I think it would be a mistake to overreact here. They need to get used to your being around.'

'I know, Greg, but slowly.'

I feel his disappointment. We say no more on the subject until he is dropping me back to the apartment.

'We'll get that car, tomorrow afternoon, then,' he concedes.

I hug him. 'Thanks. It's the right thing.'

Then he tells me he'll pick me up for breakfast. And I wonder if I got through to him at all.

8

Next morning, rather than wait to be collected and driven to the villa like a princess, I decide to walk, taking in the scenery and getting some exercise. It's a great idea, until I arrive at the front door and can't decide what to do. I have a key, but if I use it, it might seem pushy. If I don't, it'll just seem stupid. Everyone knows I have it. *Oh, what the hell.* I slip it in. I'm almost at the living room when I hear crying. I stop, afraid to walk in on a scene. I'm about to turn round when I hear Rachel's voice.

'She talks to us like babies. Is she some kind of *dork* or something?'

My stomach jumps. I can't move.

Hilary's voice is placating when she says, 'She's probably just not used to kids.'

'I don't want her to get used to us. I want her to get lost.'

'Rache, remember when I came first. You didn't like me either.'

'I did so.'

'No, Rachel, you didn't. It took a long time. But you did in the end. Lucy seems nice. Maybe you should give her a chance.'

'Why? I don't want a stepmother. Did anyone ask me? No. He never asked, Hilary. He never *checked*. He always checks big decisions with us. Always.' Her voice breaks and I feel so guilty.

I've heard enough.

I close the front door quietly and begin the trek back up the

73

hill, the sun beating down on the backs of my legs. We've made a mistake. We shouldn't have announced our engagement the way we did. We should have been more measured in the way Greg introduced me. If only I'd slipped off my ring and just been Greg's 'friend'. That way, they wouldn't have felt threatened. We could have got to know each other as individuals before bringing the whole stepmother thing into the equation. But then that wouldn't have felt right either. It would have been deceitful. If only things had happened more slowly. If only he hadn't parachuted me into their lives.

The only good thing about what has just happened is that I feel more at ease about Hilary. I'm surprised she stood up for me. And relieved. *Maybe it was my imagination. Maybe she doesn't resent my being here after all.*

I'm just back at the apartment when Greg arrives – with croissants and pain au chocolat.

'I thought we were eating at the villa,' I say.

'Well, you want to be a bit separate. So. Here I am.' He smiles.

I kiss him thanks, make coffee and we go out on the balcony. I tell him what happened.

He rubs my leg. 'You OK?'

'Yeah. Fine,' I say, not wanting him to have to take sides.

He pulls out a pack of those cigars he's started smoking since coming to France, holds it up as if to say, 'Do you mind?' I shake my head.

'She's a good kid, Lucy. But angry. She didn't mean what she said.' He removes a cigar from the pack. 'I need to sit down with her, though. I can see that. She needs to let off a bit of steam with me.' He cups his hand over the cigar and lights it slowly, ritualistically.

I look out over the trees, remembering the conversation. 'It was nice of Hilary to say what she did.'

He replaces the lighter on the table. 'Told you she was like that.'

I savour the smell of cigar smoke that always reminds me of sun holidays. 'What did she do before coming to work for you?'

'Worked in a crèche for a while.'

'How come she left?'

'She wanted to work more one-to-one with kids.' I'm about to say how good she is with them when Greg continues with 'Hilary's own marriage broke up because they couldn't have children.'

'God. That's terrible. I never even knew she'd been married.' I try to imagine what it must be like to be told you can never have a family, the finality of it, the sense of loss, especially for someone who so obviously loves kids.

'They were married five years, trying for kids most of that time. In the end the whole IVF thing wore them down. It had become their sole focus as a couple. When they finally gave up, there didn't seem anything left to salvage in their marriage.'

'That is *so* tough. When did she tell you all this?' It doesn't strike me as the kind of thing you'd unburden easily on a male boss.

He stubs out the cigar, then stands and goes to the balcony rail, placing his hands wide apart on it and leaning forward. After a few moments, he turns. He looks awkward. 'Actually, Lucy, there's something I need to tell you.' My stomach lurches. 'I wasn't sure how to bring it up before now because I didn't want to make it any bigger than it was . . .'

Jesus.

He shoves his hands into the pockets of his khaki shorts, takes a deep breath. 'OK.' He comes back and sits down. 'Way back, at the beginning, not long after she started, when I was

75

pretty low,' he pauses, 'something happened between Hilary and me . . .'

Oh, God.

'Once. Only once. It was an accident. I was so down. Didn't want to go on, felt I couldn't. I'd loved Catherine so much, Lucy. For the first few months, I drank a bit. One night, Hilary was there, saying the right things, doing the right things. And, God forgive me, I took the comfort she offered.'

Jesus.

'Afterwards, I was so disgusted with myself. I was her boss. I shouldn't have let it happen. I was ashamed, so ashamed. I apologized profusely, told her that if she wanted to leave, I'd understand, that maybe it'd be better if she did. I was straight with her, explained that what had happened was the result of grief, nothing else. She understood. Said she was grieving too, for the family she couldn't have. It was all about loss. We agreed to forget it ever happened. Never spoke of it again. Hilary does her job. And does it well. Life has just carried on. It was one of those things. I thought you should know. I just wanted to be straight with you, Luce.' He checks my reaction.

And I hide it. That they have shared this makes me feel vulnerable, makes the foundations between Greg and me a little less steady. But then he did tell me. And he was upset. And it was just once.

Still, I'd feel a whole lot better if they didn't have that history.

Greg stays for over an hour, in which time we manage to finish breakfast, have sex and a shower together. He assumes I'm coming to the villa to work from his office with him. When I explain that I think I'd make more progress working from the apartment, he looks hurt. I have my excuses ready – I like to work alone, I'd find the villa too warm, and the children need a break from me. I don't, of course, mention that I need time to digest what he has just told me, and am far from ready to face Hilary. He looks disappointed but says nothing, just that he'll collect me at twelve thirty for a swim and lunch. That would be lunch prepared by a woman with whom he's had sex, and eaten in the company of a girl who hates me.

When Greg has gone, I open my computer. But can't concentrate. I pick up the phone, needing to hear a familiar voice.

'Bonjour!' I say when Fint answers.

'Bonjour yourself! How's life in heaven?' he asks.

'Oh, you know, just hoovered my cloud.'

He laughs.

'How's Simon?'

'Long story.'

'What?'

'We broke up.'

'Aw, Fint.' There was always one issue in their relationship, a big one: Simon wouldn't 'come out'. 'I'm sorry.'

'I'm past all that angst. He needs to deal with this himself or with a psychologist. I am *not* a shrink.'

Fint is so unlucky in love. I'd hoped that Simon might be the one. He's a really nice guy. But it's complicated. And Fint is probably making the right decision.

'So how are you?' he asks.

'Fine.' That didn't sound up enough. 'Good. *Great.*'

'What's wrong?'

'Nothing.'

'Come on. This is Uncle Fint you're talking to here.'

I summarize, ending with the news bulletin about Hilary and Greg, which I admit to being concerned about.

'OK,' he says. 'I'm going to ask one question.'

I wait.

'Do you trust Greg?'

If it wasn't Fint, I'd be indignant. 'Yes. Of course. Absolutely.'

'Well, then, you've nothing to worry about, have you?'

He always was a clear thinker. 'No. I suppose not.'

'What are you going to do about Rachel?'

'Don't know. Be patient. Try not to take it personally. Remind myself I'm marrying Greg, not his family. Get out a bit more, just the two of us. I'd like to try to get to know Hilary a bit better – but I don't know, after what Greg's said –'

'Don't worry about that. Greg's marrying you, isn't he? If he'd have wanted Hilary, he'd have asked her a long time ago.'

He has a point. 'Thanks, Fint. I needed that. What are *you* going to do?'

'Work.'

I laugh. We're so alike, Fint and I.

Greg collects me for our swim. As we're heading for the pool, his mobile rings on the terrace table. It's his agent. He goes inside to take the call, leaving me standing there, watching Toby, Hilary and Rachel playing together in the water. I decide to brave it, dive in and swim the full length underwater in complete blissful silence. I pop up at the shallow end, take a long breath, flick back my hair.

'Deadly,' says a voice beside me.

In the time it has taken to swim the length, Toby has extricated himself from the others and is bobbing in the water beside me. The whites of his eyes seem so clear against the chocolate brown, his lashes clumped together with water. I smile at him.

'You're a great diver,' he says.

'Thanks, Toby. And you must be a great swimmer to get over here so fast.'

'Yeah. I am. But I can't dive.' He has a dimple on one cheek.

'It's very easy. All you have to do is relax.'

'I can relax.' He lies on his back, sticks his tummy in the air and tilts his head so far back that if it weren't for the goggles his eyes would be flooded. He stands up, just managing to keep his chin above water.

'That was very good relaxing, all right,' I say.

'Can you learn me to dive?'

'I don't know. Maybe we should ask your dad.'

'He wouldn't mind.'

I'm sure he wouldn't. But not a hundred per cent sure. And Toby isn't my child. I'm trying to decide what to do.

'Want *me* to ask him?' says the boy.

'No, he's on the phone.'

But Toby's already gone, slipping up out of the pool like a frisky otter and darting towards the terrace.

Hilary calls, 'Toby. Walk. Don't run.'

He looks at her and slows to a walk.

'Good man,' she says.

He comes running back out with a thumb in the air. 'Can we do it now?' he asks when he gets back to me.

'Sure.'

'Hey, Rach-el,' he calls to his big sister. 'I'm going to learn to dive before you.'

'I can dive already.'

'No, you can't. You're crap.'

'Ah, ah,' I surprise myself by saying. He looks at me and stops. My God. I've disciplined by accident.

I teach Toby to dive from a sitting position first. He does exactly as I say, no fear, head down, arms straight, pointing forward. I catch him every time and tell him how brilliant he is. Soon he's diving standing up. I can't believe the progress we've made in such a short time. He's so proud of himself. He can dive. But, more importantly, his sister can't. Not really. Not as well. I recognize that feeling. I experienced it the time my father realized I could draw.

The children are hungry, and Hilary takes them inside. Still waiting for Greg to join me, I decide to swim a few lengths before coming out. As I cut through the water, feeling positive about the latest turn of events, I wonder if the best way forward is to forget Rachel for a while, just concentrate on Toby. Maybe then she'll see that I'm actually an OK person. I stay in the pool another five minutes before deciding to go to look for Greg. Some phone call! I shower quickly by the pool and slip into my flip-flops, shorts and T-shirt. In the living room Hilary is on one of the sofas with Toby, rubbing sunscreen onto his legs.

'That was fun,' I call to him.

'Oh, Jesus,' says Hilary. 'You gave me a fright.' A worm of white sunscreen shoots from the tube she's holding and lands on the sofa.

'I'll get a cloth.' I rush to the kitchen. 'I hope it comes out,' I say, rubbing at it.

It does, mostly.

'Don't worry about it,' says Hilary. 'Greg won't mind.'

This I know.

'Did you enjoy that, Toby?' I ask, sitting on the arm of the sofa and smiling at him.

'Yeah,' he says with enthusiasm.

'Yes, *thank* you,' corrects Hilary.

'Yes, thank you,' he repeats.

I smile.

'Guess what? Hil's taking us to Aqua-Splash after lunch,' he announces.

'What's that?'

'This cool place with lots of pools and slides and things. D'you wanna come?'

I'm surprised and delighted to be invited. Greg and I had planned to get that rent-a-car this afternoon. But it can wait.

'Lucy has work to do, Toby,' says Hilary.

'Hilary, I'm not that busy today. I'd actually like to go with you, if it's not a hassle for you.'

She colours. 'It's just that I'm not sure Rachel is ready for you to come on trips with us yet.'

I'm disappointed. 'OK. Well, I'll take your advice on that.' I certainly don't want to push myself on her. I tussle Toby's hair. 'Another time, Toby, OK?'

'OK.'

I go to find Greg. He is in the office, on the computer.

'What happened to you?' I ask.

'What?'

'We were supposed to be going for a swim.'

'God, yeah. Sorry. I got distracted by the phone call, then had some more ideas for the book.'

9

Over the next few days I really try to get to know Toby. But it's not easy. Hilary is always there. Always joining in when I talk to him. And because she knows him so well, the conversation takes off without me. She knows what to say to interest him, how to make him laugh. By the time the conversation ends, usually by Hilary bringing him away somewhere, I find myself out at the perimeter again. If only I could just sit down and let him chat to me without interference. As for getting to know Rachel – she leaves rooms when I enter.

It is impossible to imagine myself becoming stepmother to children who already have a mother in Hilary. She does everything a mother does. Makes the meals. Cuts up Toby's food. Is naturally physical with them. She hugs and touches them in such a casual, easy way. She carries Toby when he's tired. They snuggle into her when watching DVDs. They run to her when they're hurt. Hilary can call Toby 'runt' or Rachel 'idiot' and make it sound loving. I can only imagine their reaction if I used the same words. Which is unlikely, considering I'm afraid to open my mouth for fear of sounding like a 'dork'.

Frustration leads to creativity. I hit on an idea. The solution, I decide, is for Greg and me to take the children off somewhere for a day, just the two of us. When I suggest this great idea to Greg, though, he's not so sure.

'I don't know,' he says. 'We usually bring Hilary.' He's searching his desk for a reference book and is flinging everything that gets in his way aside into a messy heap. He looks up. 'Especially over here, where she knows no one. I wouldn't want her to feel left out.'

'I understand that, Greg. It's just that I don't feel I'm getting to know the children at all. Hilary's great, absolutely great. Don't get me wrong. But, well, there doesn't seem to be a role for me when she's around *all* the time. I can't seem to get close to Toby or Rachel.'

He stops what he's doing, his eyes registering. 'OK. Let's do it.' He gets up, there and then.

OK, I think, *why not?*

But when he proposes the idea to the children, there's a problem. Rachel won't go without Hilary. So a communal trip is planned. As I get ready, though, I develop a thumping headache and a defeatist attitude. What's the point? Hilary's going to be there. I'll still be the outsider. Suddenly I'm tired of trying. And I could do with being alone for a while. Greg seems annoyed but honours his promise to the children and goes.

I return to the apartment in the little Clio I've rented, pop two Nurofen and lie down. I wake an hour later, headache-free and relieved to be alone. After happily pottering around for a while, I feel like a swim. I drive down to the villa and let myself in, revelling in its emptiness. I dive into a clear blue, perfectly still pool, feeling at peace, alone in my soundproof, underwater world. My shadow, tracking me below, is strong on the light blue mosaic, reminding me of ads for sun holidays. I come up for air and dive back under again. Life would be so simple as a mermaid.

I sit at the side, legs dangling in the water, while the hot sun beats down on my back, drying it in minutes. I lie in the shade with a book. But eventually I have enough of being alone. Greg's caretaker arriving in sarong and bare feet to clean the pool gives me the incentive to get up, go inside and ring Fint. His voice makes me realize how much I miss our wacky office with its personalities and quirky traditions. I miss Fint. The blotchy way he applies fake tan. The dapper way he dresses – the Vivienne Westwood, dark purple rugby shirt with lace collar and cuffs, the cream Jeffrey West shoes, his Brian McGinn black, rectangular glasses. The way he bursts out with 'Ooh, he's a ride' at the sight of any reasonably attractive man. I even miss the way he hears about someone's sudden illness and worries he has it too. On impulse, I tell him I'm thinking of coming over and ask when suits.

'Whenever you like,' he says, 'just give me a day's notice.' He says he was at a Pet Shop Boys concert the night before and is nursing a whopper. It reminds me that yesterday was Sunday. How the days seem to merge into each other over here. He talks of new jobs that have come in, and I volunteer immediately for two – to design the cover of a quiz book and to devise the template for a breakfast cereal company's newsletter. It's not that they're particularly exciting projects, just that the more work I have, the greater the distraction from Greg's family.

As the day goes on, my anti-family mood begins to wear off. At five, I decide to cook for them. I prepare vegetables for a stir-fry, marvelling at the natural richness of colour from the peppers, tomatoes, carrots, green beans. I chop away to the sound of a David Gray CD. My cheeriness begins to fade, though, when everything's finished and ready to be thrown into the pan, with no sign of anyone returning. I ring Greg's mobile. It goes to voicemail. I put off cooking until I'm so hungry I have to eat. I take a little of everything and make one sad portion. As light begins to leak from the sky, I worry. I keep trying his phone unsuccessfully. By eleven I'm pacing the kitchen, imagining all sorts of scenarios. When they finally return, children asleep, and adults carrying them, they look like a happy family arriving back after a long enjoyable day out. Except for one thing. Hilary does not look mumsy. Her flouncy, white skirt is up to her bum and her top is clingy and low cut. It doesn't put me in the best of moods.

'What happened to you?' I ask Greg when he comes down-stairs from putting Rachel to bed.

'Nothing.'

'Why were you so late?'

'I didn't realize there was a curfew.'

'There wasn't. I was just worried, Greg.'

'If you'd come, you'd have known there was no reason to be.'

'I'd a headache.'

'You could have taken something. I was writing, Lucy. I stopped because you wanted to go out. Then you changed your mind, and I carried on to keep the kids happy. Now you're angry I wasn't home sooner. *I* have a life too, you know. It doesn't *all* revolve around you.'

'I never said it did.'

'What d'you want me to do? Drop everything for you?'

'No.' I put my hand to my forehead. 'I don't. I just want us to get on. All of us. I want to build a relationship with your children, but I can't. Something always gets in the way. Always. I'm trying so hard to fit in to your life and get to know everyone –'

'So why didn't you come with us?'

'I had a pounding headache. I didn't feel well. And I was *tired*. This is hard. Really, really hard. How can you get people to like you when they don't even want you there?' *Shit, what I don't want to do is bloody cry.*

He takes me in his arms and for a while says nothing, just rubs my back over and over. When he speaks, it's to apologize. 'I'm sorry. I know you're trying. I should have come back sooner. I was annoyed with you for staying here. I was being an asshole. I'm sorry, OK?' He's smoothing back my hair, clearing my tears with his thumbs.

'I want it to work, Greg. I really do. I don't want to upset your kids. And I already have by just being here. I don't know,' I sigh, 'sometimes it feels like we'll never get there.'

'We will,' he whispers. 'We will.' He kisses me again and again, until I reciprocate. We make it to the bedroom, and I find comfort where I have always been able to with Greg.

Afterwards, I find myself asking about Hilary again, needing to know just how attached she is. I try to sound casual. 'How soon after her marriage ended did she come to work for you?'

'Within months.'

'She must have still been affected by it.'

'No doubt. But I think that, in all our chaos, we gave her a distraction, and a challenge.'

'It was probably good for her to keep busy, all right.'

'Not just that. I remember her saying once that she needed to feel needed.'

I don't want to think about when she might have said that.

'What age is she?'

'Thirty-two, thirty-three. Why?'

'I don't know. I suppose I'm just surprised that she's still happy to live in, at that age, especially having been married. I mean, I'm twenty-nine and I'd want my own place.'

He frowns. 'I never thought of that. Hilary's been with us so long. When she started, I needed her round the clock, with everything a mess and all the travelling I was doing promoting the books. It seemed to suit her then. Of course, she's probably changed. God, she must have. I never thought. Of course, you're right. She should be out there, getting on with her life. Not stuck with us twenty-four hours a day. Especially after we're married. Honest to God, sometimes I wonder at myself. I'll talk to her.'

I don't want to go back to the apartment tonight. I want to fall asleep in Greg's arms. I set the alarm on my mobile for six thirty and snuggle in to him.

Something wakes me. I tilt my watch towards the pool of light that floods the other side of the bed. What's Greg doing, at five past three, sitting forward, knees bent? *Writing?*

'Greg?'

He looks over. Beams. 'Behold! Athene awaketh!'

'What?'

'Athene. The Greek goddess of wisdom and victory. Fierce, fearless and righteous.'

'What are you doing?'

'Can't sleep. My mind's buzzing. I keep getting these amazing ideas. If I don't write them down, they'll be gone in the morning.'

I close my eyes to the light, the energy. *Are all writers like this?*

'Oh, and sorry about the book,' he says.

'Hmm?' I lift heavy lids.

He's holding up what looks like the novel I was reading last night while waiting for them to come home. 'I'll buy you another,' he says.

'It's yours. I found it in the living room.'

'Phew! Because I've written all over it. Couldn't find anything else.'

'It's three o'clock.'

'*Already?*'

'You'll be tired in the morning.'

He shakes his head. 'No,' he says. 'I can't seem to sleep these days. Must be getting old,' he laughs.

He looks anything but. Bright, cheery and buzzing, at three in the morning. 'Are you like this *every* night?'

'Go back to sleep. You look tired. My little Greek goddess.' He rubs my head.

I yawn again. 'OK, 'night.' I turn over, put the pillow over my head. Our earlier argument starts to trickle into my mind. I stop it. Greg has put it behind him. I close my eyes and let sleep take over.

Daylight wakes me before the alarm. My watch says six. I should get going before anyone stirs. The Greek philosopher is up and gone. I pull back the sheet. Already the air's hot. I dress quickly and clear up after myself. Then I track Greg down to his office. He is at the computer, wearing nothing but boxers, staring at the screen, his fingers racing across the keyboard. No wonder he's so good at what he does. I yawn, kiss the top of his head and tell him I'm heading back to the apartment. He glances up, his unshaven face and spiky hair giving him an almost wild look that makes me smile. He returns it, then is back to the computer, flying along. I rub my eyes and decide that, actually, it's too early to be up.

A few days later, after a morning's work, I call down to Greg, hoping that he'll join me for a swim, then lunch out, just us two. When I get there, he's on a roll at the computer. He suggests I go ahead, he'll be right out. Hilary and Rachel are finishing up their swim. Toby is getting up from the towel he has been sunbathing on by the side of the pool. It's funny to see such a young sun worshipper. He looks half feline, half French, the way he stretches out in total bliss to be warmed by the rays. As I approach, the pool is settling back to calm, the inflatable turtle, Paddy Power, still bobbing up and down. Goggles and flippers lie abandoned by the steps.

I call a friendly hello to the group headed my way. The

only person who answers is Toby. The others just walk past. Rachel's behaviour I understand. Not Hilary's. I tell myself not to worry. She's probably preoccupied. I carry on, slip out of my flip-flops at the deep end, lower my goggles and dive in. I spend a good half-hour swimming, mostly underwater. Still no sign of Greg. I shower, then go to retrieve my towel, which I've left on an airing rail on the terrace. I find it thrown to the ground, replaced on its rung by Rachel's togs. Hilary is coming back out. She holds my gaze. It's as if she wants me to know that she did this. I say nothing. Just pick up the towel, shake it and wrap it round me.

Then she surprises me.

'So you're trying to get rid of me?'

'*Sorry?*'

'I know your plan.'

'Hilary, I've no idea what you're talking about.'

'Greg told me.'

'Told you what?'

'Your plan to get rid of me.'

'What?'

'Oh, I know your game. Have me live out first. Then it's only a matter of time.'

I colour. 'Hilary, it wasn't like that at all. I just said to Greg that you might *like* to live out.'

She folds her arms, leans her weight on one leg and points the other out front. 'Yeah, well, all he can seem to go on about now is how I need a life of my own.'

'Look, Hilary. I'm sure Greg would be delighted for you to stay on full time. We both would. We just thought you might like to have a choice. That's all. We were thinking of you.'

'Oh, I'm sure *Greg* was, all right.'

'As was I.'

'If you think I believe that, you're dumber than you look.'

'Excuse me?'

She advances, hands on hips, head extended. 'You come barging into this family. No warning. Against my better judgement, I decide to give you a break. I tell the children not to worry, that they just need to give it time. I tell Rachel you're probably a really nice person. Boy, was that a mistake. Because there you were, all along, going behind my back trying to get me out of the picture.' She shakes her head. 'Unbelievable.'

'It wasn't like that. Trust me.'

'Trust *you*. Why should I trust you? You've every reason to want me gone. Sure, you've already started trying.'

'Hilary –'

'Look. Spare me the wide-eyed innocence routine, OK? I came out here to tell you something. And here it is. I'm not going anywhere. I love this family. So you can give up trying to be cute. I've been here a lot longer than you and I know this family a lot better. If you want to take me on, then do. But know one thing. I'll win.' With that, she turns and pounds back to the villa. I stand routed, heart thumping, face burning, stunned by her anger and devastated that I have just made an enemy of someone I'd once hoped might become an ally.

10

I lean against the door of Greg's office, which I've just closed behind me.

'I've just had a major run-in with Hilary.'

He looks up from his computer, a pen gripped between his teeth.

'She thinks I want to get rid of her,' I say, walking towards him.

He takes the pen from his mouth. '*Why?*'

I sit on the desk, facing him. 'You must have told her that it was my idea she might like to live out. Now she thinks I don't want her here at all. What did you *say* to her?'

He pushes back his swivel chair. 'I didn't say it was anybody's idea. But obviously I mustn't have explained properly . . .'

'Can you remember what you said?'

He frowns. 'Not exactly. Something along the lines of time moving on, her priorities changing and that I was sorry for not realizing sooner. I told her that if she wanted to move out when we got back to Ireland, that'd be fine.'

'But you didn't explain that it was just a *suggestion*, that she didn't have to if she didn't want to?'

'I thought she'd assume that.'

'She thinks I asked you to have her move out.'

His thumb plays with the top of the pen. 'OK. Let's not panic here. This is just a misunderstanding. Let me have a word with her. See if I can clear it up. After all, we were thinking about her, we were only trying to make her life easier.'

'I know, but that's not what she thinks. And she seems to

have made up her mind. You should have seen her. She was fuming.'

'She's a good person, Lucy. Honestly. Let me talk to her. We'll probably be laughing about this in a few days.'

'Yeah,' I say, without conviction. I stand up. 'Let's go out for lunch. I need to get away from here for a while.'

He smiles. 'You're not the only one.'

That night I phone Grace. Tell her everything.

'God. She sounds uptight. What's her problem?'

'She thinks I'm trying to get rid of her.'

'I know, but why? All you were doing was giving her the option of more freedom.'

'I know. I *know*. But what if she's right? What if subconsciously I suggested it because I want her gone? She makes me feel so inadequate. And I can never get near the kids with her always around. I can't even have sex without worrying that she'll hear. How weird is that?'

'What's *weird* is the way she's reacting. At her age, she should be delighted at the prospect of having a social life, not attacking you for suggesting it. I'd watch out there, Lucy. She seems over-attached.'

'She and Greg had sex once.'

'*What?*'

I start to make excuses for him. 'Way back. It only happened once. When he was upset. He told me about it. It meant nothing to him –'

'But what if it meant something to her? I'd get her out of the house.'

'I can't do that. I can't ask him to sack her. She's been with them so long. She's part of the family. The children love her.'

'All the more reason to get rid of her. She's too close. I mean, come on, Lucy, she fucked him.'

'It was five years ago. It happened once. I can't ask Greg to get rid of her. I can't. This is a very difficult time for the children. They need routine, stability now' – I've been reading my step-parenting books – 'not to have one of the people they love most in the world sent away.'

'You're taking a gamble.'

'Even if I asked him to, he'd talk me out of it. I know he would. He thinks the world of her. He's going to talk to her. It'll be all right.'

'OK. But you know what I think.'

'How's Kevin?' I ask, cutting her off.

She pauses. 'Kevin? Do I know a Kevin? Because the name rings a faint bell.'

'Still working hard as ever?'

'I'm jealous of his office chair. It sees more of his ass than I do.'

I laugh, scratching a mosquito bite near my ankle.

'How's work going?' she asks.

'Fine. I think I'll pop over soon. I miss the guys.'

'Good. I'm glad. I was worried you might quit.'

'*Why?*'

'A lot of stepmothers do . . . to compensate, you know, for not being the real thing.'

'But lots of real mothers work.'

'It's a guilt thing. And don't fall for it. Whatever else happens, *don't* give up work. Biggest mistake I ever made.'

'But you wanted to –'

'Yeah, I wanted to be the perfect mother.' There is bitterness in her voice.

'But you are the perfect mother.'

'Lucy. There's no such thing.'

'You could go back to work.'

'Are you kidding me? The kids would never see either of us. Everything would come crumbling down.'

'You could get a nanny.'

'After what you've told me? Forget it.'

Greg has spoken to Hilary. He says everything's fine. It was just a misunderstanding. Still, I'm cautious, unable to forget her rage. I'm putting clothes into the washing machine at the villa (there isn't one at the apartment) when she appears. I brave myself to extend an olive branch.

'Hilary, I'm doing a coloured wash. Would you like to put anything in?'

'No, thanks,' she says.

'I've only got two or three things here. Why don't I save you a job?'

She sighs loudly, walks from the kitchen, returns with the wash basket and drops it on the floor beside me. It doesn't take a genius to work out that she's still fuming. I'm sorry I offered now. Still, I sort the clothes and fill the machine. It's ready for the off, but I'm stuck. I don't know what cycle to select. The last thing I want to do is ask her, but, squatting in front of the unfamiliar French machine, I realize I've no choice.

'What cycle do coloureds go in at, Hilary?'

She doesn't answer. I turn around to see if she heard. She's slicing tomatoes at great speed. I'm about to ask again when she looks up.

'B,' she says.

One cycle later, I'm pulling out the clothes, heart pounding, face burning. Disaster. Rachel's pale pink top – blue-grey. Greg's yellow polo shirt – pea-soup green. Toby's Bart Simpson T-shirt – blue-grey with patches of green. I have ruined at least one item belonging to everyone, including myself.

'What did you *do*?' she asks, coming up behind me.

'Nothing. I put them in at B like you said –'

'Not B. *D*. I said *D*.'

I'm stunned, sure she said B, the opposite of my machine at home. I look at her. But her face is blank. Innocent. I don't know what to think. She wouldn't have done this on purpose, would she?

Greg doesn't care about his shirt. He's never been that keen on it, he says. Toby is very upset. Bart Simpson can't be green. He just can't. The Hulk is green. *Not* Bart Simpson.

'I'm sorry, Toby. Next time I'm in Dublin I'll buy you another, OK? I'll buy you two.' I will look in France, but, as he got it in Dublin, I'd better not make any promises.

And Rachel? Ah, Rachel.

'Are you *stupid* or something?' She stands, hands on hips, one of which is tilted forward. Attack mode.

I'm speechless. *Do ten-year-olds really talk to adults like that?*

Greg walks into the kitchen.

'*Rachel*, what's going on? I could hear you outside. How dare you speak to Lucy like that?'

'She ruined my good top.'

'And that gives you the right to be rude?'

She colours.

'Lucy's a guest here. Apologize immediately.'

'Sorry,' she mumbles.

'I didn't hear you,' he says.

I'm cringing.

'Sorry, *OK*?'

'You're getting very cheeky, young lady. You'd better change your attitude. D'you hear me?'

'Yes, Dad.' More subdued.

'Go to your room immediately.'

She does. Not before glaring at me.

Part of me wishes Greg had let me handle this, another knows I'd have made a mess of it.

'Come on, let's get out of here,' says Greg.

I don't need encouragement.

We drive to Cannes. It's my first time here and like nowhere I've ever been. Everything outside the car seems lazy and slow. In the hazy distance, pale lilac mountains could be a mirage. Yachts and powerboats cut through the water, creating lines of white through the blue. The sea sparkles like diamonds. Nowhere in the world would they be more appropriate. Lamborghinis, Porsches, Ferraris pull up outside four-star hotels. A line of upmarket boutiques, Dior, Chanel, Bvlgari, face sun and sea, their elegant mannequins bizarrely dressed for winter, more than one draped in fur.

It's too hot to walk along the seafront, so we seek shade under an umbrella in the ultra-glam Hôtel Martinez. The drinks seem to take for ever, but that might be a measure of my bad form and/or thirst. When they arrive, I press my ice-filled glass to my forehead and cheeks, then scoop out a cube and run it along my arms, legs and the back of my neck until it melts. I drink the Coke from its bottle, take another ice cube and slip it between my foot and flip-flop. I repeat with the other foot, until I begin to feel human again. I look up to find him gazing at me as if I'm a creature of great amusement.

'Don't you feel the heat?' I ask.

'No. But I'm glad you do.' He smiles suggestively.

I slap his arm.

Just then two Japanese tourists sit down at the table next to ours.

'Ohayo Gozaimasu,' Greg says to them with a mini bow. I take it to mean 'Hello'. Greg has recently taken up three languages – none of them French.

They nod and reply the same.

'Ressun sono ichi,' he says then, and I'm starting to get impressed.

They look at each other, then at him. They smile, 'Ah, lesson number one.'

And he'd sounded so good. I laugh. As does Greg. Demurely, they join in. Shortly after, though, they leave. I think we scared them away. Going out alone with Greg always returns my sense of perspective – our relationship is what's important, the rest will just take time. We get back to the apartment that evening and sit on the balcony as the light leaves the sky, watching swallows swoop and dive through the branches of the eucalyptus, like fighter pilots on manoeuvres.

The following morning there's an e-mail from Fint. Get Smart, it seems, is up for a big pitch. Four agencies, three of them international, are in the running to design the corporate identity for a shopping mall planned by a retail giant in a busy suburb of Dublin. Fint wants me home next week to meet the managing director and take the brief. Great. Action! I ring him straight away. He is as excited as I am. This is an opportunity to move us up a notch, to become one of the big guys. I pop down to the villa to tell Greg. But he's not there. According to a sour-looking Hilary, he has taken the children off on his own. I'm a bit surprised he didn't let me know. Still, he must need time alone with them, especially Rachel, so I just text him to have fun. Then I return to the apartment to try to finish the projects I'm working on, so that I can be free next week to really tackle that pitch.

At dinnertime I go down to the villa, assuming they'll be

back. They aren't. I ring Greg's mobile to find that they're still in Cannes – at the kiddies' bumper cars. He has forgotten the time but says they'll grab a pizza rather than come home any time soon. Because I know that Hilary has started to prepare dinner, I go in to tell her they won't be back. I'm tempted not to.

She is furious. 'He could have told me.'

'I think he lost track of time.'

'What am I supposed to do with all this?' She looks at the half-prepared food.

'I'm sure it'll keep till tomorrow.'

'In this heat?' She looks at me as if I'm stupid.

And I wonder what's happened to refrigeration? I walk out. At ten I call Greg's mobile, but it goes to voicemail. I drive down again. No sign of them. I'm starting to worry when the Range Rover pulls up outside. Greg bounds through the front door, an inflatable swimming ring round his neck, roller-blades in one hand, a giant blow-up toothpaste tube under an arm, keys in his mouth, eyes incredibly bright. I stop laughing when I see the children, sunburnt and laden down with shopping bags and exhaustion. Rachel closes the door with her heel. Toby lets his bags spill on to the floor and slumps down beside them.

'I'm thirsty,' he says.

'Anyone for a swim?' Greg asks, heading for the pool.

Hilary's face is thunderous. 'Can't he see they're exhausted?'

I say nothing, just go get two glasses of apple juice. Toby's favourite. When I get back to the hall, she's lifting him up, still muttering about how late it is and how children need their sleep. And routine. She wasn't upset the other night when she was out with them. Is her problem how tired they are, or that she wasn't included? I follow them upstairs. When she sets Toby down, I give him his drink and say goodnight.

Rachel refuses hers. I leave it by her bed anyway. I go back downstairs and out to the pool. Greg is churning through the water like a human propeller. I stand and watch. Up, down, up, down. Not stopping, not resting. Where is he getting the energy? Is this what happens when he hits a creative burst? He overworks, then has to blow off steam? Is that what this is, some sort of stress? Looking at him is making me stressed. I call out that I'm going back to the apartment. He doesn't seem to hear.

II

The following day I go down to the villa to see if he has recovered. But there is no sign of him. They tell me he 'popped out' three hours ago to buy screwdrivers. I ring him. 'Where are you?'

'In Nice.'

'Did you get the screwdrivers?'

'Screwdrivers?'

'You left three hours ago to get screwdrivers.'

'Oh. Yeah. Screwdrivers. God. I'd forgotten. Why did I need them again?'

'No idea, Greg.'

'OK. It probably wasn't urgent.'

'What are you doing now?'

'Oh, I've just met some people. We're having a beer . . .'

Are you, now?

'Anyway, listen,' he says. 'I've just booked a super restaurant for us for tonight. I'll pick you up from the apartment at seven.'

'Aren't you going to be back before then?'

'I've one or two things to do. Just be ready at seven, OK?'

'OK.'

I'm leaving the office when I bump into Hilary.

'Not coming back, is he?' She tut-tuts. *'Not* a good sign.'

I walk past her. *What is she talking about?*

'I wouldn't be so smug if I were you. There's a pattern, you see, with Greg. First he starts to disappear, and before you know it there's a new woman on the scene.'

I laugh. 'Thanks for the tip, Hilary.' I keep going, telling myself she's making it up.

'Well, here's another. Be very careful what you say to your *boyfriend* because it all comes back to me.'

I turn. 'Sure.' But I'm listening.

'We'd a great laugh about how you thought I'd put in a good word with Rachel for you . . . Oh, don't look so surprised. Greg tells me everything.'

I can't believe he told her when I specifically asked him not to. Were they laughing at me? No. Greg wouldn't do that. She's lying. But he must have told her. I can't believe he did that. What else has he said? And who are these people who he's having a beer with?

Back at the apartment, I put an emergency call through to Grace.

'You know what I think?' she says when I've finally run out of steam.

'What?'

'Greg thought he was doing you a favour asking Hilary to have a chat with Rachel. And she's twisted it to cause tension between you. Face it. She's trouble. I mean, can you really imagine Greg and Hilary in some corner somewhere giggling together at your expense. Come on!'

'No. I suppose not.'

'And so what if he's staying out for a few hours? He's been writing non-stop. Hasn't he?'

'Yeah.'

'She's obviously manipulative.'

'Do you think she made up that stuff about other women?' I ask.

'Do you?'

'Greg has said there was no one after Catherine. And Hilary wasn't there before that.'

'Who's Catherine, his wife?'

'Yeah.'

'So, then, you mean no one *excluding* Hilary?'

Damn. 'He doesn't count Hilary,' I say as much to myself as Grace.

'And do you believe him when he says that there was no one else?'

'I don't see why he'd lie about it. I mean, what's wrong with having relationships as long as they're one at a time?'

'You need to talk to him. Tell him what she's being saying. Because if she's saying things like that to you, who knows what she's saying to him?'

'God.' I never thought of that.

'Always beware the jealous woman.'

A wave of self-pity hits. 'What has *she* to be jealous about? She's the one the children love.'

'Come off it, Lucy. Of course she's jealous. You're going to be part of the family, a stepmother. She'll still be a hired employee. She was the mother-figure until you arrived. You've taken that from her.'

'No, I haven't. She's still like their mother.'

'But you'll be their stepmother.'

'That's just a title.'

'A title she'd probably like. Think about it. From what you say, she doesn't have much of a life outside work. No phone calls. No mention of friends, boyfriends. This family is her life. The closer you get to the children, the more she'll be pushed out of the way.'

'I'm not sure I'll ever get close to them.'

'She probably still fancies Greg. I mean, she fucked him, didn't she?'

I wish she wouldn't keep bringing that up.

'He's an attractive man. She loves his kids. Maybe you're the cuckoo in her nest.'

'Jesus, Grace. Stop.'

'Learning that she was infertile would've been extremely traumatic. It's not beyond the bounds of possibility that she subconsciously substituted the family she couldn't have with Greg's.'

'Grace, you're scaring me.' I watch a swallow zip by, its life free and easy.

'All I'm saying is, watch out. Your relationship is young. This is just another complication you don't need. Nip it firmly in the bud. Talk to him. Tell him what's going on, what she's been saying. Get him on his own. Out of that claustrophobic villa. You need to sort this out. Now. Dress up. Take him out for dinner. Take control. Enough is enough.'

'He's not going to get rid of her.'

'Let him decide.'

'If I ask him to, it would be like a showdown – what's good for me versus what's good for his family. I know who'd lose.'

'Then don't ask. Just tell him what's happening. And listen – keep working. Don't let all this interfere with your career. Don't let it swamp you. You've something you're good at, something you enjoy. Don't let that slip.'

There suddenly seems to be an awful lot at stake.

I spend the rest of the afternoon trying to work out what I'm going to say to Greg and how I'm going to bring it up. I will, though, as soon as he arrives.

But he arrives a different man.

'Your hair!'

'What d'you think?' he asks, turning a full circle.

'It's, it's certainly different.' It's white. Not blond. White. And short.

'I was just so *bored* with it.' He sounds like Fint.

Then I notice his ear. There's a diamond in it. 'Did you get your ear pierced?'

'Cool, eh?'

Now he sounds like his son. I can't understand it. *What was he thinking?* His shirt's silky. And red. His tie, black leather. He looks like a pimp. *What's got into him?*

'Here. I got you something too.' He produces a designer shopping bag and stands over me while I take out the glossy box within, then slide off its lid. I lift the crispy white paper to reveal more red silk. Slowly, I lift it out. It's a dress, though there's not much of it. So this is what he was doing.

'It's lovely,' I say.

'Try it on.'

'Now?'

'Now.'

I pretend to be fine about the possibility of wearing something so daring. I undress to my thong and slip into it. I stand in front of the mirror. Frighten myself. It's a fabulous dress – if you're Naomi Campbell. If you have her confidence, posture and poise. If you don't mind your nipples showing through the fabric, if you're comfortable with the fact that most of your breasts and legs are on display, if you want every curve of your body highlighted. *Oh, God. I'd die if I had to wear it in public.*

'Wow,' he says.

I nod. 'Very nice. Thanks. Great. Lovely.' I start to take it off.

'What are you doing? Aren't you wearing it?'

'I, ah, thought I'd keep it for a special occasion.'

'This is a special occasion.'

I think of Hilary, Rachel, Toby. What would they think if they saw me in this? What would *anyone* think, especially given how Greg's dressed?

'You know, Greg. I don't think it's me.'

'Of course it's you. You look fantastic. So fantastic you better not move.'

Before I know it, his hands are on my breasts, his mouth on mine. We need to talk. Not fuck. He cups my ass in his hands, caresses it through the silk. It's my Achilles heel, and he knows it. I'm putty. He slips the straps off my shoulders and explores my breasts with his tongue. He takes a nipple in his mouth. I groan at him to stop. He knows I mean the opposite. He lifts me and flings me on to the bed. There's something so masterful about the way he does it that it turns me on. That he looks different suddenly becomes exciting. I look down and run my hands over his white stubble. With every kiss he whispers that I'm sexy, every caress that I'm 'hot'. Which makes me feel it. He doesn't remove the dress. But he removes my inhibitions. When I see my reflection in the mirror again, I'm a different woman. Proud, confident, sexy. Up for such a dress. No problem. I'm a woman. Should I be afraid to show it?

In the car, I have to remind him to slow down. He slips a CD into the player and the car fills with a Japanese language lesson. I smile as he tries to repeat what he's heard. It's impossible but that doesn't stop him trying again after the next burst. By the time we arrive in Cannes we're sore from laughing. Parking, always at a premium, seems non-existent. The traffic is backed up. We crawl past the art deco Martinez, then the more traditional Carlton, lit up in all its glory. We inch past Christian Lacroix et al. Still no parking. Greg is getting jittery. A carousel outlined by cheery yellow light bulbs is moving faster than we are, its plumed horses rising and falling like an ad for slow living.

Finally, Greg zips into an underground car park and is lucky enough to find a Jeep pulling out. He parks, hops out and opens my door. The heat takes my breath away. By the time we're at street level, I feel like I've been in a sauna. I wipe moisture from my upper lip and turn my face to the sea in the hope of a breeze. There isn't a puff. The back of Greg's shirt is beginning to stick to him, but he doesn't seem to notice. People who pass us are flagging: children are being carried; looking flushed and tired, a man wipes the top of his head with a folded handkerchief; a woman fans herself with a street map. The only person who appears to have any energy is Greg, walking briskly and chatting non-stop. I'm relieved when we get to the restaurant, a chic, sophisticated spot that I remember passing and thinking inviting, with its great cream parasols, crisp white tablecloths and clientele of glitterati and, more importantly, locals.

Greg seems to know the maître d' and slaps him on the back with an 'Ah, bonsoir, Philippe.' Under his breath, he adds to me, looking like a boy planning mischief, 'Hope he's feeling energetic tonight.'

We're led to a quiet table in a cosy corner.

'Ah, mais non, Philippe,' says Greg, gesturing to a table we passed on the way in. It's positioned between two others. *That* one would be much more sociable.' My heart sinks.

'Greg, this is a much better table,' I say, indicating Philippe's choice.

'Aw, Lucy, let's be sociable tonight.'

I'm about to tell him we need to talk when he turns and makes for the 'sociable' option. Philippe, looking surprised but accommodating, follows him. And, reluctantly, I do too. When we're seated, Greg whips his napkin in the air to open it, almost hitting the woman at the next table. *For goodness sake!*

'Pardon, madame,' he says, bowing flamboyantly.

She shakes her head. 'Ce n'est pas grave.'

The sommelier hands a wine list to Greg, who, after a quick glance, snaps it shut and orders three bottles of champagne.

'*Three?*' I ask.

'We have neighbours,' he says, glancing from side to side.

What? 'We don't know these people,' I say in an urgent whisper.

He shrugs. 'It's a gesture of goodwill.'

Greg is not a showy person. What is he *doing?*

The dewy metal buckets arrive, and shortly after, surprised but enthusiastic thanks – 'Merci beaucoup,' from the couple on our left and a jumbled mix of 'thank you very much', 'most kind', 'you shouldn't have' and 'fantastic' come from the two couples that share the table on our right. English. They ask if we're celebrating something.

'Life,' Greg says, then, 'Salut!', raising his glass high.

'Salut,' everyone joins in, glasses clinking. They seem to have perked up considerably since Greg's arrival.

'Ladies,' he says, to the English women, 'you're both looking ravishing tonight.'

Ravishing? In this day and age, is he kidding?

But the 'ladies' seem charmed by the compliment. I wait for Greg to return his attention to our table so I can raise the subject of Hilary. He doesn't. Instead, he seems intent on involving as many people as he can in lively debate. The French couple concentrate hard for a while but soon bow out. Still, Greg has a captive audience in Tony, Felicity, James and Janet. He guides the conversation like a conductor, his cigar acting as baton. Hopping from one random topic to the next, he whips up laughter and a little heated discussion, then tops it all off with argument – seeming to disagree arbitrarily with any point, simply for the sake of argument. Once he's got everyone worked up about something, he changes the subject with a jokey, 'Well, I'm glad we all agree on that.' Interrupting is pointless. He is on a roll. And, while he can be downright funny, I might as well not be here. After my first glass of champagne I stop drinking, realizing that Greg doesn't intend to, and someone needs to drive back. For me, the evening and my plans for discussion have been ruined. All I can do is sit it out.

'You know what you look like?' Greg asks Tony.

Tony waits for the punch line.

'An Anglican parson.'

I try not to choke, remembering an Eddie Izzard comedy sketch about Anglican parsons having no arm muscles. I glance at Tony. He doesn't seem offended, joking as he is about Felicity being the one who does the preaching in their house. It's all very funny as long as people keep laughing. But what if they stop? Greg's opinions and remarks are becoming more and more risqué. It's as if he is deliberately testing the fine line between funny and insulting. Does he want to see how far he can push it with these people? Is that it, some bizarre social experiment? Well, if he's not careful, he will cross that line. And the fun will end. Someone will stand up to him and make him stop. Why am I the only one to see this? Is it because I'm not drinking? Or is it because this is the man I love, not an amusing stranger I'll never see again? I care what's happening here. Because something is happening. It's not drink. I've seen Greg drunk. This is something else. Something serious. And scary.

The restaurant begins to empty, our French neighbours leaving with a polite 'au revoir', looking unamused by Greg's behaviour.

Felicity and Janet disappear to the Ladies, leaving me with three men.

'Hey, guys,' says Greg. 'What d'you think of Lucy's dress?'

'Smashing,' says Tony.

'Stunning.' James is not far off leering.

'Well, would, you, *believe*, Lucy didn't want to wear it?'

'But you look so good in it, love,' says James.

I cringe.

'D'you know what I had to do to *convince* Lucy to wear this dress?'

'*Greg!*'

'Ah, come on, Luce, let's tell them.'

'Greg, if you say one more word, I'm leaving.' And by God I mean it.

The men are quiet, the atmosphere changing.

'Let's get another,' says Greg, jovially holding up an empty champagne bottle.

The ladies return.

'Is he *always* so entertaining?' Janet asks me.

'And cheeky,' adds Felicity, eyelashes batting.

I can't trust myself to answer without unleashing the rage I feel. He's been encouraging them all night. Flirting with them. The men too, I'd think, if I didn't know better. Unable to sit through any more without exploding, I excuse myself. In the Ladies, I catch my reflection in a mirror. It's not me. I look at the dress. *Why did he get it? To turn me into someone else? Was Hilary right? Is this the beginning of the end?* When I finally come out, the restaurant is empty. I panic that they've left without me but then see them, all five, at the top of the restaurant, Greg teaching his new buddies what look like Riverdance steps. I glance at the waiters, expecting exasperation. They are sitting at a table chatting together, drinking a bottle of champagne. I can guess who's paying. Suddenly, I wish I were back in my apartment in Dublin, in my own bed, on my own, with a quiet dependable book. *Thank God, my meeting with Fint is in the morning. Thank God, I'm going home.* Those thoughts propel me forward. I walk up to Greg and remind him of my early start. He looks surprised, as if suddenly noticing my rage. He excuses himself from the happy group and goes to settle the bill.

Once outside the restaurant, he looks sheepish, as if expecting me to lash out. *Enough scenes*, I think, making straight for the car, in the unusual position of being in front. He follows. Reaching our destination, I turn to speak to him for the first time. It's brief.

'Give me the keys. I'm driving.' As soon as we're inside, I turn on the engine for the air-conditioning but don't pull out. Instead, I demand, 'What was all that about?'

'What?' he asks innocently.

'That display back there.'

'The dancing?' He seems confused.

'No, Greg, the general behaviour. What is up with you?'

'I don't know what you're talking about.'

'Are you *on* something?'

'On something?'

'Greg, you're as high as a kite.'

'I'm in good form and you think I'm *high*. Get a life, Lucy.'

'You insulted those people.'

'I did not.'

'You don't think that telling a man he looks like a parson is insulting?'

'No.'

'You were lucky they hadn't seen Eddie Izzard. And you were lucky they were in such good form.'

'And who put them in good form? Me, that's who.'

I sigh. 'You humiliated me.'

'I humiliated you. Just how *exactly* did I do that?'

'Don't pretend you don't know. You were going to talk about our sex life – in *public*.'

'So?'

'So?' *Is he serious?* 'That was completely out of line.'

'I don't see why. Everyone has sex. I was just being open about it, that's all.'

'And it didn't cross your mind, at all, that *I* mightn't feel like being as "open"?'

'Not until you got all prissy about it, no.'

'Prissy! *Jesus*. You were flirting with those women.'

'I was being friendly.'

'Friendly!' I snort.

'What's wrong with you?'

'No, Greg. What's wrong with you? What is it – speed? Ecstasy?'

He laughs. 'You think I'm on drugs?'

'You're high, Greg. I'm not stupid. Don't sit there and tell me you're not high.'

'OK. Maybe I am high – on life.'

'Oh, come *off* it.'

But no matter what I say, he will not admit to anything. I pull the car out and speed back. I drop him at the villa and drive on. He can have the car back in the morning. Inside, I can't sit still. Out on the balcony, the whole evening replays in my head. *How dare he treat me like that?* And he *was* flirting. I remember Hilary's warning. That we never even got to discuss that makes me feel like putting my fist through a wall.

12

On the flight home, I'm not thinking about the meeting ahead.
I'm thinking about Greg. Could he really have taken drugs? It
doesn't make sense. But he was high. Why would he do drugs,
though? An experiment? Research for a book? If so, why
wouldn't he admit to it? This is more than stress. More than
the heat. I keep coming back to speed. I think back, looking
for signs. He has always been energetic. It's just the way he is.
But suddenly I remember Rob and how he said that Greg had
changed. Could he have started taking something way back
then? And Grace, I remember Grace commenting on his
energy, asking if he was all right. What if she knew something?
What if there is some medical condition that might explain
his behaviour? Maybe she does know something. I need to
talk to her . . .

As soon as I get to Dublin, I change my return flight to
allow an overnight. In a taxi to the office, I ring Grace and ask
if I can stay. She's delighted. Kevin is off at a medical conference
in Barcelona for the week, and she thinks she might be
reverting to the mental age of two.

I arrive at the office two hours before the meeting and click
into work mode, as I've always been able to do. It's so good
to see Fint. We hug and, after the preliminaries, sit at the
round table in his office.

'How're things?' I ask. 'What are you up to?'

'Busy planning a three-week holiday for when you get back.'

I laugh. 'Good idea. Where you going?'

'Don't care. As long as it's out of here.'

'I do appreciate this, you know.'

'I know.'

'I e-mailed over the first draft of the newsletter yesterday,' I say. 'Did you get it?'

'Yeah, I'd a quick look.'

'It's not the *final* final, but it's nearly there.'

'D'you want to take the jacket for Copperplate's latest chick-lit author, Tracy Hughes?'

'Sure.' In fairness to Copperplate, they let us be creative with their women's fiction. They don't insist on a picture of a smiling woman every time. He hands me the brief.

Moving on, he tells me he wants to give Sebastian more responsibility, maybe send him on a course. I think it's a good idea. We discuss various projects for current clients and what we're doing to attract new business. Then Fint briefs me about the retail giant we're about to meet and we go through our new business presentation, which has been modified to highlight the work we've done on corporate identities, particularly for fast-moving consumer-goods companies. We run out of time for lunch.

The meeting goes well. The MD seems a pleasant-enough man in his fifties. He speaks about the project. Then his marketing director gives us the brief. It will be a major job if we get it. Just the kind of account we need to stretch us as a firm. Afterwards Fint and I go for a late lunch. It takes a while to finally bring up something that has been on my mind all along – drugs.

'Remember that guy in college, what was his name again, River?'

'*That nutter?*'

'Was he on something?'

'Ye-ah.'

'What?'

'Dunno, some sort of speed.'

'Are there different types?'

'Probably. Why d'you ask?'

'No reason. I was just thinking about him today. That's all.'

'Not getting enough excitement in your life?' he teases.

'Whatever happened to him?'

'Couldn't tell you. Probably fried what little brain he had.'

'Ah, come on, Fint. Some of the stuff he did was really creative . . .'

'Yeah, but what a cop-out, having to get high to get creative.'

It's four by the time we finish up. I pop into the St Stephen's Green Shopping Centre and buy pyjamas and fresh underwear. I am thrilled to find Bart Simpson T-shirts. I get two, as promised. Rachel is trickier to buy for. In the end, I opt for a black top with a square of fabric sewn on the front, featuring a black-and-white shot of two cuddly kittens, framed with a red velvet trim. It's either that or a similar one in grey with puppies, or a completely different stripy one. I've probably made the wrong choice. I buy wine for Grace and toys for the boys. Then catch a cab there.

She's unloading shopping from the car when I arrive and, though casually dressed in a grey T-shirt and bootleg denims, looks stunning as usual. She could be Norwegian. I can see why Dad used to call us Snow White and Rose Red. Always so different. I start to help. The boys, I see, are both asleep in their car seats. They look so cute, flushed and soft-skinned, like two angels. I tell Grace as much.

'You wouldn't say that if you'd seen them in the supermarket,' she says. 'Jesus. They had me driven tormented.'

We take the shopping inside, and, while I start to unload it, Grace goes out to the car to get Jason. She sets him down in the portable car seat on the kitchen floor. I offer to get

Shane, but she doubts whether I'll be able to manoeuvre him out of his seat and upstairs to bed without waking him. I doubt it too.

'I think he's coming down with something,' she says, when she returns to the kitchen. 'He usually wakes when the car stops. And he was so cranky. He only gets that bad when he's sick. Poor little guy.'

'Poor you,' I say, putting lettuce into the crisper.

When everything has been put away, Grace says, 'I'm feeling decadent. What would you say to a bottle of white?'

'Not "no", that's for sure.'

'Right, then. We'll have stir-fry – when we've had a glass or two. Come on, let's go into the sitting room.' She carries Jason. I carry the wine. The place is in chaos. Toys everywhere. Children's feeders. Baby bottles. A heap of clothes that she must have taken out of the dryer and abandoned before sorting. This is not Grace. She catches me looking at her.

'Excuse the mess,' she says, but doesn't look bothered. 'When the cat's away –'

'I thought you were the cat.'

'Lucy. One cat in any home is enough. Anyway' – she shakes her head as though clearing the thought – 'how're tricks?'

I look down at the glass I'm twisting round and round by the stem. 'Pretty crap, actually.'

'Hilary?'

'No. Greg.' I look up at her. 'There's something wrong, Grace.'

She sits forward.

'Remember when you asked me if he was all right, and I told you he was fine?'

'Yeah?'

'Well, I thought he was. But now he's not. Definitely not. You said he was energetic then. You should see him now – he's high.'

She nods quickly, as if to say, 'Go on.'

'Is there a medical condition that makes people high?'

'Tell me more.'

I go over events of the night before.

'Wow,' she says, putting down her glass. 'That's pretty extreme.'

'What d'you think it could be?'

She removes her shoes, sits sideways with her back against the arm of the chair and pulls her legs up beside her. 'I couldn't be sure without seeing him.'

'I know, but you must have some idea.'

'He's never mentioned a tendency to get high?'

'No. Sure, he doesn't even think he is high.'

'Or low?'

'No. He's always in great form. Just not this great.'

'OK.' She thinks for a moment. 'What about his family? Have any of them commented on his behaviour?'

'Rob, his brother, mentioned how "zesty" he was, and how much he'd changed since he met me.'

'But he didn't seem worried?'

'No. He thought it was great. He thinks it's love.' What a ridiculous concept that now seems.

'OK,' she says again.

'Could it be drugs?' I ask quietly.

She takes a long breath. 'It's a possibility, though without seeing him, I'd be slow to pin it down to any one thing.'

'What kind of drugs?'

'Let's not jump to any conclusions.'

'OK, if it *were* drugs, which ones?'

'*If* it were, then most likely amphetamines. Speed. But he'd want to be taking a hell of a lot.'

'Are they addictive?'

'Yeah.'

'But not dangerous?'

'Well, not at low doses. But someone taking high doses over a long period –'

'What could happen?'

'Lucy, it may not be drugs.'

'What could happen?'

'There would be a risk of paranoia and stuff, but I *really* wouldn't worry about that at this stage. You have to talk to him, though. Get him to admit there's a problem. Because something's definitely up.'

'But why would he take drugs? It doesn't make sense.'

'I don't know. People take amphetamines for different reasons. To lose weight. To get an energy boost if they're juggling a lot of things or have a deadline. Some people use it to stimulate their minds. But we don't know what's giving him this high. The first thing you have to do is get him to admit that there is a problem.'

'But that's exactly it. He doesn't think there is.'

'Then you have to show him how his behaviour is affecting other people.'

'I tried, last night. He thinks the problem is with me. He called me prissy.'

'Show him what this is doing to the children.'

'I don't think it's actually affecting them.'

'Trust me, Lucy. If it's affecting you, it's affecting them.'

'No. They enjoy his energy. He can be great fun. Very adventurous. OK, they get tired sometimes . . .'

'He's not irritable at all?'

'Only last night, when I cornered him. Otherwise, no.'

'Something at least. Still, Lucy, you've got to do something. He's unlikely to himself. Highs are addictive. Once you're up, you want to stay there.'

'Maybe I should join him. Must be a hell of a lot better than reality.'

She smiles. 'I know what you mean . . . Just keep at him, though, until he admits there's a problem. Then get him to a doctor, preferably at home. You know I'll help in any way I can.'

It sounds so easy. I know it will be anything but. Still, at least I have a goal, a sense of direction. And I have something else: the feeling that I'm not alone. I hope I can hold on to it when I'm back in France.

13

The plane touches down at two. Cardigan off. Sunglasses on. Riviera Radio keeps me company in the car, as do Grace's words. I get to the villa, fired up and ready for positive action. But there's no sign of Greg, and I sense that something's wrong. Rachel has a face on her like a brewing storm. So does Toby.

'What is it?'

'Dad didn't come back,' he says.

'From where?'

He shrugs.

'Where's Hilary?'

'Kitchen.'

They follow me in. Incredibly, Hilary is tearing at a French stick with her mouth.

'What's happened to Greg?' I ask.

She drops the bread including the bit she had in her mouth. She brushes crumbs from her chest and turns. 'Ever think of knocking?'

'The door was open. Now, what's happened?'

She straightens up, chin high. 'He promised to bring us to Antibes for ice cream. I got the children out of the pool, helped Toby get dressed. When we were ready, he'd gone.'

'Where?'

'*I* don't know, do I? *I'm* just the hired help.'

'Did you try his mobile?'

'No,' she says, with pride.

'OK. Well, I'm sure there's a reasonable explanation.'

Somehow I suspect that may not be true. I ring his mobile, looking confident, until I hear it somewhere in the villa. 'How long's he been gone?'

'An hour.'

'Well, why don't I bring you?' I say to the children.

'Forget it,' says Rachel gloomily.

Toby is quiet. His face is flushed, and he looks languid. Hilary has all the windows and doors open to create a breeze, but the villa is stifling. This child needs to cool down.

'Toby, would you like to see my apartment? It's nice and cool and I've Magnums in the fridge.'

He looks up. 'OK.'

'Rachel, would you like to come?'

She eyes me as if I've just offered to pull a tooth. 'As if,' she says, summing up our relationship in two words.

Toby holds my hand as we leave the villa.

Hilary looks murderous.

Toby scans the apartment. 'You're right,' he says. 'It's nice and cool.'

'Would you like a drink?'

'Yes, please.'

'Sit down there and I'll get it.'

'Ooh. The seat's cold too.'

'It's leather,' I call from the kitchen.

'I like leather.'

I find myself smiling.

I return with two glasses of orange juice and hand him one. 'Cheers,' I say and hold my glass out.

'Cheers, big ears,' he says, cheerfully clinking against mine. 'It's really quiet here,' he says, looking around.

It strikes me as an odd thing for a child to appreciate.

'Is that a balcony?'

'Yep.'

'Can we go on it?'

'Sure.'

Once out, he doesn't stay long. 'Nifty,' he says and comes back in. He sits in exactly the spot he was in earlier.

'I like it here,' he says.

'Me too.'

'Can I stay with you?' He looks up at me with big brown St Bernard eyes, the puppy I've always wanted.

'Why would you want to stay with me?'

He shrugs.

'Is it a bit hot at the villa?'

He nods. 'And really noisy. Even at night-time. I can't sleep. Dad never goes to bed. He shouts on the phone and his music's *really* loud. I hate that song.'

'What song?'

'A little more satisfaction, baby. I *hate* it.' He puts his hands over his ears. I wait until he takes them down again.

'Why don't you ask him to turn it down?'

'I do. But when I get back into bed he turns it up again. So I don't ask him any more. Can I stay with you? *Please?*'

'I don't know, Toby. I think your dad would prefer you to stay with him.'

'Just for one night? Please? I'd be very good.'

I get up, go over and sit beside him. 'Would you like to go for a little sleep now? You look a bit tired.' He looks exhausted.

''K.'

'I'll be out here working, OK? Sleep as long as you like. And when you get up we'll have a Magnum.'

''K.'

I hold his hand and lead him to the bedroom. When he's settled, I cover him with a sheet and sit on the edge until he sleeps. It takes less than a minute. His little face looks so vulnerable. I go back outside and try to work but am restless. *What is Greg up to? If Toby is being kept awake, Rachel is too. She's older; she must know something's up. Because something is up. And we really, really need to talk. If only I could just get him to focus, stop for one second. Sit still. Stop talking. Stop moving. Just listen for five minutes without interrupting me or himself.*

When Toby wakes, I ask him to stay for the rest of the day. I know how much he needs a break from the heat and noise. He seems delighted. I ring the villa.

Hilary answers.

'Is Greg back?'

'No.'

'Right, well, just to let you know, Toby's staying with me for a while.'

A brief pause before she says, 'Yeah, well, just make sure he's back for dinner.'

It's like Upstairs Downstairs. *The staff running the place.*

I teach Toby to play draughts and am amused by how competitive he is. We eat the Magnums. I show him how to play Spider Solitaire on my laptop. How quickly he picks things up.

'Are you a child prodigy?' I ask.

'What's that?'

Phew, I think. *No worries there, then.*

He's such good company. I could keep him for ever. I ring Hilary again. 'Greg back yet?'

'No.'

'Right, well, when he does get back, you might tell him I've taken Toby out for pizza.'

'You can't,' she says.

'Why not?'

'He's not your child.'

I almost laugh. 'He's not yours either. His father isn't home.

He's hungry. I'm taking him out for a meal. If you've got a problem with that, I suggest you talk to Greg.'

She slams the phone down.

We drive down to Antibes and find an outdoor table at a restaurant overlooking Place General de Gaulle. Simple chrome and dark green wicker chairs lend a casual tone, though tablecloths and orange lamps add a touch of elegance. We share the same side of the table, looking out. Traffic circles the square, yet it seems distant. A woman walks by carrying a Yorkshire terrier. A long, straight parting divides its back into two glossy curtains of hair. Behind the woman skip a pair of tiny twins, encircled by a hula hoop. But the fountains opposite are what really interest Toby. Water shoots straight out of the ground around the square, alternating between wide, light sprays and single slender jets. They disappear in a pattern, leaving only wet ground and the uncertainty that they were ever there. Then they suddenly reappear, just when you'd thought they were gone for good. Toby creates a game of second-guessing the display, at which I lose miserably. He is finally distracted by the arrival of our food – spaghetti for him, as they don't do pizza. Listening to this dark little boy chat about bumper cars, piranhas and self-flush loos makes me realize how special he must be to Greg. *So where is he, then? What is he doing, disappearing off without telling anyone?*

'Are you cross with Dad?' he asks, catching me off guard.

'No. Why?'

'Hilary's cross. Dad always tells us where he's going and when he'll be back.'

'There's probably a good reason why he had to hurry away, Toby. Maybe he remembered something he had to do. He'll be back later, and we can ask him then, OK? But we're having a nice time, aren't we?'

'Yeah. When are you and Dad splitting up?'

'What d'you mean?'

'Hilary said you'd be splitting up soon.'

That stalls me. 'I see . . . Well . . . We've no plans at the moment, Toby. I think Hilary might be a bit confused.' *And an interfering cow.*

We don't rush back. I take Toby for a ride on a tourist 'train' that drives through the narrow, winding streets of the town. We buy ice creams. Then fake tattoos that we get a kick out of placing on our arms, reminding me of when I was a kid. Eventually it's time to go. Driving back, Toby 'needs a pee'. Like, now. No, he can't hold on. He has to *go*. With no other option, I pull over to the side of the road, worried about the possible existence of some obscure, French public-exposure law. But it's fine. He climbs back into the Clio, and we haven't been arrested.

'Mission accomplished,' he says.

And I laugh.

As soon as we arrive back at the villa, Hilary snatches him from me.

'Look at the state of you,' she says to him. 'You need a bath, young man.' The spaghetti and ice cream have given his T-shirt a whole new look. But so what? He's five. It will wash out. She's holding out his hands, examining the tattoos. I wink at him. And he winks back.

She starts to herd him towards the stairs.

'Goodnight, Toby,' I call. 'You were great company.'

He smiles. 'Thanks for the spaghetti.'

Red is the colour of Hilary's – entire – face.

Back at the apartment, I check my e-mails and have a more detailed look at the brief we've been given by the retail company. But before I even realize what I'm doing I'm on the

Net, doing a Google search on 'amphetamines'. I visit various sites and read list after list of the effects of speed. Alertness, increased energy and confidence, rapid movement, talkativeness, excitability – one by one I tick them off. To suffer insomnia, though, Greg would need to have been taking speed for a long time and in high doses. Worried, I read on. The sites don't give any advice on how to come off speed, but warn that doing so can lead to tiredness, depression and emotional exhaustion. Seems like a small price to pay. I'd welcome a bit of exhaustion.

At eight I ring Greg's mobile. He is back. I go down to the villa. Straight to the office. He is frantically rummaging through a drawer. What's he looking for, his stash?

'What happened earlier?' I ask.

He looks up. 'When?'

'When you disappeared.'

'What?'

'You were supposed to bring the children for ice cream, but you went off and never came back.'

'Oh, right, that. I must have forgotten.'

'Where did you go?'

He grins. 'To see a man about a dog.'

'What man? And what dog?'

'It's an *expression*, Lucy.'

'People hide behind expressions.'

'I'm hiding behind nothing.'

'So where were you? And who were you with?'

He gives me a look that says, 'What have you turned into?' But he does answer. 'I was in Monte Carlo.'

'*Monte Carlo?*'

'A little principality beyond Nice.'

'I *know* where it is, Greg. What I don't know is why you suddenly had to drop everything to go there.'

'No reason.'

'There must have been a reason.'

'Well, if there was I forget it.'

'Just like you forgot the kids. You know, Greg, they dropped everything for you. And then you dropped them.'

He starts back at the drawer, mumbling, 'I'll make it up to them, OK?'

'How?'

He pops his head up again. 'I don't know. I'll spend time with them.'

'When?'

'*Now.* If it makes you happy.'

'It's almost Toby's bedtime.'

'*So?* He can sleep in.'

'He can't sleep at all with the racket you make at night.'

'What racket?'

'Loud music, telephone conversations.'

'He's imagining things.'

'He asked to come stay with me today, Greg. He's *not* imagining things.'

'OK, OK.' He gets up, suddenly. 'Stop nagging. Jesus. I'll keep the music down, OK?' I open my mouth to speak, but he cuts me off with 'And I'll go play with the children right now, if it makes you happy.'

'Don't you want to find whatever you're looking for first?'

He scratches his head. 'I can't remember what I was looking for.'

Let me help. 'Speed, amphetamines –'

'*What?*'

'Drugs, Greg. I know you're taking them.'

He laughs. 'Well, you know more than I do.'

'Admit it.'

His face changes. 'What is your obsession with drugs? What is *wrong* with you?'

I feel like snapping the same back at him. But I don't want to fight. I want to sort this out. I try to keep calm, focus on my mission. 'Look, Greg. You've a problem. We both know it. If you could just admit it, we could do something about it –'

'The only problem I have is you, Lucy,' he says, turning and walking from the room.

He leaves me standing, winded. Hurt stops me reacting immediately. Anger propels me forward. I go after him, ready to ask, 'What do you mean I'm a problem? If I'm such a problem maybe I should leave?' But I walk straight into a happy family scene. Toby, dressed for bed, is running to get paints, while Rachel is heading my way to the office for paper. I slow down, try to lift the expression on my face. That's when I see Hilary, looking like she's ready to start fitting.

'Right,' she snaps. 'Forget routine. Fine. I'm going to my room. And I won't be back down.' She pounds up the stairs.

'What's wrong with *her*?' he asks.

I keep walking, amazed that he has the nerve to talk to me.

'Where you going?' he asks cheerily, as if the argument between us never happened.

'Bed.' The only reason I answer is that the children are there, watching.

'Don't go. You're great fun.'

I feel like clocking him.

They're sitting down to paint as I walk out the door. How long will it be, I wonder, before Greg has to do something, be with someone, go somewhere other than here.

14

A good night's sleep helps my perspective. I love Greg. Or at least the Greg I met. He brought me back to life, gave me another future. I don't want to throw that away. I didn't get another chance with Brendan, but I have one with Greg. Whatever the problem is, he reacted the way he did because I was backing him into a corner. I should have tried to stay calm, been more supportive. If I'd been smart about it, I wouldn't have mentioned drugs at all. I'd have told him I was behind him. Whatever the problem, we'd get help together.

I'm sitting on the sofa, trying to work out how to bring the whole thing up again, this time with tact, when I hear his key in the door. He breezes in, bright and cheery. Convenient amnesia.

'The kids are in the car. Are you coming up into the mountains with us?'

I have to stop myself snapping that there's nothing wrong with *my* memory. I tell myself to keep quiet. If we can just get on well today, then maybe, after we get back, we can talk. I let him take my hand and pull me off the sofa.

'Come on. It'll be great,' he says.

Hilary is in the back of the Range Rover with the children. Toby seems to be developing some kind of heat rash. I turn up the air-conditioner. Greg drives to Grasse and from there up into the Alps. As we climb, the temperature outside begins to drop from thirty-six degrees to thirty-two. The scenery is breathtaking. Sheer-drop cliffs, mountain streams, gorges, waterfalls. Tiny hillside villages perch precariously, prettily.

Higher and higher. We're almost at the top, when over the precipice float what looks like a series of tiny orange jellyfish – paragliders slowly descending in smooth arcs, like skiers down a slope, leaning to the left then right, and finally landing in a field beside the road. Without a word, Greg pulls over and hops out. We watch him approach the small group folding their wings like sails. For a moment I'm afraid he'll return with some for us. He doesn't. But he has signed up for lessons.

We make it to Gourdon, a tiny fairytale village with postcard views. In the car park we're ambushed by a very cute and amateur sales force: little blonde alpine children selling home-made bundles of lavender. We buy one for a euro and make their day. We wander through tiny streets, while Greg tears on ahead, stopping every so often to examine an item for sale or to strike up conversation with strangers. Through open windows we hear the sound of voices and crockery as families prepare for their evening meal. The children are hungry. We find a restaurant and settle in. Greg is talking on and on at high speed about some obscure subject. Another day, another monologue. The rest of us eat in silence, Hilary moving her Coke to avoid grains of rice that fly, every so often, from Greg's mouth. But then something happens to drag us from our practised inertia. Greg stops making sense. He's been talking about going somewhere in the car, but the car suddenly turns into a boat.

'. . . and when we got to Barbados . . .' he's saying.

I'm afraid he'll worry the children. So I try to jolt him back to reality. 'Greg, we've never been to Barbados. We've never been on a boat together.'

He doesn't seem to hear. Just carries on. 'The boat went twenty knots an hour, shower, power, flour.'

Gibberish.

My God!

'What's wrong with Dad?' asks Toby. 'He's talking funny.'

Greg snaps at him. 'Nothing's wrong with me. What's wrong with you?'

After that, no one talks. No one eats – apart from Greg, who finishes his meal in minutes and reaches over to help himself to mine. I give him my plate. Toby's head is bowed, his shoulders raised. He doesn't make a sound, but I know he's crying. I want to tell him everything will be all right, put my arm around him. But Hilary gets there first, with hers. He looks exhausted, his little face flushed, his hair damp with sweat. I ask for the bill and am told, by my fiancé, that I'm no crack. Once out of the restaurant, he bounds ahead back to the Range Rover. We follow behind, a quiet group. Somehow, I end up carrying Toby.

'What's wrong with Dad?' asks Rachel.

'It's hot, Rachel,' I say. 'He's been working very hard. Doing too much. He just needs sleep.'

Hilary throws me an are-you-for-real look.

'I need sleep too,' says Toby.

'I know,' I say. 'Just close your eyes and rest on my shoulder. Everything'll be fine.'

By the time we get to the Range Rover, Toby is asleep, his face damp against my T-shirt. I feel a wave of responsibility for him. Even for Rachel. Greg has the engine revving. I ease Toby on to his booster seat and strap him in.

'I'll drive,' I say, opening Greg's door.

'What do you mean, you'll drive? I'm already driving.'

'Greg, please don't make a scene. Just let me drive.' I say it quietly.

'Is there something wrong with my driving? Is that what you're saying?'

'No. I just think I should drive. You've had a beer.'

'One beer. Below the limit. I'm driving.'

That's that. Adamant.

Silently, I climb in.

Darkness is falling on the way back down the mountain. Greg insists on returning by a different route from the one we took when we came, despite my telling him that it looks like a very minor road on the map. It is, we discover, wide enough for one car only. He's tearing down it, making childish 'vroom vroom' noises and 'weees' on the hairpin bends. He takes the corners so fast I imagine us going over the edge. I hold the door handle, close my eyes and pray. My heart's pounding. My foot keeps hitting an imaginary brake. Just inches away from the wheels, the ground falls away into a gorge. A beautiful gorge that tourists snap on a daily basis. A gorge that will become world famous if Greg Millar's Range Rover ends up smashed at the bottom.

'Greg, slow down.'

He ignores me.

'Dad, please slow down,' says Rachel, sounding terrified.

It's as if he hasn't heard her.

'Greg,' I say quietly so they can't hear at the back, 'if another car comes around that corner, we're over the edge.'

'Rubbish. Where's your sense of adventure?'

'Greg, *please*. You're going too fast.'

'I'm *not* going too fast,' he snaps.

Silence now. But he does slow. I turn round to check if the children are all right. Toby is still asleep. Thank God. Rachel's face is burrowed into the side of Hilary's formidable chest. She's sucking her thumb, something I've never seen her do. My eyes meet Hilary's. Slowly, she shakes her head. I sit back and close my eyes. *No more.*

Somehow the nightmare drive ends and we get back to the villa. I carry Toby up to bed while Hilary puts her arm around a shaken and visibly upset Rachel. Together they go into her room, Hilary whispering reassurances. The door closes behind them.

I find Greg in the kitchen, knocking back a glass of water.

I'm way too angry to be supportive. 'What's wrong with you?'

'Why do you keep asking what's wrong with me? Nothing's wrong with me. What's wrong with *you*?'

'Why were you like that?'

'Like what?'

'Oh, come on, don't tell me you don't know. You were driving like a mad man. You could have killed us all.'

'Rubbish.' He slams down the empty glass. 'I was totally in control.'

'Is that right? So what would you have done if another car had come round the bend? Where would you've pulled in? How would you've stopped in time?'

'You're such a panic merchant. I'd have handled it.'

'In that case you're deluded. There would've been no way out. If you can't see that you've a serious problem –'

He laughs. 'Lucy, it's not me who has the problem, it's you.'

I can't believe it. 'Don't twist this. What's going on?'

'If you bring up drugs again, Lucy, God help me, I'll lose it.'

'You're high. Don't stand there and tell me you're not high. And, whatever the cause, it has to stop. It's got to a point where it's dangerous. You could've killed us up there. You could've killed your own children. Do you hear me, Greg?'

'Lucy, love, you really should see a doctor.'

I explode. 'There's nothing wrong with *me*. You're the one with the problem. Tearing around, awake all night, snapping at the children, living in your own fast-paced world, becoming so detached from me and yet expecting sex like it's your God given right. You're the one who needs a doctor. You!' I've given him too much rope. And he's hanging *me* with it. Holding in a scream, I storm from the villa. Tears distort the lights of the oncoming cars. Back at the apartment, I drop on to the sofa and land my throbbing head into my hands. 'I don't know what to do. I don't know what to do.' I say it aloud, over and over, torn between what I should do and what I want to. Stay or go. I cry myself out. Well into the morning, without moving from the sofa, my heavy, swollen lids finally close. Sleep, at last, takes over.

15

I'm having no impact. It makes no difference to him whether I'm here or not. But it makes a difference to me. This, *he*, is grinding me down. I have to get away. Put distance between us. Maybe then I can think, work out what to do, find a way forward, if there is a way forward. For now, I have to go. I write Greg a letter, explaining. But I won't drop it to the villa. Better for him to find me gone. To experience the shock of that. To read from start to finish what he never allows me to explain out loud. To have him react. I book the first available flight home. It leaves this afternoon, return open.

Sitting in the Departure Lounge at Nice Airport, flight delayed, I worry. *Will they be OK? What if Greg takes them out in the car again? It'll be all right. Hilary's there. Solid and reliable, Hilary. She won't let anything happen. Wish I'd thought to leave her my key to the apartment, though.* I'm wondering if there is any way I might get it to her, when I'm distracted by a woman coming through Passport Control. Weird how thinking about a person can make you see them in others. She looks just like Hilary. Even has the same denim jacket. Hair. Posture. I stare as she turns and walks into the Departure Lounge. It *is* Hilary, wheeling a small suitcase behind her. What the hell is she doing here?

'Hilary?' I call.

She looks in my direction. There's a moment of connection. Then she looks straight ahead, about to walk past.

I stand. 'Hilary. Stop. Wait. What are you doing?'

Up close, I see that her eyes are rimmed red, her face puffy. 'What happened?'

'Ask your *boyfriend*,' she spits and begins to walk again.

'Hilary. Stop. Please. Tell me what happened. How could you've left them alone after last night?'

'How could *you*?' she asks.

Instant guilt. 'I have to go home for a while. I knew you'd be there. I was relying on you. How could you've left Rachel and Toby with him when you know what he's like at the moment?'

She drops her head and mumbles. 'It's hard to mind children you no longer work for.'

'What? You *resigned*?'

She looks up, straight into my eyes. 'You always were a bit slow, weren't you?' And this time she does walk away.

After three hours of waiting, they pick that moment to call my flight. *Damn. What'll I do? I have to get on that plane. Maybe they'll be OK.* I see Toby's tired little face in my mind. *Maybe if I call them.* I dial the number. It rings out. *What if Greg's left them alone and they're afraid to answer the phone?* I call again. After five rings Rachel answers.

'Hello?' Her voice is wobbly. She sounds so young.

'Rachel? It's Lucy. Is everything OK?'

The line dies. *Oh, God. He* has *left them alone.* I dial again. It's ringing out. I imagine Toby making for the pool while Rachel stares at the phone. I panic. At the same time I wonder how I have allowed myself to get into this mess. It's ringing again. People are lining up for the flight. I can't go. I can't believe it. But I can't go. I want to kill Greg – if he hasn't already driven off a road somewhere. I want to kill the immature, irresponsible gobshite he's become. I leave Departures in a state and have problems explaining why I can't get on the flight. Major fuss. For security reasons, they need to get my bag off the plane. The flight will have to be delayed. *Encore.* But security is security. And these guys mean business. They won't let me go until I've the bag firmly in my possession. I tell them I don't care about the bag. They can keep it. I just have to get somewhere. It's an emergency. Red tape first, emergencies second, madame.

I race to the villa. Greg *is* there, absorbed in a mural he's started on the living-room wall. It's all over the place. He's covered in paint, as is the floor.

'Where are the children?' I ask.

'Upstairs.'

'Are they all right?'

'Of course they're all right, why wouldn't they be?'

'I met Hilary.'

'Where?'

'At the airport. What happened?'

'What were you doing at the airport?'

'Nothing. It's not important. What happened with Hilary?'

Leonardo abandons his fresco in favour of a whiskey. 'Want one?'

'No, I don't drink whiskey, as you know. What happened?'

He sighs. 'Hilary, Hilary, what's the fascination with Hilary?'

'*Greg!*'

'All right, if you're so concerned – I let her go.'

'Why?'

'I was sick of looking at her. Moody cow.'

'And that's a good enough reason to sack her?'

He doesn't answer, drains his whiskey and returns to the wall.

'Rachel and Toby love Hilary. They need her. Especially now.'

He twists round. 'What do you mean especially now?'

'Nothing.'

'They'll get over it,' he says.

'Will they? Are you *sure*?'

He looks straight at me. 'There was nothing great about Hilary.'

'She's been with you since Catherine died. She helped you through that –'

'I helped myself through. If you think I can't survive without Hilary, you're mistaken. I'm perfectly capable of looking after –'

'Did something happen?'

'*No*,' he says too quickly, too loudly.

'Then why?'

'I'd enough of her, OK?'

'When did this happen, when did you sack her? It must have been last night, if she managed to get a flight today.'

He ignores me, daubing buttercup yellow on the wall.

'Did you even bring her to the airport?'

No answer.

'She was your responsibility. Did you even check to see if she'd enough money to get home?'

'If you met her at the airport, she obviously did.'

'What is the matter with you? You used to be thoughtful. You used to appreciate people.'

I pull out my mobile, look up her number and dial. Her phone goes on to voicemail. I leave a message asking her to call me, telling her the children miss her (which is a given) and that Greg's sorry.

'I'm not fucking sorry,' he says before I can hang up. 'I don't want her back here. And you better not ask her again if she rings back.'

'So what're you going to do? Who's going to mind the

137

children while you write? Who's going to keep the place tidy? Who's going to cook the meals?' *And who's going to be here when you do your disappearing stunts?*

'I'll hire someone else.'

'Just like that? An English-speaking nanny who the children will love as much as they did Hilary. You better start looking in the sky, Greg, because I hear Mary Poppins is good.'

He ignores that.

'You need Hilary. She's been with you for five years. If she calls, then I'm inviting her back.'

'She won't come back. Trust me.'

What has he done? What has he said? He isn't telling me everything. That much I know. Something must've happened. Something definitely happened.

I go upstairs, check Toby's room. Nothing. I go to Rachel's. I hear nothing but sense they're inside. I knock gently. No answer.

'Can I come in?'

Still nothing.

I open the door a fraction, peep round. Rachel's sitting on the bed, Toby's head in her lap. She's smoothing his hair, over and over.

'Hi,' I say.

Rachel doesn't budge. Toby sits up but says nothing. He's been crying. I smile at him and go to sit on the edge of the bed.

'Get off my bed,' Rachel says, with hate in her eyes.

I stand. 'Sorry.'

I squat down and talk to Toby. 'Are you OK?'

Nothing.

'Are you sad about Hilary?'

'Yeah,' he says.

'*Toby,*' says Rachel.

'Sorry, Lucy,' he says, 'but I can't talk to you.'

'I'm so sorry about Hilary. It's hard when someone goes away –'

'*Goes* away?' Rachel's chin is jutting out. 'You mean, is *sent* away, *sacked*. You got Dad to fire Hilary.'

'Sorry?'

'You heard me.'

'I heard you, but you're wrong. I'd nothing to do with this.' How did she get that notion into her head?

'Yes, you did. You were jealous because we love her, not you.'

'Rachel, I wasn't even here.'

'You told Dad to sack Hilary before you left. Hilary told me, and *she* doesn't lie. You're the liar. You're the one who spoils everything. You.'

So Hilary told them it was my fault. Why? She's not even going to be around. What does it matter to her? What is this, her parting shot? 'I'm sorry you think that, Rachel.'

'No, you're not. You're happy, 'cause Hilary's gone. You think we'll like you now. But we won't. We won't even talk to you. And we won't cooperate.' She folds her arms.

Despite my distress, I spot the big word. You can always tell the readers.

'Well, I'll be downstairs if you need me,' I say.

'Don't worry, we won't.'

I go back down, furious with everyone: with Hilary for everything she's done, with Rachel for being so difficult and with Greg for creating this whole bloody mess. I prepare dinner, because I know that *he* won't have thought of food all day.

My efforts are wasted. Greg has gone to get turpentine for the mural and hasn't returned. Toby has a sick tummy. And

Rachel? Rachel's response to what I put in front of her is 'I'm not eating *that*.' So I eat alone. Not that I'm hungry either.

All of a sudden, I need to hear Dad's voice. I go outside and ring from my mobile.

Mum answers. 'I thought you'd forgotten about us,' she says.

'Sorry, Mum. It's been a bit hectic. I've been busy on a pitch for Get Smart.'

'Oh, I'm glad. I wouldn't want you to fall down on your job just because you're engaged. I was a bit worried when you said you were spending the summer in France.'

'Is Dad there?'

'Always look after yourself, Lucy – in any relationship.'

'Yeah, OK. Is Dad around?'

'He's here beside me. I'll hand him over in a sec.'

'Mum, I'm on Greg's phone,' I say, fingers crossed.

'Oh, sorry, you should have said. Here he is now.'

I hear her tell him not to be long and feel guilty then.

As soon as Dad gets on the phone, I sit down.

'Hi, pet. How're you doing?'

I smile at the sound of his voice. 'Good. And you?'

'Never better. How's Greg?'

'OK. He said you'll have to organize another game of golf when we get back.'

Silence.

'I'm joking, Dad.'

'You old codger.' He chuckles. 'How are the kiddies?'

'They're all right.'

When he says, 'These things take time,' I realize I should have been more enthusiastic. 'How's Greg?' he asks again.

'Good.' No point worrying him.

'How're you coping with the heat wave? It's all over the

news. People have died in Paris. Others are leaving the country.'

'It's OK.'

'No doubt Greg has the place air-conditioned.'

I could cry.

'Better let you go,' he says. 'This must be costing Greg a fortune.'

'No. No. It's fine.' My voice starts to crack, my eyes to smart.

'You all right, love?'

'Yeah, yeah, fine,' I say, a little too high. 'Actually I think I'll go. I haven't talked to Grace in ages.'

'Good idea, love. Ring your sister.'

'Bye, Dad. Love you.'

'You too.'

I can't ring Grace. I can't do anything. Except burst into tears.

It's eleven, and there's no sign of him. I'm livid, now. *What if I walked out, behaved as irresponsibly? Would he cop on then? No, probably not.* I punch his number into my mobile. And seethe as it rings out. *Where the hell is he? In a nightclub, music pumping? With these 'other women' Hilary mentioned? Or speeding along the motorway, radio blaring? Or maybe he's looking at his phone right now, seeing it's me and ignoring it? Or on his way home, hearing the phone, reaching for it, going over a ravine, the car sailing through the air in slow motion and ending upside down, wheels spinning? Stop, Lucy. Stop it. He'll walk through the door any minute without a scratch. And what good will all the worrying have done? None. Get some sheets, make up a bed. Sleep. Don't think.*

I carry bed linen to one of the guest rooms. *I'm not going to worry.* I make up the bed, go find a fan. *I, am, not, going, to, worry.* I look at my mobile. *He's fine.* I get under the sheet.

141

Pull it back, again. Check my watch. *Where is he?* I close my eyes. Open them. Get out of bed. Check on the children. Return to bed. When the phone rings, at three, I know without looking, what time it is. I get to it before its fifth ring.

'Hello?'

Silence.

'Bonjour? Bonsoir? *Hello?*'

There is someone there. I sense it.

'Greg?' *It's not Greg. He never remembers the number of the villa.*

The line goes dead. I wait by the phone in case it rings again. After five minutes I head back to bed, relieved that the worst hasn't, in fact, happened. Relief changes to anger when I think of what he's putting me through. As soon as I see him, I will tell him two words: I'm leaving. He'll have to cop on then, he'll have to remember his responsibilities. This is his problem, not mine.

Somehow, at some stage, I fall asleep.

At nine I wake to hear hushed conversation and light footsteps on the stairs. Rachel and Toby are up. I throw back the sheet. Go to Greg's room to check if he's there, though I already sense he isn't.

And I'm right.

Back in my room I dress, then give the children a comfortable few minutes before heading down. I find them in the kitchen. Toby is sitting at the table, legs dangling, still unable to reach the floor. He's looking down at his cereal bowl, into which Rachel is pouring Coco Pops. There is protectiveness about the way she's standing over him. She looks like a very vulnerable mini-mum. To me, they both look like they need protecting. Rachel turns. I'm graced with a scowl. Then it's back to the business at hand. I'm not here.

'Good morning,' I say brightly, walking in.

No answer.

'Would anyone like some toast?'

No eye contact.

I busy myself making coffee, then sit at the table. Expecting continued silence, I'm surprised when Rachel speaks.

'Did you stay here last night?'

'Yes.'

'Why?'

'Because your dad was out and I didn't want to leave you on your own.'

'Oh.'

Eyes narrow again. 'Where did you sleep?'

'In one of the guest rooms. Why?'

'No reason.'

I let the silence return.

'Where's Dad?' asks Toby. Chocolate stains the edges of his mouth.

'Gone again, as usual,' Rachel says, with the exasperation and bitterness of a long-suffering wife. I know how she feels.

I sip my coffee, hoping they don't work out he's been gone all night. 'So, what would you like to do today?'

Toby glances at his sister. She frowns a silent warning. He looks down at his bowl, which is now empty apart from a few soggy Coco Pops floating in brown milk.

'How about Aqua-Splash?'

His head pops up. 'Yeah,' he says. Then 'Ow,' as his sister kicks him.

He looks down again, gives a quick nod as if telling himself to be quiet.

'We're not going,' she confirms for both of them.

He closes his eyes.

'Look,' I say, 'are we going to get on with life or are we going to mope around?'

'Mope around,' says Rachel victoriously.

'OK,' I say, 'suit yourself. I've plenty of work to do. I was just trying to make your day more enjoyable. But if you want to hang round here, fine.'

Toby looks pleadingly at his sister. I feel sorry for him. But she won't budge. They're going nowhere. Despite my attempts to be blasé, I keep an eye on them, dragging my laptop around wherever they go. If they're in Rachel's room, I'm in mine. If they're downstairs, I am too, usually at a sneaky vantage point. I'm trying to be subtle about it, but when they go for a swim, this becomes impossible. I appear in the water two minutes after they do. Rachel glares at me, then turns to her brother. 'Come on, Toby, let's go,' she says, without taking her eyes off me.

'But we just got in,' he whines.

'Come. On.'

'*No.*'

'*Fine,*' she says, furious at having to leave her accomplice behind.

I wink at him.

He smiles.

It's the one thing we share. We're the youngest of two and don't always like it.

They spend the rest of the morning in Rachel's room, door closed. When they emerge, she is fussing over him, getting drinks and food or putting him in the bath to keep him cool. She even trims his fingernails. She's becoming a little Hilary, with Hilary expressions and mannerisms. And, just like Hilary, she doesn't want me here. Let's face it: I can think of a lot of places I'd prefer to be – all of them child-free. I could kill Greg, out there in his own colourful, interesting, *loud* galaxy, while I'm stuck here struggling with his children. *Come back, Hilary, all is forgiven.*

16

Round about lunchtime, Fint calls. He wants me back in Dublin to brainstorm for the big pitch. There is no way I can commit to that. Not now, with Greg gone and no idea of when he'll be back, not when I can't trust him with the children if he does return, and not when there is the possibility of his leaving them alone if I go. But I don't want to let my partner down. He has been so good to me.

'What do you mean you can't come? We have to brainstorm on this. It's a *major* opportunity.'

'I know. I just can't come over straight away. The children's nanny has walked out.'

'*So*? Whose children are they, Lucy?'

'Greg isn't well.'

'What's wrong with him?'

'I . . . I don't know.'

'I see,' he says, sounding like he doesn't.

'Look, let me see if I can find someone, a childminder. There must be agencies over here. Give me a week, OK? Just give me a week to find someone, then I'll be over.'

'We can't afford a week. Our deadline is tight enough as it is.'

'I'm really, really, sorry, Fint, but I can't come over right now.'

'Can't or won't?'

'*Can't.*'

'Well, then, I really think you need to look at your priorities. Your personal life is taking over here. I can't keep making concessions. You made a commitment to come home for meetings. Well, this isn't just any meeting. This is huge. This is an opportunity to bag the biggest, most prestigious account we've ever had, and you're prepared to blow it. We're supposed to be a team.'

'I know and I'm sorry.'

'So come.'

My stomach is knotted so tightly I could throw up.

'I'm carrying this partnership, right now,' Fint continues, his voice barely holding his anger together. 'You know, if you can't keep up your business commitments, well, I don't know, maybe it's time to start talking about –'

'Fintan, you know that if I could come, I would. I said I was sorry. And I am. But I can't help it. I'm worried sick about leaving those kids.'

'You're putting babysitting before Get Smart. This is a partnership. The effort is supposed to be fifty-fifty.'

'If you want me to quit, I'll quit. OK? I can't take this. I've had enough. I'll ring you tomorrow and we can sort this out.'

'Right, that's really mature. First you back out of your commitments, then you quit –'

I hang up. What's the point? What's the fucking point?

I ring Grace in a state. My relationship, my career, my *life* is falling apart. I'm practically hysterical.

'I'm coming over,' she says.

'What d'you mean you're coming over? You've the kids . . .'

'I'm bringing them.'

'Grace, there's a heat wave.'

'Have you air-conditioning?'

'In the apartment.'

'Fine.'

'I don't expect you to drop everything . . .'

'I might as well be over there as here for all I see of Kevin. I'm bored out of my tree, stuck in the house for the last week because of the rain. It's not as if my diary's full of prior engagements. It's not as if I *have* a bloody diary. Lucy, I need a challenge. And let's face it, you could do with a hand.'

I say nothing. I need her to come but don't want to pressure her.

'I am *not* going to let you give up your career,' she says. 'One in the family is enough.'

'Grace, I'm sure there are nanny agencies over here.'

'So, how are you going to find them?'

'They must have a yellow pages.'

'So. You find an agency, what then? Is your French good enough to wade through CV after CV, conduct interview after interview in a foreign language? Even if you manage to get someone, will they last? I mean who'd want to work for a person in Greg's condition?'

I feel like wailing.

'Look. I'll talk to Kevin. But, in the mood I'm in, fuck Kevin and the horse he rode into town on.'

'Grace, I warn you, it's a circus over here.'

'Lucy, I think I've a fair idea.'

Mid afternoon, Grace calls to confirm that she's coming. I can feel my body deflate, my breathing ease. In one week they'll be here. My form improves enough to call Fint before he leaves the office.

'It's me,' I say.

'I thought you'd quit.'

'Don't you watch *any* movies? You weren't supposed to accept my resignation. You were supposed to shower me with compliments and beg me to stay.'

'Are you kidding? I was furious with you.' He stops. 'But it's

147

OK. I've calmed down now.' He pauses. 'What's happening?'

'Grace is coming over to give me a hand.'

'Grace?' He sounds surprised, as if there really might be a problem after all. 'Is everything all right?'

'Yeah.'

'Greg OK?'

'Yeah. No. Look, I'm sorry about earlier. The last thing I want to do is let you down. You've been great, really great.' I'm starting to get upset.

'Forget about it, Lucy. I had a brainstorm with the guys. Sebastian sat in. He was amazing.'

'Really?'

'Yeah. Incredibly creative. We had a very productive meeting.'

'That's good,' I say, beginning to feel left out.

'Look, if things are so difficult over there right now, we may be able to manage without you. We've some really good ideas to go on now.'

'No, no. It's fine. I'll be over. How's Friday next week?'

He checks his diary. 'Fine.'

'OK. Friday it is. I'll let you know when I've booked a flight.'

Within minutes of hanging up, I get a call on my mobile from Emma, the managing editor at the Copperplate Press. She wants to know where Greg's overdue corrected proofs are. She can't get Greg, so she's using her clout as one of my biggest clients to see what I can do to 'hurry things along'. Pushed to the limit, and Greg still out, I check his desk. It's chaotic, cluttered with mounds of paper, books, half-eaten food, three overflowing ashtrays, CDs, newspapers, *Asterix* comics. The mess spills on to the floor and along it like a creeping virus. Hand-written notes and computer printouts are covered in doodles, diagrams and cartoon sketches, all outlining ideas. He's written on everything from paper to receipts, napkins to toilet paper. Instead of his usual loose scrawl I find tiny letters and words all jammed together, as if he's trying to condense an epic on to a postcard.

When I move the keyboard and mouse out of the way, what Greg's been working on comes up on screen. It seems to be a novel. But the sentences don't follow on from each other in the usual way. They're unlinked in thought, connected only by words: either words that rhyme or the same word at the beginning and end of two adjacent sentences. Impossible to follow. Is it some sort of experiment? One thing's for sure, no publisher is going to accept it. No publisher is going to *understand* it. Better to show them nothing than this.

Becoming increasingly despondent, I check the drawers of Greg's desk for the corrected proofs. Without success. What will I tell Emma? A wave of hopelessness crashes down on me. I realize that whatever's wrong with Greg, it's way too big for me. Maybe even for Grace. I rest my forehead against the cool mahogany of the desk and close my eyes.

There is a rumble of distant thunder. I open my eyes and see how dark it has become. I go to the window. Angry storm clouds, the colour of charcoal, are gathering on the horizon like soldiers preparing for battle. The air is heavy. Without sun to scorch the villa, I swing open all the shutters. Out on the terrace, I gather in bone-dry clothes, towels and togs. A weak flash of lightning. Then the sound of a bowling ball running along a wooden floor. *Faites attention! Nous venons!* I stand on the terrace, arms folded and wait. The rain, when it comes, is torrential, blotting out all other sound. The children come to the doorway and watch. And there we stand, transfixed by the storm, my only thought how much trouble we are in.

The storm rages all evening until it loses its novelty value for the children. At nine Rachel decides it's time for bed. When Toby starts to protest, as he always does, she says she will read him *Captain Underpants*. As they climb the stairs, I hear her telling him that they should brush their teeth first to get it over with. I call 'goodnight'. Only Toby turns. He gives a little smile, then carries on up the stairs, his sister holding his hand.

Apart from intermittent lightning flashes, it is fully dark outside when the sound of a loud and unfamiliar engine out front alerts me. I go to the window. Headlights dazzle, then die, leaving darkness. Someone's coming to the door. I switch on the outside light and peer out. Sitting in the drive is a beautiful silver sports car, top down in the middle of a thunderstorm. I open the window and stick my head out to see who is at the door.

Greg.

He's soaked through, white hair glistening under the light, as he fumbles with his keys.

I go to open the door.

'Oh. Hello!' he says, surprised.

'Whose is that?' I ask.

'The car?' He turns to admire it. 'What do you think? Porsche Boxter. Cool, eh?'

'Yeah. But whose is it?'

'Mine.' His chest expands.

'You bought it?'

He nods proudly. 'Nought to a hundred in six seconds. Put that in your drum and bang it.'

'Where's the Range Rover?'

He runs a hand through spiky, albino hair. 'I traded it in.'

'Where's all the stuff that was in the boot?'

He bites his lip.

'Where'll the children sit? How'll we fit anything into that little boot?'

He digs two distressed fingers into his forehead and drags them across. He looks down at his open-toed sandals and tanned, sandy feet. Then lifts his head, throws his arms in the air in a who-cares gesture, as if the process of thinking is just too much.

'And you remembered to change your insurance, right?'

He looks like he's about to blow, an android reaching meltdown from circuit overload.

'Greg. We need to talk. This has gone on too long. You need to stop, OK? You need help.'

'I buy *the coolest car* and I need help.' He rolls his eyes, then turns one hundred and eighty degrees.

'Where you going?'

'For a run.'

'We're in the middle of a thunderstorm,' I call.

He legs it down the drive, his shirt clinging to his back.

I slam the door. Kick it. An angry crack of thunder causes the windows to vibrate. The car alarm goes off. I'm amazed he remembered to put it on. Lightning lights up the entire room. Less than a second later, thunder sounds like a giant plank of wood cracking. Blue light invades the room again. Flash, waver, flash. Smack. The rain is heavier than ever. I check on the children and find them out cold on Rachel's bed, back to skinny back. I can't believe they're sleeping through this. I cover them with a sheet, turn off the fan. Do all children look so innocent when they're asleep? I gaze at them and sigh. They don't deserve this. Nobody does. How can such a great father just lose interest in his family? Can drugs really do that to a person?

I go to my room, sit on the bed, wrap my arms around my knees. I never thought I'd say it, but if only I'd never met him.

My world was safe. I controlled it. Why did I have to go and expose myself to this? Wasn't it enough to lose one man? Do I have to go through it again? Because I'm losing Greg. I may already have lost him. He is living his own life now, separate from me. To him, I am a bore. So why not offer me the drugs? Maybe he did, the night of the red dress and the restaurant. If so, he got his answer when I told him I didn't want to be treated like that. And I don't. I want to live in the real world. And I want the man I love to want the same. Is that too much to ask? Apparently so. Which leaves me with only one option. To end this, to leave the man I love because he has chosen such a meaningless, hurtful and destructive path. That I have made that decision breaks my heart. My tears are more relentless than the rain outside. It is a long, long time before I sleep.

I wake early and immediately sense change. I feel Greg's presence. I can't see him, but I know he's near. I hear his breathing. Sit up. And there he is, asleep, *finally asleep*, on the floor beside the bed, still in the clothes he was wearing during the storm. He looks so vulnerable, like someone who needs rescuing. I slip my pillow under his head and cover him with the sheet. That he came and found me and lay beside me softens something in me. It's daylight but dark. The rain has eased but thunder continues to rumble and lightning flickers, pale pink against a dark grey sky. I check on Rachel and Toby. They're at the window looking out. I stand in silence beside them. Toby starts a stream of questions about forked lightning, sheet lightning and people getting electrocuted. Rachel just wants to know if her dad's home.

'Yes,' I say. 'And he's asleep.'

There is hope in her eyes when she looks at me. For the first time, we've something in common.

17

At twelve, Greg is still in a deep sleep. I'm sitting at the kitchen table nursing a coffee when, on the table, next to the keys of his Porsche, his mobile begins to vibrate. I pick it up, ready to take a message. The screen tells me it's Hilary.

'Hello, Hilary.'

She hangs up.

When I do the same, I notice that the sign for missed calls is displayed. I hit it. And nearly drop the phone. She's been ringing him non-stop for days, at all hours, day and night. *Why? To get her job back? Surely she's too proud for that. And anyway, all she had to do was ring me.* I look at the silver, brand-new Sony mobile phone and wonder why Greg hasn't been answering. *He must have heard some of the calls. Why didn't she try the villa?* That's when I guess the source of those silent calls – Hilary, ringing for Greg, and hanging up when I answer.

It's lunchtime when Greg surfaces. Dark circles ring eyes that seem sunken in a pale, drawn face. A long red line runs down his cheek where he's slept on a crease. He's changed out of his wet clothes but still looks shabby, unshaven with T-shirt and trousers hanging off him. I realize how much weight he's lost. He looks burnt out, as if the last two weeks of sleepless nights have finally caught up with him.

'Hi,' I say.

'Hi.' He half smiles, half looks at me, pulling out a chair and slumping on to it.

I plug in the kettle, then turn, folding my arms and leaning against the worktop. Neither of us speaks; just watch the rain through open doors.

'Hilary's been ringing your mobile – constantly,' I say.

'Oh?' He doesn't look at me.

'What does she want?' I ask.

'Dunno.' He gets up, goes to the fridge, pulls out a carton of juice and drinks directly from it.

'She's been calling here too and hanging up. What's going on?'

He shakes his head. Shrugs.

'She must have got through to you at some point?'

Again he shakes his head. 'She said something about wanting her job back. I told her it was out of the question.'

'Why?'

'I don't want her back. That's all. Where are the kids?' He looks to the door.

'Upstairs.'

'What are they doing?' He puts the carton back. Yawns. Scratches the side of his face.

'Avoiding me.'

'Both of them?'

'They think *I* told you to sack Hilary.'

'*Why?*'

'Because she told them I did.'

'Jesus. What did she do that for?'

'Who knows? Revenge. A parting shot.' I look at him. 'Greg, can you sit down for a sec?'

His eyes register that he knows something's up. But he doesn't argue.

'We're in trouble,' I say.

I can see him swallow.

'I can't go on. Not like this. You're not yourself. You snap at me, the children. Sack Hilary. Then disappear whenever you want for hours, *nights*, at a time, without any explanation. I don't know where you are, who you're with, what you're doing. You won't talk to me. You don't care. Just leave me here minding your children as if I'm some kind of idiot. They are your responsibility, not mine. At this stage, the only reason I'm still here is so that nothing happens to them. I can't trust you to mind your own children, Greg. You've lost all sense of responsibility. You have a family, a successful career, a fiancée, commitments, but you just don't seem to care. It's like all you want is to be out having a good time, getting high, and to hell with the people who love you. We're not exciting enough for you any more. Did you know that I've had Emma hounding me for the proofs for *A River Too Wide*?'

He opens his mouth to say something, but I don't give him time. 'I've had enough, Greg.'

'I'm sorry, Lucy. I, I haven't been myself. So restless. Always something else to do –'

'You used to be a great father. I admired you for it.'

'I don't know what's got into me. I'm sorry. You're right. I'll change. I won't go out –'

'What is it? Are you bored with us?'

'No.'

'Isn't life exciting enough for you?'

'Of course it is.'

'Is there someone else?'

'No. *No*.'

'Please. Just tell me what it is – I want to know what ended our relationship.'

He gets up, comes to me, squats down, takes my hand. 'There's no one else, Lucy. Just you. I love *you*. I won't go out. I, I'll stay in. I'm sorry. I just don't know how I've let things get this out of hand. I don't understand it myself.' He sniffs. 'I promise I'll stick around, be here for you, for the kids.' He rubs his bristly chin back and forward.

'How do I know I can trust you? You say you'll do all these things and then you don't. I'm tired, Greg. So tired. I need to go home now. Get Rob over here to help you with the kids. They're not my responsibility. I've tried to make this work, I've tried so hard. But I can't do this any more. I just can't.' I look down at the beautiful triangular solitaire that reminds me of another time, another man. I close my eyes as I begin to remove it.

'No, Lucy. You can't. I promise you, there's nowhere else I want to be, just with you and the kids.'

'Then why aren't you?' I manage to prise the ring off a finger swollen from the heat. Immediately, I hold it out to him. *Take it. Please take it.*

He looks desperate. 'I love you, I swear. Give me a chance to prove it, Luce, please. Give me a week. You'll see.'

Can I believe him? Can I trust him?

'One week,' he says.

I enclose the ring in my fist. For once, we are talking. He is actually listening. Promising to try. All he wants is a week. And, much as I want to, I can't deny him that. 'One week, Greg. That's it. One week.'

He hugs then kisses me. 'Thank you, Lucy. Thank you. You won't be sorry, I swear.'

Neither of us moves. He hasn't held me in a simple hug like that for what feels like a very long time. Eventually I ask him to call the children for lunch – they might come for him.

They look wary, not sure what to expect.

'Hi, guys,' Greg says.

Toby looks at me. I smile reassurance.

'Hi,' he says quietly, taking his place at the table.

'Hi, Dad,' says Rachel, eyeing her father carefully.

We sit down to eat. For a long while no one speaks. The children look like they're on full alert, as though expecting an outburst or sudden ingenious idea that spells disaster.

'Maybe when the rain's stopped, we could go for a swim,' he suggests in a voice that sounds very calm for him.

Toby looks at Rachel, unsure. She seems to mull it over. 'Can Lucy come too?' she asks without looking at me.

Though I know why she's asking, I'm still surprised.

'Of course,' Greg says.

After lunch, the children go upstairs to change into their swimming costumes. Greg helps me clear the table.

'They hardly said anything over lunch,' he says.

'They didn't want to upset you.'

He stops halfway between the table and the sink, glasses in hand. 'Why would they upset me?'

'Greg, everything upsets you lately. Especially the people who love you.'

He looks bemused.

He needs his next hit. Any minute now, he'll go.

But he doesn't. There is no next hit, no more high. Instead, over the next few days, he glides slowly back to earth, to us, his boundless energy fading like a dying wind, his restlessness with it. He seems content with our company again, no longer desperate to befriend the world. Gradually, he resumes the simple acts of living that I once took for granted – eating, sleeping, *listening*. At times I wonder if I imagined it all. But then there is a silver sports car out front, an unfinished mural on the wall, an office that looks like a hurricane hit it, a diamond earring, white hair and a red dress.

And there are worried children.

'Dad, what was wrong with you before?' asks Toby, one night, sitting on his father's lap having his toenails cut.

Greg doesn't take his eyes off Toby's feet. 'When?'

'Before. When I didn't know what you were saying.'

Now he looks at Toby, confusion and worry written on his face. 'You didn't know what I was saying?'

'No.' Toby's eyes search mine for confirmation.

'None of us did,' I say.

Greg seems stuck. 'I don't know,' he says finally. 'Must have been the heat. Yes, that was it. The heat.'

No way. Not just heat.

'But it's still hot, Dad,' insists Toby.

'Not *so* hot, though. It's cooled down a good bit, hasn't it? And you can understand me now, can't you?' He smiles and ruffles his son's hair.

'Yeah.'

'Well, then. That's what matters, isn't it? Everything back to normal.'

Is it, though? I'm still waiting for the next disappearing act. Despite how wonderful he's been over the last few days – staying at the villa, cooking the meals, swimming with the kids, listening – I can't allow myself to believe that this is over. After all that's happened, for Greg to stop, just like that, seems too good to be true. Still, I ring Grace to let her know. No point in her embarking on a wasted journey. She's relieved that Greg's feeling better, but, as she has the flights booked and could do with a change of scene, she is going to stick to her plan. I was hoping she might.

The following day I go to pick them up from the airport. When they come through Arrivals, I feel almost teary to see them. My own, personal cavalry. With one hand, Grace is pushing the trolley. With the other, she is carrying a heavy-looking Jason. Shane is sitting on the cases like he's king of the castle. I wave like mad. Grace has to stop the trolley, as Shane suddenly decides to disembark. I squat down, and he runs to me. I squeeze him tight and stand with him in my arms. I plant a raspberry on his cheek. When Grace reaches us, I pop Shane down and take Jason from her. It is good to feel his podgy little arms around my neck, though it reminds me of the enormous gap between Greg's children and me.

18

When I arrive back at the villa after settling Grace and the boys into the apartment, I walk in on a phone call.

'You have to stop ringing here, Hilary,' Greg says, the back of his head visible above the top of the chair.

I can't move.

'No,' he says. 'That's impossible. No. This is for the best . . . There's nothing here for you . . . I'm sorry. I love Lucy . . . You need to start a new life, for your own sake . . . I'm sorry about what happened. Really I am . . . but there's no future for you here.'

Why did he have to say he loved me? What was she asking of him? And what did he mean, 'what happened'?

Then I get a call myself.

'Lucy, hi. It's Hilary.'

'Hello, Hilary.' My voice is cold, flat.

'I was just wondering. You know when I left and you offered me my job back?'

I say nothing.

'Well, I'd like to take it.'

Why is she only calling me now – because all else has failed? 'I'd have to talk to Greg about that, Hilary.'

'Why? Why do you need to talk to Greg?'

'Because Rachel and Toby are *his* children.'

'Oh, forget it –'

'No, I'll ask him.'

'I said forget it.' She hangs up.

Later I bring it up with Greg. We're sitting out on the

terrace, children in bed, cigar smoke floating on the balmy air. Down in the bay, the sea is flat and glassy. Lights along the coast look warm and cheerful, and signify life.

'Hilary rang me today,' I say, interrupting the peace.

He looks at me in shock, then his eyes dart away. He starts to roll his cigar between his fingers.

'What did she want?' he asks, his casual tone sounding fake.

'Her job back.'

'What did you say?'

'That I'd have to check with you.'

'Good.' There's relief in his voice.

'What's going on? Why's she so anxious for her job back?'

He reaches for his bottle of Kronenbourg. 'I don't know. I guess she's so attached to the family.'

'The family or you?'

'The family,' he says firmly, but instead of meeting my eyes he rubs condensation from his bottle. 'She's been looking after Rachel and Toby for five years. You know her history. You know she can never have kids of her own.'

'Then why did you sack her? And why won't you take her back?'

'She needs a life outside of us. For her own sake.'

'I know that. But why are you suddenly so adamant about it? There was no need to fire her. Couldn't she have just lived out?'

'She needs a clean break.'

'Did something happen between you again?'

'*No.*' Abruptly, he stubs out the cigar.

'She's in love with you, isn't she?'

'Don't be ridiculous.' He stands suddenly, his back to me.

'Am I? Am I being ridiculous? Or are you hiding something?'

He walks away, head down, hand on the back of his neck. Then he stops, turns. And finally meets my eyes. 'OK. All right,' he says. 'Maybe she does have . . . feelings . . . for me. What can I do about it? Nothing except keep her away.'

'Is that what all this is about?'

He doesn't blink when he says, 'Yes.'

'So, something did happen the other night, the night you fired her?'

He nods slowly.

'What?'

He sits back down, takes a moment. 'She came on to me . . .'

I sit forward, gripping the sides of the chair. 'Jesus, Greg.'

'Nothing happened, Lucy, I promise you that.'

'Then why didn't you tell me?'

'I just wanted to get rid of the problem. Deal with it. Fast. I thought that if she wasn't around, that would be the end of it.'

'But it's not, is it?'

'She'll get tired of ringing.'

We're quiet. I look out at the pine trees, silhouetted black against a colourless sky. That is when I tell him. 'She told me you were seeing other women when you started disappearing.'

His head swivels in my direction. '*What?*'

'She said it happens every time you get bored with the person you're with. You take off and before you know it there's another woman on the scene.'

He looks stunned, unbelieving. 'Why would she say that? And what would she know anyway? She wasn't even *around* when I was married to Catherine. And there's been no one since –'

'Except Hilary.'

He looks hurt. 'I told you about that. I explained.'

'I know,' I concede.

'I can't believe she said that. What was she trying to do? You didn't *believe* her, did you?'

'No, I didn't. But then you kept disappearing, no explanation. And I kept remembering that time at the restaurant when you were flirting with those women. And I didn't know what to believe –'

'What women?'

'Those *ravishing* English women.'

'Jesus, Lucy. I don't even remember their names. I was out for the night, in good form. I was *not* flirting.'

I'm quiet.

'Lucy, you know I'd never cheat. Not on you. Or on Catherine. Why didn't you talk to me about this?' he asks.

'You haven't exactly been the easiest person *to* talk to.'

He looks away. Quietly he asks himself, 'What the *fuck* was I up to?' He leans forward, placing his elbows on his legs, and his hands in prayer position in front of his mouth. He stays like that for a long time. Then speaks. 'I'm sorry. For everything. For being so hyper, always on the go, for taking off, and' – he drops his head – 'not being here for you.' He stops, looks up straight into my eyes. 'But I have *never* been unfaithful to you. Not once.' And now his eyes look sad at the thought that I might have doubted that.

The pressure of the last few weeks suddenly hits. My throat burns, my eyes fill. 'She told Toby that we were going to split up.'

'*Hilary?*'

I nod and the first tear falls. 'And she said you both laughed together about my wanting her to talk to Rachel.'

'*What?*'

I glare at him, all my anger finally escaping like a flare. 'I asked you not to tell her, Greg. Why did you?'

He runs his fingers up and down his forehead. 'All I did was ask her to have a word with Rachel. I thought I was doing you a favour. Of course I didn't laugh at you. Why would I do that?'

I shrug. Then a sob grips me.

He seems to know not to come to me. 'Jesus. This is a nightmare. I can't believe Hilary said all those things.'

'I'm not making this up,' I snap.

'I know. I know you're not. It's just hard to take in, that she was capable of this kind of manipulation. I'm just, I don't know, I'm just stunned.'

'Weren't you *stunned* when she came on to you?'

He looks hurt by the knife in my voice. 'Yes. Of course I was. But that was impulse. What you're talking about is *calculated* manipulation.' He stops. Then, quietly and slowly, he says, 'I trusted Hilary. I trusted my family with her.' Then he looks guilty. 'And I exposed you to her. I don't know what to say, Luce. Except that I'm *so* sorry.'

When Greg arrives down the following morning, he no longer has white hair. All that's left is dark shadow. He makes two calls, the first to his caretaker, whom he asks to paint over the mural, the second to the garage where he bought the Porsche. The salesman who sold it to him thanks him again for the generous tip. He will indeed have a look at the car with a view to taking it back. On our way there, a thought strikes. *Here we are in a sports car that does nought to a hundred in six seconds and Greg is driving more slowly and carefully than I've ever seen him.* The salesman buys back the Porsche for a considerably lower price, rain having damaged the interior. The old reliable Range Rover is returned. As it was still waiting to be serviced, the contents of the boot remain untouched. Never has a full boot seemed such a sane and normal thing. On our return journey, Greg calls at the jewellery shop where he bought the diamond earring. Yes, they can have it made into a pendant for the 'madame'. Later that afternoon Greg arranges to get air-conditioning installed. And it's true, I realize, what they say about actions and words.

'*So?*' was Rachel's reaction when I told her my sister and her kids were coming over. Toby wanted to know if they were bringing toys. Greg wondered why they weren't staying at the villa. I drive to the apartment to collect them for dinner. Grace comes to the door laden with the usual paraphernalia that goes with small children. I help her get everything, including the boys, into the car and apologize in advance for the meal: a basic pasta dish. She tells me it's a treat not to have to cook. Shane and Jason's noisy exuberance makes me realize just how quiet Rachel and Toby have become. Shane marches up to them with presents – water guns almost larger than he is. They look surprised.

'Cool,' says Toby, checking his out.

'Thanks,' says Rachel, squatting down to him and smiling. 'How does it work?'

As Shane demonstrates, Rachel gives her dad isn't-he-cute looks. Grace asks her to help screw the portable baby seat on to the table. She seems to revel in the challenge and offers to put Jason in. Carefully she secures the straps. We sit down to eat. Shane's lively, innocent chatter is a relief. Everything has been so intense here. So brittle. Grace picks up pieces of penne that Jason has scattered over his tray and places them back on his plastic plate.

'Food's for eating, Sonny Jim.'

Shane finishes first. Grace reaches into a giant patchwork bag and pulls out crayons and paper. Everyone concentrates on what he is producing. It's so good to have someone other than Greg to focus on. I pick up a crayon that has fallen to the ground and put it back beside my busy nephew.

'Like my picture, Rachel?' he asks with the confidence of someone who knows she's going to say yes.

'Yeah, it's brill,' she says. 'What is it?'

'Poo,' he says proudly.

She laughs.

'A word of advice, Rachel,' says Grace, smiling. 'Never ask Shane what he's drawn.'

'I was thinking that,' she says, still laughing.

After dinner, out by the pool, Rachel, Toby and Shane have a water fight, the boys teaming up against the only girl. Shane, though only three, is pretty handy with a weapon.

'I will experminate you,' he shouts, running after a laughing Rachel.

After the war, they cool down in the pool, Grace and I joining them with the baby, who is decked out in a sun-proof costume that covers most of his body. Under his little sun hat is a smiley face. Jason loves the water. Rachel asks to play with him for a while. And so, while the boys mess around together, she finds a shaded part of the pool and starts a game, pushing the baby away in his bright yellow float, then pulling him back towards her, talking in a high-pitched voice and making expressive faces. He is gurgling and chuckling.

It's official. Grace and the boys are a hit.

That night, when Greg comes to my room, he is as gentle and caring as he used to be before a whirlwind took over his body. After, when he holds me close and tells me he loves me, I do believe him. And when he tells me there has never been anyone else, I believe him too. In the morning, the one week I promised to give him is up. And I'm not going anywhere.

When the phone rings around eleven next morning, I half expect the line to die.

It doesn't.

'Hello,' says an older male voice I recognize but can't pinpoint immediately. 'I wonder if I could speak to Greg, please?'

'Eh, I'm afraid Greg's not available right now. Can I help?'

'Is this Lucy?'

'Yes.' It's Ben, I realize.

'This is Ben Franklin. We met –'

'Oh, yes, of course, Ben. How are you?'

'Well, thank you. I was hoping to have a word with Greg.'

'Actually, he's in bed. I'll just run up and see if he's awake.'

I do. He isn't. I run back down.

'He's out cold. Can I have him give you a call when he gets up?'

'When do you think that will be?'

'I'm not sure.'

'Actually, Lucy, perhaps you could pass on a message. If you could just tell him that Ruth and I are popping over to Antibes for a few days and we were hoping to meet up with him. Perhaps we could take you both out to dinner tomorrow night?'

'Oh,' I say, surprised, knowing how things are between them. 'That sounds lovely. I'm sure it would be fine. When Greg gets up, I'll ask him to give you a call.'

'How is everything?'

'Fine, thank you.'

'How are the children?'

'They're well. Would you like to speak to them? They're just upstairs . . .'

'No, no, I won't disturb them. I'll see them tomorrow or the day after. Well, I'd better go.'

'Thanks for the call. And the invite.'

★

'Odd,' Greg says, when I tell him. 'Ben hates the South of France. You should've heard him when we bought the villa. In all the years we've had it, they've never been out.' His eyes narrow. 'I wonder what's on his agenda.'

'Does he have to have an agenda?'

'Ben Franklin *always* has an agenda. Just wish I knew what it was.'

19

On the Cap d'Antibes, we drive through the pillared entrance of the exclusive Hôtel du Cap Eden Roc. Never has a name seemed more appropriate. It *is* like arriving in Eden. Tall pines tower over us as we wind our way down to a sparkling blue sea. It's the perfect place for anyone – rich – wanting to avoid the fast pace of the Riviera. Must suit Ben and Ruth, then. The car is valet parked, but we're early, so Greg suggests a stroll up to the bar at the main hotel, explaining that we've arrived at the restaurant, a separate building, on the water's edge. Walking through paradise, we pass people who seem close to perfection, immaculately dressed and very beautiful. Almost unreal. At the terrace bar we find more of the same. Men in blazers and crisp open-necked shirts, hair slicked back. Stick-thin, tanned women with long straight hair wearing floaty, designer dresses and high strappy sandals. There is a definite look. Greg has it. Grace would if she were here. In my fitted black shirt and long white skirt, I am the country mouse.

'Wish you'd told me it was so dressy,' I whisper, when we've sat down.

'You look lovely,' he says.

'I look *ordinary*.'

'Thank God for that. Have you ever seen so much collagen per square inch? You look natural, Lucy. Like you've a bit of spunk.'

An American at the next table, who has just come off his boat, is telling his skinny fan club about a party he's attending, hosted by a Hollywood star's ex-wife. Greg rolls his eyes.

At eight thirty we head down to the restaurant, also on a terrace. I can see why. The view is incredible. The sea is no longer the Mediterranean but a private lake belonging to the hotel, or so it seems. The sky is a wash of pale blue and pink. Lamps have been lit around the perimeter of the restaurant, and candles glow on every table. A pale yellow moon and sidekick star hover overhead, the sky the ultimate ceiling. It is magical.

Breaking the spell, the maître d' informs us that our hosts are at the table. We follow him. They stand when they see us. Ben is in a blue and white striped shirt with white collar. So corporate big boy. Ruth, in a three-quarter-sleeved beige linen dress, looks as out of place as I do. Neither has broken into an automatic smile, which is not unexpected. Ben's greeting is a formal handshake. Ruth follows his lead. We have our linen napkins opened for us by waiters and menus slipped into our hands. We let Ben steer the conversation. Though the wine flows and the atmosphere in the restaurant hums, our table is formal and stilted. There are polite questions about the children, France, the weather. It's tough going. And, for some reason, I feel we're being judged.

As it happens, I'm right.

Just as we're finishing coffee, Ben says, 'We've had a visit from Hilary.'

My heart thuds.

'She seemed worried. Is everything all right, Greg?'

'Everything's fine, couldn't be better, Ben,' he says, flashing a wide smile. 'I'm not sure what Hilary's worried about.'

'She's concerned about the welfare of *our grandchildren*.'

Jesus.

'The children are fine,' Greg says, without faltering. 'You can see for yourself tomorrow.'

170

'Yes, yes. And how are *you* feeling?'

'Never better.'

'And the driving? No problems there?'

'None.'

'Good. Good. Getting plenty of rest?'

'What is this, Ben?'

'Nothing. Nothing. Just making sure you're all right. Not getting too much sun, that sort of thing.' He's fiddling with his tie.

'Well, thank you for your concern,' Greg says through gritted teeth. 'But, as you can see, I'm a big boy. Quite able to look after myself. And *my children*.' He smiles and slams down his coffee cup. 'You know what? Let me get this, Ben.'

'No, no. I wouldn't dream –'

'I insist.' He calls the waiter, pulling out his wallet.

He pays without checking the bill.

Nothing more is said, apart from curt goodbyes.

Greg doesn't speak until we're pulling away.

'That was humiliating,' he says.

I look at him. 'You were right about something being up,' I say, strapping in.

Greg yanks at his belt and it jams. He tries again, slowly. I know he wouldn't bother with it if I weren't beside him.

'Who does Hilary think she is, upsetting them like that?' I ask. 'I mean, she must have really freaked them out, to have them hopping on a plane to France.'

He sighs. 'Of all the people to freak out.' At the top of the drive, he turns left.

'You really don't like each other, do you?'

'Lucy, he can't even look at me.' We pass tiny beaches, families still swimming and picnicking in the moonlight.

171

'It isn't just that he's a snob, though, is it?' I say, remembering how Ben had directed all his comments to me, practically a stranger, until the final confrontation with Greg.

'He blames me for Catherine's death.'

'*What?*'

'They both do.'

'They said it was your fault?' I'm appalled.

'No. They'd never do that.' He pulls in behind a parked car to let another pass on the narrow road. 'I just knew. Sensed it. They couldn't look me in the eye. Not then. And not since.'

'But how can they blame you? Catherine died in childbirth.'

He pulls out again. 'Who got her pregnant?'

'Oh, come on.'

The traffic slows as we reach throbbing Juan-les-Pins. Before long, we have to stop at lights. He looks across at me. 'They knew we'd been warned against having another. When Catherine got pregnant, she told them it had been her idea, that I knew nothing. They still looked at me as if I were a complete idiot for allowing it to happen. I was as worried as they were. When she . . . died . . . they couldn't face me. And, to be honest, I couldn't face them. Hilary used to bring the children over to see them. It was easier for everyone.'

'So that's how she knows them well enough to do this.'

'Oh, they *love* Hilary. She looked after their grandchildren while the oaf tried to pick up the pieces.'

The yellow licence plate in front moves forward and we follow.

'Weird the way he said "our grandchildren", though,' I say, 'as if they're actually *his* kids.'

'They're his last link to Catherine. They couldn't be more precious to him. And, though, at times, he drives me spare, I suppose I can understand where he's coming from.'

★

Next day we drop two open-mouthed children off at the Hôtel du Cap for an afternoon at the poolside with their grandparents. They are in awe of the spill-over pool, the edge of which blends with the horizon. Regardless of the luxury, there's no way Greg will hang around. And I get the impression we're not welcome. We return to the villa, where Greg decides to clear out his office. How, he wonders, did he let it get into such a state? He starts at the edges and works his way in. Black bag after black bag appears outside the door, reassuring me that things are on the mend. After two hours I go in to drag him out. The computer is on, but he's sitting at his desk, head in his hands.

'You OK?'

'No.'

'What is it?'

He looks up. 'It's rubbish. Everything I've been writing is rubbish. It just doesn't make sense.' He picks up page after page and shoves them at me. 'Look. Look at this. Does any of this make sense to you? Because it sure as hell doesn't make sense to me. And I wrote it. *Apparently.*'

I pretend to read it for the first time.

'See? *See?*'

'Well, it's . . . it's just very, very *creative.*'

'It doesn't make sense. Did I write that? Did I really write that *shit*? I must be losing my mind.'

How can he not know what he's written? 'Come on, take a break.'

'Did you know I was writing this?'

'No,' I lie. 'Come on. Come away from it. Start again later.'

'What if I produce the same crap?'

'You won't. Just do the proofs for *A River Too Wide.* They're straightforward enough. It'll get you into the swing of things.'

'I don't know.'

'Go out to the pool, have a swim, clear your head. I'll tidy your desk. I won't throw anything out. I'll just file it –'

'Dump it. Dump the whole bloody lot of it.'

'OK. I'll dump it. Now go.'

It kills me to shred what he's written, but I do it, then clear away books, magazines, CDs, DVDs, returning them to their cases. Any real rubbish, I bin. The only thing that remains, apart from his computer, are the proofs for *A River Too Wide*.

Later that afternoon we collect the children. I drive.

'How did that go?' asks Greg, twisting round in the front passenger seat.

'All *right*,' says Rachel.

'Just all right?'

'Boring,' says Toby.

'Yeah. They wouldn't let us do anything. They wouldn't let me go on the rope ladder or the swing, even though I'm *ten*.'

'They wouldn't let us dive.'

'They kept putting sunscreen all over us,' says Rachel. 'Even though we had some on. And even though I can do it myself.'

'Oh,' says Greg.

'They wouldn't let us have Coke,' says Toby, 'even though I said you let us.'

'Or chips. And they kept asking were we happy.'

'I hope you pretended to be,' says Greg.

'No. Not with them. With you.'

I stall the car. Behind, a horn blows.

'With me?'

'Yeah. They kept asking questions about you.'

'What kind of questions?'

'Were you cross with us? Were you talking funny? Were you driving funny?'

'And what did you say?' he asks quickly.

'I lied,' says Rachel. 'I said you were fine.'

Greg and I exchange glances. He looks so guilty. He turns back to her. 'Well, thanks for sticking up for me, Rache,' he says, his voice gentle. 'And I'm sorry, guys, if I've been a bit, you know, snappy. It won't happen again. I promise you that.'

''S OK, Dad,' says Toby. 'At least you let us have Coke and chips.'

Just the reassurance he needs.

On the day of the brainstorm, I leave for the airport by taxi, giving my Clio to Grace for the day and turning down Greg's offer of a lift – he seems to really need his lie-ins lately, and I feel guilty enough about giving in to his insistence that he pay for all the flights. Anyway, it's nice to get time alone even if it is only in a taxi, driving to the airport.

Last time I was back, I never really got a chance to sit in my office and take a few moments. This time I do. I swivel round in my chair. Flick on my computer. Slide open my drawers and peek inside. It seems ages since I used my Tweedy Bird stapler. I pick up a chain of coloured paper clips I probably made during some brainstorm or other. When the screensaver comes on, it's a picture of Greg and me grinning at the camera. It seems so long ago since I installed it, but it's only weeks. We look so happy, vibrant, *together*. I run my finger over his face and sigh. We have been through so much in so little time. I make a wish that it's all over, then hold my turquoise mouse and click. I spend half an hour preparing for the brainstorm.

Fint's looking great, tanned and relaxed. Sebastian too is the picture of health.

'So what did you think of my proposal?' I ask Fint, when we gather in the meeting room.

'Good.'

'Only good?' In the Dictionary of Fint, good means, well, bad.

'No, no. It was good . . . Sebastian had some ideas too. Do you want to present them, Sebastian?'

A presentation? I thought this was a brainstorm.

Sebastian looks awkward, for Sebastian. He takes us through a PowerPoint presentation, his confidence building as he goes. I'm stunned by the freshness of his ideas, so innovative they show mine up as jaded, tired. Which, I realize, they are. I look across at him as if really seeing him for the first time. Whatever happened to my enthusiasm? How have I lost it? I was fine before I left. Fine while I was a free spirit. I've never been the kind of person to applaud after presentations. But I do after Sebastian's.

'Sebastian, that was amazing. You're a genius.'

He beams. 'Thanks, Lucy.'

'He is, isn't he?' says Fint. 'And to think that if you hadn't gone to France, we'd never have discovered this Natural Born Designer.'

I feel a stab of something, regret maybe? A touch of envy? It isn't that I resent his having talent, far from it; I just wish I knew where mine had gone . . . I realize I don't like being away from the office. Too much is happening without me. I'm losing my handle on things. I should be right at the centre of this project, not out at the perimeter. I need to come home more often. No, I need to be home, full stop.

As the plane touches down, I move my watch forward an hour. The flight has been uneventful but late by half an hour. With no baggage, I'm one of the first to reach Arrivals. I'm disappointed: Greg's not here to lift me up and swing me round. I check my watch. He won't show at this late stage. I feel flat. He could have made an effort. Then I begin to panic. Could something have happened? Could he have taken a step back, reverted to old behaviour? I'm about to pull out my mobile when I catch sight of a blonde beauty rushing in the door, carrying a baby. Grace, as usual, is oblivious to the heads she is turning.

'Sorry I'm late,' she says, out of breath. 'I tried ringing to let you know I was coming but your phone must still be off after the flight.'

'Oh, yeah. Sorry. Thanks for coming. It's good to see you.' We hug. 'Hey there, handsome.' I kiss Jason. 'I was just going to get a taxi.'

'You should have known one of us would be here.' We walk out into the sun, me fumbling in my briefcase for my mobile and switching it on.

'Is Greg OK?'

'Yeah. Fine. Though he seems a bit drained today. Didn't feel up to coming. He should probably take a tonic. He looks as if he might be coming down with something.'

'He's probably run down. If we stop at a pharmacy on the way back, would you be able to pick out something?'

'Assuming my French holds up.'

We get to the car and strap Jason in the back. Grace hops into the driver's seat. I throw my briefcase in the boot, then sit in beside her. 'How'd your meeting go?' she asks.

'All right.' I sigh. 'Some bright young spark showed me up.'

'*Lucy.* You're not exactly old and dull,' she says, before reversing out of the space.

'Oh, yeah?' That's exactly how I do feel. Doesn't matter that Sebastian's older.

'Is everything OK?'

'Yeah. I just should be back there more often, though.'

177

She's quiet for a second or two. 'Maybe you should go over more regularly. Once or twice a week, say.'

'Humm. Maybe . . . Where's Shane?'

'At the villa. Rachel's making up games for him and Toby. They're in their element. She's very good with them, isn't she?'

'Yeah,' I say, still surprised at this upbeat side to her.

'God, the way Shane trails around after her. It's so cute. It reminds me of how you used to follow me around when we were kids, remember?' She looks over.

'All I remember is how you wouldn't let me play with your friends,' I tease.

'You know I still feel guilty about that,' she says. 'Let me take this moment to officially apologize.'

'It's OK, Grace,' I laugh. 'I think I've recovered without major psychological scars.'

'You were great, though. Remember when you were five, that was it, no more being my personal slave. You'd had enough.'

I smile, remembering. We stop at lights. I glance at the car next to us. A guy in a bandana is nodding his head, presumably to music.

'You never really liked me, though, did you?' I almost don't hear.

'*What?*' I turn to stare. 'Don't talk rubbish. Of course I liked you.'

'You called me Little Miss Perfect.'

'Not to your face.'

'Which is even worse.' She pulls away from the lights.

'We were kids, Grace. Just because I called you a dumb name doesn't mean I didn't like you.'

She looks at me. 'So why did you do it?'

'I don't know,' I say, irritable at being cornered. 'Because you *were* perfect. And everyone loved you. And you did everything right. And I didn't . . . OK, I admit it, maybe I was a bit jealous.' I can't believe we're discussing this, and that I'm admitting to something I've never admitted even to myself. I never meant to hurt her. It was just a name.

'Well, you got it wrong. I wasn't Little Miss Perfect. I was Little Miss Wanna Be Perfect. And that's how I've spent my life – trying. Trying to impress a mother who can't be impressed, followed by a husband who can't be impressed. Which is a bloody big waste of a life, I can tell you.' Her voice breaks.

Oh, God.

'I've wasted my life, Lucy. I married someone because my mother liked him. How stupid is that? What about me? What about what *I* liked? Why didn't I think of that? *She* doesn't have to live with him. *She* doesn't have to listen to him.'

'Do you want me to drive?'

She shakes her head.

'You sure?'

She nods.

I rummage in my bag for a hankie and hand it to her. 'I'll hold the wheel.'

She nods again. And blows. Then drops the hankie in her lap. 'I'm fine,' she says. 'Fine.' She sniffles. 'I just needed to blow off steam. Tell someone.'

I rub her arm. 'Well, I'm glad it was me. And I may only be your sister, but I think you're perfect. You've always been there for me, Grace. You've always listened, encouraged me, complimented every drawing, every sketch, urged me to go to art college. You were there for me after Brendan. And you're here for me now. I'm *embarrassed* it's taken so long to appreciate that. You couldn't be more perfect.'

And then she smiles. 'Thank you.'

'No, Grace. Thank *you*.'

She just needs a break, I tell myself. *She's been under a lot of pressure, handling the boys by herself, Kevin working so hard. It'll get better. He'll miss her while she's away. He'll be more attentive when she gets back. More loving. It'll be fine.*

Grace wants to clean up before facing everyone, so she drops me at the villa and goes on to the apartment with Jason. I find the children indoors, playing an old board game of Rachel's, *Frustration*. Rachel is sitting up on the back of the sofa. Toby is draped across it. And Shane is surreptitiously picking his nose.

'Hi there,' I call.

They all look up. The boys say, 'Hi.' Then Shane asks where his mum is.

'Just gone up to the apartment to let Jase have his nap.' Rehearsed excuse, and partly true.

''K.'

'Would anyone like a drink?' I ask.

I've two takers – the boys. I quickly sort them out.

'Where's your dad?' I ask Toby when I hand him his blackcurrant juice.

'Outside.'

'Thanks.'

Greg's on the terrace. Just sitting. Not reading and sitting, or doing a crossword and sitting, not jotting down notes and sitting. Just sitting. He seems miles away.

'Hi!' I kiss his cheek.

'Oh, hi.' His smile is low voltage.

'You OK?' I ask.

'Mm-hmm.'

'I got you a tonic on the way back from the airport. Grace was saying you're feeling a bit drained.'

'I'd have come to collect you. But I just didn't have the *energy*.'

'Not to worry.' I pull up a chair beside him. 'Miss me?'

'Mm-hmm.'

'That much?' I joke.

When he smiles, it seems forced.

'How did you all get on?' I ask.

'Fine,' says the man who never uses one word if fifty will do.

'So what did you get up to?'

He thinks for a moment, then abandons it. 'Nothing much,' he says.

'Are you pissed off with me or something?'

He looks surprised. 'No.'

'Well, what's wrong? You're very quiet.'

He shakes his head. 'I'm fine.'

I try a few openers, including how the 'brainstorm' went. He barely blinks. The only time he shows any interest is when I tell him that Grace is unhappy with Kevin. He is sympathetic to the point of appearing personally sad about it. I take out the tonic and suggest two spoonfuls as a kick-start. Later, when everyone's asleep, I slip into his bedroom. And bed. In all the weeks we've been together, this is the first time I have initiated sex. He does get into it, eventually, but his enthusiasm doesn't see him through. He cannot maintain an erection. This has never happened before. I don't know what to say or even if I should say anything. He doesn't want to talk about it, just turns from me, saying he's tired. I blame myself. I should have just accepted the fact that he was exhausted. And left it at that. I wait until he is asleep to leave.

The children have not commented on the fact that I'm still staying at the villa, perhaps because they've become used to my being around – as long as I stay in the guest room. And perhaps they too are nervous that their father might revert to old habits. In any case, there's no room at the apartment, for me to stay or to work. Not that I'm complaining. The villa's a very different place now – with air-conditioning, without Hilary, and with Greg back to normal. The office has changed too. Gone is the chaos and noise. I work alone in the mornings while Greg sleeps. Grace insists on minding the children, though it's not as difficult as it sounds, with Rachel a willing and able helper.

One morning I'm busy working on the shopping-mall job, which, to my humiliation, I'm now doing in conjunction with Sebastian, when Greg appears. He's getting later and later. It's practically lunchtime. I smile hello and watch him settle at his computer. His proofs are finished, and he's attempting the new novel, afresh. At first I don't notice that he's having problems. It's the silence that draws my attention to it. There is none of the usual frantic keyboard tapping I associate with Greg and his computer. There is no sound at all. I look over. He is sitting, staring at the screen, fingers ready, but there's no action. I pretend not to notice and try to carry on with my work. But then he slams a fist on the desk, saying, 'Just one clear thought, is that too much to ask?' And leaves before I can react.

After half an hour I go to look for him. I find him lying on his bed, staring at the ceiling. I don't go in. Just close the door. He needs peace, a quiet place to think about Cooper and plots and pace and all those things writers have to get right. I wonder what it must be like to be expected to come up with something fresh and creative and not be able to. What am I talking about? I do know. I'm going through it. And appreci-ate that you just have to keep pushing yourself until you come out the other side. Then again, a design isn't a whole novel. Maybe that's what's stopping him, the magnitude of what's ahead. Knowing there is nothing I can do to help, I return to my own problems.

Over the next few days Greg spends less and less time in his office and more and more time 'lying down'. When he's up, he mopes in a chair, doing nothing, nothing at all. Except smoking.

'Dad, are you coming for a swim?' Rachel tries.

He doesn't appear to hear.

'Dad?'

'Hmm?'

'Are you coming for a swim?'

'No. No, thanks. You go ahead.'

She shrugs. 'OK.' She walks away, looking back.

I sit beside him.

'You OK?'

'Yeah, fine.' I know he's not.

'I'm sure all writers go through this. I wouldn't worry about it, Greg.'

'I haven't been a good father, have I?'

I'm confused. 'You're a great father.'

'I've neglected the kids. Neglected you.'

'Come on. Forget about that. You've been fine since we talked. Everything's OK now.'

'No.'

The word seems to reverberate in the silence that follows, making me see the truth. This is more than writer's block. This is more than Greg being 'run down'. I remember the Internet site on amphetamines. I remember the list of symptoms associated with coming off the drug. It is like receiving confirmation and a blow to the chest at the same time. Now

I'm convinced. All of this has been about drugs. It takes a few moments before the implications dawn: one, he has stopped; and two, he lied.

'I think I'll lie down for a while,' he says.

I could do with bed myself. 'You're just up.'

He heaves himself out of the chair as if it takes all the energy in the world and makes his way to the stairs. And, as I watch him go, I find a reassuring thought. *It will be OK. In a few days it will be OK.*

But it is not OK. Over the days that follow, rather than improving, Greg stops communicating completely, not only with us but with the world at large. Phone calls, letters, e-mails, all are ignored. It's the same with TV, radio, newspapers, even books. The only thing he embraces is drink. From mid afternoon on, he's nursing something. If it's to lift his spirits, it doesn't work. And it sure doesn't do anything for mine. Down, down, down everything goes – his head, shoulders, the edges of his mouth, his mood, even his voice. Every movement looks like it requires huge effort. Everything he does is in first gear.

He is still in bed, one afternoon, when his father-in-law rings.

'How is everything?' he asks me.

'Fine, Ben, thank you.'

'And the children?'

'Very well, thank you. Would you like to speak to them?'

'Yes, yes, in a moment. I wonder could I have a quick word with Greg first?'

I'm not going to tell him Greg's in bed, not when he's so obviously rung to check up on him. 'Just a moment and I'll find him.'

I go up to the room. It's dark, stifling, shutters *and* windows closed. Air-conditioning off. He's lying on his side, a pillow over his head.

'Greg?'

He doesn't answer.

'Ben's on the phone.'

'Tell him to fuck off.'

I laugh, assuming he's joking, then open the window, turn on the air-conditioning.

'Go away,' he says.

'I'm *sorry*?'

'Please. Leave me alone. Please.'

'What is *wrong* with you?'

'I just need peace. Is that too much to ask?'

'OK, *OK*, I'll tell him you'll call him back.' *Jesus*.

'And turn the air-conditioning off. The noise drives me mad.'

Resisting the urge to answer back, I do as he asks. Then head for the door.

'Lucy?'

'What?'

'Can you keep them a bit quieter?'

Honest to God, the children aren't making a sound. I say nothing, just go back to the phone. Ben's hung up. I look up his number on Greg's mobile and call him back.

'Ben. I'm sorry for keeping you waiting there. I was working and didn't realize that Greg's actually taken the children to the beach. I'm sorry. I'll get him to call you when he comes in.'

'Is everything all right?'

'Everything's fine. I'll get Greg to call you, all right?'

'All right.' He doesn't sound too happy.

'Thanks for calling.'

When Greg does appear, an hour later, he looks like a man

who could do with spending the day in bed. I remind him of the phone call. This time he talks to Ben. And I hope he's a bit more charming than he was with me. At dinner he won't eat. Instead, he drinks. Wine. Then whiskey. Later, on the terrace, while he stares off into the distance or absently watches two geckos scale the wall of the villa in search of light-seeking moths, I try to read. I go inside to get a drink. When I come back out, he's picked up the autobiography I've been reading and is examining the cover. He opens it and runs his finger under the first line. He goes back over it. Can't seem to get beyond that. Over and over it he goes, until he slams it shut. I watch as he flings it through the air. Landing in the pool with a splash, it disappears.

I stand up, furious. 'I was reading that.'

'*That?* What the fuck was it about? The guy's a writer, you'd think he'd know what plain English is.'

'Maybe I'd have liked to have decided that for myself. For God's sake, Greg. You've just ruined my book.'

He runs his hand across the lower half of his face, his eyes registering what he has done. 'I'm sorry, Lucy. I didn't mean to destroy it. I just got so *frustrated*. I couldn't get beyond that first line. Here, let me do that.' He reaches for the net I'm holding and goes to fish the book out of the pool.

'You might as well bin it,' I say, when he gets it.

He apologizes again.

'What's wrong with you? Why are you like this?'

He walks back to the table, reaching for the whiskey bottle.

'Drinking isn't going to help.'

'I'll drink if I bloody well want,' he barks.

'Right. Fine. You do that. Just don't expect me to hang around and watch. I'm going. I can't take this any more.'

'Where?' he sounds panicky. 'Where are you going?'

'I don't know . . .' Then, suddenly, I do. 'To the apartment.'

'Don't.'

He's got to be kidding. 'I'm sorry, but I've had enough for one night. If you insist on being miserable, fine, be miserable, but don't take it out on me.' I leave, wondering how I ever thought that depression would be more acceptable than a high.

20

'You OK?' Grace asks when she opens the door.

I shake my head and the tears come.

'Greg?'

I nod.

She puts an arm around me and walks me into the living room, where she sits me down on the sofa.

'It's all gone wrong,' I say, covering my eyes with the heels of my hands. 'He's miserable. He's drinking. He snaps at me for the least little thing.'

'Shhh, it's OK,' she says, rubbing my back.

'He's so down. He's no energy, can't work, won't eat. He's grinding to a halt, Grace. I keep telling myself it's because he's come off drugs, but he's getting worse, not better.'

'Did he *tell* you he was on drugs?' She sounds surprised.

'No. But what else could it be? He has all the signs –'

'Have you ever *seen* any evidence of drugs?'

'No. But it has to be . . . He was talking gibberish. His writing was bizarre.'

'Can I ask you a question?'

I don't like the sound of that. 'Yes.'

'When he was high, was he overspending, making any impulse buys?'

Now that throws me. How could she possibly know about that? 'Why?' I ask. 'It's not a medical symptom. Is it?'

She takes a breath. 'It can be. Sometimes.'

'Of what?'

'What kind of things did he buy?'

'A Porsche.'

She raises her eyebrows.

'A diamond earring – for himself.'

She nods. 'He also dyed his hair white, didn't he?' I watch jigsaw pieces click together in her eyes. She scratches her hand, the way she always does when nervous. 'Lucy, there is *one* other thing that maybe we should consider –'

'What? What is it?'

'I've seen patients with symptoms similar to Greg's.'

'*And?*'

'Well, something I *might* have considered with them was bipolar disorder. Have you thought of that?'

'What is it? I mean, I think I've heard of it but I don't know.'

'Manic depression,' she says, as if that'll clear it right up.

'He *is* depressed. But he's no reason to be. I mean, a bit of writer's block –'

She clears her throat. 'Lucy. *Manic* depression is a little different from being depressed.' She is starting to scare me. 'It's caused by a chemical imbalance in the brain and leads to mood swings, often from very high to very low.'

'Oh, God, Grace, I *do* know what you're talking about now. I *have* heard of it. On the radio or in an article or something. Someone famous had it.' Head down, I tap my forehead, actually wasting time trying to think who.

'It's not important, Luce.'

'Spike Milligan! Spike Milligan had it. I remember now. Oh, God. It never goes away,' I say, remembering. 'You have it for life, don't you? And it's up and down and up and down. And you can get hallucinations. And . . . Oh, my God . . .' I've pulled my hair to one side and am twisting it round and round until it's tight like a rope.

'Lucy. It can be treated – successfully, with medication. And I'm just saying it's *one* option. There are others –'

'But if he has it, this manic depression, why didn't he tell me?'

'*If* he has it, he probably doesn't know. It can come on at any stage.'

'What if he does know? What if he's just not telling me?'

'No, Lucy. I've thought about this. If Greg had been diagnosed with bipolar disorder, Rob would have been alert to the symptoms. Families have to be. If he'd noticed a change in behaviour, as he did at the barbecue, he'd have been very concerned, seeing it as a warning of an approaching high. No. *If* Greg has bipolar disorder, this is his first episode.'

'Oh, God, Grace, a mental illness . . .'

'I'm not *saying* that this is the problem. There are so many other reasons Greg could be depressed – coming off speed, if indeed he was on it, ME, glandular fever, brucellosis . . . Bipolar disorder is just one possibility. Greg does need to see a doctor, though, ideally back in Dublin. You should try to get him home. The sooner the better. I'll come back with you, if you like, speak to a friend of mine, Karl, a really great GP. He's so copped on. He'd examine Greg from top to bottom . . .'

One of the boys starts to cry. Sounds like Jason.

She rolls her eyes. 'Timed beautifully, as usual,' she says. 'Back in a minute.'

I watch her disappear down the hall and try not to envy her the normality of her life. Try not to envy her relationship, a relationship that may be under pressure but at least is normal. *This is the kind of thing that happens to other people, not to me. Mental illness. I'm not strong enough for it. I don't want to be. I want to run. Far, far away. But wait; it may not be bipolar disorder. It may be brucellosis . . . brucellosis, I thought cows got brucellosis . . . or ME . . . or . . . If it is bipolar disorder, then none of this is his fault. He hasn't lied. He can't help it. He doesn't even know what's going on. Oh, God, the thought of that, of his not being able to control his moods and not understanding why . . . If that is what's happening, how can I walk out on him? I wouldn't expect him to do it to me.*

The following day Grace takes Rachel and Toby off, so I can talk to Greg. He is still in bed.

'Let's go out,' I suggest, hoping that we might be able to talk better away from the villa, a place that seems to have absorbed Greg's negative energy.

'I don't want to go out.' This is the man I couldn't keep in.

'Come on. Your proofs are done. No more deadlines. Let's forget our responsibilities and just go to the beach like normal people.'

'What do you mean, normal people? Are you saying I'm not normal?'

'No. I just said we should go to the beach, not work so hard.'

'You said "like normal people", implying I'm not.'

'That's not what I meant. I wasn't implying anything. We work too much and I just think we need to take a break.'

'There's nothing wrong with me.'

'I know. I know that. Of course there isn't. I just think that maybe you could have a shower, get dressed and we could go out, the two of us, get a bite to eat. We haven't been out in ages.'

'I don't want to.'

'It'd do you good.'

'I. Don't. Want. To. Go. Out.'

'OK, OK. Jesus.' I get up to go. No point talking to him when he's like this. 'It doesn't matter that I might like to go out, I suppose?' I grumble my way to silence.

'You don't love me,' he says.

That stops me. I turn.

'And I don't blame you. I've been a bastard.'

I come back to him, sit back down, take his hand. 'Greg, of course I love you.'

'I'm old, incompetent. I can't even get it up, for fuck's sake.'

What I say now seems very important. I take a deep breath. 'Greg. Every man goes through that at some stage. You can't be expected to perform one hundred per cent of the time.'

'Perform. That's it. I can't perform. On any front.'

I'm not letting the conversation down that particular route. 'I love you.' I lie down beside him, facing him. I put my arm round him.

'You're lying.'

I sit up. My voice is firm when I say, 'I am not lying. If I didn't love you, I wouldn't be here.'

'You're going.'

'Greg, I am going to Dublin tomorrow for the shopping-mall pitch. That's all. I'll be over and back in the same day. If I could get out of it, I would. But I can't. This is a big deal for Get Smart. I can't let Fint down. Grace will be here.'

'You're going to leave, like Catherine left . . .'

What's he talking about? 'Catherine died.'

'Because of me.'

'That's your father-in-law's logic. Not yours.'

'I made her pregnant.'

'Stop this.'

'I killed her.' He squeezes his eyes shut. I've never seen him cry.

'Greg, please. Don't do this. It wasn't your fault. You know it wasn't.'

'If I'd only kept my stupid dick to myself.'

'OK. Now *stop*. That's enough. You're being ridiculous. And you know it. Let's go home. Let's just go back to Ireland.'

He's silent.

'You're depressed.' I'm amazed I haven't actually said it before.

'I'm fine.'

'No, you're not fine. You're definitely not fine. I'm worried about you.'

'I'm not going anywhere.'

'I think you need to see a doctor.'

'What kind of doctor? A shrink, is *that* what you mean?'

'No. I don't mean anything. All I know is that you're depressed. And we need to do something about it. We need to see a doctor. Any doctor but preferably an Irish one, OK? Someone who can just tell us what's wrong.'

'I can handle it.'

'Please, let's go home.'

'I *said* I could handle it.'

'Well, *I* can't, Greg. I'm about to crack up here. We have to go home. We have to sort this out.'

He closes his eyes, blocking me out.

'Is it drugs? Were you taking drugs? Are you having withdrawal symptoms? Is that it?'

He looks at me slowly. 'Lucy, I have never, in my life, taken drugs.' His voice sounds tired, but I think honest. And suddenly I believe him.

'Have you ever been depressed like this before, Greg?'

'When Catherine died . . .'

'No, I mean when there was no reason to be?'

He suddenly seems to gather where this is leading. 'I'm not depressed. I'm just exhausted. Burnt out. I'll be fine. Just let me sleep.' He turns his back on me.

I leave the room feeling like a failure. When Grace arrives back with the children, she looks at me expectantly. I shake my head.

'I feel I shouldn't go tomorrow,' I say in a low voice.

193

'You must . . . I'll be here. Don't worry . . . And Lucy?'

'Yeah.'

'I didn't expect him to say yes immediately. It's not easy to admit you're in this kind of trouble.'

Colour is leaking into an indigo sky when the alarm goes off. Careful not to disturb anyone, I get ready but can't pass Greg's room without checking on him. I know, instinctively, that he's awake.

'Are you OK?' I whisper.

No answer. He's breathing through his mouth, head turned into the pillow. Silently crying.

I sit on the bed beside him, take his hand in mine. 'I'll be back later. Grace'll be here.'

He nods.

'I love you, Greg. You know that, don't you?'

He turns to me. 'Why, Lucy? Please, tell me why.'

The need in this once confident voice almost breaks my heart. I think back to when we met. 'I was asleep until I met you. You made me see the world from a different place. You taught me so much – how to let go, take risks, have fun, laugh. You inspired me. Taught me passion. Love without fear.' I am in tears now. I miss him so much.

'Do you know that I wake up every morning with such a sense of dread I can't move, thinking *how* I am going to make it through another *entire* day? I don't know what's wrong with me, Lucy. I'm so lonely.'

'How can you be lonely?'

'I don't know.' He sounds totally exasperated with himself.

'You've Rachel and Toby and me. And we love you *so much*.'

He sighs the deepest most hopeless sigh.

'I won't go,' I say, suddenly deciding.

'No, you have to.'

'No.'

'Lucy, go. Please, I want you to. I'll see a doctor while you're gone.'

'You will?'

'Yes.'

'Oh, Greg, that's great. That's great. It's the right thing. I know it is.' I hug him, believe him.

21

Normally, I'd be thrilled to see Fint. Today, I feel nothing. He's flapping around, wearing his favourite suit, his lucky tie. A pep in his step. It's pre-pitch fever, a bug I usually catch. Not today. Sebastian's making up for me, though. We don't dwell on the personal stuff, just focus on running through the presentation. I can't work up the necessary enthusiasm. Fint suggests that Sebastian should present the company blurb, while he pitches the proposal. Fine by me.

As soon as the potential client walks into our meeting room, I get a bad feeling. The MD hasn't bothered to turn up. It's just Frank Haddon, the marketing director. And he's late. He doesn't apologize. His attitude is rude and superior – he has something we want and he knows it. His air is one of practised disinterest. Typically, this would stimulate me into action, motivating me to convince him he'd be mistaken to go with anyone else. Now I'm just furious. His is the attitude of a person who has already decided, without even seeing our pitch, not to go with us. Oh, I know the type – insecure exec wanting to make the right decision, going for the safe option – the biggest, most expensive firm. The internationals. That way, if things don't work out, he has a fallback for his boss: 'I picked a blue chip.' So why didn't he just go with the big boys first instead of using up our man-hours? Because the smaller houses often have the best ideas, ideas that can be 'adapted' to such an extent that no one can be accused of stealing them.

He has wasted our time. Not just the time we're spending

looking at his ugly mug or the time all three of us have put into preparation, but the time I could have spent with Greg, convincing him to come home. Well, I am sick of being pushed around by people like him. Does he think he can just swan in here and treat us like this without *any* repercussions? When Fint has finished his presentation and Haddon hasn't come up with one question – interesting or otherwise – I ask, with an innocent smile, 'So, where's your managing director today?'

He looks surprised, marginally uncomfortable. 'Important meeting he couldn't get out of, I'm afraid. Sends his apologies.'

'Pity he didn't try to reschedule.'

'Didn't want to put you out, I expect.'

'Nice of him.' My tone is sarcastic.

'Quite.' He looks annoyed.

Fint is looking at me, eyes wide in warning.

I ignore him. I want to show this guy. 'So, how many other agencies are you seeing?'

He clears his throat. Smiles. 'Two or three.'

'And will you turn up late for them too?'

'Excuse me?' He laughs at my audacity.

'I was just wondering if you'll turn up half an hour late without an apology for them too?'

'Well, I . . .' He looks at Fint and Sebastian, presumably to be bailed out.

'Thank you, Lucy,' says Fint and looks at me as if to say shut-the-fuck-up.

I carry on. 'It's just that I wonder if you appreciate our *time*, Mr Haddon.'

He starts to shove his mobile phone, car keys, and the jotter and pen we supplied into his briefcase. He stands abruptly. 'Well, then, I won't keep you another moment. Thank you for your presentation.' He nods at Fint and an appalled Sebastian. He starts to leave, without a glance in my direction.

'Eh, I'll just show you out,' says Sebastian.

As soon as the door closes behind them, Fint rounds on me.

'*What* was that about?'

'I'm sorry. He just got my goat. We've been here before too many times. Snotty-nosed marketing hot-shot with his yaw-yaw accent. We all know where *he* went to school.'

'So you decided to take him down a peg or two? That showed him, all right.'

'We weren't going to get the business anyway.'

'Is that right?'

'That's right.'

'And how did you work that one out?' he asks.

'I knew the minute he walked in the door. Didn't you? Rude bastard. Didn't even apologize. And the *attitude* of him. Who did he think he was? These people think they can just waltz in here and steal our ideas. I really think we should stop getting involved in competitive pitches –'

'Do you know how much *work* Sebastian and I put into that pitch?'

'Do you know how much work *I* put into that pitch?'

'So why did you just go and blow it? Did it make you feel better to watch him squirm? So what if he's an asshole? So what if he's rude? A lot of our clients are, but they pay the wages. We're in no position to start getting fussy.'

'I know. OK, I'm sorry . . . I'm just not in good form.'

'Just don't take it out on the business, Lucy.'

'Sorry.'

'Fine for you,' he says. 'Jetting back off to the Riviera to your millionaire lifestyle. Some of us still have to earn a crust.'

'That is so not fair.'

'You've lost your edge. You've lost your hunger. You used to be good. Better than good. You used to be great. Where's it all gone?'

'Stuff you,' I say. And walk.

Flying down the stairs, feet pumping, I visualize that little pipsqueak sitting there so smugly, *stealing* our ideas, *using* us, and Fint fooling himself – he knew, deep down, that we hadn't a hope. Well, I'm glad we didn't get the business. Imagine working for that wanker. But by the time I'm fastening my seat belt, ready for take off, I'm seeing the situation from outside. What was I doing? What was I hoping to achieve? I was completely out of line. Get Smart is not my business. I'm a partner. I should behave like one. If I want to go blowing contracts, then I should work for myself. Poor Fint. I'd be livid, if he'd done the same to me.

In the taxi, on my way to the villa, the sun is sinking behind cypress trees, bathing everything in warm, glowing, optimistic light. *If only I'd never left. I wouldn't have ruined everything, behaved like such a lunatic.* It's nine when I finally push in the front door. All is quiet.

Grace comes to greet me. 'Hey! How did the meeting go?'

'Disaster.' I drop my briefcase as though it weighs a ton.

She opens her mouth to speak.

'Don't ask.' In the kitchen, I pour myself a juice. 'Where is everyone?'

'Bed.'

'Already?'

'Rachel's reading in her room. Jason's asleep in his chair.'

'Where's Shane?'

'Having a sleepover, in Toby's room.'

I smile, imagining them.

Grace's face is suddenly serious. 'Lucy, Greg is really low. You have to get him home.'

'What did the doctor say?'

'What doctor?'

'He said he'd go to the doctor today.'

'He didn't budge out of bed all day. I brought him up lunch, but he didn't eat. He barely drank anything. All he did was smoke. I hid the whiskey.'

'Shit.'

'This is very serious.'

'I *know*. But what can I do? He won't listen to me. I can't force him.'

'You'll have to.'

'How?'

'Scare him. Bluff. Give him an ultimatum – either he goes home with you or you leave – for good.'

I look at her. 'What if he tells me to leave?'

'You have to get him home. Concentrate on that and you will.'

'He doesn't listen to me.'

'You have to make him. If he has bipolar disorder, and I'm not saying he does, but *if* he does, his moods, feelings are out of control. It's up to you to get him home. Be brutal if you have to. But get him home. I'll come with you. I'll help you through.' She takes my hand in hers. 'Promise.'

'But you have your own life, your own marriage –'

'I know. And I need to get home to try to sort that out. I can't do it from over here.'

'Oh, Grace, I'm glad.' I hug her. 'I knew you just needed a break from each other for a while. That's all.' She doesn't look convinced.

'Let's just get Greg home, OK?'

I nod. 'OK.'

There's never going to be a good time. So I pick the best time. Late afternoon, next day. Greg's up. And hasn't started drinking – the whiskey's still hiding. (I can't believe I never thought of that myself.) Grace has taken the children to Aqua-Splash. Greg's sitting with his head leaning back over the top of one of the sofas, eyes closed.

I sit beside him.

'What did the doctor say?'

He lifts his head with great effort. 'What doctor?'

'The doctor you were supposed to go to yesterday.'

'Oh,' he says quietly. 'I didn't go.'

'It's time to go home, Greg.'

'Not this again.' He pushes himself up from the chair and leaves the room. I follow him, trying to keep calm. He stands at the window of the office, arms folded, staring ahead. Blotting me out.

'This isn't going to get better by itself.'

He ignores me.

'It has to end. Now.'

'*Really?*'

'Yes. We're going home. And we're going to a doctor.'

'The last person who tried to bully me was sacked.'

What is he talking about? He fired Hilary because she came on to him. But I'm not going to think about Hilary now. I'm not going to get distracted. 'Here's the thing, Greg. If you don't come home to Dublin with me now, I'm leaving you. I'm going.'

'You wouldn't.'

'That's where you're wrong. I'm not going to stay and watch you ruin yourself. And I'm not going to let you take me down with you.'

'All right. Go, then.' He doesn't budge.

'Fine. I will.'

I turn and walk, thinking *damn, damn, damn*. How I hoped he would crumble. He hasn't. I've gone this far. I have to keep going. He has to believe I mean it. Maybe I do. Maybe I *have* had enough. I pull my case out from under the bed, march to the wardrobe, grab everything down from the hangers. I throw the clothes on the bed and start to fold and pack them. *Am I doing the right thing? How far will he let me take this? All the way? Just like that? Relationship over.* I've almost finished. I sense him at the door. I don't look, afraid he'll see weakness in my eyes.

'Don't go,' he says, his voice gentle.

I keep packing.

'I just have to control it,' he says. 'I *can* do it Lucy. It's mind over matter.'

I put my not-so-red sandals into their canvas bag. 'I meant what I said, Greg.'

'Don't force me, Lucy.'

This is so hard. I can't look at him. I have to keep busy, not let him see my face. When I start to cry, it's because I know, all of a sudden, I'm going through with it, all the way. I turn to him, convinced. 'I'm going. I don't want to, but I am.' Back to the case. I zip it up. Remember my toiletries. Go to the bathroom and start to fill my make-up bag. My hands are shaking, legs weak. This is it. It's over. I reach into the bathroom cabinet, fingers, like the rest of me, trembling. Toiletries begin to tumble out, land in the sink and clatter to the tiled floor. *Damn.* I stoop to scoop them up. *Why does nothing ever go right for me? Time to face the pattern, Lucy. Time to go home and crawl back into your cocoon.* I pull myself up using the side of the bath and see him at the door, looking wretched.

'All right,' he says, letting his head fall, as if conceding victory. 'I'll come home.'

It takes me a second to adjust. I look at him, waiting for the catch.

It comes.

'But I'm not making any promises about a doctor.'

'No, Greg. Not good enough. All or nothing.'

I walk past him, open the case and squash the make-up bag in. I zip it shut, lift it off the bed, pull up the handle and begin to wheel it behind me as I make for the door.

'All right. *All right*. I'll see someone. OK?'

'You mean like you promised to do when I was away?'

A wave of guilt crosses his face. 'I will go. In Dublin. I will. I promise.'

'You really promise?'

He crosses his heart like he did when we first met. And I want to cry.

'Thank you.'

22

I grab the moment and seize the day, or grab the day and seize the moment. Whatever the hell it is. I move immediately to get us out of there. If I delay, a mood might pass, a mind might change. We'll be home on the first available flight. It doesn't take long to organize. I book Grace and the boys on the same flight and let my sister know. Greg tells Rachel and Toby we're going home.

'Already?' asks Rachel.

'Why?' asks Toby.

'I'm not feeling the best. The heat – it's making me tired.'

'Oh,' says Toby. 'So if we go home will you be able to play with us again?'

'Mm-hmm.'

'You won't stay in bed all day?'

'No.'

'Is it a deal?' he asks.

'Deal,' says Greg.

'Shake on it.'

He shakes.

Toby nods. 'OK, so let's go.'

'What about the guys?' asks Rachel. 'Are they going back to Dublin too?'

'Yes.'

'Will we see them there?'

Greg looks at me.

'Sure,' I say.

Rachel takes Toby off to pack their things.

My future stepdaughter walks ahead of us at the airport, posture perfect, like a mini-airhostess, pulling her case on wheels behind her. Her sense of purpose makes me, for the first time in a long time, feel positive. We're sorting this out, whatever it is. On the plane, Greg eases back his seat, closes his eyes and opts out. Toby, next to me, is busy with an activity book. Rachel is playing peek-a-boo with Shane, who is seated in the row in front with his mum and brother. When we get to Dublin, Kevin is there to pick up his family. Shane runs to his dad and is scooped up. When Grace, carrying Jason, reaches Kevin, I detect a tension between them I've never noticed before. When she turns to me to say goodbye, all she says is 'I'll call you.'

'Thanks, Grace, for everything.'

She smiles and turns to go. As I watch them head out through the sliding doors, I hope that they'll be all right.

The rest of us get a taxi, leaving the airport under a grey sky, everyone quiet. Returning to Dublin is like returning to reality. It feels like an episode in our lives is over, and another beginning. I hope it will be better. A lot better. When we get to the house in Dalkey, though, there's a crisis. Toby runs to Hilary's room, expecting her to be there. It's empty, everything gone, cleared out. She's taken her things. Of course she has. It makes total sense. Not to Toby.

'But where is she?'

It's Greg who should explain. But he's downstairs, slumped in a chair. I squat down. 'Hilary's working somewhere else now, Toby.'

'But why?'

'Sometimes a time comes for change, for people to move on. But other people come instead, like Grace and the boys.'

'They're gone too. Everyone goes.' The corners of his little mouth turn down and his eyes fill.

'No, Toby. They're not gone. You can see them any time you like. They're kind of like your cousins, really,' I say, to cheer him up.

'Really?' he asks.

'No,' says Rachel. 'They're not our cousins. Because Lucy is not related to us.'

'Oh,' says a disappointed Toby.

'Well, Toby,' I say, trying to move on from my stupid mistake, 'your dad's not gone. Your dad's still here. He'll always be here.'

'Why did Hilary go?' he asks.

'It was just time for a change –'

'That isn't true,' says Rachel. 'You asked Dad to sack Hilary, remember?'

'No, Rachel. I didn't –'

'Forget it,' she snaps. 'Come here, Tobes, I'll look after you. I'm not going anywhere.' She glares at me as if to say, 'But you'll be.'

Grace has made an appointment for Greg with her GP friend Karl Brennan. Apparently, he has a special interest in psychiatry. Greg knows nothing of the special interest. And I hope he won't need it, that this will be something simple, easily explained away. All Greg cares about is discretion and getting it over with. This guy's a stranger who has taken the Hippocratic oath – fine, then, bring him on.

He wants to go alone. And I have to trust that he'll get there. He takes a taxi, lacking the energy or concentration to drive. I can't stay still from the moment he leaves. By the time he gets back, the place is spotless; the holiday clothes washed, and in the process of being dried, cases put away. He walks past me, on into the kitchen. I follow. He's standing at the window, staring out at the incredible sea view. I go up to him.

'How did it go?'

'I thought he was supposed to be good,' he says, looking at me as if I've done something wrong. 'He hadn't a fucking clue.'

'What did he say?'

'He wanted me to see a shrink. A fucking shrink.'

Everything stops.

'Today,' he laughs. 'Would you believe that?'

I force the next question. 'Did he say what he thought it was?'

He doesn't answer. And to be honest, I don't want him to. We're stuck.

'Maybe he's making a mistake,' I say, hoping.

'Of course he is. *Bloody quack.* I thought Grace knew what she was doing. Why the fuck did she pick *him*?'

'Did he think you were depressed?'

He turns to me, his face contorted by bitterness. 'Oh, no. Nothing *that* simple. He thinks I'm *manically* depressed. He thinks I've *manic* depression. No, no, *sorry* . . .' He curls his fingers into quote marks. 'Bipolar disorder. The politically correct tag. I mean, who're they trying to protect? Do they think that by changing the name it changes what it is? It's a joke.'

His anger makes everything clear. He does believe the GP. Otherwise he'd simply have dismissed him. He believes him, but he doesn't want to. And, my God, I don't blame him. I want to put my arms round him. I want to say that everything will be OK. But I'm paralysed. Will it? Manic depression. It seems so huge, like a dark grey rug being thrown over us.

'What time is your appointment?' I have to assume he's going. It's my only hope of getting him there.

He throws me a look that says, 'Are you mad?' 'I'm not going. Waste of time.'

'Greg, you have to go. You've got this far.'

'I said I'd go see a doctor and I did.'

Think, Lucy, think. 'Yes, but you have to do what he recommends or else it's as if you haven't gone at all. I know it sounds like he's making a mistake. I'm sure he is. But go to the psychiatrist and get the all clear so we can move on with our lives. Please, Greg.'

'What if he's right? Do you want that? Do you want me to have manic depression?'

'You either have it or you haven't. And if you have, let's just deal with it, OK?'

'He thinks the psychiatrist will admit me.'

'To *hospital*?'

'St Martha's Hospital.' His head lowers. 'Psychiatric ward.'

No. No way. This isn't happening.

'He wants me to bring my stuff in case I have to go in.'

I want to scream 'stop'.

'When? When's your appointment with the psychiatrist?'

'As soon as I'm ready. He's expecting me.'

I can see why denial seems like the easiest option.

'What about the children?' I ask. *What will he tell them? Who will mind them? And how will they cope with yet another separation, this time from the most important person in their lives? I've just told Toby he'll always have his father. Jesus.*

'That's what I'm saying, Lucy. If I go in, I won't be coming home. Not for weeks.'

Weeks? I'm too shocked to speak. But I have to, to pretend I'm not shocked. 'Oh-kaay? We can manage that. Let's think. We'll have to get someone to mind the children, someone they know and trust, someone who's free . . . Rob. Of course! He's still on summer holidays. We'll ask Rob.' I'm relieved. A solution.

He looks hurt. 'Why not you?'

'Me?' I'd be useless. They're not my children. Rachel hates me. 'Greg, they need family.'

'You are family.'

I truly believe he's making a mistake.

'Please, Lucy, look after Rachel and Toby for me, and I'll go in.'

His eyes are searching mine. He's waiting. If I say no, he won't go.

I close my eyes and find my head nodding, my voice agreeing, 'OK. I'll do it.' I try not to think about what will be involved.

'Thank you.' I hear the relief in his voice.

We gaze out to the children, busy in the garden, Rachel trying to save the plants from drought, and Toby reaching under a shrub for something. We stand in silence for a long time, neither of us wanting to move forward.

'D'you want me to pack some things?' I ask eventually.

'Hmm?'

'Should I pack for you?'

'Would you, Luce? I can't seem to get my head round what I need.'

'I'll make some tea, then throw a few things in a case, OK?' I try to sound casual, not think about the fact that this'll be the last tea we'll share for, well, I don't know how long.

I bring a packed bag downstairs and start to look for the car keys.

'I'll go in on my own.'

'Oh, Greg. Let me drive you.'

'No, Luce. I need to handle this myself . . . I'll get a taxi.'

The thought of him heading off alone makes me worse. But I call the taxi. Because he has his pride. We call the children in. Toby comes running, shouting. 'D'you want to see my snail collection? It's brill. There's five of them. My favourite's the small one, but I like them all, really. D'you want to see, Dad?' I marvel at how quickly children can get distracted. For the moment, he's forgotten about Hilary. Greg looks at me, a question on his face. How can I leave my little boy?

We sit, the four of us, at the kitchen table. Rachel regards us carefully, suspecting something's up. Toby's oblivious, poking his box of snails under Greg's nose. 'Dad, can I've some lettuce for them? They ackshilly love lettuce.'

'Guys,' says Greg. 'I've something I want to tell you.'

Toby stops, looks up at his dad, big brown eyes wide. Rachel looks like she wants to run.

'I haven't been feeling the best.'

'I know,' says Toby. 'But you're home now. And it's freezing. Are you better yet?'

'No.'

'But you said –'

'Yes, I said that when we got home it wouldn't be hot and I'd be fine. But I was wrong. I'm not fine.'

'But you shook on it.'

'I was wrong. I'm sorry, pet. I'm still sick and have to see a doctor.' He ruffles Toby's hair. 'I might have to go into hospital for a while.'

'No,' says his son. 'You can't. You have to stay here with us. You can't go away. I won't let you.'

'Come here, Tobes.'

Greg sits him up on his lap. 'You can't go, Dad. You just can't.' He clings to Greg, cheek against chest. Greg wraps him up in his arms.

'You want me to get better, don't you, Tobes?'

Toby doesn't answer.

'And you're a big man now, aren't you?'

Silence.

'What's wrong, Dad?' asks Rachel.

'I just haven't been feeling the best.'

Toby sits back from Greg. 'D'you have a pain in your tummy?'

Greg rubs Toby's cheek with the back of his fingers. 'No, no. No, pain.'

'Well, what is it, then?' asks Rachel. 'Not *cancer*?'

How does she know about cancer?

'No,' says Greg. 'Not cancer. It's just that I'm exhausted and I need to rest. That's all.'

'Go to bed,' says Toby.

'Stop, Toby,' orders Rachel. 'If Dad has to go to hospital, Dad has to go to hospital.'

Toby's little face crumples.

'Ah, don't cry, pet,' says Greg, hugging him. 'It'll be OK. I'll be back soon.'

'When?'

'In a few weeks.'

'*A few weeks?*' Toby and Rachel say together.

'Why weeks?' Rachel asks. 'Eva had her whole appendix out, and she wasn't even in for one week. What is it, Dad? Is it really bad?'

His smile looks forced. 'I have to see this doctor, OK? And he'll decide if I have to go into hospital or not, and if I do, how long I'll stay. Let me go to see him and hear what he says, OK? Let's just take this one step at a time.'

'So you mightn't be going in?' Rachel.

'I probably will, pet.'

'Who'll mind us?' she asks. 'Rob?'

'Lucy, of course. Rob will help out.'

Both heads swivel in my direction. Then Rachel shakes hers. 'No *way*.'

'*Rachel*,' says Greg.

'But I don't want her –'

'Look. I'm only going to say this once. I don't like being sick, and if I had my way I'd be staying right here. But sometimes we have to do things we don't like to make things better for everyone. Lucy will have a lot on her plate, and the last thing she needs from you is trouble. Do you hear me?'

She lowers her eyes. 'Yes, Dad.'

'I want you both to help Lucy. OK? I want you to keep your rooms tidy, clean up after yourselves and help out. Is that clear?'

'Yes, Dad.'

'Now, give me a hug.'

And they do.

'I'll ring as soon as I know what's happening, OK?'

'OK,' we all say together.

The taxi pulls up outside. Looking like a man who's lost a battle, Greg gets in. I put his bag on the seat beside him. Even *it* looks sad. The two of them just sitting there, in a heap, lost, deserted. I don't want to fuss, just say, 'Talk later,' but then I can't let him go without kissing him and adding, 'Love you.' He's looking straight ahead, as if finally accepting his fate. I close the door and stand back as the taxi pulls away. The sound of a lawn mower coming from a nearby garden seems at odds with what's happening. Nothing else should be normal. Not today.

'He didn't wave goodbye,' says Toby.

The taxi is at the top of the avenue now. It indicates and turns right, taking with it the only thing we have in common.

For a moment we just stand, not looking at each other. Flattened. Then Rachel lifts her brother, turns and walks towards the house. I look back up the avenue. A young couple stroll by, bodies glued together, each with a hand slipped in the other's back pocket. They stop to kiss and gaze into each other's eyes. *Wasn't that the plan?* I look away and make for the house.

Rachel hasn't closed the door on me.

It's a start.

23

I assume that the children are off limits, hidden away in Rachel's bedroom, a place that, when I first saw it earlier today, reminded me of what an enigma she is to me. I've never met a child so tough and sassy, yet her room looks like it belongs to a girl who dreams of turning frogs into princes. It is pale pink with a blue chandelier and a muslin drape falling over brass bed knobs. Her colour-coordinated furniture is prettily ornate, as if taken from a doll's house and magnified.

Should I go in? Or not? I take a step towards the door, then stop, think. What could I possibly say that would reassure them? With Toby, I mightn't have to say anything. I could just hold him. But with Rachel, I need answers. With Rachel, I need a miracle. Wringing my hands, I walk away. In my room, I can't sit down. In the end, I pick up the phone and call Grace.

'I'm coming over,' she says when she hears of Greg's possible hospitalization.

'Grace, there's no need,' I say, well aware of her own problems.

'I think there is.'

'What about Shane and Jason?'

'I'll drop them at Mum and Dad's.'

'Don't tell them,' I say in a rush, remembering how Greg reacted when he discovered Grace knew – it took him a bottle of wine and half a day to calm down.

'Don't worry. I'll come up with something.'

She arrives half an hour later. I'm at the front window,

214

pacing like a sentry. I open the door before she gets to it. We hug and I burst into tears. She just holds me. Eventually she asks where the children are.

'Upstairs.'

'Where's the kitchen?'

I point down the hall.

'Right. Come on.'

She closes the door behind us.

I find some kitchen paper and use it on my face. We sit at the table. Sharing what happened makes me feel better. Marginally.

'*Will* he be admitted?' I ask, willing her to say 'no', 'probably not', 'unlikely' or any version of negative.

'To be honest, Luce, while Karl has a lot of pull with the hospital, he wouldn't have got Greg seen today if it hadn't been urgent. And he wouldn't have asked him to pack unless he expected him to be going in.'

I close my eyes. 'That's it, then. It's definitely manic depression.' I wait for her to say something. But she doesn't. I open them again. 'But why hospital? Can't they just, I don't know, give him some antidepressants or something and send him home?'

'He's very low, Luce.'

'We've all been low. Doesn't mean we have to be admitted to a psychiatric ward.'

'This isn't just being low or feeling down. There's an imbalance of chemicals in his brain. That takes time to readjust. And they'll need to keep an eye on him while they do it.'

'But weeks, Grace. He said it'd be for weeks.'

'Hospital's the best place for Greg now.' She holds my hand. 'I know it's hard, but when you're as low as Greg is, ordinary life can seem too much to cope with. Hospital can provide an escape, a sanctuary. And, Lucy, he won't be in there for a solid block of weeks. As soon as he starts to improve, they'll begin to send him home for short periods to see how he gets on. Weekends at first, then maybe longer. The good thing is, they'll only discharge him when he's ready.'

'How'll I manage? I've the children and work and I'll have to find time to visit him – '

'I'm here. Mum and Dad, too.'

'I can't tell them.'

She nods. 'I understand that . . . Well, you've got me. And Rob. I'll help with Rachel and Toby, the house, whatever. You'll probably have to talk to Fint about work, though. There's no way you'll be able to go back full time.'

'I know, but how'll I tell him? I'm in his bad books at the moment. He's put up with a hell of a lot from me already.'

We're preparing dinner when the phone rings. I rush to answer it, calling to Grace, 'Must be Greg.'

'Hello, is this Lucy Arigho?' A female voice.

'Yes?'

'This is Staff Nurse Betty O'Neill, from St Raphael's Ward at St Martha's Hospital.'

My heart skitters. 'Is Greg all right?'

'Yes, he's fine. Professor Power, one of our psychiatrists, has just admitted him. He's resting now. He asked me to call you to say he'll talk to you tomorrow.'

'Oh.'

'He's tired. It's been a long day. And of course a bit of a shock.'

'I was going to come in and see him in a little while . . .' I look at Grace. She's offered to stay with the children.

'Well, perhaps not this evening. Maybe let him settle in a bit.'

'He's all right, though? It's just I was expecting him to call.'

'Yes, I know. But he doesn't feel up to much at the moment.'

'I'll come in first thing.'

'Actually, if you don't mind, we usually encourage visitors to wait till after five.'

'*Why?*'

'It allows patients to rest, attend group sessions, have time to talk.'

'OK. Thanks for ringing,' I say, dropping the phone and once again bursting into tears. Grace is with me in seconds.

'Shh,' she says, hugging me. 'It's OK. This is the worst time, Lucy. It'll get better. I promise.'

'You said that already,' I wail.

When I look up, Rachel and Toby are standing in the doorway.

'Was that Dad?' Rachel asks.

I quickly wipe my eyes. Grace lets me go.

'It was the hospital. They were just ringing to say he's fine.'

They speak together.

Toby: 'So why are you crying?'

Rachel: 'He said *he'd* ring.'

I answer Rachel. It's easier. 'He's resting.'

'Can we go see him tomorrow?' asks Toby.

'Maybe not tomorrow, Toby. Let me just go in and see how he is –'

'Why do you get to go and not us?' Rachel.

'Can we ring him tomorrow?' Toby.

I don't need this. I really don't. But I look at them and see how distressing it must be for them. At the ages of ten and five, their only security in life gone. 'We might just let your dad rest tomorrow, Toby,' I say. 'When I go in, I'll bring my mobile. And if it suits everyone in there, I'll call you so you can talk to your dad. I can't promise, though. Because I'm not sure yet, OK?'

'OK.'

'But I'll do my best.'

'Yeah, right,' says Rachel.

Grace looks at her. Then at me.

No one eats. Grace goes home. I suppose she'll tell Kevin.
Rachel mothers Toby, putting him to bed and reading to him.
By ten I'm locking and bolting up the huge, unfamiliar house.
Outside, it's twilight and the garden is full of shadows. I wrap
my cardigan around myself and go to my room, hoping that
things will seem more manageable in a smaller space. Two
things keep me awake – fear of not being able to cope and
guilt that I don't want to have to.

I wake early and get up, intending to occupy myself with
something, anything, rather than think. On the landing, at the
airing cupboard, is Toby. He's jumping up trying to reach
something. He's naked.

'Toby, are you OK?' I ask quietly, trying not to startle him.

I don't succeed. He covers himself with his hands. 'I . . .
I . . . was just getting some sheets.'

'Here. Let me help.' I reach into the airing cupboard and
pull out what looks like Bart Simpson bed linen. 'These
yours?'

He nods, holds his arms up for them. His skinny body is
covered in goose bumps.

'It's OK,' I say. 'I'll carry them for you. They're heavy.'

In his room, the smell of urine lingers. He has tugged off
three corners of his sheet. The fourth is held fast in against the
wall. His soggy pyjamas are in a heap on the floor.

'I'm sorry,' he says, head hanging.

'Toby, that's OK. It's just a little accident. Everybody has
accidents.'

'Don't tell Rachel.'

'Cross my heart.' It's catching. 'I'll just go get you a towel.'

I return with a warm bath towel and wrap him in it. Eye to eye, I say, 'Everything'll be all right, Tobes.' I hold his chin between my finger and thumb and give it a little shake. 'I bet you're the kind of man who likes bubbles in his bath.'

He follows me into the bathroom, where I put down the toilet lid for him to sit on, while I fill the bath. Cold first, I remember from Grace and the boys. As it fills, I nip back to his room to remove the evidence in case Rachel stumbles on it. I open the windows, close the door. Back in the bathroom, I can't find bubble bath. I retrieve my Molton Brown shower gel. To think that I once thought things like this precious seems like a joke to me now. I could dump the whole bottle in. I test the water with my elbow the way you're supposed to do with children, or is that babies? Toby is in charge of pouring in the 'bubble bath'. He isn't stingy. Slow to leave him alone yet not wanting to be too obvious a presence, I busy myself tidying. Without directly looking, I notice that he's just sitting there, surrounded by bubbles.

'D'you want to mess around with this?'

I hold up the empty Molton Brown bottle, not expecting him to be interested.

'Yes, please.' He submerges it, watching it fill with bubbly water, lifts it up, tips it over. He starts to hum.

'Can you wash yourself, Toby, if I give you a cloth or do you need a hand?'

'I can wash myself.'

'What about your hair?'

'I might need a *little* hand.'

'OK, handsome.' I smile.

I wrap him in a fresh bath towel and carry him to his room. We pretend he's a baby dinosaur that's newly hatched. And suddenly I feel just as protective as a mummy dinosaur. Later, as I'm giving him breakfast and he's chatting about snails, Rachel appears with her usual cloud. She ushers her runaway fledgling back under her wing. I wish she'd allow herself to be the child she is, rather than the adult she insists on being. I'd look after her, if only she'd let me.

In the afternoon Grace arrives with the boys and I leave for the hospital. When I get there, I stand in the lobby, unable to ask where the psychiatric ward is. I try to remember the name the nurse used on the phone, then run through the list of wards displayed. St Raphael's sounds familiar. I follow the signs. The doors are closed, I assume locked, it being a psychiatric ward. I'm searching for a bell when someone just walks through. I do the same. And I'm in. The mad bustle of the corridor outside dies. The walls are lavender. I wait for the impression of peace to be shattered as I edge along the corridor, half afraid someone will suddenly appear at my side, grinning. I pass a television room to my left. Its occupants – a young, attractive man and a tiny, grey-haired woman – are dressed in outdoor clothes and occupy armchairs about five chairs apart. They ignore each other, staring instead at the TV. A woman is coming towards me, dressed in black – polo-neck top, trousers and flat shoes. I stop. Try a smile.

'Hello. Excuse me. Eh, I was wondering where I might find a nurse?' As I say this, I realize my mistake. I don't know anything about this woman apart from the fact that she's in a psychiatric ward.

'You're talking to one,' she says. 'I'm Betty O'Neill. Can I help you?'

'Oh. Yes, Betty. I think we spoke yesterday? I'm Lucy Arigho. You rang me about Greg Millar?'

'Yes, of course.' She smiles. 'I'll take you to him.' We walk side by side in silence, until she stops at a two-bed room. She gestures to the bed nearest the door. It has the curtain pulled round it.

'Is it OK to go in?' I whisper.

'Yes. It's fine. He just wants privacy. Go on in.'

He's lying with his back to the door, still in the clothes he was wearing when he came in. If he hears me, he doesn't react.

'Greg?' I whisper, in case he's asleep.

He turns.

I smile. 'Hi.'

He drags himself into a sitting position, his clothes crumpled, his pillow flattened behind his back. 'Where are the kids?'

'At home. With Grace. I didn't know whether they'd be allowed. And I didn't think you wanted them to come in yet.'

'I don't.'

'Maybe we could ring them in a little while? I've my phone.'

'Yeah. OK.'

'Can I sit down?'

When he nods, I perch on the edge of the bed, facing him.

'You didn't tell anyone else, did you, apart from Grace?'

'No.'

'Well, don't. OK?'

'What about your family?'

'No.'

'What if they're looking for you?'

'I said *no*. Make up an excuse. Lie if you have to. Just don't tell them. Especially not my mother. Do you understand, Lucy?'

'Yes, yes, of course I understand.' *I'm not stupid.* 'But I really think you should tell Rob.'

'No.'

221

'Greg. You'll be in here for weeks. Won't you?' I hold my breath, make a wish.

'Looks like it.'

Damn. 'Well, what if Rob calls over and the children tell him you're in hospital? What'll he think? And don't tell me to keep him away. Rachel and Toby need all the familiar faces they can get just now. You're suddenly gone. And they're left with me. It's not like I'm their favourite person in the world.'

He taps four fingers on his leg for what seems like ages. 'OK. Just Rob . . . But *I'll* tell him.'

'Fine . . . What'll I tell your mother if she calls?'

'Let me think about it, OK? Let me think. *You* can't tell her . . . Promise me you won't.'

'I promise.' *Jesus. What's the problem with her?*

'And warn Grace not to tell anyone.'

'OK. OK.' He's not exactly making this easy. I change the subject. 'Rachel and Toby made these for you,' I say, opening my bag and pulling out two cards. Rachel's has a smiling happy sun. Toby's has a rocket. He peers at them. They've the opposite effect to what was intended. He puts them down as though they're made of stone. His once blue, now pewter eyes fill. It kills me to see him like this. I pick up the cards and stand them on the locker. I reach for his hand. He pulls it away.

'We've done the right thing. I know we have. This is the first step to your recovery. Things will get better from here.'

Cynical is the look I get.

'What was Professor Power like?'

'Does it *really* matter?'

'Did he start you on medication?'

He sighs. 'For what it's worth.'

I give up. Look around. Dinner tray untouched. Case unopened.

'Will we ring the kids now?' I ask.

'OK.'

I dial the number, expecting Grace.

Rachel must have beaten her to it. 'Hello?' she says so hopefully.

'Rachel, it's Lucy. Your dad wants to have a word.'

'OK.'

As I pass the phone to Greg, I hear her calling Toby.

'Hello, pet,' says Greg. 'I'm fine. How're you? . . . It's fine . . . Soon . . . I'm not sure . . . She's doing her best, Rachel . . . I'll call you tomorrow, OK? . . . Love you too . . . How's my man? . . . I miss you too, Tobes . . .' His voice is rising. 'I know . . . Very soon . . . I'll talk to the doctor, OK . . . And I'll ring tomorrow . . . Are you minding your sister? . . . Good boy, good man.'

I know he's not up to me staying and doesn't want to be touched. So I say goodbye, tapping the bed with my hand. On the way out, I see Betty walking up ahead. I catch up with her.

'Betty? Hi. Would you have a moment?'

'Yes, of course. Why don't you come in here?'

I follow her into some kind of office.

'How is he?' I ask.

She folds her arms, smiles in an apologetic way. 'I'm sorry, Lucy, but Greg has asked us not to talk to you about his condition.'

'*Excuse me?*'

'Greg has asked us to respect his confidentiality. He doesn't want us to talk to anybody about his condition.'

'Not me, though, surely.' *He loves me. He trusts me.* 'I've been living through this with him. I'm his fiancée.'

Her voice softens. 'I understand that. But I'm afraid he was very clear. And we have to respect our patients' wishes. I'm

223

sorry. If he doesn't wish us to talk to you, we have to respect that.'

'I don't understand.'

'This isn't unusual. Greg's very down at the moment, but, as his condition improves, I'm sure he'll rethink. For now, though, we have to respect his wishes.'

I can't believe that he's excluding me.

'I can't talk to you about Greg specifically,' she continues, 'but I can give you these.' She holds out a bundle of leaflets and booklets. 'You might find them helpful.'

I have to stop myself telling her where to shove them.

24

Evening. In a house that is not my own, with none of my things around me. Where I can't lounge on the sofa or leave the toilet door open. Where there are too many rooms, none small enough for me. Where the shadows and creaks are unfamiliar. Where my bedroom is the only place I can feel in any way cosy. I take out my latest step-parenting book. It is the second time I've read it. It's either that or the leaflets.

My mobile rings. 'Dad' comes up on the screen.

'So you're home,' he says accusingly.

'Yes.'

'When were you going to tell us?'

'I was just about to ring you.' Slight exaggeration.

'We wouldn't even have known if Grace hadn't let it slip. It is nice *occasionally* to know what country your daughters are in. Your mother's upset, Lucy. You're home days and you never called.'

'Three, Dad.'

'She may not be your favourite person in the world, but she is your mother. She does love you. She does get hurt.'

'I know. I'm sorry. I'll call around. OK?'

'When?'

'I don't know. Tomorrow . . . I'll bring Rachel and Toby so you can meet them.' No choice.

'Aren't you back at work?'

'Eh, no. Not yet. I'm working out of the office for the moment.'

'Oh, why?'

'I don't know. It just suits. So how are you?'

'Fine, fine, grand. Hang on a minute, your mother is saying something . . . Why don't you all come over tomorrow for dinner, save you cooking?'

'It might be difficult. Greg's very busy at the moment.'

'Surely he has to stop to eat?'

'Well, it's just he has this deadline coming up and he's way behind. He's working flat out.' I hate lying but am surprised by how easy it is. 'I'll come with the children sometime tomorrow. OK?'

'Won't you be working?'

'I can take a little break.'

Speaking of work, I have to face Fint. I've already put it off one day. It's impossible, though. How can I tell him I'm home but not office bound without admitting the truth? Does Greg realize the extent of what he's asked me to do? Fint's my best friend. We've always shared our problems. Outside of that, he deserves an honest explanation as to why I can't go in and why I behaved so appallingly at the pitch. But I have promised to respect Greg's privacy. If a nurse at the hospital can do it, surely I can. And so the only way to talk to Fint is as a partner, not as a friend. I'll wait until morning, when he's in the office.

When I finally work up the courage, I go to my room, close the door, pick up the extension, and take a breath. Dial.

'Ooooh, it's the globetrotter, gracing us with a call.'

I force a laugh. *He's joking, right?*

'Let me guess, you're ringing from Monte Carlo, where you're visiting dignitaries.'

'I'm home.'

'Oh. Great. So what's keeping you? It's eleven.'

'I can't come in, Fint. I need to continue working out of the office for August. I hope that's OK.'

'No, actually, it's not. I need you in here . . . We might be able to win the odd pitch if we could actually put our heads together on something.'

'Fintan, I am so sorry about that pitch. I was way out of line –'

'You sabotaged the whole thing.'

'I know. I'm sorry. I was under a lot of pressure.'

'Pressure? *Pressure?* You don't know the meaning of the word . . . So when are you actually going to grace us with an appearance? I've been very patient, Lucy, but this is a business. It requires *some* effort. New accounts don't just sail in without a bit of blood, sweat and tears.'

Speaking of tears . . . Everything's coming to a head – Greg's diagnosis, the responsibility of the children, Rachel's stubborn rejection of me and now Fint's fury. I lose it. 'You have no *idea* how much effort I've been putting in. You haven't a clue what's going on in my life; how this is the last thing I need right now. Oh, forget it.' I hang up.

It rings. Guessing it's probably Fint, but equally afraid it might be the hospital, I pick it up and wait for the person to speak.

'I'm sorry,' says my business partner.

I say nothing.

'Are you OK?'

'No.'

'What is it?'

'Nothing. Forget it.' I stifle a sob. 'I just need to be around here for a while.'

'OK. Fine. Just tell me why.'

I sigh. 'Things are tricky right now. I'm minding Greg's children.'

'Why? Where is he?'

'I can't say.'

'What do you mean you can't say? This is me, *Fint*.'

'It's awkward.'

'Is he all right? Are *you* all right?'

'I'm OK, but I'm not "swanning around" anywhere, I'm not having a good time; I'm trying to cope. And because Greg's children are my responsibility now, I have to work from home. Or quit.'

There is a brief pause. 'That's not an option . . .'

The thought of even working seems too much.

'I wish you'd confide in me. I might be able to help.'

'Believe me, you wouldn't.'

'Is he ill?'

He deserves to know that much. 'Yes, he's ill. Very ill. But, Fint, don't ask me any more. Please. I promised him I wouldn't talk about it.'

He is silent for a moment. 'Can I do anything?'

'Just hold the fort for a little while longer. I'll be back in a few weeks. And I'll make up for it. You can take months off. A year. I don't care.'

'That's the only way I can help, work?'

'Yes.'

'OK.' His voice is tight, hurt.

'I'm sorry, Fint. I want to tell you, and I will when I can, but I promised Greg.'

'No. *I'm* sorry,' he says. 'I've been . . . a bit . . . uptight. I shouldn't have snapped.'

'You have every right to. I haven't exactly made life easy for you lately.'

'Forget about it. Do what you can, OK?'

'I could make client meetings.'

'Let's just see how it goes.'

'Fint, there is another option.'

'What?'

228

'Buy me out of the business.'

He doesn't hesitate. 'Forget it, honey. We're a team. We're stuck with each other. Wouldn't trust anyone else.'

How can I bring Rachel and Toby to my parents without their mentioning the hospital? I'll have to ask them not to. But they'll want to know why. I'm mopping the kitchen floor, trying to help the thought process, when the doorbell rings. Rob. Looking innocent. *Does he know or doesn't he?*

'Are you OK?' he asks, his voice full of concern.

I nod. 'He told you, didn't he?'

'Yeah. Though I'm not to tell anyone else.'

I half smile. 'Come in.'

The children come bounding down the stairs. 'Rob, Rob,' Toby shouts, hurling himself at him like a lonely koala.

'Hey, bud,' says Rob, rubbing the top of his head with his knuckles. 'How's the champ?'

'Fine. Dad's in hospital.'

I'm sunk. There's no way I can bring them to my parents now.

'He's exhausted,' Toby continues.

'I know,' Rob says, nodding slowly, probably trying to gauge how much they know. 'Lucy,' he says to me. 'I was thinking of taking the guys out for the day, if that's all right with you. Might give you a bit of time to catch up on things and maybe see Greg later if you want.'

'Are you sure?' I ask, hoping he won't change his mind.

'Sure I'm sure,' he says, beaming.

'Well, thanks. That'd be great. I'm sure they'd love a break from me.'

'Yeah-ah,' says Rachel.

Rob throws her a surprised look.

'Where're we going?' asks Toby.

'Up to you. We can decide in the car.'

Rob is so at ease around them. I feel tense, my neck stiff, my shoulders two inches too high. I am, I realize, holding myself as though expecting a blow to the back of the head.

He winks. 'See you later.'

'Eh, Rob? What time'll you be back? Just so I can make sure to be here.'

'Eight OK? Would that give you enough time?'

'Yes, that'd be great. Thanks, Rob.'

'No probs. See you later.'

I ring my parents to say it'll just be me. They invite me to lunch. I call Grace.

'What did you tell them?' I ask.

'Nothing.'

'They knew I was home.'

'Sorry, I let that slip but I didn't say anything else. I swear.'

'Did you tell them I've lost weight?'

'*No.*'

'Well, then, why does she keep inviting me for food?'

'I don't know. Doesn't she always?'

I think about that. 'Well, yeah, I suppose . . . Look, I'm sorry. This is impossible.'

'What?'

'Keeping everything secret. It's impossible.'

'Are you OK?'

'Who knows?'

'Want me to come over?'

'No, thanks, I'm fine. Oh, and don't worry about later. Rob's taken Toby and Rachel off until tonight. So you're off the hook.'

'I never felt I was on it. I'll come tomorrow, OK?'

'Thanks, Grace.'

'Don't mench.' An expression of our mother's.

Mum's made my favourite: home-made quiche and salad. It's so good to be home in our old kitchen, with its familiar smell of baking. Seeing my mum in her Alpen apron, I'm close to tears – obviously cracking up. Mum's questions no longer seem like nosy interference but come across as concerned. Although I want to answer truthfully, admit I'm in trouble and need help, I can't. I promised. So I put on an impressive performance, tell them that Greg's busy and in good form. I steer the conversation to safe topics like the South of France, with its towns, beaches, mountains. It's exhausting trying to sound enthusiastic about things that seem so unimportant, but more exhausting trying to watch everything I say, to avoid slip-ups.

Somehow I pull it off.

My second hospital visit, the following day, is worse than the first. The man I have promised to spend the rest of my life with won't talk to me. He won't even look at me, making me feel that it might be easier for him if I wasn't there. And that hurts. My attempts at optimism sound trite, even to me. I get back to an empty house feeling drained. And cold. I climb the stairs and crawl under the duvet fully clothed. If only I could get warm.

I wake. It's dark. The house is quiet. It takes a second to find my bearings. When I do, I sit bolt upright. *Damn. I wasn't supposed to sleep. I just closed my eyes for a second.* I jump from the bed and tear downstairs. *I'd have woken if they'd knocked. Maybe Rob has a key. I can't believe I didn't think to take his number . . .*

I bump into him in the hall.

231

'Jesus,' I say, my hand going to my chest, 'I'm sorry. I didn't know anyone was here. How did you get in?'

He holds up a key, smiling.

'Where are Rachel and Toby?'

'Asleep.'

'I am *so* sorry. I didn't mean to nod off.'

'You must've been tired.'

'Cold. I was freezing. Anyway, sorry. Thanks so much for looking after them today. It was such a great help.' I'm walking him to the front door.

'Don't I get a cup of tea?'

'Yes, yes, of course. Sorry.' My hand touches my forehead. *What's wrong with me?* We make our way to the kitchen. He pulls out a chair and sits back, one leg casually thrown across the other. I make for the kettle.

'How was he?' he asks.

My back to him, kettle under tap, I wonder what to say – be honest and have him know that Greg wouldn't talk to me? Or start some charade that'll exhaust me as I try to keep it up? I sigh, turn off the tap, re-lid the kettle, plug it in and turn to him. 'To be honest, Rob, I don't know.' I join him at the table. He pulls his chair closer. I pick up a drinks mat and rotate it. 'He won't talk to me. He says *he* wants to handle it.'

'Now why doesn't that surprise me?' he says, surprising me.

'What d'you mean?'

'Well, it's just typical Greg. He doesn't rely on anyone, especially family. When Catherine died, I got the same – "I can handle it." The only person he allowed to help was Hilary, and that was because it was her job. I bet he talks to the nurses and doctors in there.'

'I don't know. Nobody'll tell me anything. He won't let them talk to me.' I get up abruptly with the excuse of making tea, keeping my back to Rob. When I've managed to regain control, I bring the teapot and jug to the table. Rob gets up to collect the rest – mugs and sugar bowl. When we've settled, I ask, 'Why is he like that, Rob? Why is he blocking me out? All I want to do is help. We're engaged, for God's sake.'

'It's the way he is. Survival instinct or something. Since he was ten, he's had to be the responsible one. It's a habit, I guess.'

'But he should trust us.'

'I think he's afraid to. It's as if he feels our father let us down and now the only person he can depend on is himself. I don't know. I sometimes wonder if what's happening now has anything to do with the pressure of that.'

'If only he'd talk to us.'

'He thinks he's protecting us. He's been doing it all his life for me, for my mother. Now you.'

'But it means we can't help.'

'You *are* helping, Lucy, by being here, by looking after the children. When Catherine died, that's how I helped – with Rachel. I'd take her off, distract her, give him time for himself. It did help. I know it did. Of course, I couldn't let on I was deliberately helping.'

'Is that what you were doing today?'

'Absolutely. Helping you is helping him. I was thinking, what if I take Rachel and Toby for a few hours every evening? You could go see Greg.'

'That's too much, Rob. I'm sure Grace will do some nights. You have a life.'

'I'd like to do it, Lucy. It's always been one way with Greg and me. I don't just want to help, Lucy, I need to.'

I can understand that. 'But you'll want to see him yourself.'

'I'm off for another few weeks. And when school starts again, I'll work something out – either get to him before or after you've been.'

233

'Well, then, have dinner with us when you come to collect them.'

He agrees on the spot.

I wake three times during the night from the same nightmare. I leave the children to sleep on the street overnight while I check into an upmarket hotel. I go back out on to the street where I left them, tuck them up in sleeping bags and leave them, hoping they won't wander off or be attacked. It never once occurs to me to bring them into the hotel with me.

25

In the morning, on my way downstairs, I notice that Rachel's bedroom door is open. It's a rare occurrence, allowing a glimpse of the bombsite within. Her pretty room is over-flowing with clothes, books, CDs and dirty plates scattered in random heaps. I know it's partly my fault. I should have been able to say no when she headed upstairs with her self-made dinners, lunches, breakfasts. I should have been able to say no to a lot of things. But I've a problem getting the word out with Rachel. Her dad's in hospital. I'm not her mum. And I'm afraid of scenes. She is a landmine. And I am a foot. But there's no sign of her now, so I pop in to rescue uneaten food at the pre-fungal stage.

From across the corridor, I hear the toilet flush, the door open. A heap of clothes under one arm, a stack of plates in one hand and four glasses in the other, I turn. She's standing at the door looking like she's ready to blow.

'Get out of my room.'

'*Sorry?*'

'Are you deaf? I said get out.'

'Don't talk to me like that, Rachel.'

'Then don't go into my room. It's my room. You can't just go in whenever you want.'

'Rachel, I was just bringing down your dirty plates and the clothes that needed washing.'

'Did I ask you to?'

'No. But if you don't want me to come into your room, then please keep it tidy, so I don't have to.'

'I'll do what I like in my own room. It's my room.' The tilt of her head and hips say more than the words.

'Rachel, honestly,' I say, in what I hope is a reasonable voice, 'how do you expect your clothes to get clean lying here on the floor?'

'*I'll* clean them. At least *I* can, without ruining everything.'

'Fine, Rachel. Clean your own clothes. And leave your room whatever way you want. Just keep the door closed so I don't have to look at it.'

'Don't tell me what to do,' she shouts. 'You're not my mother. You can't make me do anything.'

'I wish you could hear yourself.'

'I can. *You're* the one who's deaf.'

Now I know why Hansel and Gretel's stepmother left them in the forest. I count to ten. In French.

'Why won't you just go away?' she says, when I get to six.

'And why won't you be fair?' My arms and fingers are aching now. If I don't put something down they'll slip out of my grip. I rest the glasses on my forearm. 'All I was trying to do was help. All I've ever tried to do is help. And you've been nothing but ungrateful. You won't eat my food. You insult my clothes. You give out about the mess the house is in but never lift a finger to do anything about it.'

'*Look*. Nobody asked you to do anything.'

'That's where you're wrong. Your father asked me to look after you while he's in hospital. If I had a choice, by God, I wouldn't. Once upon a time, Rachel, I had a life. I don't need this from you, day in, day out –'

'So go.'

As soon as we arrive at this point, I realize it was her intended destination. I've just given her what she wanted, an admission that I don't want to be here. Despite knowing that it's too late, I try again. 'Why can't we be friends? Why can't we get on? I only want what's best for you and Toby.'

'You just said you *didn't* want us.' She looks triumphant.

'Rachel, what I meant to say was that it's hard to enjoy looking after you when you're deliberately being difficult. That's all I meant to say. Actually, I didn't even mean to say that.'

She doesn't budge, standing there, arms firmly folded.

'OK, you win,' I exhale. 'I'm going.' *How could I have said that? Why couldn't I have just kept my mouth shut? She's a child. Remember that, Lucy. A child. Remind yourself every time she scowls at you, every time she pushes your buttons. Or just face facts – you're not cut out for step-parenting.*

In the hall, Toby has the phone to his ear and is pressing down the buttons. It melts my heart. I go to him, put down the glasses and plates, and let the clothes drop to the floor.

'You all right, Tobes?'

He's been chewing his sleeves. The cuffs are wet. Little holes have started to form, as if a family of moths has been on a picnic.

'What's Dad's number?'

'It's a little early to ring the hospital, Toby.' *And Greg's worst time of day.* 'I'll tell you what, why don't you come into the kitchen with me and help me make a . . . *what the hell can I interest him in making* . . . a Slush Puppy.' He loves Slush Puppies.

'Can you *make* Slush Puppies?'

'We can *try*.'

When Grace discovered that no one would tell me what was going on with Greg, she asked Karl to call the hospital to check on the patient's progress.

'It mightn't be the most ethical route in the world,' she said, 'but fuck that.'

Now she arrives with news, the boys and lunch. Shane runs uninhibited into the house. Jason, on hands and knees, isn't far behind. I catch Rachel looking down from the landing. I pretend not to notice. Toby comes out from the kitchen.

'Hi, guys,' he says to the guests.

'Hi, Toby,' everyone replies, in various stages of language development.

'Hey, Rachel, you coming down?' calls Grace.

'Yep,' she says, all smiles.

'D'you want to take Jase and Shane out the back to the swing boat?' Grace asks her.

'Sure,' she says obligingly. She picks up the baby. He looks at her, grins, then yanks her hair.

She laughs. 'OK, everyone, follow me.'

Grace and I watch them from the kitchen.

'Remind me to ask you round more often,' I say.

'I invited myself, remember?'

'Well, do it more often, then.'

We exchange smiles.

'So,' she says, all business suddenly, 'as I expected, they've started him on lithium and an antidepressant.'

'Oh, God, Grace. Hang on.' My stomach lurches. 'Let me sit down for this.'

'Sorry. We can see the guys from the table, can't we?'

'Yeah.'

'Will I make tea?'

'No, no. I'm fine now. Sorry.'

We sit, Grace keeping an eye on the children.

'Right, well you know that lithium stabilizes mood?'

'You told me.'

'And it's the standard treatment for bipolar disorder?'

I nod.

'Right, OK. Well, they've also started him on an antidepress-ant for the moment.'

'How soon will it start working?'

'It'll take a week or two to build up in the blood.'

'It would, wouldn't it?'

'They're also going to try to involve him in group therapy. So far, they haven't had much luck there.'

'What's that?'

She waves to one of the kids. 'Oh, just where some patients come together to talk about things.'

'Then I'm not surprised. He won't even talk to me.'

'These would be general conversations, you know, like what's in the newspapers.'

'What good would *that* do?'

'Get him out of his own head . . . But never mind that. They seem to be having some success on a one-to-one level. He's been allocated one nurse as a main point of contact. Someone called Betty. He seems to be opening up to her.'

'Oh. *Betty.*'

'You've met?'

'She was the one who told me Greg didn't want me speaking to them.'

'Right, well, he seems to speak to her, which is a start . . . Hopefully, in time, she'll be able to convince him to go along to psychotherapy . . .' She sees the confused look on my face. 'You know, group therapy, art therapy . . .'

'Art therapy?'

'Expressing yourself through art.'

'Sounds good.'

'At this stage, Lucy, Greg probably couldn't care less. Hope-fully, once the drugs kick in, and once he begins to trust Betty, he'll get more involved.'

At that, the children burst into the kitchen looking for juice. Grace gets up to get lidded beakers for hers. Rachel takes over from there. We wait till they've gone. It takes a while. Rachel's making a picnic.

'When can he come off the drugs?' I ask, when the door closes behind them.

'Once he's out of the depression, they'll probably try weaning him off the antidepressant. The lithium is for life, Lucy.'

'Life.'

'For most people, yes.'

'What's most?'

'Fifty to seventy per cent.'

'What about the others?'

'The lucky few who don't relapse? They might try weaning them off after, say, five years. But I don't want you to get your hopes up. For your own sake, you need to assume Greg'll be on it for life . . . But let's not think about that now. At the moment he's in a very, very dark place. If he says anything hurtful, tell yourself that it's the illness talking. Try not to take it personally.'

'Easy to say.'

'All the more reason for you to have your own life outside this. Your job. Your interests.'

'Interests! Are you kidding? Where'll I find time for interests?'

'I'm here, Lucy. You know that.' She takes both my hands in hers. 'You'll get through this.'

I said something similar to Greg. Had he felt as hopeless, hearing it?

'This doesn't have to spell disaster. I know lots of people who lead fulfilled and happy lives with bipolar disorder.'

Happy and fulfilled. Not normal, though. Not normal.

★

240

Art therapy's my chance to get involved. Or so I think. When I suggest it to Betty, she has a different view.

'Lucy, with all due respect, while Greg needs your support, he doesn't need your *involvement* in his care. You're not a therapist.'

'I need to help.'

'I understand that. But Greg has to be allowed to regain his strength at his own pace. If he'd a broken leg, you wouldn't rush him to hop out of bed and run around. Think of this the same way. Greg's in competent hands. You should be concentrating on your own health now. This is a difficult time. You need to keep your strength up – get plenty of sleep, fresh air, good food. Have you thought of joining a support group?'

'So there's nothing I can actually do?'

'Have you read those leaflets I gave you?'

'Well, eh . . . not yet.'

'It would help you to understand some of what Greg's going through and why this takes time.'

And so it seems that everyone's telling me the same thing. I have to let Greg fight his fight alone until he's ready for me to join in. But it doesn't feel right.

On my way back to Greg's house, I call in at home.

Dad's in the garden.

'Hi, Dad, is Mum in?' I ask, walking past him.

He looks surprised. 'Everything OK?'

'Yeah, yeah, fine. Is she inside?'

'Kitchen,' he says, his trowel suspended in mid-air.

In I go, a woman on a mission. She's at the sink.

'Mum?'

Her rubber-gloved hands lift out of the water as she turns.

'Lucy,' she says. 'Is everything all right?'

Is it so weird I want to talk to my mother? 'Everything's fine, Mum. Can we sit down?'

Looking concerned, she starts to peel off the gloves, never an easy job, though she has it perfected.

When we've settled, I say, 'I just wanted to say thanks for everything.'

She looks confused.

'Everything you've ever done for me, every meal you've ever cooked, every pair of jeans you've ever washed. I mean it, thank you so much, Mum.'

Her face relaxes into a smile. 'What's brought this on? Had a bad day?'

'You could say that. I'm finally seeing parenting from the other side.' I think of Rachel. 'Was I *very* difficult?'

'No, Lucy, you weren't.'

'I was, though, wasn't I?' I remember years of arguments.

'You weren't any more difficult than other teenagers, including myself.'

I can't imagine her a teenager. 'I'm sorry, Mum.'

'For nothing.'

'How did you do it?'

She sighs. 'Well, not perfectly, that's for certain. I've made my mistakes, Lucy.'

'No, no, you haven't. You were great. I just never appreciated it.'

'I pushed you too hard. So hard I pushed you away.'

I'm amazed to hear her speak like this. I never thought she noticed.

And she seems to see that in my face. 'Your father and I had a long chat when you were in France. I know you don't call home much at the best of times, but when you were away and didn't call, I got a bit down. It made me face up to the way things really are between us. I talked to Dad about it.'

Wow!

'I'm one of life's worriers, Lucy. When it comes to my children especially. The minute you tell me something, I'm worrying about the implications. And instead of keeping all those useless fears to myself, I blurt them out. I'm trying to be helpful. But all I'm doing is interfering. In trying to protect you, I'm telling you how to live your life. And I'm sorry.'

I'm too stunned to speak.

Then she smiles. 'But I've been "working on it", as he'd say himself. I don't know if you've noticed?' She looks hopeful.

I don't tell her that I've noticed little outside of Greg lately. What I do say is: 'Dad used to tell me how you only wanted the best for us. I saw that as a negative. Until now. God, it's so *hard* to do it right, isn't it, Mum? All I could ever see was what you were doing wrong. Never what you were doing right. And never the effort you put in – or the worry.' I take a deep breath. 'Well, I appreciate it now, if that's any comfort.'

'It is, Lucy. It is.'

We're holding hands across the table when Dad peeps into the kitchen.

'Crisis over?' he asks.

'No crisis,' says Mum, smiling at me. And for the first time in my life I think I see pride in her face. Maybe it was there all along, and I was too stubborn to notice.

'Good,' says Dad. 'Good. Any more of that rhubarb tart left?'

'Something arrived for you,' says Rob as soon as I get back.

Lying in the kitchen sink, immersed in water, is an enormous bouquet of sunflowers. I look at him. *Who could be sending flowers?*

'There's a card with them,' he says. I can tell he's curious.

I open it. And smile. Fint, offering his services in whatever way he can.

'Secret admirer?'

'No. Just a very good friend.'

26

Rachel won't do anything for me. Neither will she go any-where. Until I suggest that we visit Jason and Shane. That she'll do. And so we go.

'Hi, guys,' says Grace. 'What a lovely surprise!' She opens the door fully and stands aside. Walking down a particularly messy hall, she adds, 'Dad's here.'

Damn. 'His car isn't outside.'

'Mum's gone shopping in it.'

It's too late to turn round. How can I keep Rachel and Toby from talking to him? He answers that himself, tucked away as he is in the dining room, surrounded by bits of Grace's hoover.

I stick my head in. 'Hi, Dad.'

He looks up. 'Oh, hi, love.' He catches sight of the children behind me. 'Hello,' he says, smiling, 'you must be Rachel and Toby.'

I open the door wider.

'Hi,' they both say.

'You don't mind if I keep going here, love? If I leave it now, I'll never get it back together.'

'No, no, that's fine. OK, come on, guys.'

'Would you like a hand?' Rachel asks him.

He looks up at her, a strip of black grease running down his nose. 'You know, that'd be great. I love a bit of company when I'm working. Lucy used to be my helper when she was a little girl.'

She ignores that.

'Right, then. Hand me that screwdriver over there. The one with the red handle.'

Like a shot, she obliges.

Toby starts to look interested, so I offer him a drink. That works. I close the dining-room door and cross my fingers. In the kitchen, Jason's busy gnawing on building blocks. Toby finds a truck and begins to race Shane, who has a Ferrari. It's good to see him with children closer to his own age. No one to take over, smother him. Grace makes coffee, and the two of us sit at the table, keeping an eye on the boys. I ask her what they're doing to the kitchen cupboards. Work seems to be in progress.

She lowers her voice. 'Don't talk to me about those bloody cupboards. If I hear the words "preparation is nine tenths of the law" one more time, I'll scream.'

'What are you doing, painting over them?'

'Oooh, no, not just painting. That would be sloppy. First, we're sanding them down, *then* we're going to paint them. Sorry, *I'm* going to paint them. Kevin will project manage the job, supervise the entire operation. Give me practical little tips. Honest to God, there are times when I could throttle him. D'you know what I spent the morning doing? In between feeding and changing children, that is?'

'No.'

'Filling in holes and irregularities in the woodwork. I told him that it's wood, it's supposed to have irregularities, and do you know what he said? There's other people's wood and there's *our* wood.'

I smile. To me, that's sounds like such a simple, straightforward argument. No one being accused of not loving, not caring, deserting.

'If I suddenly jump up and start filling in the children's

chicken pox marks with stopping, you'll know I've finally flipped.'

'What's stopping?'

'You don't know what stopping is?' she says in mock horror. 'Lucy, you haven't lived. You use it on wood instead of Pollyfilla. It's *fantastic*. I'll have to get you some.'

I laugh. Then stop myself. 'Outside of the cupboards, how's it going?'

'I don't know. I'm trying, Lucy. I am really trying.'

'Maybe it's not the best time for DIY, though. Maybe you should just get out of the house, have fun together.'

'Kevin? Fun?' She looks at me as if to say, 'You must be joking.' 'Anyway, forget the perfectionist, how are you?'

'Freezing.' I run my hands up and down my arms. 'You don't have a jumper I could borrow, do you?' I feel shivery and tired. Grace disappears and returns with a jumper and socks. I'm especially thrilled with the socks. They're so snug, and homely. I start to get teary. I know she's going to talk about it, so I stop her before she does. 'Let's not,' I say.

After coffee, she shoos me away. 'Go on. Show your face in the office. They'll be fine here.'

'They'll be *happier* here. But what about you?'

'Lucy. You're doing me a favour. Shane and Jason are occupied. And when Rachel's finished in there, she'll take over. Honestly, go. It's actually easier for me with them here.'

I hope that Dad will work in his usual way – in silence – and that my mother will be back shortly to collect him.

Fint and I hug, everything forgotten, forgiven, without a word. He cancels his plans for the afternoon and takes me through all that's been happening – staff issues, proposals they've been putting together, current clients. We troubleshoot, brainstorm. Work. It feels good to have my opinion sought and listened to as if it counts for something, to feel the adrenalin of an office environment, to be reminded I have a brain. I leave with two not-so-major jobs to get working on. Grace was right. I needed another focus.

I'm not the only one. Back at the house, having collected the children, I'm lifting a pile of laundry from the wash basket when I feel someone behind me. It's Rachel. I brace myself for a complaint, an unreasonable request, a problem basically.

'You've a nice dad,' she says, almost shyly.

I remain cautious. 'Did you have a good time?'

She nods. 'I like helping out.'

I smile. 'Good.' I go back to the wash basket.

'I used to help Dad all the time . . . Before.'

I straighten up, turn back to her, surprised that we're still involved in what might be becoming – I'm still not sure – our first proper conversation.

'Do you think your dad would ever need a hand with anything else?'

I hide my surprise. 'I'm sure he would, Rachel.'

'Can you ask him?'

'Yes, of course I'll ask him.'

'Thanks.' And then she's gone.

Later when they're asleep, I call Dad.

'You were a big hit today.'

'Ah, she's a little dote.'

Strange. Though she's a child, I've never seen Rachel as little. And never as 'a dote'.

'She reminds me of you.'

'She's not a bit like me.'

'No?'

'*No.*'

248

'She's very quiet,' he says.

I say nothing, which I realize, too late, probably proves his point.

'Angry,' he says.

'You can say that again.'

'I used to know a little girl like that.'

Listen to the psychologist. 'If you're talking about me, you're wrong.'

'Your mother didn't make you angry?'

I'm not going to admit to anything.

'And your sister?'

'Wrong. I was *never* angry with Grace.' *I might have been jealous . . .*

'What did you call her again? Little Miss Perfect? Don't tell me you weren't the teensiest bit angry?'

'Guess who's making me angry now? Anyway, I just called to say thanks. You seemed to cheer her up.'

'That's all right, love. I enjoyed her company. As I always did yours . . . my little helper.'

Why does that make me feel weepy?

'You know,' he continues, 'maybe you should think about letting her help around the house.'

'She'd never do anything for me.'

'Let her think it's her idea.'

'I don't know.'

'Well, why don't you let her come over here some afternoon? I'll think of something she can give me a hand with. And you could probably do with a break from each other.'

'You can say that again.'

'That settles it, then. And sure, bring the young lad as well. Toby. Your mother took a big shine to him. He's a looker, isn't he?'

'Like his dad.'

'How *is* Greg? Now that you're back, you must bring him round.'

'He's kind of busy at the moment.'

'Oh, yes, I'd forgotten.'

'It's not like that, Dad. He'd love to call round. He's just busy. Up to his eyes.'

'I know,' he says, not sounding convinced.

'Listen, I gotta go. I'll see you soon, OK?'

'Bye, Lucy. Good to see you today.'

'You too.'

The following morning my mobile rings.

'Is that Lucy?'

'Ben.' Inside I groan. I forgot to tell them we were home.

'I got your number from Hilary. I've been ringing the villa for days. I've been trying Greg's mobile phone number . . .'

Damn. 'Oh, I'm sorry, Ben, I think it needs recharging.'

'Why haven't you been contactable? We've been so worried. We were going to fly over when Hilary gave us your number.'

Hearing Hilary's name has the same effect as always. It's like receiving bad news. 'Ben. We're home.'

'You're home? In Ireland?'

'Yes. I'm sorry we haven't got around to calling you. Things have been a bit hectic.'

'How long are you back?'

'A few days.' Over a week.

'And you didn't think to let us know our grandchildren were in the country? We *do* have a right to know where they are, Lucy.'

'I realize that,' I say, struggling to remain calm. Why is he talking about 'rights'?

'What are you doing back? Was there a problem?'

'Yes.' I've worked it out. 'The heat. It was way too hot for the children.'

'Ah, yes. As a matter of fact, I'm surprised you didn't come home sooner.'

'Well, we're back now.'

'Is Greg there?'

'Not at the moment.'

'Why is he never available when I call?'

Do I really need to answer this? 'Bad timing, I guess.'

'Is something going on, something I should know about?'

'Ben. Nothing is, as you put it, going on. You can see your grandchildren any time. I'm sorry you had a problem getting through, but everything is fine. We're just settling back in. If you'd like to call over and see the children, that would be fine.'

'Eh, maybe you could drop them to us. We'd be more comfortable with that.'

'Fine.' *What am I, his personal slave?* 'When would suit?'

'Next Saturday?'

'What time?'

'Three?'

'Fine. Rachel will be able to show me where you live?'

He gives me the address anyway. Just in case.

I have five days to figure out what to do.

Professor Power picks that day to convince Greg that he should explain to his children why he's in hospital, the rationale being that it would be good for Greg to start seeing them again and for the children to know the truth, rather than build imaginary fears. It makes sense. It's the timing I'm worried about. Couldn't we leave it until after they've seen Ben and Ruth? I'm not sure they're ready to hear that Greg's in hospital suffering from a psychiatric illness.

The children are so excited at the thought of seeing Greg. They try to think of things that will cheer him up. And so we buy a hanging fern and little red watering can – Rachel thinks that Greg should have something to look after. Toby remembers wine gums. We make posters for the room. Toby hums while he works. Rachel forgets to snap at me. Art therapy has a convert.

I drive up to the hospital entrance, where we've arranged to collect Greg. *Will he be there? Will he look OK? Will the children worry when they see how pale and gaunt he is? Has he remembered to shave? Stubble emphasizes everything.* All three of us peer out for the first sight of him.

There he is! Waiting. A lone, thin figure. When he smiles, I see the effort he's making. We pull up. The children jump out and run to him. They cling to each other. A car honks behind me, reminding me we're in zero-tolerance Dublin. Rachel gives the driver the finger. I'm shocked but strangely proud of her gutsy attitude. I get out to help Greg into the car, as if he's some kind of invalid. What am I *doing*?

Driving off, I'm gripped by a *Thelma and Louise* urge to keep on going. Never come back. The children bombard their father with questions, and he struggles to keep up. It's a short trip across town to Sandymount strand, the only obstruction being the south city traffic. When the car doors open, the salty sea breeze rushes in. We walk down on to the strand. The tide is so far out that the balance of sand to sea seems wrong, as if the moon has pulled too hard, leaving a margin of blue at the edge of a golden page. The sky seems to stretch for ever in all directions. The sand, at first, is dry and loose, then damp and corrugated. Little saltwater streams and pools, left by the outgoing tide, glisten in the sun, reminding me of milk on a surface of porridge. We take off our shoes, roll up our trousers and walk. Huge brown jellyfish lie stranded, looking like alien spacecraft that have landed for a convention. A giant seagull struts by as though he owns the beach. As we get closer to the sea, the line of white dots at the water's edge becomes a flock of seagulls. A dog runs among them, causing them to lift and fall like a Mexican wave. No matter what the beach has to offer in terms of fun, adventure or excitement, the children never leave their father's side. Toby slips his hand into his father's and starts to skip, his skinny body light and carefree. It is so good to have Greg back with us again, breathing the salty air, experiencing the breeze on his face, in his hair. We spend at least an hour on that beach.

Almost back at the car, Greg stops at a wooden bench that looks out on to the strand.

'Let's sit for a while.'

This is it.

He settles at one end, Toby on his lap, Rachel next to him. I'm at the other. Bookends.

'Guys,' he says. 'I want to explain why I'm in hospital.'

'It's OK, Dad. We know,' says Toby. 'You're exhausted.'

'Well, there's a little more than that.' He takes a breath. 'I have a sickness that makes me sad sometimes. Other times it makes me very excited.'

They take time to digest that.

Toby is first to speak. 'But it's OK to be sad, Dad. You said.' He looks at Greg for confirmation.

'I did. And it's OK to cry when something happens to make you sad.'

'Yeah, you're always telling us that.'

'It's just that if there's no reason to be sad and you're sad anyway – all the time – well, that's not good, is it?'

Toby shakes his head wildly. 'No, that'd be . . . sad.'

'And not good,' says Greg.

'No,' agrees Toby.

Rachel's quiet. Taking it all in.

'And it's OK to get excited too,' continues Greg. 'Lots of things are exciting –'

'Like Christmas and birthdays and fireworks and when you get on to the next level with your Game Boy.'

'Exactly,' says Greg, smiling. 'But being hyper isn't good.'

'No.' Toby shakes his head again. 'When you have Coke or Skittles or something you get hyper. And that's not good 'cause you go bananas. Isn't that right, Dad?'

'Yes, son.' Greg kisses the top of his head. 'But you eventually go back to normal, don't you?'

'Yeah.'

Rachel's eyes are fixed on her father. She is oblivious to the breeze whipping her hair across her face.

'Well,' says Greg, 'I have a sickness that makes me hyper for weeks. And that's not good.'

'No . . . Why not, again?'

'Well, it can make me do silly things, and can make me hurt people.' He looks at me meaningfully.

'Did you hurt someone?' asks Toby.

'I think so,' Greg says, without taking his eyes from mine.

My throat burns. Tears well. I smile.

'Who did you hurt?' asks Toby.

'In France. I think I hurt you all.'

'No, you didn't,' rushes Toby. 'You never slap us.'

'I wasn't very nice to you, though, was I? Do you remember? I was hyper and I forgot about you, the people I loved. And that wasn't right, was it?'

'Is that *hurting*?'

'Yes, Toby.'

'Is that because you were sick, Dad?' asks Rachel. 'I thought you were just cross with us.'

He puts his arm round her. 'No, Rachel, I wasn't cross with

you. You didn't do anything wrong. If I snapped at you, it was my fault, not yours. I wasn't well. I had, still have, this sickness. This sickness called bipolar disorder.'

'Dad?'

'Yes, Tobes?'

'Was it the sickness that made you talk funny?'

Greg nods. 'Anything I did in France that I don't normally do was all because of the sickness. And I'm sorry. So sorry. I didn't mean to frighten you or upset you . . .' His voice falters. I'm afraid his tears will upset them. But that only shows how little I know about children. They put their arms round him. 'It's OK, Dad. It's OK.'

And so four people sit on a bench. Two crying – the adults. And two comforting one of the adults and thankfully not noticing the other. Greg pulls a handkerchief from his trouser pocket and runs it over his face. He sighs. 'You're such good kids. I'm glad we had this chat. I wanted to explain, in case you were worried about what happened in France. Were you?' He looks from one to the other.

'Kinda,' says Toby.

'Yes.' Rachel.

'Well, everything's going to be OK. I'm taking medicine. And I'm not so sad now.'

'And you're not hyper,' reassures Toby.

'No.'

'Poor Dad,' says Toby, snuggling into him.

'Hey, guess what? The doctor said you can come and see me every day now, if you like.'

'*Great*,' they both say.

'And soon I'll be coming home for a weekend.'

'When?' asks Rachel.

'Well, maybe not this weekend. But next weekend. Maybe. How's that?'

'Great,' she says.

'Good,' says Toby. 'Can we go and get your presents now? They're in the boot. They're really good.'

'Let's do that.'

The children hop up. Greg reaches out and takes my hand, the first time in weeks that he has voluntarily touched me. In doing so, he has touched my heart. As we return to the car, I marvel at how straightforward bipolar disorder can be when explained a certain way – a sickness that makes you sad and excited. Not something to be ashamed of. Just something that happens. Of course, that's when you're talking to children. With adults it's different. With adults it's more complicated. And with Ben and Ruth, I guess, it's impossible. They'll never understand. At the hospital entrance, I'm about to start the goodbyes when Greg asks the children if they'd like to see where he sleeps. Another surprise. Another step forward.

That night, as darkness falls, I have a visitor. I'm surprised to see Hilary but more surprised at how she looks, almost unrecognizable because of the amount of weight she has gained. I have never before appreciated the extent to which fat can distort a person's appearance. Her face has changed shape, the lower half dominating, her features losing prominence. It doesn't help that her hair is greasy and scraped back.

'I need to talk to Greg.'

I notice a stain on the front of her sweatshirt. 'I'm sorry, Hilary, Greg's not here.'

'Yes, he is. I know he is. He just doesn't want to talk to me.' She steps closer.

I hold the door and am firm when I repeat, 'Greg isn't here.'

'Well, where is he, at this time of night?' she asks, as if trying to catch me out.

'Hilary, I don't think that's any of your business and frankly you've a nerve showing up here after what you did.' I suddenly understand my mistake. The last thing I should be doing is engaging in conversation with her.

'What *exactly* am I supposed to have done?'

'Nothing. Forget it. I'll tell Greg you called.' I make to close the door.

'If you're talking about Ben and Ruth,' she rushes, 'I just told them the truth.'

'What do you want, Hilary?' I make myself sound tired.

'To talk to Greg.'

'Fine. I'll tell him you called. He has your number.'

'Why isn't he answering his phone?' She takes another step forward.

Nervous now, I slip my foot against the door. 'I don't know. I'll get him to call you, OK? Now goodnight, Hilary.' I close the door. Lean against it. Don't move. Listen. Hoping she'll go. I hear nothing. Then, after what seems like an age, I hear footsteps walk away. I breathe a sigh of relief. *It's just Hilary*, I tell myself. *Hilary. What can she do?* But there's something invasive about her coming to the house. It reminds me that she could do so at any time. During the day when the children are here. Any time. It would be so easy to make a scene.

27

Dad needs a hand to re-grout the bathroom, fix a doorbell and a leaking tap. Mum could do with help in the kitchen. Rachel is called in on maintenance duty. Toby's culinary expertise may stem the domestic crisis. I'm told to clear off. I make a much needed appearance at the office, where I complete one of the jobs I've been working on and make good progress on the other. When I get back to collect the children, they nag me to stay for dinner. After all, Toby has cooked it single-handedly, with just a bit of guidance.

'I'd love to stay, but we're having Rob for dinner.'

Poor Toby, his little face.

'Why don't you just ring him and invite him here?' Mum asks. 'And Greg, of course. We've made plenty. Or should I say, *Toby's* made plenty.' She puts her hand on his skinny little shoulder.

He looks so proud.

'Greg can't make it, Mum. He's up to his tonsils.'

'Yeah, he's in hospital,' explains Toby helpfully.

Both parents look at me, then at each other.

Damn.

'In hospital?' asks my mother.

'Yeah. He's sad but not hyper and he'll be able to come home, not this weekend but next weekend,' announces Toby matter-of-factly.

'It's bipolar disorder,' confirms Rachel.

'Yeah. He has to take medicine,' says Toby. 'I saw his bed. It's boring. But we brought in lots of stuff, so it's much nicer now.'

In fairness to my parents, they say no more. Mum opens her mouth but shuts it again.

'Come on,' I say, defeated, 'let's go. Thanks, Mum and Dad.' I kiss them both. What'll I tell Greg? And how can I bring them to Ben and Ruth's now?

'Wait a minute,' says Mum, and she disappears into the house. She hurries out with a big Tupperware container filled with dinner.

'You have to try this. It's delicious,' she says to me, looking at Toby. 'Would you like to carry it, Toby?'

He nods shyly but is silently proud.

'Bye, my darlings,' she says, kissing them both. The warmth she has for them is something we never experienced as children, and I wonder if that's because she doesn't feel responsible for them in the way that she did for us. She can enjoy their company without worrying for their future.

'Can we come again?' asks Rachel.

All eyes on me.

'Of course, if it's OK with you,' I say, addressing my parents.

'We'd love to have them, any time.' I almost hear them thinking, *Especially as . . .*

When we're in the car and driving off, Rachel says, 'Is it a secret that Dad's in hospital?'

'Eh, well . . .' *Think, Lucy, think.* 'It's not a *secret . . . as such* . . . It's just that . . . your dad . . . well . . . he isn't ready to tell everyone.'

'Why not?'

'He just wants peace and quiet . . . at the moment. And . . . if everyone knows he's in hospital, they'll all come and visit and he's not ready for that yet.'

'But he's sad,' says Toby. 'Visitors will cheer him up. They can bring presents, like us.'

'I know. It's just that . . . well, your dad doesn't have the energy for any more visitors other than us and Rob at the moment.'

I can't look them in the eye. Whatever Toby may think, I know for a fact that Rachel doesn't believe me.

Since Greg's chat with the children, our routine has changed. Rob comes with us to the hospital now. We collect Greg and go for a walk or coffee. When it's almost time to head back, Rob takes the kids off for ten or fifteen minutes, while Greg and I have time alone. Having everyone there makes things easier for me, as Greg makes more of an effort. I worry, though, that it tires him.

We're feeding ducks in Herbert Park when I tell him about my parents knowing. 'Greg, the only way to keep this a secret is to lock up the children.'

He's quiet for a moment, then looks at me sideways. 'Where'll we lock them?' he deadpans.

I do a double-take. *Is he joking? Is he actually joking?*

He shrugs.

I smile.

'Forget about it,' he says. 'Nothing you could have done.'

'No.'

We circle the pond slowly, then Greg speaks. 'Rob says you're doing too much.'

For him to think like that, outside his own head, is major progress. Even I know that. Of course, he *is* worrying. But I can do something about that. 'Greg, I'm fine. I'm great. I don't know why Rob said that.'

'I asked him.'

'Well, he's wrong. Really.'

'Is he, though? Your job, the kids, the house, me. You can't do it all.'

'I can. Honestly. It's not a problem.'

'Cut back on something. Maybe you don't need to see me so often.'

'Are you kidding? You're my priority in all of this.' That, I see now, gets forgotten in the day-to-day hassle of survival. 'I love you, Greg. I want to be with you.'

'What about work? You don't need to, you know. I can support you, Luce.'

'I like my job. I need to work.'

He scratches his head. 'Thought you might say that.'

I watch our feet as we walk in silence.

'How're you paying for things?' he asks.

'Greg, please, don't worry about money, everything's fine.'

'We should have a joint account. No, sure, why don't I give you my card and pin number?' He stops, begins to tap his pockets. It's weird. I did resent paying what seems a huge amount to run a house that size and look after two children, but, now that he's offered, I don't want his money. We're supposed to be a team. 'Greg, please.'

He finds his wallet, pulls out his card. 'Here take it. The number is . . . Hang on. What's the fucking number? Jesus.' He hits his forehead with the heel of his hand. 'OK. Don't worry. I'll sort something out with Rob . . . And I want you to get a cleaner. Catherine always had a cleaner.'

'I don't need someone to pick up after me.'

'There's more than you . . . Rob will sort it. Don't worry.'

Maybe it would be good.

'What about a part-time childminder?' he asks.

'No, Greg. Let's not land someone new on Rachel and Toby right now. Let's see how we cope alone. In a weird way, it's an opportunity for us to crack this – it's them and me. Sink or swim.'

*

The inevitable phone call comes at nine. Dad. Timing it beautifully. I can picture him working it out: 'What time d'you think she'll be back from the hospital?'

'Hi, Dad,' I say, tired.

'Hello, love.'

I wait.

He waits.

Then, 'Why didn't you tell us?'

'I'm sorry. I wanted to. Greg doesn't want anyone to know.'

A second's silence. 'Understandable.'

I don't have anything to say.

'So, how's he doing?'

'He seemed better today.' I yawn.

'Will I come over?'

'I'm a bit tired, Dad.'

'All right, love. I just wanted to say that your mother and I want to help.'

'I'm fine, Dad, thanks.'

'Are you getting any time on your own?'

'Grace takes the children if I've to go into the office.'

'Grace knows?'

'Yes, Grace knows. I asked her advice before I knew what was wrong. Then I had to ask her not to tell. Sorry.'

'Lucy, there's nothing to be sorry for. I understand. I'm glad you've had Grace. We want to help too. We'd like to take the children for a few hours a day. We'd love to have them. We've been feeling a bit lonely lately, and they're dotes.'

'And that's the only reason?'

'Well, you *could* do with a bit of time on your own, even just to spend it at the office. At least you'd be getting away from things for a while. You're still a young woman.'

I need the reminder. 'I suppose I could do with showing

my face in there a bit more . . . actually, Dad, that would be great . . . If you don't mind.'

'We wouldn't have offered –'

'You would.'

'Put it to the children. See what they think. If they're all right with it, that's what we'll do.'

I feel my shoulders relax a little.

Rob hires a cleaner through a local agency to do three hours twice a week. Tracy arrives like a fairy godmother. All she's missing is the gold dust. The wash basket stops overflowing. The Mount Everest of ironing vanishes. It's possible to see whole pieces of furniture again, to see a room as it's supposed to look. Dust and cobwebs I've always meant to get to, simply disappear. Hearing the hoover is a relief. I managed to keep up with the kitchen floor, but all other rooms are suffering serious neglect. Next time, she says, she'll do the brass on the front door. *There's brass on the front door?* I've been struggling on an endless production line of cleaning, ironing, cooking, Internet shopping (which I'm *convinced* is no quicker), so tired that my head has become hard to hold up. The number of times I've caught myself leaning my forehead against walls, tables, the steering wheel, the wooden slats in the airing cupboard. So hard to lift back up, so much energy required. Even listening takes such *concentration*. And now here's Tracy. Like the sun coming out.

Over a two-week period I've fielded four calls from Phyllis, Greg's mother. Rob made the mistake of telling her we were back. He had the sense not to mention where Greg was, though, and for that I suppose we should be grateful. When she calls, I tell her Greg's out. I ring the hospital. Greg leaves it a while, then calls her back. It's been working, except for one thing. Why, she wants to know, hasn't he invited her round for Sunday lunch? So, instead of Greg using his first day at home to relax and to settle back to normality, he decides to put on a performance. Without consulting me, he invites her to lunch. When I hear, I nearly explode. He doesn't need that pressure. What if he can't handle it? What if the children mention the hospital? What if she cops that something's up? And what if my cooking isn't up to scratch? There is no way I can handle Ben and Ruth on the same weekend. I'm only human. I phone to cancel. Ben's not pleased. He wonders if he should worry. I feel like telling him to go right ahead, he seems to enjoy it. Instead, I arrange their visit for the following Saturday and try to put worrying about it on hold.

We collect Greg around ten. He's looking better, his blue shirt picking up the colour of his eyes. It makes him look less pale. He had a hair cut yesterday in honour of the event. He's cleanly shaven. All round, a big improvement. But enough to fool his mother? We get to the house in plenty of time, wander down to the sea, something Greg misses. Toby and Greg roll up their trousers and paddle on the steps. Rachel collects stones for skimming. I sit perched on a rock, hands around my knees, staring out at Bray Head and Sugarloaf Mountain. A cormorant colony, on an island rock close to shore, spread their black wings to dry. They look ominous.

After an hour or so Greg starts to explain to the children why we shouldn't upset 'Gran' by mentioning that he hasn't been well. I slip away to the kitchen. She likes pork steak, cut into slivers, covered in flour, then fried. Can't be *that* difficult. I make a start, just in case. I take it from the fridge, cut open the plastic wrapping and watch watery blood ooze out. No matter how many times I've cooked it, I still haven't got used to raw meat. There's no getting away from the fact that it has been a living, breathing thing. It smells, but, as I've never experienced the pleasure of raw pork steak before, I can't tell whether it's a normal or an abnormal smell. I check the fridge. No alternatives. I check my watch. Too late to nip to the supermarket.

I ring Grace.

'What does raw pork steak smell like?'

'Jesus, Lucy, how can I describe the smell of raw pork steak? It smells like raw meat, what can I say?'

No help. 'I know but how d'you know if it's gone off ?'

'It smells gone off.'

Getting nowhere here. 'What else?'

'Does it look sort of greeny-grey?'

'No,' I say, lifting it with a piece of kitchen paper and slowly twirling it around. 'It looks OK.'

'Then it probably is, Luce.'

'I don't want to poison her.'

'You sure?' she laughs. 'Listen, I've got to go, they're killing each other.'

'Hurry, Jason's only a baby.'

'He's doing the killing.'

'Oh, right.'

'Cook it, Lucy. It's fine. Got to go.'

Phyllis, as is her custom, arrives by taxi. I stay at the door while Greg and the children go to greet her. Greg helps her from the car. She has gifts and hugs for Rachel and Toby.

'Come meet Lucy, Ma,' says Greg, his arm around her.

Here they come. She's about ten years older than my mum but looks more. Thin, short and slightly stooped, her face a road map of lines, her silver hair yellowing at the front. Still, she's wirier than I expected. When she speaks, her voice is deep and hoarse. 'Lucy,' she says, with a quick nod. That's it.

'Lovely to meet you,' I say with a smile. I put out my hand.

She shakes it, initially loosely as if testing my grip, then finishing off with a tight squeeze before letting go. I catch her looking at my toe ring and can't believe I forgot to remove it.

Once inside Greg pours drinks.

'Aren't you having something yourself, Greg?' she asks.

'Nah, not today,' he says. 'Rough night, Ma.'

'I know it's a mortal sin to smoke inside, but would it be all right if I'd a quick one?'

'Go ahead.'

I remove myself to the kitchen, where I make a semi-success of lunch. Rachel, under her father's instruction, helps me serve. We sit down to eat. While Phyllis asks the children if they're looking forward to going back to school, I check faces as they bite into their pork.

She turns to me and smiles. 'And what do you do, Lucy?'

'I'm a graphic designer.' The children eye me with interest. We've never discussed my job.

'And what's that when it's at home?' Her laugh is husky.

'We design packaging, logos, book covers, pretty much anything, really. We . . .' She has stopped looking at me. Has she stopped listening? Am I boring her or going too fast? Maybe design is too modern a concept. I stop. If she wants to know more, she'll ask.

'Don't stop now. This is fascinating,' she says in a bored tone.

Confused, I look to Greg for help.

'Lucy's an artist,' he says, smiling at me.

'I *knew* you were good at drawing,' says Toby.

'I'm learning how to sew, Gran,' says Rachel. 'Lucy's mum is teaching me. She's really good.'

'You go to Lucy's parents?'

'Yeah, we go all the time, when Lucy's at work,' says Toby cheerfully.

I shift. I've never brought them to see her.

'What?' she asks, looking at her son. 'Is Lucy *living* here? Where's Hilary?'

There's an awkward silence.

'Yes, Lucy is living here,' says Greg.

'Just until Dad gets out of . . .' Rachel stops when she sees the warning look her father is giving her.

'And we let Hilary go,' Greg says.

She looks at me, then back at her son. 'You sacked her? Why?'

'It wasn't working out,' he says.

'But she was *so good* with the kids.'

'I *know*,' says Rachel, narrowing her eyes at me.

'I'm shocked,' says Phyllis.

No one speaks.

She lifts a piece of pork with her fork and examines it. Shakes her head. 'They make such good meals at the home.'

Greg looks at me as if to say, 'Don't mind her.' But he doesn't say anything in my defence.

'*Catherine* was a *great* cook,' she says, staring off into space as if dreaming of wonderful times gone by. 'Speaking of food,' she says, turning to her son, 'are you eating properly? You've lost weight. You don't look well.'

He pretends he hasn't heard, cutting into a piece of meat.

'You work too hard, Greg. Always have. You should let Lucy take care of you. Ah, but Lucy has her own priorities.'

What have I done to the woman?

'It's Catherine's anniversary next week. I think we should do something.'

'We'll talk about this another time, Ma.'

'I think we should put an announcement in the paper.'

'We'll discuss it *later*.'

The children's knives and forks have paused in mid-air.

267

'Such a great loss, she is. She was such a good wife. And mother.'

'*Fine*. Ma.'

'She could handle anything, could Catherine. Then again, she was older.'

'Excuse me,' I say and leave.

Greg follows me into the kitchen.

'Don't mind her.'

I turn to him. 'How can you let her talk on and on like that?'

'She's my mother.'

'Catherine this, Catherine that. As if I'm chopped liver.'

'She's just lonely. She doesn't mean it.'

'She means every word. I'm not going back in there. I'm going for a walk.'

'OK, fine. Run away.'

'Don't think I'm not tempted, Greg Millar, a million times a day.'

He looks wounded.

'I'm sorry, Greg. I didn't mean that.' But, in a way, I did. And he knows it.

He turns and goes back to his mother.

28

I stand, looking into dirty pots, reminders of the cooking frenzy I naively entered into earlier: the remains of potato I carefully mashed, pork steak I fussed over, broccoli I didn't overcook, carrots sliced longways, the way she likes them. *The old bat.* She's probably in there planning another offensive. I'd been doing so well with Greg, fighting all urges to admit how hard I'm finding everything. And now I've gone and sabotaged that with one thoughtless remark.

I go back. Try to make eye contact with him. Mouth 'Sorry.'

'Oh, Lucy, you're back,' she says.

Round two.

'I was just telling Rachel about the time her mother discovered she was pregnant with her. She was so happy . . .'

What about Toby? How can she even bring up pregnancy?

'Toby, are you finished?' I ask.

He nods.

'Come on, I want to show you something in the kitchen.'

'OK.'

'We'll see you later,' I say into the general air.

'What d'you want to show me?' he asks when we get to the kitchen.

I haven't a clue.

'Bubbles,' I say.

'Bubbles?'

'Yeah, let's make some. Let's make a load. Let's fill the kitchen with bubbles.'

'OK,' he says, perking up.

I sit him up beside the sink, put in the plug, hand him the washing-up liquid and blast on the water. As I watch bubbles multiplying like sparkly, happily dividing cells, I begin to see things in perspective. She doesn't matter. Only Greg does. And I've hurt him. Which is the last thing he needs. When she's leaving, I bring Toby out to say goodbye. As the back of her tiny head disappears up the driveway, the children go inside.

'I'll get a taxi,' Greg says, without moving.

'Greg, I am so sorry. I didn't mean that. I was just upset.'

'I wouldn't blame you if you did.'

'I didn't, though. Honestly. Why don't you come in and I'll make a cup of tea?'

'I need to go back, Lucy. This was a mistake.'

We drop him at the hospital, everyone silent. When we get home, the kids turn on the TV. I'm stacking the dishwasher when I hear someone's runners squeak on the floor behind me. I wipe my eyes and turn. It's Rachel, carrying a heap of plates in from the dining room. The gesture seems enormous.

'Thank you,' I say.

She half smiles and goes back out. When she brings in her grandmother's plate, she heads straight for the bin with it, as if trying to hide the fact it's hardly been touched. We work together in silence.

Eventually she speaks. 'She was kind of mean to you, wasn't she?'

'A bit.' I shake my head. 'But it doesn't matter.'

'Especially when you made her favourite dinner.'

I attempt a smile.

She tucks the hair that usually shields her face from me behind her ears, then fiddles with the coloured charity bands that adorn her wrist, before looking up at me with those dark eyes of hers. 'It's not just you, you know,' she says. 'She's like that with Rob's girlfriends too.'

'She is?'

'Yep.'

'Well, that makes me feel a whole lot better, Rachel. Thank you.'

'It's OK.' She looks out of the window.

Suddenly I feel for her. 'Things will get better, Rachel.'

'I'm going now.'

'OK.' I'm disappointed. 'Thanks for the help. And for what you've told me . . . You're a good kid.'

She gives me a you-can't-be-serious look.

That evening, round about ten, the doorbell rings. I think of Hilary and peer through the peephole. It's Rob. How does he always manage to look so cheery?

'Kids in bed?' he asks, as we walk down the hall.

'Rob, if they're not at the door two seconds after you arrive, assume they're in bed,' I say, smiling.

'So how did it go?' he asks when we reach the kitchen.

I look at him, realization dawning. 'That's why you're here, isn't it? You knew it'd be a disaster.'

'Well, let's just say I know my mother.'

I pull a Heineken from the fridge. This I need. 'Want one?'

'Only if you're having one.'

'Try and stop me.' I crack open two cans and pour. 'Let's go inside.' I need to get out of that kitchen.

'So,' he says, once we've settled, 'how awful was she, on a scale of one to ten?'

'Five hundred.'

'Ouch.'

I give him a rough outline.

'If I *ever* get married, remind me to live abroad,' he says.

'I don't know. You might be OK. She liked Catherine.'

He throws his head back and laughs. 'Are you serious? Catherine and my mother? They hated each other. Catherine refused to be in the same room with her.'

'But she said –'

'Lucy, if my mother was talking Catherine up, it was to bring you down.'

It takes a second for that to sink in.

'Don't take it personally,' he says, topping up his drink. 'Nobody's good enough for her boys, especially her eldest.'

So Rachel was right.

'Catherine was a hoot,' he says. 'She wouldn't put up with any crap. If the Old Dear was visiting, she'd arrange to be somewhere else.'

'And Greg was OK with that?'

'Yeah. I think so. Less tension. Sure, even if he wasn't, he didn't have much choice. Catherine was her own woman. Did her own thing. In fairness, I think she was right.'

I feel such a wimp.

'Catherine was straight. No bull. But no saint. Not till she died. That's when my mother canonized her.'

'Well, I'm not about to keel over to keep Phyllis happy.'

'Take my advice and stay out of her way. She's happiest when she can have her sons, especially her eldest, all to herself.'

'But why didn't Greg tell me that?'

'You have to understand something, Lucy. Greg has always been protective of her – ever since Da died. He lets her get away with anything. Won't have a bad word said against her. I don't see that changing. Take a leaf from Catherine's book. Love him but don't take any bull from his mother.'

I stare into my beer. 'I should be more like her, shouldn't I, Catherine?'

'No.' He looks bemused.

'Sometimes I think Greg was looking for another Catherine when he met me.'

'What makes you say that?'

'Don't you think we look alike?'

'*No*. You're dark like she was, but that's it. Your face is softer.'

'Maybe he didn't fall for me at all.'

'You've lost me.'

'Greg was probably hypomanic when we met.'

'Come again?'

'Hypomanic: in the earliest stages of mania. Remember the barbecue? Remember how you thought that he was acting out of character? Well, maybe he was. Maybe he was at the beginning of his first high. Maybe he didn't fall for me at all, but an idea of what I was.'

'Now *that* I don't believe.'

I lean forward. 'I've been reading all this stuff the hospital gave me and going into web site after web site and things keep hitting me. Like the fact that his depression might be my fault.'

'How d'you work that one out?'

'Rejection can trigger depression. After his high, I told him I was leaving. I couldn't take any more. What if I caused his depression?'

'Lucy, I think you're being deliberately pessimistic –'

'And then today I sent him tearing back to the hospital. Do you know what I told him? I told him I thought of running away a million times a day. Like that's just what he needs – more rejection. I'm afraid of what I might have done to him.'

He's quiet. 'Look, Lucy,' he says, 'I'm no expert. But I do know that Greg loves you. Even when he's down, he's thinking about you. He's always asking after you. "Is she doing OK? Is she doing too much?" He's never asked for my help before.

All of a sudden, he's asking me to organize money, a cleaner . . . I mean, no offence, I'm delighted to do it. You know that. I'm just making a point. He rang me about an hour ago and asked me to call over to make sure you were OK. He's about as low as a man can get, and he's still thinking about you. In my book, that says something.'

Of course that makes me worse. There he is, still caring for me after I told him I wanted to run away.

'Greg loves you, Lucy; I know my brother. Maybe you should stop reading all that stuff. Just go see him. And steer clear of my mother. Keep close to wonderful people like me.' He grins.

I produce a lop-sided smile.

'You'll get through this. I know you will. Trust me. I'm a teacher. We know everything.'

Funny how, of all people, it's Greg's happy-go-lucky brother who is helping to hold our relationship together, allowing me to understand why he stood by his mother, and why underneath it all he still worries about me.

Next day, walking up the quiet hospital corridor with Rob and the children, I'm terrified. I don't know what to expect. Will he have regressed? Will we find him lying on the bed, a pillow over his head, curtains drawn?

We get to the room. He isn't there. His roommate directs us to the exercise room. *An exercise room, really?* We find it. And Greg. He is pummelling a large black punch bag. I don't know whether it's all that action or the fact that punch bags automatically make whoever's laying into them more masculine, but he looks great, moving with determination and force. Rocky Millar. Well, not quite.

'Dad,' says Toby. 'Can I have a go?'

He turns. Smiles. 'Hey,' he says, very Rocky. 'OK. Come

on, a quick one.' He stands behind his son as he throws a few quick punches.

'Cool,' says Toby.

'Right. Let's go,' says Greg, grabbing a towel, running it over his face and throwing it across his shoulder. We follow as he strides from the room. Where has this energy come from, this confidence, determination? Rob and I exchange surprised glances. We drive to Greg's favourite destination, Sandymount strand, where we walk. Rob takes the children off for an ice cream while Greg and I sit together on the very same bench where he told Rachel and Toby about bipolar disorder.

'I started group therapy today.'

'Oh, Greg, that's great.' I can't understand it. I rejected him. The opposite is supposed to be happening.

'I made a decision. I'm going to get out of this mess. I'm going to do the art therapy, the group therapy, the psycho-therapy, every bloody therapy they have.' There is colour in his cheeks. Better than that. There is determination in his eyes.

'That's great.'

'I'm sorry, Lucy. I've been an idiot. I should have involved you. But I thought I was doing the right thing – protecting you from it all – when all I did was push you away. No wonder you wanted to leave. I don't ever want you to feel like that,' he says, taking my hand in his two. 'I'm so sorry about Phyllis. I should never have invited her. I should have known she'd be difficult.'

'Don't worry about it.'

'In future I'll take her out to lunch with the children, and maybe Rob. If that's OK with you.'

'That's a better idea.'

'It was Betty's.'

'Clever woman.'

'She said something else.'

'What?'

'Most first trips home end in disaster.' He bumps me with his shoulder.

Hilary is making me increasingly nervous, phoning the house in search of Greg and then slamming down the receiver when I tell her he's not there. When she turns up at the door again late one night, I decide to finish this before either of the children ends up answering a call of hers.

'Greg's not here,' I say, beating her to it.

'I don't want to talk to Greg. I want to talk to you.'

I fold my arms. 'I'm not sure I can help you, Hilary.'

'I don't want your help. I want to tell you something. About your precious boyfriend.'

Should I close the door now? I don't want to hear this. But I do.

'Can I come in?' She moves forward.

'No. You can stay where you are.' My hand holds the door, my foot against it.

'Suit yourself,' she says with a tilt of her head. 'He hasn't exactly been faithful to you, you know.'

No matter how untrustworthy the messenger, it's never something you're in a hurry to hear. I work hard at sounding bored when I say, 'Hilary, your lies are getting predictable. Don't you think Greg and I talk? Don't you think I know there were no other women? No private jokes about me?'

'OK. Maybe not *women*, but there was *a* woman.'

'*Sure.*'

'Oh, I'm sure all right. Because it was me. Why d'you think he sacked me?'

'He told me why he sacked you. You came on to him.'

She laughs. 'Actually, he came on to me. But it doesn't matter. The result was the same. He fucked the hired help and didn't feel too good about it. Why d'you think I've been ringing him? Because he can't get off that lightly. You think you're so goddamn wonderful. Well, you're not –'

'OK, Hilary. Mission accomplished.' I try to hold my voice steady and keep myself from crumpling until I close the door. Once inside I lean against four inches of mahogany and slide down, wrapping my arms around my legs. I place my chin in the safe place between my knees. *He didn't do it*, I tell myself. *He wouldn't* . . . But I remember back. *He was out of control, fired up, over-sexed . . . And it wouldn't have been the first time . . .*

29

I ring Grace in a state of high anxiety.

'I have to ask him, straight out.'

'No, Lucy. You can't confront him now. You have to wait till he's able. *Then*, you can talk. For now, you have to believe that whatever he did when he was high doesn't count. Off limits.'

'I can't. If he and Hilary –'

'Stop, Lucy. What's important is how Greg is normally. That's all.'

'So I should let him off? He can do anything he likes when he's high and I can't say anything?'

'You're actually accusing him of something he probably didn't do.'

'You don't know that.'

'Lucy. Stop. You said yourself, you can't believe anything she says.'

'This time I do.'

'Talk to Rob.'

'Why? He wasn't there.'

'No, Lucy. But he knows what Greg's normally like . . .'

My God. I don't. I say it slowly: 'I don't know what Greg's normally like.'

'That's not what I said.'

'But it's true. If he was hypomanic when we met, then I don't know what he's like when he's not.' *It's possible. Of course it is. Not only possible, probable. The very things I fell for in Greg are also symptoms of hypomania: his enthusiasm, optimism, impetuousness, wit, energy, adventurousness, busy mind. What if I didn't fall for Greg at all, just a bunch of symptoms? What if I love an illness, not a man? Do I even know him?*

'Lucy? Are you there?'

I can't speak.

'Give him the benefit of the doubt. Be fair.'

'I'm sick of being fair.'

'Talk to Rob.'

'No. This is too big for me. I don't want it. It's not worth it.'

'Talk to Rob.'

'No, Grace. I've had it. I want out.'

'Lucy, listen. If anybody should leave their relationship, it's me.' Her voice goes quiet. And slow. 'I don't have what you have, Luce. I never did. You're mad about each other. The way you look at each other, the way you touch. The first time I saw you together I knew what was missing between Kevin and me. Passion, love . . .'

'But –'

'You've been through so much and you're still together. Don't give up now, when things are about to get better, just because that manipulative bitch shows up on your doorstep. Wait till he's ready, then hear his side. Don't give up on what you have. Because not everyone has what you have.'

'But *do* I have it?'

'Trust me, Lucy. You do.'

'How does this always happen? How do I consistently end up in a mess?'

'At least you didn't create it, like I've created mine. I have no excuse. I walked into this marriage, trying to do the right thing for the wrong person. It's not going to get any better for me. Kevin will always be Kevin. He'll still be checking my legs for cellulite when I'm ninety. He'll still be expecting perfection

– from me, from the boys. Greg will improve, Luce. And you can try again. Give yourselves that chance.'

'But what if it doesn't work out?'

'Then it doesn't work out. But you'll never be able to blame yourself for not trying. Not all relationships can withstand the pressure of bipolar disorder. There's no shame in it not working out. But I think you should, at least, see how things go when Greg has stabilized. I think you should give your relationship that chance.'

Four times I dial the number. Four times I hang up. On the fifth attempt, I manage to speak.

'Hi. Hello. Yes. I was just wondering. Are they *completely* confidential, your support groups?'

'Yes,' answers a soft voice. 'Completely.'

'You don't have to say who you are or who the person is who has depression or anything? It is *totally* private?'

'Totally. All our groups are run on a first-name basis. And, if you like, you can even make that up. Confidentiality is important to everyone who comes here. And we ensure it.'

'And who runs the groups, a doctor?'

'Well, it depends. Which group were you thinking of attending?'

'The one for families of people with bipolar disorder. You do run those, don't you?'

'We do. Our facilitators are people who've experienced living with someone who has bipolar disorder. They know what it's like. And they're just there to help things along. It's all very relaxed.'

No matter how comforting that voice is, I'm still afraid. So it's not logical that I find myself, three days later, standing outside a Georgian building in the city centre, obscuring a brass plaque that announces the mental health charity that organizes the groups. When I'm buzzed in, I don't hang around. The facilitator is reassuringly normal-looking, the kind of person you'd imagine as somebody's mother, neighbour, friend. She's real. Her short dark hair is peppered with grey, her eyes pale blue and knowing. She does not hide her high colouring with make-up. Her dress is casual – a round-neck, lime-green pullover and white cotton trousers. She extends her hand, smiling hello. 'You must be Lucy. I'm Christine. Good to meet you.'

'You too,' I say, not sure yet that I mean it.

'Sure, we might as well go in.' As we make our way towards a door that has been left ajar, she explains, 'There'll be eight of us tonight, including yourself.'

'I won't talk,' I say. 'If that's OK?'

'Whatever you're most comfortable with.'

I follow her into a large room with a high ceiling, a Georgian fireplace and threadbare carpet. Around a long table sits a mixed group of men and women of various ages, sizes and presumably social backgrounds. Simple mathematics tell me I'm last to arrive; an empty chair is positioned between Christine and a teenager who is wearing a yellow T-shirt with *Dirty Girl* emblazoned on it. With a head of tiny blonde black-rooted plaits, eyes darkened by kohl and a swallow tattoo on her upper arm, she looks like she has attitude, not problems.

How wrong can I be? Minutes later I know her as Amy. She speaks of what it's like to live with a mother who genuinely believes she's Tina Turner when manic, and totally worthless when depressed. Amy's voice is tired, worn out. Mary is next to share her story. A quietly spoken woman in her fifties, she lives with a sister who has tried to commit suicide four times, despite having all she wanted in life. Mary knows she can't be there round the clock. Frank, a pale, thin man in his thirties, is struggling to forgive his wife who had an affair with a neighbour she'd never even liked. I lean forward, concentrating on every word.

'I know she didn't mean it, and she's as gutted as I am. But it still hurts. I have to look that smug bastard in the face every day. We're thinking of moving. I love Miriam, but not when she's high. I keep telling myself it's not her fault. But it is. She stopped her lithium. She wanted that high. Regardless of what it would do to me. Or the kids. I want to forgive her,' he says, shaking his head, 'but don't know if I can. Part of me just wants to walk away.'

I didn't want to speak, but now the process seems to start by itself. 'I'm so tired of telling myself "it's the illness". So tired of not being able to confront him about things. Of being excluded. Of not knowing what he's thinking, feeling, whether he loves me or not. Whether I love him. I am so tired of mental illness. It's a thousand times worse than any physical one.'

Heads are nodding in agreement. I look around. These people know. It isn't just me. I'm not a freak. They understand. Rob's great. Grace is great. My parents are great. But they don't *know*.

'I feel so stupid, so guilty, for not recognizing what it was sooner, for denying that anything was wrong, and when I couldn't avoid it any more, for thinking . . .' I search my mind for a name. '. . . Jim . . . was on drugs. But the worst thing is, I caused his depression. I rejected him. After his high, I told him I wanted to leave.' I drop my head and mumble, 'I caused it.'

'Lucy, you don't know that,' interrupts Frank. 'If Jim had already experienced a high, the depression was probably just the disease following its course. Or maybe something else triggered it, a stressful event. You don't know that it was you.'

'He may have had an affair.'

A person who hasn't spoken before, Charles, I think, says, 'It's not uncommon.'

'I know, but I'm like Frank. I don't think I can just say it doesn't matter. I don't think I can just forgive and forget. Even the *thought* of him with her hurts.'

Charles says, 'Of course it does. But what you have to ask yourself, Lucy, is, are the good times worth the bad?'

'I don't know. At this stage, I'm not even sure that there were good times or whether we were just living off his high. I don't know if we've had enough real good times to judge.'

Whatever else, walking back to the car, I feel different. Not so alone. Not so weird. Not so weighed down. My steps are lighter, faster. I'm looking ahead, not down. My shoulders are back, chin up. I've done the right thing. I'd felt so isolated, unable to call friends to tell them I was back because I couldn't talk to them. Now I know I'm not alone. And in a lot of ways, my situation could be worse.

Later, though, lying in bed, I change my mind. How could I have told our business to a room full of strangers? Do I really need to know about hallucinations, suicide attempts, sexual indiscretions? Frank's story lends credibility to Hilary's. Can I put that aside until Greg is better? Will I ever, realistically, be able to forgive him if what she says is true? And do I really want a future of such uncertainty?

Still, I can't do it. I can't leave him. Not yet. Work provides a temporary solution. It distracts me, presents challenges I can handle, lessens the guilt. While Greg struggles alone, I'm not out having a good time; I'm being constructive. Every morning I drop Rachel and Toby at my parents', where Rachel learns how to use a sewing machine, electric screwdriver and wire plugs, while Toby becomes a master chef and gardener. It's good to know that they too are getting a break from reality, and that Rachel is getting a break from me. I revert to my old corporate self. Every few days Fint asks how Greg is doing. Guilty I still haven't been able to tell him, I keep my answers vague but honest. 'Good day, yesterday . . .' That kind of thing. When I pick the children up from my parents', we're all in better form. We leave with our dinner in Tupperware. The few hours we have free before going to see Greg are often spent in the company of Grace and the boys – at parks, the beach or her place. Keeping ourselves busy and out of the house seems to be a workable solution.

30

It's three weeks since Greg was hospitalized, and he is due home for a full weekend. Considering the disaster that was the last visit and what's going on in my mind, I'm dreading it. The children and I spend the afternoon making a vegetable curry. At five we collect him. We eat together, and Greg spends time with his kids while I clear away.

'I can't get over Rachel,' he says after they've gone to bed. 'She's making such an effort.'

'She's making a *huge* effort, Greg. Tidying her room, helping round the house . . .'

'You seem to be getting on better?'

'I can't believe it. Ever since your mum's visit.'

'Don't mention the war.'

He can still make me smile.

'Maybe her behaviour made Rachel see how unfairly she's been treating you?'

'She wasn't that bad.'

'Come on. Rob told me.'

'OK, well, maybe she had her moments. But she was so good to me after you left, that day.'

'I'm sorry I wasn't up to staying.'

I remember what Grace said about hospital being a sanctuary. Suddenly it makes sense. 'I'm sorry too – you know I didn't mean what I said.'

We're quiet for a while.

'How's Tobes?'

I smile. 'The best thing you did was tell him what was going on. As soon as he started seeing you again, he's been so much better.' I never told Greg about the bedwetting, but it has stopped.

'Lucy, I want to thank you. For everything. For sticking by me, for taking such good care of the kids. I knew you would . . . At times I may not sound like I appreciate you, but I do. So *much*.' He closes his eyes.

'I know.'

'I'm sorry for anything I've said or done to upset you . . .'

I think of Hilary. 'It's OK. Forget it.' *Can I?*

'When I think of what I've put you and the children through, I just can't . . .' His voice is crumbling.

'Greg, we understand. Honestly, we do.'

'I love you.'

'I know. I know you do.'

'And I know you love me,' he says.

Jesus.

'You wouldn't still be here if you didn't. You wouldn't be minding my children, coming to see me every day . . . I've been trying, Lucy.'

'I know. I know you have.'

'Attending every therapy session, talking myself stupid. Forcing myself to get up, shave, get dressed, make an effort, eat . . . OK, I still can't sleep, but it's a matter of time. It's just a matter of time.'

'You're doing great.'

'I have to fight this, keep fighting it. I'll get out of it. I know I will.'

'You've already started.'

'Never thought I'd be the one they'd be telling, "Keep taking the tablets." '

He *has* been trying, even refusing wine with his meal. Given how he'd been drinking, I know it's another thing he's struggling with. We go to bed early, to our separate rooms. Outside mine, he stoops to kiss me goodnight. Our first kiss in weeks. A simple peck. I force a smile but break down as soon as the door is closed behind me.

I'm heading for bed when the phone rings. I don't know if I should answer it, with Greg home. It *is* his house. But then it could be Hilary. I make a grab for it, but it goes quiet. I pray it wasn't her and that she isn't hounding him right now. I haven't told him about her calls in an effort to protect him from that stress, but if that is Hilary now, I've wasted my time. To distract myself, I root around in the drawer for another dog-eared book on step-parenting and climb into bed. There's a quiet knock on my door. Greg pops his head in. 'Sorry for disturbing you, Lucy.'

I hold my breath.

'That was Ben.'

'Ben? What did he want at this time?'

'To know if it would be OK for Hilary to be there tomorrow when we bring the kids over for their visit.'

My heart skips a beat.

'He read somewhere that cutting off contact abruptly with nannies can be' – he puts his fingers in quote marks – '"traumatic". He thought it'd be good for them to see her.'

My voice is cynical when I say, 'And he didn't mention, at all, did he, that Hilary might like to see them?'

'He might have mentioned something about that too.' A corner of his mouth lifts.

'I hope you said no.'

'Of course I said no. I haven't *completely* lost my marbles.'

I smile at that. 'What excuse did you give?'

'I just told him you don't like Hilary.'

'You *did not*.'

'No, I didn't.' He smirks.

Before I know what I've done, I've hit him with a pillow.

'Careful,' he says. 'Delicate man here.' He makes a poor-me face.

And has me smiling again. 'So what *did* you tell him?'

'Just that I'd prefer it if she wasn't there. And, in his usual reserved way, he didn't ask why.'

'So that's that, then.'

'That's that.'

I'm about to say goodnight.

'You look nice,' he says.

No make-up, grey T-shirt and tartan pyjama bottoms – I don't think so.

He leans towards me and pecks me on the cheek. 'Goodnight,' he says.

''Night.'

I close the door and decide that I need to talk to Rob.

Unfortunately, the visit to Ben and Ruth's can't be postponed for ever, and the Saturday I've been dreading is suddenly here. Though Greg has had a 'chat' with the children, I'm terrified that something will slip out, especially with Ben being the inquisitive (to put it politely) man that he is.

Their Glenageary home, a two-storey-over-basement red-brick, is on one of Dublin's most prestigious roads. It is in mint condition, with a glossy black door and gleaming brass work. Rich, heavy drapes are visible through the windows. Perfectly maintained box plants fill the matching metal window boxes that adorn each sill. We climb the dust-free granite steps.

Both grandparents appear at the door almost immediately.

'Children, Lucy, Greg,' exclaims Ben. 'Good to see you.'

'Hi, Grandad, hi, Gran,' say Rachel and Toby together, walking past them into a hall with a black-and-white tiled floor. Ruth follows, chatting to them, quietly stroking Toby's hair. It's clear she loves them.

'Bye, guys,' Greg calls.

'Bye, Dad.'

'Would you like to come in?' Ben says, his voice empty of welcome.

'No, thanks, we're off to the movies,' says Greg.

'Good, well, I'd better go in. We'll see you later, then? What time will you be here to collect them?'

'When the movie's over. Six-ish?'

I feel that Ben would like the time pinned down, which is probably why Greg is keeping it open.

'Good, good,' he says. 'See you then.' And closes the door firmly.

'I wish we didn't have to do this,' I say as we get into the car.

'Don't worry. They won't say anything.'

Much to my relief, Greg turns out to be right. When we collect the children, Rachel boasts of how she stopped Toby from spilling the beans. Toby denies this and a fight breaks out, each claiming to be best at keeping secrets. I worry about how much we are asking of them.

Sunday. Greg brings his mother out to lunch with Rob and the children. I make a long-overdue visit to my neglected apartment. So glad to be home, I kick off my shoes. Throw my keys on the counter. Open all the windows. Check what's in the DVD player. Barbara Streisand and the Bee Gees. That'll do. I take a Coke from the fridge and lounge across the sofa. My eyes take a slow trip around the familiar, alighting as though magnetically on the paintings I have collected over the years, ever since my first pay cheque – the sparseness and simplicity of Robert Ryan, the richness of Stephen Cullen and the special attachment I feel to works done by friends. I gaze at the Shona sculpture Brendan bought me from a dealer in Sonoma Valley on that magical Californian holiday when he proposed. 'The Lovers' is carved from soapstone and features a man with hair like ropes, his arms wrapped protectively around his woman. I love it. Always have. I close my eyes and think of Brendan, try to visualize his face, his smile. In the end, I have to find a photo. I run my finger over his tanned, vibrant face, then close my eyes. *Help me, Brendo. Please. Tell me what to do. Keep going? Or come home?*

I'm afraid to open my eyes. I've done this before – and nothing. As long as I keep them closed, I can believe that a sign is on its way, to take the decision from me, leave it to someone else. But I do open them. And again, nothing. At first. Then, in through a window, flutters a tiny butterfly in chaotic bouncy flight. It is such an unusual colour. Iridescent blue. I don't remember ever seeing one like it. It seems to have no goal, no sense of direction – and it doesn't seem to care. Its flight is light, optimistic, happy. And I know what to do – give Greg and our chaotic relationship a chance, talk to Rob, try harder to understand. I stay watching that butterfly until it flies free, then it's time to go. I begin to lock up. On my way out, I stop at the Shona sculpture, run my hand over its cool, smooth surface and lean to kiss it.

Thank you, I say to the man who was my life.

Mid afternoon, Rob returns to the house with the children, having dropped his mother at her home and Greg at the hospital.

'He's great, isn't he?' he says.

'Much better,' I agree.

'So much fitter, brighter. I know a lot of that's pure effort, and he'll probably fall into bed when he gets back, but still, at least he's trying.'

'True . . . Rob?'

'Yeah?'

'Have you any plans for the rest of the day?'

He eyes me, knowing something's up. 'Nope.'

'Will you stay for a while?'

'Sure.'

The children don't want to go out again, so we just hang out. I wait for the right time to talk and learn that there won't be one until two pairs of small ears are in bed. I try to relax and enjoy the entertainment they're providing. Rachel's acting as seamstress. Mum has given her needles, threads and, for some reason, felt. Her current assignment is uncommissioned – a pair of white felt underpants for Toby. She's opted for a simple design: two pieces of (stiff) cloth cut into the shape of a T. Without realizing it, she's making her brother a thong. She holds it up against his skinny little body. Yep, right size. She stitches it up with big blue stitches and bribes him with sweets to model it. When he tries it on over his trousers, it bursts. But he's done the job and wants the sweets. No sweets, she insists, until she stitches them up and he tries them on again. He's having none of it. I broker a deal: one sweet now and the rest after the next and final trying-on session. I feel like a Mafioso. In the meantime I make pasta. Then, freeing the thonged superhero from his sewing-enthusiast sister, I give him a quick bath. Wrapped in a towel, with another draped over his head, he looks like a nun. A cute nun.

'Who are you again, Sister Alfonsis Xavier or Sister Glorious Halleluiah? I can never tell you apart.'

He produces that cute smile of his. 'Fonsis Zavier.'

'You're a dote. D'you know that?'

'Yeah.'

I smile, kiss the top of his head, read *Captain Underpants*, hug him goodnight. It's great – we've moved on to hugging. He started it.

''Night, bub,' he says.

''Night, Captain Underpants.'

Alone with Rob, children in bed – it's what I've been waiting for, and simultaneously dreading, all afternoon. Sitting on the couch, he looks so trusting, *so bloody balanced*, I know I can tell him.

'Rob, I need your help.'

'Sure,' he says. 'What's up?'

I try to organize my thoughts. Take a deep breath. Let it out. 'Remember the other day, when I said I thought Greg may've been hypomanic when we met?'

'Yes, Lucy, but, I know he loves you –'

'It's not that.' How am I going to say this? 'It's just that if he was, then I've never known him otherwise – well, except depressed. I've never known him just as he is. And I need to. I need to know what was a symptom, and what was really Greg when we met. You know him, Rob. He's your brother.'

He opens his mouth to speak.

'There's something else,' I say before he can, 'something I can't get out of my head. Hilary told me that something happened between her and Greg on the night he sacked her. I keep telling myself that whatever he did when he was high doesn't count, that it's what he's normally like that's important. But I don't know what he is normally like with women. I don't know what he's normally like, full stop. I need to and I don't know where to start, except to ask you . . . I can trust you, Rob, can't I? Please tell me you won't go back to Greg with this.'

'Come on, Lucy. Give me some credit. This is the last thing Greg needs to hear.'

'I know,' I say, feeling guilty. 'I want to trust my love for him, Rob, I really, really do, but I need to get to know him all over again, to learn what's real, solid, what I can believe in.'

'I don't know where to start.'

'What's he normally like with women?' Trust, I suddenly understand, is the biggest issue. Without it, there can be no relationship. 'Be honest, please. Don't keep anything from me. I need to know.'

He shifts in his seat. 'There's nothing to keep. After Catherine, there was no one. I tried to set him up a few times, and he told me where to go. How did he put it? He'd a wife to remember, children to raise and a book to write. If someone flirted with him, he skedaddled. He was a one-woman man, Lucy. And that woman was Catherine. Until you.'

It's like Greg said. And I chose to believe Hilary over him. Why? To protect myself by thinking the worst?

'Do you think he and Hilary ever –?'

'God, I doubt it. There was never any hint of anything. Their relationship revolved around the children.'

But they did have sex. I decide that Rob's not the person to ask about Hilary.

'Tell me about him, Rob.'

'What d'you want to know?'

I remember what attracted me to Greg and start with a favourite quality. 'Was he always an optimist?'

'An optimist? God.' He makes a face. 'I wouldn't say an optimist . . . more a realist . . . He's always looked to a better future but knew he had to work for it, you know?'

Immediately, I rationalize. To be optimistic in their situation would have been naive, lazy even. Blindly believing that good will happen negates the need to work for it. It strikes me that not only do I have to uncover the real Greg, but that I have to re-evaluate the qualities I once thought important. Can I do that with *everything*?

'He was always sharp, though?'

'Sharpest tool in the shed. Always.'

'But took life pretty seriously, didn't he?' I don't want a yes here.

'Yes, he did. But he could be fun. He's always had a sense of humour. When we were kids, if I'd had a really bad day at school, and he was trying to cheer me up, he could be so fucking funny. He'd take off one of the Brothers, any of them; he'd them all down to a T. I swear to God, he'd have me cracking up.'

I smile, remembering how he used to do that with Matt. How simple and uncomplicated everything was then, when he was just this great, fun guy who embraced life and me. I miss him so much.

'Lucy. I could talk and talk about Greg. But you'll see for yourself, if you just wait. He's the best guy. I've seen him through the best and worst times, and, to be honest, I wish *I* were more like him. That's all I can say. You just have to hang on – like he has to. Just hang tight till he gets through this. The good times will come again.'

He's right. And Grace is right. I might not be able to trust the times we've had, but if I wait, hold on, until Greg has stabilized, then I can judge. Like Grace said, if Greg comes out of this and it's not working, then we can end it, knowing we gave it our best shot. So I will wait for the boy who brought up his kid brother. I will wait for the man who survived the loss of his wife and raised his children on his own. I will wait for Greg to fight his biggest fight – this impossible, unfathomable illness that has taken his mind hostage. If anybody can get through it, he can. And yet the insecurity of not knowing exactly who will emerge at the other end remains. Maybe Greg Millar doesn't need to be impulsive, fun, impetuous, gregarious for me to love him. And yet those are the things I fell for. If they're gone, what'll be left?

31

A few days before the children return to school for the autumn term is way too late to get organized, I discover – the hard way. I have to queue with them for books, uniforms, shoes and haircuts. First day back, we're twenty minutes late, teaching me the valuable lesson of how long it takes to get two children ready to a deadline. School has its tests too. When collecting Toby, first day, I stand alone, watching mothers (who all seem to know each other), one after the other, stoop to kiss and hug their children. I wait, unsure. When he sees me, he starts running. I squat. And he nearly knocks me over. Can what I'm feeling really be love? When Rachel comes out, half an hour later, it's a different scene. The older children talk together in small groups until they see their parents, then just walk to them. No big deal. No hugs. The relief I feel reminds me that, while Rachel and I may be getting on well, our relationship does not extend to physical contact.

Now that the children are back at school, my parents take to minding them in the afternoons instead of the mornings, allowing me to return to a full day at the office. I nip out from work to collect them and drop them over at my parents' for a few hours. Dad would willingly do this, but I want to be there for them when they come out. I also want, I discover, the same things for Rachel and Toby that a real parent might – for them to like their new teachers, find work easy, be happy, fit in.

One day I overhear a woman invite her daughter's friend over for the afternoon. I ask Rachel if she'd like to do the same. She would. And does. I take a half-day, and a girl called Keelin comes to visit. To distract Toby from following the two of them around, I decide to take the stabilizers off his bike and teach him to cycle. I hold the saddle, instructing him to keep his weight in the centre and look where he's going rather than at the pedals. The girls potter around, in and out of the house. I so like this, and I so don't like that. It reminds me how young Rachel is but how old she tries to be.

It never occurs to me that Greg might like to have been the one to teach his son to cycle, until I see his face when I tell him I have. It's only then I appreciate that, in trying to do my best, I've started doing too much. Roles are blurring. And it's time to unblur them. When Toby decides to take up hurling, I see my chance. Maybe Greg would like to be there for his first lesson.

He would.

It's a Friday. I collect Greg. Together we pick the children up from school. We drop Rachel at hockey and make our way to the Gaelic sports grounds in Dalkey with Toby. In the car he changes into his little red-and-white jersey. He jumps out, all set, then chats to some friends from his class. He's given a bright blue helmet and a hurley stick. I try not to laugh – the helmet's almost bigger than he is. Before long there is a hall full of what look like mini-aliens racing around in circles. They have no fear, tearing around after the ball, sticks flying and the sound of clashing wood echoing. Toby is a little flier. And a great man for stopping the ball. He isn't like I used to be at sport – an eye-closer. I'm so proud of him.

'Come on, Toby, *whack* it.' *Was that me?*

I catch Greg looking at me. He's laughing. Actually laughing.

In the car on the way back to collect Rachel, Toby is animated.

'That was the best day of my life,' he says. 'I was Man of the Match, Dad. Did you see that?'

Greg turns round to him. 'You were great, Tobes.'

'Was I?'

'Exceptional.'

'Was I better than exceptional?'

'You were spectacular.'

'Was I better than spectacular?

'You were splendiferous.'

'That good?'

'That good.'

I look in the rear-view mirror.

He's beaming.

And I've a flavour of what it must be like to be a real mum.

That evening, while two exhausted children watch *Finding Nemo*, Greg decides to go for a swim. I throw on a sweater, and we make our way to the end of the garden. The breeze carries a September chill, and already the light is beginning to fade. The water is grey, choppy and unwelcoming. The surface is thick with bladderwrack. He wades in, knee-deep on the steps, prepares to dive off.

'You're mad,' I tell him. Then my face drops as it dawns on me what I've said.

'And you're only realizing that now?' He dives in and swims out with a strong over-arm. 'Come on in,' he shouts. 'It's . . . *freezing.*'

'Tempting. But I think I'll pass.'

He swims for a good five minutes, then back in, runs up the steps and shakes himself on me. I scream, jump out of the way and throw him his towel. He snatches it mid-air and begins to dry himself. I'm surprised by what good shape he's in. Visits to the exercise room have really toned him up. I feel something I haven't felt in weeks. And it catches me by surprise, as it did that first time, in a snug in a pub, on the outskirts of Dublin.

'I'll tell you, that'd cure any man's depression,' he says, dragging on his trousers. I hand him his shirt. He takes it from me and kisses me quickly. His lips are cold and salty. Alive. I look into his eyes and kiss him back. Properly. He pulls back, his eyes searching mine as if to say, 'Do you really want what I think you do?'

'Don't stop,' I breathe.

Then his mouth is on mine, icy fingers cupping my face, then running through my hair. *Oh, God. I've missed this.* Freezing hands slip up under my T-shirt. He groans when he reaches my breasts. My hips arch towards him, and he responds by pressing me close. Our kisses are urgent now, caresses frantic. He lifts my T-shirt and sweater up over my head together, then pulls me to him. Our mouths meet again and stay that way when he lifts me up, my legs wrapping round his waist and my nipples brushing against his chest. *Oh, God.* He carries me to the changing area, where in the company of the swirling September breeze, he lays his damp towel on the ground and we, at last, let go of our worries, our fears and thoughts of tomorrow.

Saturday. The children visit Ben and Ruth. And, as usual, I worry. There is a keeping-secrets competitiveness between them now, which reassures me a little that they won't divulge anything but has me feeling guilty about the need for them to hide things from their grandparents in the first place. I tell myself that with Ben, there is no other option and try not to think about it. When we collect them, though, I feel I can breathe again. We have lunch together, then Greg spends time alone with them, while I go shopping. Later Rob babysits, while Greg and I visit a local restaurant where we end up having a normal conversation about nothing in particular. Like old times. Which are still relatively young times. Sunday we get up late and take it easy. Greg, Rob and the children go out for lunch with Phyllis. But this time Greg returns to the house. Only at the very last minute do we prepare for him to head back to the hospital. I feel like a school-hating child on a Sunday night, longing for just one more day. That changes when Greg says, 'I'm ready to come home.'

I stop folding the sweatshirt I've been packing. *Is* he ready? Am *I*?

'I'll tell Betty when I get in,' he says, with a certainty I don't share.

We've discussed the *logistics* of his coming home. I'm supposed to stay on in the house until he's feeling better. I'm to monitor his moods and call the hospital if I feel he's becoming too animated or too down. I was fine with that, happy even, finally to be included in his care. But his sudden announcement changes that. I panic. Am I really the right person to do this? Wouldn't Rob be better? He's known Greg so much longer. How can I tell the difference between a normal mood swing and an abnormal one? I don't want to ring the hospital, worried, only to discover he's just fed up about something anyone would be.

'OK,' I say with a brightness I don't feel. Now that he's finally making progress, I'm not going to be the one to stop it.

He comes home on the Tuesday for a trial period of a week. As advised, we try to settle into a routine. With Fint's agreement, I go back to working from home but regularly calling into the office. I think it best that the children continue to go to my parents in the afternoon, although for shorter visits. I don't want to land too much on Greg, and, although

I don't say it, I feel it wise to stick to the routine, in case things don't work out. After three days I ring Betty, worried about his progress. She establishes that he's getting up in the morning, eating and sleeping, then hints that the problem might be mine. She talks of letting him 'take his first steps himself', 'encouraging him all the way' and appreciating that 'even the smallest steps will be monumental to him'. She suggests I get out of the house for a few hours in the morning. And so it's back to half-days at the office.

When Greg is officially discharged one week later, he does everything by the book. Takes his little white tablet every night and the coloured ones during the day. Attends every appointment. Professor Power fortnightly. Anxiety management once a week. Outpatients every two weeks to have his lithium levels checked. Getting better seems a full-time job. I do my bit, keeping a nervous eye out for mood swings.

Betty's right. The small steps, when made, do seem monumental, even to me. An offer to help with homework. A dinner prepared. Another quiet but firm refusal to drink. The very first time he gets up before eleven. Especially that.

'Thank you, Dad, for the lovely dinner,' says Rachel.

'Thank you, Dad, for the story,' says Toby.

They notice every little thing he does for them. And he notices their noticing. It makes him try harder. He starts to swim every morning. It gets him out of bed, kickstarts his day. We buy a punch bag like the one in the hospital exercise room and install it on the landing, so we can all have a swing at it whenever the mood grabs us. Which is pretty often. Toby takes a particular shine to it, contributing as it does to his ambitious muscle development programme.

As the weeks pass, Greg begins to collect the children from school. Twice a week he takes them to my parents'; otherwise he brings them to whatever activity they have on, or else home. That the children are increasingly happy is evident from random snatches of conversation that I catch.

'What's Mr Incredible called again?' Toby asks his sister.

'Bob.'

'Oh, yeah.'

Not so long ago Mr Incredible wouldn't have mattered.

With every new responsibility Greg takes on, he moves closer towards recovery, towards regaining his pride, towards getting his life back. Not yet ready to resume writing, he finds an outlet for his creativity in the garden, a place that is tolerant and forgiving of his lack of concentration and slowed mental agility. He and the children begin to plan a fruit and vegetable patch. They look up books, consult the local garden centre, map out a section of the garden. As a matter of pride, Greg doesn't seek the advice of his own gardener, just tells him they will be 'cultivating' a plot. This is their baby. Finally, they get going. To look out and see three backs hunched over together busy planting is to imagine a brighter future.

When Greg finally feels up to greeting the outside world, he recharges the battery on his mobile and switches it on. It's a big step. One that is ruined by Hilary. Within hours she calls. The first I learn of it is when Greg comes to my bedroom, all the colour gone from his face. 'Did Hilary call here?' he asks.

I put down the book I've been reading, knowing instinctively that this is it. The Hilary showdown. It has arrived, I fear, before he's ready. 'Yes.'

'What did she say?' he asks quietly.

One thing I've learned is that when you're dealing with Hilary, it's wise to be straight. 'That you sacked her because you and she . . .' I finish the sentence with my eyes.

'Shit. Why didn't you say anything?'

'I was waiting till you were ready, Greg.'

'God, Lucy.' He runs his hand over his mouth. 'What exactly did she say?'

'That you came on to her, not the other way round.'

'Not true.' He comes to me. Sits on the side of the bed.

'She said that it didn't matter either way because the result was the same – that you fucked her, then sacked her because you couldn't face what you'd done.'

'Jesus.' It's a whisper.

'What happened that night? I need to know – every detail.'

He nods slowly. Then takes a breath. 'When you left the villa, Hilary came down. She started the same thing, about my needing to see a doctor. I didn't want to hear it. Not twice in one night, not when I knew there was something in it. But she kept going. Then started on about your not understanding me like she did, not seeing that anything was wrong. She said I was making a mistake with you. And then, well, basically, she . . . started to get physical.' He checks my reaction.

I hide it. Say nothing.

'I'm going to be honest with you, Lucy. I was tempted, not because it was Hilary, but because I was high as a kite. I'd have jumped on a goat. But I didn't. I swear. I left. Drove. Tried to sort my disorganized, wired-to-the-moon mind into logical thought. I decided she had to go. It was the only way. To keep her on, knowing how she felt, would have been dishonest. To everyone.'

'Why didn't you tell me the next day when I asked what had happened?'

'You know the way I was. Everything was spinning out of control. I couldn't organize my thoughts. I couldn't trust myself to tell you and not botch it. Lucy, I love you. I'd never consciously do anything to hurt you.' His eyes are sad when he says, 'But somehow I always seem to manage it.'

'But why does she keep ringing?'

He sighs. 'I was hoping to protect you from this.'

I give him a look that says, 'Enough protecting.'

'OK. When the calls started, she was looking for her job back, saying she'd made a mistake. I felt a bit sorry for her then. I didn't know how she'd been with you. I knew she missed the kids. But I couldn't risk her coming back. I tried to explain that she needed a life outside of us. She wouldn't listen. Then she changed her attitude completely. Started to threaten me. She said if I didn't take her back, she'd sue me for sexual harassment.'

'My God!'

'I hoped she was bluffing. Waited for the solicitor's letter but none ever came. Then one day she rang to ask if I enjoyed the visit from Ben and Ruth. I felt the pressure build. I was dealing with a loose cannon. She seemed intent on trouble. I sometimes wonder if the pressure of all that sent me into the depression.'

'I can't believe the sexual harassment thing. God!'

'It would've ruined everything – our relationship, my reputation, career. God knows how I'd have kept it from Rachel.'

'Why do you think she didn't go through with it?'

'I don't know. Maybe she got legal advice. Maybe it'd have cost too much. Or maybe it was just a threat she never intended to carry out. I don't know.'

'What did she say just now?'

'That she hoped you'd got over the news OK.'

I shake my head. 'I can't understand how she thinks that this kind of behaviour will get her her job back.'

'It's gone beyond that, Lucy. She knows there's no hope of that now. It's moved up to another level. She wants to cause as much damage as she can.' He reaches for my hand. 'Thank God you didn't believe her. Thank God you had faith in us.'

I can't look at him.

'Lucy?'

I meet his eyes.

'You do still love me?'

I nod.

'If you've changed your mind, I'll understand. I've put you through so much, Luce. And who knows what's ahead? If you want to leave, then maybe now would be a good time.' He's looking at me as if he knows everything that has been going on in my mind.

'I'm not leaving.'

'Think about it. Your life would be easier, freer, less complicated. You could start again with someone else – someone who doesn't have this –'

'I don't want anyone else.'

'We're not married; we're not tied to each other. Don't feel guilty if you want to go. Just do it. Please. I don't want to live with a martyr.'

I leave my spot on the bed, crawl to where he is sitting and put my arms around him. 'I love you, Greg. I'm going nowhere.'

We hold each other for a long time until one thing leads happily to another. I fall asleep with his arm around me.

In the morning, when Greg is returning to his room before the children wake, he speaks as though he has found a solution to the problem.

'It's time we put a stop to Hilary. We need to talk to her, as a couple, present a united front. The reason she has got away with this for so long is that we haven't been united. We are now. And we need to tell her that nothing she does will break us. She'll give up, she'll have to.'

I look doubtful.

'We have to end this. For once and for all.'

★

Hilary's not looking well when she calls at the house the following morning. Overweight. Spotty. She has made an effort with her clothes, though, wearing a clean white blouse and a long navy skirt. She has also washed her hair.

'You never said *she'd* be here,' she says, as Greg shows her into the living room, where I'm waiting, nervous as hell.

'Hilary, why don't you sit down,' says Greg, taking control. She does. We all do.

'Hilary, the reason we're both here is to show you that we are still very much a couple. Whatever you try to do to spoil that only brings us closer. I'm sorry if you ever got the impression that your job was more than a job. That may have been partly my fault. I made one mistake a long time ago, and I'm very sorry for that. You were a great nanny. The best. And I'd be happy to state that in a reference. But you stepped over the line on a personal level, Hilary. I love Lucy. And that's that. It's time you moved on now, built your own life, around yourself.'

'End of lecture?'

He raises an eyebrow.

'I've invested five years of my life in this family,' she says. 'I won't be discarded like a used cloth. I love Rachel and Toby. You can't keep me from them. And let's not forget, *you* were the one who stepped over the line back then, not me.'

Greg winces at that but lets it go, taking a different tack. 'Hilary. There wouldn't have been a problem if you hadn't tried to turn the children against Lucy. We can't trust you.'

'You can, you can. I'm sorry about that. It was a mistake. I was afraid.' She's leaning forward, clutching her mini-rucksack. Her fingernails have been bitten so low that the fleshy parts of her fingers are peeping over the top.

Maybe if we really were the strong couple that Greg claims

we are, we would give in. But we're not. We're so vulnerable now. We can't risk her interfering. We just can't.

'I'm sorry, Hilary,' says Greg. 'You need a clean break. You need to start your own life. Separate from us.'

'Don't sit there so smugly and tell me what I need. How do you know what I need? Who are you to decide? Who are you to take the children from me? You can't just dismiss me with a snap of your fingers after all I've done for you. I'm a person. I have feelings. You can't treat me like this.' She breaks down. I remind myself of what she's done, how she's created this situation for herself. She wipes at her tears impatiently, stands suddenly.

'This isn't over,' she says. 'I'll find a way. I will. I won't give up. I'll bide my time. Do it right. You'll see.'

She storms from the house.

'Oh, Greg!' My heart's hammering. 'This was a mistake. It was like two against one. Maybe you should have met her alone.'

'No. She had to see that we're a couple. She had to see that we won't be bullied.'

'But we've only made her madder than ever. She wants revenge. I feel she's going to do something. I really do.'

'Don't worry.' He puts an arm round me. 'It'll be fine.'

I want to believe him. But can't.

32

When we don't hear from Hilary for weeks, she begins to fade from our minds. The run-up to Christmas is upon us before we know it. Toby's questions begin as soon as the decorations make their first shimmer in the shops. 'Are Santa's elves slaves? Can he fly on his own, without his reindeers? Is there a Missus Claus?' It's the first real build-up to Christmas I've enjoyed since I was a child. And I'm loving it. Rachel makes a crib out of three black cardboard sheets. You can tell by the care she takes that it isn't just a crib but a home for Mary and Jesus. It is their first year without Joseph, who met an untimely death last time round when he fell and his head rolled under the fridge. So Mary stands guard behind Jesus. The three wise men and shepherds line up on the right hand side. The animals, on the left. Nice, orderly crib.

As soon as Toby sees cars going by with trees strapped to the roofs, the requests begin for ours. Before long we are inhaling pine, listening to Frank Sinatra and imagining chestnuts on open fires. It makes a change from 'The little Lord Jesus lay down his sweet head . . . The little Lord Jesus asleep on the hay,' which has been sung over and over by Toby ever since he began to rehearse the school play.

Greg and I shop together when Rachel and Toby are at school. That they both want surprises forces me to really think about their personalities. That Toby is easier to buy for comes as no surprise. Still, walking around the shops, picking things up, discussing them, I feel we are, at last, on the way to becoming a family.

The children's Christmas plays signal the final run in. Toby's is first. He is Rudolph. The spotlight is on his nose when he picks it, demonstrating that even legends have bad habits. To hammer home the point he removes his cardboard antlers and begins to chew them. We're so proud. When we go up to the stage to collect him after the show, we overhear him say to another antlered boy, probably Donner or Blitzen, 'I'm so proud of myself. Are you proud of yourself?' Sadly, Rachel's class has been corralled into a much more sophisticated production: in-tune carol singing from lines of uniformed children, nothing out of place, no mistakes. It doesn't feel right to go straight home afterwards, so into town we troop, to visit the live crib. Greg decides to make it a tradition. I sneak a peek at Rachel. But she hasn't flinched at the thought of my being included in future plans.

It is customary, on Christmas Eve, for Ben and Ruth to break with tradition and come to Greg's house with their gifts. It is a simple enough evening. Their focus is on the children. They sit, a little less straight-backed than usual, sipping politely on sherry, commenting on the decorations and the weather. They leave before nine. On Christmas morning the children's excitement is like a present in itself. Greg slides an arm round me as we watch them rip open their presents. While they're busy with their newly discovered treasures, Greg and I quietly slip into the kitchen to exchange gifts. I found it hard to choose for him – everything has been so delicate between us – but, in the end, I settled for a giant telescope so he could look to the stars. So big was it, I nearly broke my back carrying it from the shop. He loves it, he says, then jokes that it will be great for spying on the neighbours. Greg's gift to me, a painting, means so much. Not just because it is beautiful and done by one of my favourite artists, but because for the first time I have an excuse to hang something of my own here. I will have my own little space. A place for me.

We go to Mass, then on to my parents. As requested, the children have made, rather than bought, their gifts. (Toby, an apple tart for Dad and shortbread biscuits in the shape of angels for Mum. Rachel has sewn a pink gingham apron for Mum. For Dad, she has fashioned a kind of holder for his tools. Made from heavy fabric, it ties around the waist, so that when he's working, everything is at hand.) My parents are thrilled. Grace and Kevin arrive with the boys, and the tempo moves up a notch. I study Grace and Kevin. There is little eye contact between them. Independently, they focus on the children. Neither smiles at the other as if to say, 'Aw, look at that.' All the time I am hoping for a look, a word that will reassure me. I find none.

We arrive back to the smell of turkey. Rob and Phyllis arrive for Christmas dinner. I've had a few glasses of wine by now, which softens the edge to Phyllis. I let it all run off me, concentrating on how far we have come in the last few months.

On St Stephen's Day I go horse-racing at Leopardstown with Fint. It is a tradition that started way back, and one I try not to miss. As usual it is mobbed and overpriced. But we do not care. He scoffs a steak sandwich, and we warm our insides with port. And I make an early New Year's Resolution to spend more time with friends.

New Year's Eve sees Greg and me return to the restaurant of our first date. I look across at him, still as handsome as ever, but with eyes that seem at the same time more knowing and more humble. So much has happened between us in so little time. And there is a temptation to say, 'Let's forget it all and start over.' But neither of us does. We've seen each other raw, laid bare. And, hard though that's been, to lose it would be a mistake. It is part of who we are now. Still, at midnight, we toast to a year that will be nothing like the one we've just been through.

January sees Greg knuckling down to start writing again. He has begun researching his next Cooper book, trying to establish a pattern of work. But, he says, he can research for ever and still end up with nothing, unless he concentrates on the business of putting words on paper. He sits at the computer and waits, stares at the screen and waits. And I think, *Oh, no, not again.* I silently urge him to type something, anything, just to get going.

'I can't do this,' he says eventually. 'How can I be creative with my thoughts reined in by lithium?'

I don't have an answer.

'It's cotton wool in here,' he says, tapping his head.

I try to think of a solution. 'Maybe if you just write something to get started. Anything. And just keep going till you reach the end, then worry about what you've written. Isn't that what Stephen King says?'

'Stephen King. The fucking expert. Bet he's not on lithium.'

'Well, coming off isn't an option, Greg.'

He pushes back his chair. 'Why not? I'm fine. If I stop and get a bit high or low, I'll just take it again.' He's looking at me as if it's a great idea.

'If it was that easy, they wouldn't spend so much time warning you against it.'

'They just say that to be on the safe side. I bet some people can control it, once it's been tamed. I bet I can. I know I can.'

'Greg, I don't think you should risk it. Everything's coming together for us now, finally. The only problem is the writing and –'

'Writing's my life. If I can't write I *will* get depressed.'

A point.

311

'Have you any idea what it's like to have to take pills every day of your life?'

Another point.

'D'you know that each time I reach for one, it reminds me I've a mental illness?'

Make that three.

'Lucy, if I come off, you can keep an eye on me, tell me if I'm heading up or down. I'll go straight back on them. I promise.'

I've made my own New Year's resolution to move back to the apartment and return to full-time work at the office. That won't happen if Greg stops his lithium. I'll have to hang around the house watching his every move. And so, because my motivations aren't entirely pure, I feel guilty. Which weakens my resolve. Especially as he keeps on and on about it over the next few days.

But then I speak to Grace.

'Lucy. This happens all the time. As soon as people feel fine again, they think it's OK to stop. It isn't.' She's unpacking Shane's lunchbox.

'But the lithium is making his head muzzy.'

She turns to me, Tupperware in one hand, bread crusts in the other. 'No, it's not. It might be slowing things down a bit, but it doesn't cause muzziness. It's probably the antidepressant.' She throws the crusts in the bin, the Tupperware in the dishwasher, rubs her hands together and sits opposite.

'He's convinced it's the lithium,' I say.

'Well, unconvince him. You have to make him stay on it. It's that simple.' She sips the coffee I've made her.

'He thinks he's different from everyone else. He thinks he can control it, that he can take the lithium again if his moods start to change.'

'And that's exactly what has sunk so many people. The next

up could be way up, the next down, further down. And harder to get out of. Greg needs to keep taking the lithium. And it's up to you to convince him to.'

'How, though?'

'Remind him what he was like. Warn him you won't go through it all again. Tell him you'll leave.'

'Do I have to spend my entire life bullying him?'

'If it means him continuing to take his lithium, yes. Look, no matter how sensible or rational or *frustrated* he gets, you can't let him stop. Go see Power. He'll know a way round this. Maybe he'll cut down the dose of the antidepressant.'

'Hmm.'

'Don't make the mistake of forgetting how bad it got. Don't forget what it was like coming down that mountain.'

I let out a long breath. 'OK. I'll try to get him to see Power.'

'Well, do. Otherwise he might just stop and *not* tell you.'

That wakes me up. She has me convinced. Now all I've to do is convince Greg. And I do. I take him back in time; make him relive his high, from our point of view. Remembering it all, I get upset, distressed. When I say I can't go through it again, I mean it. Together we go to see Professor Power, who reduces the dose of the antidepressant and explains that this is the beginning of weaning Greg off. He suggests waiting a week or two before trying to write again.

'Why did you stay with me?' Greg asks that evening, staring into the fire.

I sit on the arm of his chair. 'Because I love you.'

'But I treated you so badly.'

'No, Greg. You didn't. The illness did. I only told you how bad it got so you'd stay on the lithium. It's over now. I just want it to stay that way.'

'I knew it was bad. I knew I hurt you. But –'

'It wasn't you.'

'But you didn't know that.'

'I loved you.' It's the truth. And I love him now. Does it matter that I had moments of doubt? It may be a different kind of love than the one we started out with, but it's stronger, I think.

33

After two weeks Greg tries writing again, abandoning the computer and trying longhand. One evening I'm glancing across at him. Spiral notebook on his lap, he's spending more time sucking his pen than using it. I've an idea.

'Why don't you forget Cooper? Write something else.'

He takes the pen from his mouth, looks over. 'Like what?' The question lacks optimism.

'I don't know. Something really different. Something from the heart.' I think for a second. 'What it's like to have depression.'

He groans.

'Why not?'

'Too depressing.'

I rethink. 'All right. But you could write about what you've just been through.'

'I couldn't put that in a book.'

'Then don't do it for publication. Do it for yourself.'

'*Why?*'

'Just to get you writing again.'

He seems to consider it.

'You could give it a simple structure. Something short, like a letter . . .' I check his reaction.

He's listening.

'You could write to me. So I can understand what it was like for you.'

He's starting to look hesitant. 'I don't think so.'

'You've always said writing is easier than talking. So write it.'

'I don't know, Lucy. Let me think about it, OK?'

'OK.'

Two days later he begins to write. I don't ask what. He's off, that's the main thing. He writes slowly at first, longhand, then transfers back to the computer and seems to take off. I don't say a word. We settle into a new routine. Greg drops the children at school and writes in the morning while I head to work. On the two afternoons the children are at my parents', he also writes. Otherwise he's there for them. Sometimes, after dinner, he disappears to his office for another hour or so. Two months after the coming-off-lithium scare, it seems the furthest thing from his mind. He is engrossed in his writing and his life. I feel it's time for him to become fully independent. After discussion, I move back to the apartment.

It seems very quiet there.

For months Greg writes. In April he gets a call from his editor wanting to know how he's getting along with the next Cooper book. That focuses his mind.

'What'll I tell her?' he asks me.

'That you're working on another project.'

'That would make me in breach of contract.'

'Oh.'

'And anyway, what I'm working on isn't for publication.'

I look at him.

'It's for you. My trip through psychosis,' he says. 'I'm bringing you with me. If you still want to come.'

'I do.'

'There won't be a Cooper book this year, at the rate I'm going.'

'I suppose you'd better tell them.'

He does. They're not impressed. They've promised the book trade another Cooper book. What will they give them instead? That's when I remember a book cover I've done for

316

a collection of articles and essays by a well-known novelist. I thought it a bit of a cop-out at the time. Now I see it as a way out. I suggest it to Greg. His agent passes the idea on to Copperplate like a relay baton – embellishing it before hand-over. Copperplate buy it. It means nothing to them that little effort will be required from Greg. All that matters is that the book will sell. His international publishers share Copperplate's enthusiasm. Greg is off the hook.

We spend summer in Dublin: Greg writing, me working and the children happy to attend summer camps with their friends, something they've always missed by going to France. I'm relieved not to be going back. It's too close, too raw.

By mid August Greg's finished.

'Are you sure you want to read this?' he asks.

'Try and stop me.'

'There are things in here I haven't told you. Couldn't.'

'That's OK.' I sound more confident than I feel.

'I love you, Lucy. I want you to know that before you read it. I've always loved you, however low I got. I want you to understand that.'

'I do, Greg. I do.'

He hands over the heavy wad of A4 pages, more manuscript than letter. *Do I really want this? We've been doing so well. Will this just bring it all back?* Still, I have to know. I tell Greg I need to read it privately, and he understands. I take it home to the apartment. And, though it's only nine, I climb into bed with it.

He starts by taking me back to when we met. He tells me that driving to that meeting, he was feeling the best he'd felt in his life, the most energetic, powerful, alive. Why? Because he was hypomanic. I let the manuscript drop. So he didn't love me, not really. *I was right. Reading this was a mistake.* But then I remember his face when he handed it to me, how he

317

made a point of saying he loved me, as if he knew I'd need to hear it. He wanted me to keep going.

I pick it up again.

Greg explains that had he not been hypomanic when we met, he'd never have had the confidence to pursue me. He'd have taken my refusal at face value. I am ashamed. Here is the person with manic depression taking an optimistic view. Rather than doubting his love because of hypomania, he appreciates it for making him more gung-ho.

Reading on, I learn what Greg's high was like from his point of view: how he wanted everything to happen immediately, including marriage; how he believed he was indestructible and could outsmart, outwrite, outdrive anyone. He truly believed he could do *anything*. And excel at it. Bring on the adventure. Bring on the challenge. Nothing couldn't be conquered. The world should know of his genius, his way with words, his great sexual feats. I remember that time in the restaurant. If I could have looked inside his mind back then, it would have explained so much. I would have seen how unreal his world was. I would have been more understanding. How easy it is to pigeonhole the actions of others.

I have to keep readjusting my perception of the past. Intense experiences we shared, I'm reliving from Greg's point of view. The time I confronted him about drugs: he wished he *had* been on something because he'd have had *some* explanation for his behaviour. When he accused me of having problems, he wasn't just trying to deflect attention away from himself; he really did think there was something wrong with me. I was doing everything so *slowly*. And I never knew, never *imagined*, that one of the reasons Greg avoided us during that time was because he couldn't take the fear he saw in our eyes.

I spend almost a full weekend locked away, reading, unable to detach, no appetite for anything else. Greg doesn't call. I know that he is waiting for me to call him. And he's probably terrified. I won't pretend that reading this isn't hard. It's like having my past rewritten. After the thunderstorm, when I told Greg I couldn't go on, he began to behave reasonably again, but he wasn't actually responsible for that. He had started to come down from his high, naturally. It had nothing to do with our conversation. It was the result of brain chemicals.

I learn the enormity of what I was asking Greg to do in seeing a doctor. I was urging him to admit failure, to relinquish his role as hero to his children. How could he be their hero and have a mental illness? And how could he look after the people he saw himself as responsible for if he couldn't look after himself. Despite all that, he went to the doctor because he loved me and didn't want to lose me. And I doubted his love. How easily I had given up.

When Greg told me he was trying to protect me by isolating me, I never imagined the extent of what he was protecting me from. When he was admitted to hospital so quickly and for so long, I never dreamed it could have been because he was suicidal. He thought of it constantly. He even planned it. Actually planned to take his life, leave us. It is like receiving a physical blow. Pages fall and scatter. A wave of nausea takes hold, and I race to the toilet and watch as the contents of my stomach disturb the stillness of the water. I wash my face and then cry all over it. I want to grab Greg and shake him, scream why. But the answer is lying silent on the bed. Waiting.

He struggled to keep going, to keep doing those simple things that had once been automatic. Everything that had given him joy became impossible – writing, reading, communicating, *living*. The man whose life had been books could no longer read to the end of a sentence, let alone steer his thoughts into writing one. The people he loved became a reminder that something was wrong. He felt *so far away*. He wasn't just down; he was underground, in the dark, cold earth, already in the grave but living. There was no escape in sleep, because he could not sleep. He'd lie awake watching the sunrise, wondering (as he'd once told me) how he'd get through another *entire* day. Greg was in a tunnel with no light at the end. Then suicide became a light. It seemed to him the only way out. What was the point in living when he already felt dead? Better to end it and save everyone the *pain*.

That I lived with him through that, without any clear understanding of what he was going through, makes me feel insensitive, clumsy, stupid and of course guilty. Thankfully it does not end there. Greg took his medication with absolutely no hope that anything would improve. But slowly, very slowly, the opaque screen that had been shielding us from him began to fade, and he remembered why he loved us. He realized that he needed to fight for us. There were things that helped: certain things I inadvertently said; seeing the children and being able to explain what had gone wrong; being able to talk to Betty; then me; exercise; the hospital chaplain; getting home; and yes, even group therapy.

He has changed, he writes: quicker, now, to give people the benefit of the doubt, more appreciative of his family and the people who stuck by him, and more than willing to take one day at a time.

34

I put the last page down. Outside it's dark. And quiet. One question rings in my mind: how could I ever have considered leaving this person? I check my watch. Eleven. I grab my car keys and run.

I let myself in and find him in the living room, reading by a blazing fire.

'Hey!' I say.

He looks up.

I beam at him to let him know that everything is OK. Then go to him, take the book from his hand and place it upside down on the table. I ease myself on to his lap and snuggle up to him.

'You're wonderful,' I say.

'So you're not leaving me, then?'

'Not for the moment.' I stretch up to kiss his cheek, then rest back against his chest. 'I can't believe what you've been through.' My voice starts to crack.

He puts his arms round me, kisses the top of my head.

'Thank you for telling me.'

He rests his cheek against my hair.

'I love you so much,' I say.

For a while we are quiet. Then something important occurs to me. I sit up from him. 'You have to publish it, Greg.'

He smiles as if humouring me.

'It's brave, honest, from the heart . . . and it'd help so many people.'

'It's private. I wrote it for you.'

'I know, but think of the people out there who're going through what you've been through, not knowing what's going on, their families totally at sea. If someone as high profile as you stood up and said, "I have bipolar disorder and it's not the end of the world," think of what it would do.'

'End mine. People would run a mile. From me. From my books. There goes my income, our security, up in smoke.'

'I don't think they would. I think that, OK, maybe they'd buy the book out of curiosity. But once they read it they'd see the reality – you're the same person, only stronger from what you've been through. Imagine what that would do to the stigma of mental illness.'

He looks dubious.

'Look at the alternative. Spending our lives hiding, covering it up, pretending, hoping the children won't say anything . . . Greg, publishing this would help us too.'

'Lucy, you're overestimating it.'

'Don't you want to help people?'

'I don't want the world knowing my business.'

'Even if that helps men and women out there on the verge of suicide?' OK, I'm overdoing it. I have to.

'Whatever about the rest of the world, I can't tell my mother I've manic depression.'

'Why not? Better to hear it from you than the children. If you tell her, you control the way she hears it.'

'Lucy, I need to get up.'

I get up, so he can.

He paces up and down in front of me. Eventually he stops. 'There's something I haven't told you, Lucy. Something that happened when I was a child.'

Oh, God, this is it, whatever he has been hiding . . .

'My father had depression. He committed suicide. If my mother hears I have depression, it would kill her.'

'My God, Greg . . . I'm so sorry.'

'Never mention this to Rob. OK? He doesn't know. No one does, except my mother and the GP.'

'But how do *you* know?' I can't believe she told one child and not the other.

Pain passes over his face and the realization dawns on me.

'Don't tell me you found him, Greg.'

He puts on a fake smile. 'Hanging from his dressing-gown belt . . . My mother sent me to call him for breakfast. He never could get up in the morning.'

'Oh, Greg.' I go to him, take him in my arms as if he's still that ten-year-old boy.

'That's what he left me, Lucy, that memory. It's blotted out all others. I can't think of him without thinking of that. It's too powerful. So I don't think of him. Don't talk about him.'

Everything begins to slot into place. How Rob can chat endlessly about growing up, while Greg refuses to revisit the same childhood. Of course it's not the same childhood. Rob has his own cloud-free version while thunderstorms rumble above his brother's head. Something else clicks into place. Greg's depression is hereditary. But that means he must have had some awareness of it. 'Greg, when you started feeling depressed, didn't you worry you had inherited it from your father?'

'It crossed my mind,' he says bitterly.

I pull back from him, needing to see his eyes. 'But I don't understand. How could you have even *considered* suicide, when you knew what it does to the people left behind?'

'My logic was very different.'

I wait.

He lets out a long breath. 'I thought, better to get the inevitable over quickly. Save all that pain.'

★

That Saturday, Rob calls Greg. To apologize. He has accident-ally let slip to Phyllis about Greg's hospital stay last year. They were trying to remember the date that Phyllis's nursing home increased its fees. Thinking aloud, Rob recalled that it was about the time Greg was in hospital. Then, apparently, she pounced, saying she knew something was up. She demanded to know what. In fairness to Rob, he didn't know the full significance of keeping the news from her. And, also in fairness, he has told Greg straight away.

I'm not sure Greg appreciates either of those points as he hammers the punch bag, something he hasn't done in months.

'I can't believe it. I can't fucking believe it.' Wham!

'You better get over to her,' I suggest.

Another punch. 'I knew we shouldn't have told Rob.'

'Greg, I couldn't have coped without him. And you can't hide everything. This just proves it.'

'Fuck,' he says. Smack!

'Come on. It's not the end of the world. Maybe it's for the best. At least you can be honest with her now. I mean, that's good, isn't it?'

No answer.

'All those secrets, Greg. No wonder you got sick.'

'Manic depression is *biological*. It has nothing to do with secrets.'

'Your mother is a coper. Look what she's lived through.'

'I'm responsible for her.'

'You can't protect her from everything. You can't pro-tect her from *life*. You're human. You can't manage the world.'

'That's for sure,' he says in a defeated voice. He pats his trouser pocket for his car keys. 'I better go.'

I kiss him. 'Good luck.'

★

'Will you braid my hair, Lucy?' Rachel asks, as she usually does on Saturdays.

'Sure,' I say, remembering back to a time when she'd have died before asking me to do anything. She has grown up so much in one year. She holds herself so straight, so elegantly. Clothes are a big thing now. She has developed her own unique style. Trousers long and flared like those of her friends, but instead of the crossover tops they wear, she opts for summer dresses that have grown too short but still fit. They become mini-smocks, under which she wears plain, long-sleeved T-shirts. My favourite's the denim. She has let her fringe grow out, taking her face out of the shade, exposing it at last. She is a beautiful girl. She sits on her bed and I kneel behind her, holding brightly coloured braiding in my mouth.

'Remember when you were five and you climbed out your bedroom window and sat on the ledge?' she asks.

'Who told you that?' But I know the answer. Dad. Ever since Rachel and Toby first started spending time with my parents, he has taken it upon himself to tell them stories of when I was a child. Not all of them cute. His rationale, I discovered when I confronted him, is to make them see me as a real person rather than as some stranger who has landed in their lives without their say. The whole thing has mushroomed. I find my life being thrown back at me on a regular basis.

'Did that really happen?'

'Mm-hmm,' I say, the braiding still between my lips.

'Was it because you were looking for attention?'

'No. I was just getting fresh air,' I insist, beginning to wind the braid around a thin plait.

'But Joe said you were looking for attention. He said you were jealous of Grace.'

325

'Well, he's wrong. I sat out on the window ledge because it was peaceful and quiet and away from everything.' I've made it sound too tempting. 'But of course it was very dangerous.'

'*Were* you jealous of Grace?'

'I don't know. Maybe. Sometimes.'

'Are you still?'

'No. I appreciate Grace now.'

'And were you really engaged before?'

'Yep.'

'And did he really die?'

'Mm-hmm.'

'Were you sad?'

'Very.'

She is quiet for a moment. Then she turns her head, causing me to move my hands to avoid pulling her hair. 'If he hadn't died, you wouldn't be here now on my bed, would you?'

'No.' I smile so she doesn't think I regret it.

'So sometimes, good things can happen, can't they, because of bad things?' How wise she is for her years.

I think about Greg's illness. Would I have ever become so close to him or the children without it?

Toby bursts in.

'You're supposed to *knock*, Toby,' says his sister.

'I've got on to the Genie level,' he shouts, holding up his Game Boy for inspection. He looks like a skater boy, his top hooded and his extra large trousers long and baggy. He sees me doing Rachel's hair.

'Will you spike mine? I'll get the gel.' And off he runs.

When Greg hasn't returned, I take them to a movie showing at the local cinema. I leave a note for Greg and bring my mobile. Even so, we get back before he does. It's late afternoon when he returns. The children are upstairs. I'm enjoying a quiet moment with a book when Greg walks into the living room. I put down the novel.

'D'you want a cup of tea?' he asks.

'Please,' I say, trying to work out from his face how it went. I follow him into the kitchen. He puts on the kettle, leans against the worktop and reaches for a schoolbook. He flicks through it. 'Jesus, I was crap at Irish.'

'*Greg*. I'm dying here. What happened?'

He looks up. Smiles. 'She was actually OK. Knew something was up all along. Strangely enough, my voice was the give-away. Poor Rob. He didn't stand a chance. She dragged it out of him.'

'Well, mothers are supposed to know everything. And when you think about it, she *has* seen depression before.'

'True.'

'So, she was OK about it?'

'Pretty much.'

'Phew! That's a relief.'

'She was upset I hadn't told her. And wanted to know everything. Once I got talking, I kept going. It felt right. For the first time in my life, I stopped trying to protect her. She had so many questions about depression. She really wanted to understand. We'd never talked about what happened to Da. We've spent our lives trying to pretend. It was a heart attack, plain and simple. When he died, I was *terrified* some-thing would happen to her or Rob and I would lose them too. So I tried to make sure it didn't. I've never stopped. She doesn't want that, she told me. That's why she moved into a home rather than here. She needs her independence, not my protection. She can look after herself. She *wants* to.'

'You look relieved.'

'Lucy, you have no idea how relieved. I told her about what I've written. She wants to read it.'

I'm not sure that's a good idea. 'Does she know that you planned suicide?'

'We talked about it. I told her about lithium. And how you keep an eye out for mood swings, and how supportive you are to me.' *Not that she'll hate me any less.* 'So, yeah, I think I'll let her read it.'

I nod. Hope she's up to it.

'It's weird,' he says. 'I thought her finding out would be the worst thing in the world. It might just be the best.'

I think about that. 'Greg. Maybe it's time to do the same with Rob, tell him how your father died.'

His voice changes. 'That's different. I've kept it from him for so long. All these years.'

'You've spent your life protecting him. And I understand why. But there *is* a downside to it, Greg. When you're in trouble, you don't let him close. He's wanted to help so many times, pay you back for everything you've done for him. But you turn him away. When Catherine died, especially. This time round at least you asked him to look out for us. He really appreciated that.'

'How do you know all this?'

'He's such an open guy. He's been so good to me, so good to the children. And so loyal to you. You said your mother is a grown woman. Well, Rob's a grown man. He's able for this. Tell him. It would explain a lot. I think he needs it. And I think you do too. You all do, as a family.'

And, for the first time, he isn't dismissive.

35

Greg gives Phyllis the manuscript. For days we hear nothing. He's beginning to regret his decision when she rings. She wants him to come over. And talk. After more than thirty years of asking herself why, Phyllis has, at last, gained a deep insight into her husband's depression and ultimate suicide. The manuscript was a shock, but it has brought her a kind of peace. It wasn't her fault after all. If they'd argued less, it wouldn't have made a difference. If she'd been a better wife, it wouldn't have stopped him. Thirty years of guilt. Thirty years of self-blame. All because she didn't understand depression. It has to be published, she insists, for people like her who've had their lives ruined by an illness they underestimated. She is adamant. And hounds him for two weeks until he relents.

He sends it to his agent, hoping it'll be sent back so he can tell her he tried. Doesn't happen. Jack is hopping up and down like a child on Christmas morning. He immediately sells it to Copperplate Press and Greg's international publishers. From being a contract-breaker, Greg has become a champ. Publication will be rushed to have it out early next year, appearing simultaneously in the UK and America.

Greg hasn't included anything about his father in the book. That's his father's business, he says, nobody else's. Still, he does tell Rob – who reacts with anger: anger that Greg didn't feel he was up to the truth, anger that there has been something between them all these years and he never knew, anger that the two most important people in his world conspired to keep him living a fantasy. He goes away to try to take in a new reality. And slowly begins to appreciate that they were only doing their best to protect him from something that had traumatized them so much. Ultimately, he looks on the positive side, as only he can. He does know now and has an explanation for all those times Greg pushed him away. Most importantly, he is glad that there's no longer a need for Greg to do that.

The book is delivered and requires little editing. Greg makes a light-hearted remark about it being a good time to squeeze in a quick wedding. That he has given me an opt-out clause – the option of laughing it off or simply ignoring it – makes me love him even more. We set a date in October.

Once I dreamt of proper wedding gowns, tuxes with carnations, official photographs, video recordings, a string quartet. That dream involved another man. With Greg, none of that is important. In fact, it would be a distraction. What matters is family. And friends. The smaller the group, the more special. Words: low key, informal. Dress code: casual. As for official photos: guests, all thirty, are handed disposable cameras and instructed to be adventurous. The local church in Dalkey does the business, and a marquee in Greg's garden the trick. In Rachel we've a beautiful flower girl who has been creative with denim, and in Toby a handsome pageboy who looks just like the groom, in shirt and chinos.

Mum, Fint and Sebastian are rebels and glam up. Dad, in jeans and white shirt, looks very Paul Newman. Grace, in a simple floral dress, looks like an ad for Timotei. Shane and Jason appear Nordic and restless. Kevin, Ben and Ruth, uncomfortable. Rob, as best man, wears his most faded denims in an early Marlon Brando way. It's almost sacrilegious. But it is the groom who takes my breath away, my man, facing me now at the top of the church, eyes bluer than ever thanks to his open-necked navy shirt. Rob passes him the platinum band, and he stops to hold my gaze before slipping it on to my finger and taking me in his arms.

And then it's over. We've done it. Outside, everyone's clapping. And hugging us. Taking photos. Throwing confetti. The press must have found out, because here they are with cameras. I almost laugh at the disappointment we must be to them – no posh dress, no glam. Will their readers even believe it's a wedding? A journalist with a spiral notebook asks about my 'unusual' dress. I try to keep my face straight when I point out the 'designers' – Rachel and my mum. We smile for a few shots and let Greg's agent take it from there. Poor Jack is *not* supposed to be working. Back at the marquee, the atmosphere is party. The speeches are short. Dad's no sooner up than he's down. Greg is touching, if embarrassing. And the best man? Well, Rob is outrageous – despite the presence of his mother. She and I are still avoiding each other. And I guess that's the way it will always be. But I'm used to the idea now. Just because we both love the same man, doesn't mean we have to love each other.

Rachel and Toby stay with my parents while we escape for the first time ever. We have a week in Sicily. I feel like a new bride, not a stepmother or a bipolar-disorder casualty. We share a bed knowing neither of us has to sneak away or keep guard. Hand in hand we stroll along narrow, steep, cobbled streets, wandering in and out of tiny shops, buying each other gifts that involve thought, not extravagance. We visit small harbours, Greek temples and beaches with views of Mount Etna. Swimming in the sea, I discover my favourite place – my legs wrapped round his waist, my arms round his neck and my lips on his. We keep to ourselves, reverting to the way we were when we first met. The excitement is back, the passion, and the freedom of living without interruption or expectation. We are so happy. It's such a surprise, like a warm sunny spell at the end of a disappointing summer. Our relationship will always surprise me, I decide.

When we get home, we are an official family. We can relax. Just be ourselves. Greg's house is home now. I rent out my apartment, and we settle back to work and our new lives together. There is something fresh about our lives. It's as if we've started again with a clean slate. The world has become an optimistic and friendly place.

In March I'm in a production studio of the country's leading radio station, looking at Greg through a window. Headphones on, he's being interviewed about his new book, *At Least I Don't Snore*, chronicling his experience of manic depression. It's his first time to speak publicly about it. He spent last night awake, terrified that he was on the verge of ruining his career. Will people think him mad? Will he lose his readers? Will publishers shun him?

When we got to the station half an hour ago, Greg was going to back out. Wasn't it enough to write the book, without having to talk about it as well? He was getting up to leave when the presenter appeared in the cafeteria, where we'd been asked to wait. Greg had been interviewed by Gerry Glennon before and liked him. He came over to chat, so down to earth you'd never think he was a rising star. He told Greg the type of questions he'd be asking. I could see him begin to relax. Gerry asked us to go back to the studio with him. I stayed with the production team in one room, while Greg followed Gerry into the studio. As the pre-show news bulletin came over the air, Gerry readied Greg at his mike, explaining that he need only wear headphones when taking questions from callers. Greg paled but was stuck. No escape. He looked out at me with a grimace, and I smiled encouragement. Gerry introduced Greg to the listeners, then eased Greg into the questions.

Now it's as if they're having a quiet chat between themselves, not in a studio with a large chunk of the population listening. Greg considers each question as if searching for a precise and accurate answer, as if he wants to get it exactly right, be understood. He's not trying to entertain, impress or be funny. Just get it right. I can't take my eyes off him.

Texts and e-mails begin to flood in. The studio phones are hopping. How immediate radio is. People all over the country are wishing him well – fans, sufferers, doctors, even people with no connection who want to show support. Greg speaks about his high, his low, his plans for suicide. To emphasize the importance of staying on lithium, he relates the story of our mountainside descent, and admits to putting his family in danger. The producer begins to reorganize the programme, cancelling other guests and letting the interview run. Gerry starts to take calls, and Greg answers each question with the same concentration that has characterized the interview. When he finally emerges, he looks exhausted. I stay in the background as Gerry and his team thank and congratulate him. Calls are still coming in. As soon as Greg turns on his mobile, it starts to ring. And keeps ringing all morning until he has to turn it off again. At some point I fit in how proud I am of him.

Over the next few days Copperplate's publicist is on to him constantly. Newspapers want interviews; the late-night TV talk shows compete with each other to have him on. It's like he's become a commodity. Which makes him nervous. He didn't expect or want this level of attention. But public reaction is such that within days of the launch, a second, much larger printrun of the book is ordered. Stocks are almost depleted when the next batch arrives at Copperplate's warehouse. Matt personally helps deliver copies to wholesalers and bookshops. He takes all his staff off current assignments for a week to handle the flurry. Hundreds turn up at Greg's Dublin book signing. Reviews are positive. Greg's reaction is relief. It doesn't seem to have been a mistake after all. He'll be able to hand over a decent cheque to the mental-health charity that has been promised the Irish royalties.

The following week, when I'm back at work again, Fint sticks his head around my door.

'Hi,' he says.

I smile hello. 'Come in.' He usually doesn't need to be asked.

He closes the door behind him, also unusual, then sits on the corner of my desk. 'I wish you'd told me.'

'I wanted to. But I couldn't.'

'I never imagined . . .' He pushes his glasses up his nose. 'It must have been a nightmare.'

I sit back, fold my arms. 'It was. But it's almost two years ago now. And, thank God, he hasn't had another episode.'

He picks up my stapler and begins to fiddle with it. 'If only I'd known, I would have been more patient.'

'Fint, you were great, once you knew I was in trouble. You've been really great. I'm sorry I couldn't tell you.'

'I heard him on the radio. He had me in bits. What he went through!'

'Yeah.'

'Suicide.'

'Well, he didn't actually –'

'I know.' He puts the stapler down, gives me a loaded look. 'You'd be surprised the people who think of it at one time or other.'

'*You?*'

He raises his eyebrows and nods. 'A long time ago. When I was at school.'

'*Why?*'

'I was having a rough enough time of it. It was your typical all-boys' school. Rugby, rugby, rugby. And more rugby. If you weren't into it, you weren't one of the lads. And if you weren't one of the lads, you were pretty much crucified. So you'd pretend to be like them. But you weren't. You knew that. They knew that. You hated yourself. And so did they. They called you girls' names. Tripped you up. Let air out of your bicycle tyres. Laughed in your face. For years. You couldn't see a way out. You couldn't tell anyone, especially your parents, because they had their expectations and homosexuality wasn't one of them. It was against the law.'

'God.'

'I saw one solution. A quick one. Dad, as you know, was in the army. He'd guns locked away at home. I knew where he hid the key. We all did. I got a gun, went to my room, loaded it as he'd taught me, put it to my head. But I couldn't do it. I left it on the bed and ran. For miles. I wasn't going back. But I did – at some point. When I got to my room, the gun was still there on the bed. No one had found it. I put it back, locked the drawer, returned the key to its hiding place. No one ever knew. I never tried again. I stuck out school, went to art college and began to see that there were lots of people like me, and they were normal. It was OK to like beautiful things. It was OK to be myself.'

'What age were you?'

'Sixteen.'

'I'd never have met you.' The shock of that. 'I'd never have known you, Fint. We'd never have had all those laughs, set up our business, created all those designs –'

'I'd never have fallen in love, never have tasted champagne. Forget that, I'd never have had a massage . . .'

His weakness.

'Your parents would've been broken-hearted.' I *love* Fint's mum. As does Fint. 'When did you tell them you were gay?'

'Second year in college, I finally got the courage.'

'How did they take it?'

'Nobody reacted like I thought they would. My father, who I thought would blow up, put his arm around me and said, "You poor bastard." My mother, who I thought would be OK, was gutted. She saw me as having a family. She thought being gay would mean a harder life.'

I think about that. 'Are you sorry you'll never have a family?'

He shakes his head. 'I don't think about it. It's just the way it is. I've nieces and nephews. They're my kids in a funny way.'

It isn't something I've considered, children of my own, struggling as I've been with Rachel and Toby. But they accept me now. Things are easier. What would a child of ours be like, I wonder. What would Greg think of a baby? What would Rachel and Toby think? *On second thoughts, maybe it's something for the future.*

'But you're fine now, right? You're happy?' I ask.

'God, yeah. It's such a relief to be able to go home and be myself. And Mum's great about it now.'

'I know. She's a dote.'

'Of course, I wouldn't say no to a stable, long-term relationship. It's what we all want, isn't it? To have someone to love and be loved by.'

36

A month later Greg and I are having coffee in the kitchen. He's exhausted, having just returned from a whirlwind book tour of America and I've taken a few days off to catch up. The doorbell rings. Being jet-lag free, I hop up to get it. Standing outside is a small, thin, birdlike woman in her thirties with mousy hair and a forgettable face. She's dressed in a grey business suit that has seen better days. I've never set eyes on her before.

'Hi. Can I help you?'

'Yes. I'd like to speak to Greg Millar, please.'

I see that she is delivering a package.

'Do you want me to just give him that?' I ask, trying to avoid having him get up.

'No,' she says. 'I have to give this to him in person.' There is something about the way she says it that makes me nervous.

'Just a second, then.' I go to get him, leaving the door open.

'Who is it?' he asks.

'I don't know. Someone delivering something who says she has to give it to you in person.'

I go back out with him.

'Greg Millar?' she asks when he gets to the door.

'Yes?'

She holds out a large yellow padded envelope. Greg is about to take it from her when she taps him with it, saying, 'You are served.'

My heart jumps.

'Sorry?' Greg says, looking at the envelope that has been thrust into his hand.

But she has already turned and is hurrying to her dusty Nissan Micra. She starts the engine after two attempts and drives away, spewing exhaust. Greg looks at me, 'Probably some chancer trying to get money out of my publisher or something. Wouldn't worry.'

In the kitchen he examines the envelope. Turning it over, he starts to remove the numerous staples that hold it together. As soon as he starts to read the legal-looking documents contained within, his face changes.

'Shit.'

'What?'

'Fucking hell.'

'What?'

'They want the children.'

'Who? Who wants the children?' My hands are at either side of my face.

'Ben and Ruth. They want custody of Rachel and Toby.'

'*What?*'

He looks up, wounded. 'They think I'm an unfit parent. They heard me on the radio. They've read the book. They think I'm a danger to their grandchildren.'

'No. There must be a mistake. They wouldn't do that.'

'They think I'm going to top myself in front of the children, that I'm going to drive off a mountain with them in the car.' He slams the document on to the worktop, runs his fingers through his hair. 'Fuck.'

I pick up the papers as if they might spontaneously combust. The first page is a solicitor's letter explaining that it's 'a court order, made *ex parte*, granting interim custody to the applicants, with a motion for a court hearing, grounded on an affidavit'. Whatever that means. It's like a foreign language. Which makes it even more scary. 'Are you sure that's what it means?'

'Read it. If we don't hand Rachel and Toby over to them within twenty-four hours, we'll be in contempt of court. They can get a bench warrant for my arrest for failing to comply with the terms of the court order.'

Jesus Christ! I can't believe this is happening. 'But they can't do that. They can't just take the children.'

'Here, give me the letter.' He takes it. 'It says here' – he underlines it with a finger – 'that, according to the Guardian-ship of Infants Act, they can.'

My hand presses against my chest.

'They think I'm mad. They think their grandchildren are in danger.'

I can't speak. I can't do anything. Except panic.

'I shouldn't have written that stupid book. I should have kept my mouth shut . . . This is what I get for messing with stigmas.'

I realize how stupid we've been. 'We should have talked to them before the book came out,' I say. 'We should have explained. How could we have forgotten them?'

'Exactly. How the fuck could we have forgotten Ben of all people?'

I think back. 'We were focusing on your mother. And then everything happened so quickly with the book. Then the wedding. We just didn't think. Everything was going so well with them, the children visiting every week, we forgot what they were like when they thought there was a problem, the way they hounded us, fussed over the children, the way he called them *my grandchildren* as though they were his. How could we have forgotten Ben?'

Greg's pacing the kitchen. 'I'm calling our solicitor.' After a brief conversation, in which my husband does most of the listening, he hangs up.

'Well?'

'We need a family law solicitor. Harry knows someone. He's giving her a call and will get straight back to us.'

'But they can't do this, can they? They can't just take the children from us?'

He opens the drinks cabinet and slams it shut again. The phone rings and Greg has a longer conversation with Harry. He replaces the phone.

'What did he say?'

'They've gone to the High Court and convinced a judge that I'm a danger to my children. Without our being there, she granted them temporary custody until a court hearing decides who they should stay with for good.' His voice falters.

'Well, it's a mistake. You're not a danger. And that's that. The family law solicitor will fix this. It's all just a mistake. It has to be. When's she coming?'

'She's in court all day and usually wouldn't be available after that, especially to call out here, but apparently she owes Harry one. She'll be here as soon as she's free. In the meantime she's sending a courier to collect the legal documents. She'll try to look at them over lunch, in between cases and on her way over to us.'

'Why're they doing this? Why?'

'We lied to them, Lucy. We told them everything was OK. And they believed us. Now they know the truth. Hilary wasn't exaggerating. They think I'm a danger. And I don't blame them.' He sounds gutted. He finally sits, cradling his head in his hands.

'You'd never do anything to harm Rachel and Toby. This is ridiculous.'

'I've a mental illness,' he says. 'They heard me loud and clear on the radio saying how I put you all in danger. They heard me say I was suicidal. As far as they're concerned, it could happen again. And they're right. It could.'

'But you haven't had an episode in almost two years.'

'It doesn't make any difference.'

I start leafing through the stack of legal documents as though I can somehow single-handedly solve a problem I don't even understand. But I have to do something. 'I don't believe it,' I say. 'There's something here from Hilary.'

'*Hilary?*' He gets up and comes over.

I hand him a document. He speed-reads it. 'That's great. That's just great. Hilary's made a sworn statement, going into vivid detail of how terrified she and Rachel were in the car in France, how out of control my driving was, how I wouldn't listen to reason. It's all here. Black and white.' He slaps it with the back of his hand.

I feel sick. She has finally found a way. 'Sexual harassment seems minor by comparison.'

We look at each other.

'I think you should ring Ben,' I say. 'Try to explain everything. Tell them we didn't want to worry them.'

'Why should he believe me now?'

'You could bring a letter from Professor Power saying everything is under control, that you haven't had a relapse in almost two years.'

He looks doubtful.

'It's worth a try, Greg. Anything is.'

'Maybe I should check with Harry first.'

'OK. Yeah. Maybe.' I haven't a clue. I'm so out of my depth, I'm drowning.

He rings Harry, who says it should be fine as long as we don't make any threats or say anything that could be used

341

against us. Whatever that means. We interpret it as 'be nice'.

Greg picks up the phone, dials, waits, then drops the handset. He looks at me. 'It was Hilary. What's she doing over there?'

What is going on?

We need that solicitor. But have all day to wait. We can't stay still, have to get out of the house. We find ourselves on Dún Laoghaire Pier, walking its length over and over, oblivious to the cold wind that has others stooped, heads down, hands in pockets. We're quiet, each of us trying to work out a solution. Every so often the silence is broken by one of us bursting out with an idea. But it doesn't get us anywhere. Law is something you either know your way around or you don't. We don't.

When it's time to collect the children from school, we go together. We do our best to act normally. But it's hard not to cling to them. It's hard to be casual when they're silent on the way home, as they always are. It seems such a waste of time not to be talking. At home we notice every little thing they do, every word they say. We cook their favourite, tuna pasta. It reminds me of that first day in France when Rachel said she hated me. It seems so far away. We let them watch whatever they want on TV and wonder how important homework really is in the scale of things. I try not to think that they could be gone in less than twenty-four hours.

Freda Patterson has a strong handshake. Instead of hello comes a brusque apology for being so late – crisis at home. Her crisis means that Rachel and Toby are asleep by the time she arrives. It also means that, presumably, she has a family. *Good*, I think. *She'll have more empathy. Won't she?* Her curt demeanour makes me wonder. We show her in. She slips out of her mackintosh. When I attempt to take it from her, she shakes her head.

'It's fine,' she says, sitting and folding it over the side of the armchair. She's still in her business suit, pale grey with a pencil skirt. She looks efficient.

'Sorry,' I say, getting up from where I've just sat down. 'I never offered you tea or coffee.'

'No, no, I'm fine.'

I sit down again.

Greg looks at me as if to say, 'Relax.'

She clears her throat with an almost masculine sound. 'Now.' She pulls the documents from her case.

'Can they do this?' I ask.

She looks up, seems to consider me for a second.

'Yes. I'm afraid they can.'

'*How?*'

'Well,' she says, putting her briefcase back on the floor, 'they've based their claims on a published book, a broadcast radio interview and a sworn affidavit from what looks like a reliable childminder, given that she worked for you for five years.'

Even to me, it doesn't sound good.

'By granting this injunction,' she continues, 'the judge has, I'm afraid, already indicated that she considers the children's father a danger. And in family law, the welfare of the children is the primary concern.'

What does she mean 'the children's father'? He's sitting opposite her. He has a name. 'Greg,' I say. 'The children's father's name is Greg.'

'Yes, of course. Greg. I'm sorry.'

'Is there anything we can do to stop them being taken tomorrow?' Greg asks.

'No, I'm afraid not.'

'There has to be something,' I say. 'You can't just go into court and swear that someone is a bad parent and have their children taken away. There has to be some safety net against that happening.'

'I'm afraid, in this case, Greg has publicly admitted to endangering the children's lives by driving dangerously with them in the car. The fact that he still has the condition that caused him to do that means that technically there is a risk it could happen again. In situations such as this, where a serious yellow flag has been raised in terms of the welfare of a child and a relative or health board mounts a legal challenge, the courts will look at it. And they will consider the welfare of the child a priority.'

I am sick, totally stalled, like a person in a nightmare who can't move when faced with danger.

'What about Lucy?' Greg asks, his voice urgent. 'Lucy is my wife and the children's stepmother. Doesn't her being here count for anything?'

Freda doesn't look optimistic. 'Lucy was in the car during the dangerous driving incident and allegedly unable to influence your behaviour. Her role in protecting the children could be legally challenged. Aside from that, step-parents are not considered, in law, to be as significant as flesh and blood. Legally, grandparents have a stronger claim on the children because there is a blood link.'

Greg interrupts. 'But that's ridiculous – doesn't it matter at all who the children are closer to, who would do a better job at parenting, who the children would *prefer* to be with?'

'Greg, if you were to die in the morning, Rachel and Toby would be removed from Lucy's care, immediately.'

We look at each other, eyes wide.

Then Freda adds, 'Unless, of course, you have *adopted* the children?'

'Adopted? Why would I need to adopt if I'm already a stepmother?'

Greg interrupts. 'Would it make a difference?'

'It would have, yes,' she says, speaking in the past tense. 'It would have created a direct line between Lucy and the children.'

'Why don't people tell you that?' I ask. 'How are you supposed to know?'

Again Greg interrupts. 'Lucy could adopt them now.'

'I'm afraid there would never be enough time. It is a long and arduous process.' Seeing our distress, her face softens. 'Having said all that, in *this* case, one thing has gone in your favour. Their solicitor has made, in my view, a slight cock-up . . .' The word startles me coming from Freda. 'He has included Lucy's name on the order. That increases your relevance to the case,' she says, looking at me, 'and puts you both in a stronger position because they are effectively acknowledging your position as that of a parent. A parent who does not have bipolar disorder.'

'But then –' starts Greg.

'Legally, it could still be undermined because the blood link is stronger. But it's *something*.'

I look at my husband, guilty that I never offered to adopt the children, and even more guilty that I am considered a better parent simply because I don't have bipolar disorder.

But Greg hasn't given up yet. 'Can't we argue that taking the children from their home would be extremely traumatic? They've already had to suffer separation when I was in hospital. Surely a court should recognize this? And surely Ben and Ruth must come across in a bad light for seeming not to care about that?'

'You can argue it but not until the hearing. Temporary custody has been granted. A decision has already been taken in court that indicates that the judge is concerned about the children's welfare.'

'Couldn't we appeal?'

'Yes. You could. But it wouldn't be in your interest. An appeal would be based on a short affidavit only – not enough, in my opinion, to convince a judge. A full hearing is what you need, and that is already planned for three weeks' time. What we should concentrate on now is being as prepared as we can for that hearing. We need to get a report from your psychiatrist . . .'

But Greg has stopped listening, 'Are you saying that the children have to stay with Ben and Ruth for three weeks? That's a *ridiculous* amount of time to separate children from their parents. It's unjust.'

'That's why I'll begin negotiations for access tomorrow,' says Freda in an assured tone. 'We should get daily access. It may have to be supervised. Indeed, we should request supervised access. It would increase our chance of getting it. I will argue for supervision to be carried out by a relative.' She makes a note of that.

'So hang on,' I say. 'We can't get the children back for another three weeks, and there's a chance we may not even see them in that time, and then a court hearing will decide who they will be staying with permanently?'

'That would be a pretty accurate summation.'

Jesus.

'With whom will you negotiate for access?' asks Greg, who has started to take notes himself.

'The applicants, through their solicitor.'

'Who are the applicants?' I ask.

'The children's grandparents. They are the applicants. You are the respondents.'

'What if they don't agree to access?' Greg continues.

'Unlikely. Their solicitor will advise them to agree. Judges

346

don't look favourably on denial of access. Even in child abuse cases, access is granted. Supervised access.'

Child abuse? This is nothing like child abuse. How can she even compare the two?

'But,' she continues, 'as there have been cases where applicants have not agreed to access, I will prepare a replying affidavit to bring a motion, returnable on the date of the court case, seeking interim access that day.' She makes a note of that.

'Sorry, what?'

'If they don't agree, the question of access will be before the courts in three weeks.'

'That's all we can do?' asks Greg.

'For the moment.'

'What about speeding up the hearing?' It's Greg again, asking all the right questions.

'I must warn you,' she says. 'The case may in actual fact be postponed.'

'What? Why?' I say, not believing.

'Their side is likely to apply for a Section 47 Report as soon as the hearing opens. If that happens, and don't be surprised if it does, then nothing can be decided until the report has been prepared. It may take weeks.'

'I'm sorry, you've lost me,' I say. 'What's a Section 47 Report?'

'It's a report carried out, for the benefit of the court by an independent expert – a child psychiatrist or psychologist usually – recommending which party custody should go to. The – probably psychiatrist in this case – will be professionally trained to interview the applicants and respondents. He will also want to see how the children interact with both. He will, almost certainly, look for access to your medical records, Greg.

These can, I'm afraid, be used as evidence against you.'

'If they're going to apply for a Section 47 Report anyway,' says Greg, 'would there be any advantage in our being the ones to request it, you know, to show we've nothing to fear?'

'No, the courts will make their decision on the welfare of the children only. And no, I wouldn't request one. Once evidence goes in, that's it, you can't take it back,' she says, leaving us in no doubt that a Section 47 Report would not be good news.

'Is there anything we can do to influence the report?' Greg asks.

I think it a wasted question. Surely there's nothing we can do.

'Two things,' she says. 'First, it is well known that some psychiatrists are more pro-men than others.'

'Really?' I can't help saying.

She nods. 'I'll go through the list of psychiatrists who do these reports and contact one I feel would be appropriate and see if he could start work ASAP. If the applicants request a Section 47 Report, they'll suggest a psychiatrist. If we don't agree with their selection, we can put forward the name of our man on the basis that he'd be ready to start immediately. Saving time would be seen as hugely advantageous to the court.'

'You said there were two things we could do?' Greg is ready with his pen.

'Yes, we should also ask the psychiatrist you attend to prepare a report on your condition, treatment and prognosis. You're his patient. He's likely to give you a favourable report. However, I should warn you that a Section 47 Report, should it be requested, will override all others.'

'Is there anything at all in our favour?' I ask.

'Well, there's Greg's history as a good father.' She turns to

Greg. 'You've been a parent for twelve years and nothing untoward has happened to the children in your care. There is the fact that your condition is well-controlled . . . I *assume* it is?'

Empathy of a stone.

'I haven't had an episode since I was diagnosed almost two years ago,' Greg says, flushing under her scrutiny. I hate Ben, Ruth and Hilary for putting him through this.

'Good, well. We have that in our favour. And the fact that Lucy has been included on the order.'

'Thank God for "cock-ups",' he says bitterly.

'What do we do now?' I ask.

'First thing in the morning I'll get on to their solicitor to negotiate access.'

'Could you let us know how the negotiations go as soon as you can?' It's Greg. 'We need to talk to the children.'

The thought of telling Rachel and Toby nearly chokes me.

'Yes, of course,' she says.

'When do we have to hand them over?' asks Greg.

'I'll find that out tomorrow . . . Right, I'd better be off. It was good to meet you both.' She holds out her hand. 'Till the morning, then?'

'What d'you think of her?' asks Greg as soon as we get back to the living room.

'I don't know. What d'you think?'

'I like her,' he says.

'You do?'

'She's straight. Says it as it is. No bull.'

'She doesn't seem to have much of a heart, though, does she?'

'We don't need a heart, Lucy. We need balls.'

'Well, she certainly seems to have those.'

'Let's hope so. We're totally in her hands now.'

'I still can't believe it,' I say, shaking my head.

'I shouldn't have written that bloody book.'

'No, Greg. That book had to be written. It shouldn't be used against you. Millions of people have manic depression. It's not a licence to take their children away.'

'Not unless they're dumb enough to go on record showing how out of control they were. That driving thing is going to sink us, Lucy. I know it. I can convince anyone I'd never commit suicide so that the children could find me – not after my experience. But the driving thing – I can't argue that.'

'Your condition is under control. Your psychiatrist will vouch for you.'

'I know, but what about that bloody Section 47 Report? It's going to hammer us.'

'That's if they go for it.'

'You heard Freda. They'll go for it.'

'We need access. We have to be able to reassure the children. All I can think of is what Hilary might say to turn them against us, the lies she'll come up with. She had so much control over them once. We need to see them. We need to keep in touch.'

'I know.'

We watch Rachel sleep, safe and secure in her land of dreams, cheeks flushed, features relaxed and trusting. There's no trace of the gutsy little girl who once declared war on me with a fury I later came to admire – only a softness that reminds me of how she came to my rescue after her grandmother's visit, how she's always looked out for her little brother, how she did the same for her father as soon as he came home. She looks so peaceful, and I know there's nothing we can do to protect her.

Toby, in his room, looks so innocent. Vulnerable. This is the boy who has always made me smile, who likes *Horrid Henry* and *Captain Underpants* and who says, 'Hello, sir,' to every dog he passes in the street. The little boy I couldn't bear to lose.

It doesn't seem right for us to be sleeping apart. We should be herding together, safety in numbers. But there is safety in nothing. A process has been set in motion, without our say, to take the children from us, for at least three weeks, maybe for ever. A person we've never met will decide our future.

Neither of us sleeps. Every few minutes one of us sits up, flicks on a bedside lamp and scribbles something down – an argument in favour of us as parents, an argument against them as guardians, a word or phrase that might help explain all of this to Rachel and Toby. Rachel and Toby, the children I once wished away but whom I've come to love as if they were my own.

37

Greg takes Rachel and Toby to school as though it's a normal day. I wait by the phone. When he returns, we wait together. At eleven, just as we're trying to decide whether it's a good or bad sign that Freda hasn't yet called, she does. And it's bad. Access denied. The most they'll do is let us talk to the children over the phone twice a day, at allocated times. Greg, who has been so patient, loses it.

'Who gave them the right to make the rules?'

I sigh. 'The law.'

He looks at me. 'This means war. This means fucking *war*. If they want to play the bully, let's see how tough they are. Let's see how fit they are to be parents, how mentally stable.'

'What'll we tell the children?' It's all I can think.

'Well, I don't know about you, but I haven't a clue what to fucking tell them. Sorry, guys, but we don't make the decisions any more. Out of our hands. Don't look at us.'

'Greg, they're coming at three. We have to think of something. We have to pack.'

'I can't believe this. I can't fucking believe it.'

We pack first in the hope that it'll clear our heads. But it turns out to be a bad idea. Putting away their things in cases and bags – Game Boy, books, sewing things, drawing stuff, pillows, clothes, uniforms, togs, hurley stick, hockey gear, skateboard, helmet and protective pads – makes it all real. Definite.

We discuss and argue and argue and discuss what we should

or shouldn't tell them. There's no way they should learn how out of control things are. Still, we can't lie, invent some three-week holiday they're not invited on. Even if we wanted to, it wouldn't work. A strange man will come asking questions. Who knows what Hilary will say? And what will we tell them if, after the three weeks, we don't get them back? They'll never trust us again. Somehow, we have to give them as much of the truth as we can, without the accompanying worry. Impossible, considering *we* know the truth and we're terrified.

We hear Rachel's quick footsteps echoing in the corridor. She rounds a corner shoving her second arm into her coat, her school bag slung over one shoulder. She beams when she sees us, looking delighted to be let out early. Then she sees our faces.

'What is it, Dad?' she asks as soon as we reach each other.

He hugs her tightly. I pick up her bag, which has fallen to the floor.

'Is Toby OK? What is it?' She looks from Greg to me, back to Greg.

'Toby's fine,' Greg says at last. 'He's still in school.' He rubs her cheek. 'We wanted to talk to you about something.' His voice is so gentle.

'What?'

'Wait till we get outside, pet,' he says.

She looks at me.

I force a flat smile. How are we going to do this?

There's a park opposite. 'Let's go in here,' I suggest, realizing how awkward it would be to talk in the car. We sit on the edge of a fountain, Rachel in the middle. All around us, spring is adding optimistic touches. Bluebells spreading out under trees, daffodils in cheery clumps, crocuses and snowdrops reminding me of Easter. Cherry trees are showering the paths with their superior blossom, birds are preparing for family life. A red balloon floats high over the buildings on the other side of the park. In the distance a mother lifts her toddler out of a safety swing. Beyond the railings people run for a bus.

'Rachel, sweetheart,' starts Greg. 'We've something to tell you.'

'I know,' she says. 'Is it bad?'

'You know Gran and Grandad Franklin?'

'Are they OK?'

'Yes. Yes, they're fine.' He looks at me as if to say, 'I wish they weren't.' 'No. It's just that they want you to stay with them for a while.'

She's surprised. 'For a sleepover?'

'Well,' he looks at me again, then back at Rachel. 'For a bit longer than that.'

'How long?'

'About three weeks.'

'*Three weeks?* But that's *ages*. What about school?'

'You'll still be able to go to school.'

'But why do they want me to stay for three weeks?'

'Not just you, honey, Toby too.'

'But why, Dad?'

'It's a long story, Rache.' When his eyes seek mine, I encourage him with a smile. He turns to his daughter. 'It's kind of hard to explain . . .'

She waits.

'Remember when I was sick?'

She nods.

'Well, Gran and Grandad don't really understand about bipolar disorder very well, and they think I can't be a proper dad if I have it. So they want to mind you for a while.'

'But you're better now, Dad. Just tell them.'

'They won't listen.'

'I'll tell them. They always listen to me.'

'Sweetheart, there's something else I have to tell you.'

'What?'

'For those three weeks Lucy and I won't be able to see you. We'll talk on the phone twice every day, but we can't go to see you and you can't come home.'

She looks very wary. 'What's going on? This doesn't sound right.'

'Well,' Greg struggles, 'it's just that Gran and Grandad want you to live with them for good –'

'*What?*' She stands suddenly, turning to face her father. '*No way.*'

He stands too. 'Now, Rachel, that's the last thing Lucy and I want. We want you with us –'

'So why aren't we, then? Why do we have to go for three weeks? I don't want to go at all.'

'Rachel, the thing is,' Greg says with obvious difficulty, 'actually, honey, could you sit down for a sec. I'm trying to tell you something.'

She leans back against the fountain. Not exactly sitting.

Greg sits back down. 'You see, Gran and Grandad have asked a judge to decide who you should live with.'

'*A judge? Why? This is crazy.*'

'Rachel, remember that time in France when we were driving down that mountain?'

She nods sullenly.

'That was because of the illness. You know that. You under-stand. But Gran and Grandad don't. They're worried that I might do it again, and they think they're protecting you by having you live with them. They don't understand that I'm taking my medication now and that I'm fine. Lucy and I have to explain all that to the judge. A very clever lady is going to help us do that. She's a solicitor and really knows her stuff.

Together, we're going to convince that judge that we're the best people to look after you.'

'What if you don't?'

'We will.'

'How do you know?'

'I just do.'

'Dad. This doesn't sound good.'

'It's OK, Rachel. I promise, you'll only have to stay with them for three weeks.'

Don't promise, Greg. We said we wouldn't.

'But I don't want to,' says Rachel. 'What if I tell the judge that? He'll listen to me, won't he? It should be up to me who I live with, shouldn't it?'

'It should, pet. But it isn't.'

'But I'm twelve. I'm almost a teenager. I know what I want. And I want to be with you. I want to stay at home.' She begins to cry.

'Rachel. Rachel, sweetheart. Please. Come on. You have to trust me. We'll sort this out. You just have to be patient. And do this one thing. Just go there for three weeks . . . Remember when I had to go into hospital. That was for longer. And we managed then, didn't we? It was tough for a while, but we managed. And you looked after Toby so well for me, didn't you?' He lifts her chin. 'Remember? You were great. I need you to do that again, pet. He's too young to understand. We can't tell him as much as we've told you. He'd be too afraid. Poor little fellow.'

'*I'm* afraid.'

'I know. But you have to trust us that we are going to convince that judge that your home is with us. We will. It might take a while, but we will do it. After three weeks, we'll see you every day until we get you back for good.'

'Promise?'

'Promise.'

She sighs. 'All right, then, I'll do it.' As if she has a choice.

We sit with Rachel and discuss what we should say to Toby. It gives her a focus outside of her own misery. Toby's a pretty copped-on seven-year-old, she reminds us. We should be honest with him. And so, to the boy with the brown eyes, we offer a simplistic, optimistic, watered-down version of what we've told his sister. Rachel helps us through it.

'I'll be with you all the time,' she says. 'And I'm going to make it like a holiday. Wait till you see. I'm going to bring my pocket money and buy you a treat every day.'

'Really?'

'Yeah.'

'Even chewing gum?'

'Yeah. And when we get home, Lucy and Dad will get you loads of treats. They might even get you a new Game Boy game.' She looks at us hopefully.

'Absolutely,' Greg says.

'And I'll still be able to go to school?'

'Yep,' says Rachel.

'And hurley?'

'Yep.'

'Can I bring my Game Boy?'

'You can bring anything you want,' says his father.

'But what if my tooth falls out?' he says, wobbling one of his bottom set.

'The tooth fairy will find you.'

I hope Greg's right. I look at Rachel, and she understands. She'll take care of it.

'What time will you be ringing?' he asks.

'Before you leave for school. And just before bedtime. OK?'

'OK. And when the judge decides, we're definitely coming home?'

'Definitely,' says Greg.

It was wrong, I know, to promise. But how could he not? He had to give them something to look forward to, something to keep them going. Three weeks is a long time in a child's calendar. And maybe, just maybe, they won't ask for a Section 47 Report. Maybe the hearing will go ahead, and the judge will send them home. I try not to think of Ben, the man used to getting his own way, and try not to think of Hilary, who is finally fulfilling her promise to us. What a good witness she'll make – the caring nanny of five years.

The doorbell goes at three, on the button. We all look at each other. The children shrink back, suddenly seeming smaller, younger.

'I don't want to go,' says Toby.

Greg bends down to him, puts a hand on his shoulder. 'You have to be a big boy now, Tobes,' he says gently. I imagine similar words being said to Greg many years ago.

'Come on, Toby,' says Rachel. 'The sooner we go, the sooner we'll be back.'

How I wish that were true. We trundle into the hall with the luggage. Open the door to another surprise.

'Hilary!' four voices exclaim, two angry, two happy, all surprised.

'What are you doing here?' Rachel asks.

'I'm going to help your grandparents mind you,' she says with a warm, warm smile. She looks more like her old self, her eyes bright, focused. Her posture, confident. She is back in the driving seat. Plan A, executed. Now on to Plan B.

I look at Rachel. Her face is alight. 'How did you know Gran and Grandad would be minding us?'

Ah, the innocence of a child.

'They told me,' she says brightly. 'And then they asked me to help them. And of course I said yes.'

'Of course,' says Greg with sarcasm.

She smiles at him.

'The children's *grandparents* have been granted custody,' Greg says. 'And that is who will get it.'

'They're just in the car,' she says, standing her ground.

'Well, you'd better get them, hadn't you?'

'Whatever,' she says in a tone that implies it'll all have the same result. She turns and walks down the steps to the car.

Rachel looks up at Greg. 'What's wrong, Dad?'

'Nothing, pet.' His voice softens. 'It's OK. It's just that if your grandparents want to mind you, then they should come to collect you. That's all.'

In the car they're staring straight ahead, no doubt thinking they're the goodies, saving their grandchildren from a deranged parent. Hilary bends down as they lower the window. Then SuperBen steps out to the rescue. He walks tall and proud, Hilary following.

'Hello, Greg,' he says curtly. 'What seems to be the problem?'

'Don't start me off, Ben, or so help me . . . You wanted the children? Well, have the decency to come for them in person.'

'Children!' their grandfather calls. He swivels and starts down the steps, expecting them to follow. Far from the Pied Piper . . .

'Come on, guys,' says Hilary cheerfully, 'wait till you see what Gran and Grandad have got you. A hamster, a PlayStation . . .'

'A hamster?' asks Toby. 'Deadly.'

They chat together as we follow them to the car.

'You can pick a name for him,' says Hilary, 'and feed him and look after him.'

'*Really?*' he asks.

'Yeah.'

'*Deadly.*'

'It's really good to see you, Hilary,' says Rachel. 'Why didn't you ring us?'

Hilary makes a point of looking at me, then says to Rachel, 'I'll tell you later.' I bet she will.

Greg loads the suitcases into the boot, his face tight. Rachel and Toby stand obediently by the car as Hilary opens the back door. I hug each of them, not wanting to let go. But their arms slip away. Greg lowers himself to one knee and draws them to him, eyes tightly closed. He kisses them. 'I love you, OK? Just remember that. I love you. You'll be back soon. I promise.' Slowly, reluctantly, they climb in. Greg stoops down at the back window. Toby, closest to him, stares out, his hand on the glass, fingers splayed. I will him to lower it, but he doesn't. Rachel, at the far side, leans forward and looks towards her father. Hilary sits between the children. I want to punch that triumphant look right down her throat. Rachel is stretching out her hand and placing it on her brother's leg as the car pulls away from the kerb. Toby's crying, calling his dad. I bite my lip as they disappear up the avenue. I put my arm round Greg, and he pulls me into such a tight hug, I know it's for him as much as for me. For a long time, it is all we can do. There is nowhere we want to go, nothing we want to do, except be with them.

38

Greg heads for the punch bag. I make for the phone.

'Surely there's *something* we can do?' I ask Freda.

'Keep in touch with the children. Keep every prearranged phone call. And . . . try to be positive.'

'But can't we be doing *anything* to strengthen our case?'

'I'm working on it, Lucy. We've already lodged the replying affidavit. We've contacted Professor Power's office to request a report. And we're tracking down a suitable psychiatrist for the Section 47 Report. At this stage all you can do is wait.'

'If only we could see them. Two phone calls a day . . . It's just not enough. Even if we could write to them, send them little things, just to let them know we're thinking of them . . .'

'I'll talk to their solicitor.'

'Thanks, Freda.'

'You just have to be patient now, Lucy.'

So easy to say, so impossible to do.

We can't stay in. Everything reminds us of them. Their favourite foods are in the fridge. Rachel's pink Groovy Chick mug peeps out from the cupboard. Toby's frog Wellington boots lie abandoned in the cloakroom. Their clothes are entwined with ours in the washing machine. We have to get out. Get air. Keep moving. There is only one thing we can talk about, think about, only one thing that matters. We can't eat, sleep, work. We can't do anything, except regret. And that's too easy. Writing the book and sacking Hilary were mistakes, according to Greg. But I think our only mistake was

361

not explaining to Ben and Ruth about the illness once Greg was better. We regret in private. Doing so out loud only leads to argument.

Stunned questions are repeated over and over by my parents, Grace, Rob, Fint. Answering them is exhausting, depressing, humiliating and many other things, none of them good. Their fury is appreciated, but doesn't help. I think I must be Freda Patterson's most annoying client, ringing her constantly.

'Has Professor Power's report come in yet?' I ask, in yet another phone call to the poor woman. I'm going through the checklist I drew up at three this morning.

'No, not yet. If nothing's arrived by the end of the week, I'll have someone chase it up. These things take time. Psychiatrists are busy people. To them it's just paperwork.'

'Have you had any luck finding a psychiatrist for the Section 47 Report?'

'We're on to it. If I've any news, you'll be the first to know.'

'Thanks, Freda.' I know she thinks me obnoxious or highly stressed. Or both. But maybe she's used to this. Maybe everyone acts out of character if they think their family is under threat.

As soon as I hang up, I call Power to explain how much more than paperwork this is.

Short, awkward telephone conversations are all we have to keep close to Rachel and Toby. We live for them. As the minutes edge closer, we perch by the phone, silent, tense, hoping it will go well, that we won't mess up, say something to upset them, make them more homesick than they already are.

'So how are you?' Greg asks Toby. 'Did you have a good day?' Pause. 'Did you have a good day at school?'

362

It's so unnatural. Question after question just to get him to talk. It makes us sound hyper. And probably makes the children nervous. If only we could see them, be with them, we'd know what to say, what they'd need to hear. We'd sense it. We mightn't have to talk at all. But on the phone every word counts, every word has to be chosen carefully. And it isn't just the words. It's the tone. Too happy and they'll think we're fine without them. Too low, they'll worry.

'Hi, Rachel,' Greg says. As he listens, his smile disappears and he looks at me. 'It's a long story . . . We had our reasons, pet . . . I can't talk about them now, OK? You have to trust us on this, Rache.'

When he finishes the call, I ask what she said.

'She wanted to know why we'd stopped Hilary from seeing them.'

'Didn't waste much time, did she?'

Night-time calls are the worst: Toby is tired then and wants to come home. It makes me feel like marching over there, banging on the door and *demanding* them back. One night he is sad because Greg's not there to read his story. Greg decides to do it over the phone. He puts me on to Toby while he runs upstairs to get a book.

'Hey, Tobes. How's Hammy?' The one thing guaranteed to excite Toby is his new hamster.

'Great. He ackshilly yawned today. Like a baby. I could see all his teeth.'

'Wow.'

'Yeah, and he jumped off the first level of his cage and landed on the sawdust.'

'On purpose?'

'Yeah, 'cause he did it again. He keeps doing it. He's mad.'

Thank God he has something to care for and distract him, even though it is another notch in *their* belts. Greg's back. He begins a story about owl babies who miss their mummy. Halfway through, Greg stops.

'He hung up.'

'Ring them back.'

'Can I do that? The agreement is two phone calls. I don't want to risk it. You know what Ben's like.'

'You were cut off.'

'Still. I'm not sure I should risk it.'

'Why did he hang up?'

'I don't know.'

'He was probably tired,' I suggest.

'Or upset. I hadn't got to the bit where the mummy comes back.'

'He knows the story. He knows she comes back.'

'Well, then, maybe he was bored.'

'Or needed a pee. Who the hell knows? This is impossible.'

'Maybe Rachel will call us back?'

We wait. In vain.

Waiting for news from Freda turns out to be like waiting for a Dublin bus. Nothing, nothing, nothing. Then, ten days after the children have been taken, we receive three pieces of news together. One: Ben and Ruth have agreed to our posting things to the children. Two: Freda has found a suitable psychiatrist, available at short notice to do a Section 47 Report. Three: Professor Power's report has arrived. She's sending it over by courier.

Greg waits at the house while I rush out to buy bits and pieces for the children. I want to get a package out to them today by SwiftPost. For the first time since that yellow envelope arrived, I feel positive. Suddenly there's something I can do. I buy a calendar of *The Simpsons* for marking off the days and a new Game Boy game for Toby featuring one of his favourite cartoon characters, *SpongeBob SquarePants*, an appropriate nickname for his grandfather, I think. I buy the remaining five books in the *Lemony Snicket's* series. Rachel can read them to Toby. I get DVDs of the old Charlie Chaplin movies and the *Home Alone* series for Toby. I'm in the car before I notice the theme: vulnerable characters coping in adversity.

I rush back.

The report has arrived.

'Well?'

'It's fine. As long as they don't call for a Section 47 Report.'

'Can I've a look?'

'For what it's worth,' he says, gesturing to the table. His tone is defeatist. I look at him, hoping he isn't heading for a low. Then I realize that I was the same until the phone call from Freda.

To Whom It Concerns:

Greg Millar has been a patient of mine for twenty months, initially as an in-patient at St Martha's Hospital, where he was diagnosed with bipolar disorder, subsequently as an out-patient, regularly and consistently attending my clinics. Mr Millar's condition is extremely well-controlled on lithium, the standard treatment for bipolar disorder.

Prior to admission and treatment, Mr Millar experienced one episode of mania (which led to the dangerous driving incident outlined in the legal documentation) and one episode of severe depression, which was accompanied by suicidal urges. He was admitted to St Martha's Hospital at that point and commenced on treatment. Since then, for a period of almost two years, Mr Millar has been entirely free from episodes of either mania or depression. This bodes very well for the future.

Mr Millar has an excellent understanding of his condition

and the need to adhere to medication. He has returned to an excellent quality of life and is very well supported by his wife. He has published a well-respected and, I would say, widely helpful book on his experience of living with bipolar disorder. The extent and demands of such a project are indicative of his return to good health.

It is my professional opinion that Mr Millar is a highly respon-sible and loving father who does not present any danger what-soever to the children he has brought up single-handedly since the death of his first wife seven years ago. I recommend that Mr Millar be reunited with his children immediately. I am happy to give evidence to this effect.

Yours sincerely
Professor Con Power

'But that's great, Greg.'
'Better than nothing,' he says.

We send Rachel and Toby one new item each a day. It's a simple exercise, and I don't expect much from it. And so I'm surprised when it starts conversations flowing rather than jerking along. Every day there's something new to talk about – the surprise they've received. They *love* the fact that when they get in from school there's a package waiting, personally addressed to each of them. They've never received anything by post before. Now with every day comes something new to look forward to. It reminds them we're thinking of them, and that we care about them more than anyone else.

It's bizarre. We have to prepare for a court hearing that is, more than likely, going to be postponed. Freda sets up a meeting at her office, which turns out to be as austere and cold as her personality. Still, anything to get away from the house. She introduces us to our 'counsel'. Jonathan Deale is in his forties and already completely grey. He holds himself so erect and looks so sure of himself that, buck-naked, you'd guess his profession. He smells of cigarettes and mints. I've more confidence in Freda, and wish she could be the one to represent us in court. She's solid. And I trust her. But a barrister it has to be.

We're here to build an affidavit, a sworn written statement putting forward our side of the story. It's Jonathan Deale's job to write it. And so there are a lot of questions. When did Greg become high? Was I there then? Did I do anything to prevent the dangerous drive down the mountain? Did I know of the suicide plan? When was Greg diagnosed? How has he been since? Career-wise, what has he achieved since? Did Greg in any way ever hurt the children? On and on he goes. He looks edgy. I suspect he needs a fag. At this point I'm tempted to have one myself.

In between all the questions, we learn a few things. Some judges are more sympathetic than others. And it's potluck who we get. I can't understand how that's justice. There won't be a jury. Just a judge. Less intimidating, says Freda. Depending on the judge, I reply. I'm not sure what Greg's social standing and career success have to do with anything, but Jonathan points out that they should impress a judge. I will be sold as the 'stabilizing influence', regardless of the fact that I'm far less skilled as a guardian. Ultimately what this affidavit must show is that Greg's condition is well-controlled and that we, as a couple, are not only responsible and capable of looking after the children but are the best people to do so. From the questions Jonathan Deale has asked, it will take a small miracle to prove that.

The meeting lasts an hour but so much is covered it feels

longer. Just as we're finishing up, I start to worry about media attention. I can see the headline: BESTSELLING AUTHOR BATTLES TO KEEP CHILDREN.

'That won't happen,' reassures Freda. 'The parties in family law cases cannot be identified in order to protect the children.'

One small thing.

39

The morning of the hearing I open stinging eyes and panic. I'm not ready. I've wished for this day for three weeks. Now that it's here, I need more time. I dress in the clothes I laid out the night before. Like a criminal going to trial, I wear a formal suit. In the mirror my face looks drawn, older. In general I seem faded, as though I've lost substance. I also seem to have shrunk, not just lost weight but bulk. I mean, is it possible to lose *height*?

On the way to court I think of Rachel and Toby who will be at school, Toby not completely aware of the day's significance, Rachel knowing only too well. I pray that we will be able to cope with the outcome. I hope for a specific one. The children returned. Case dismissed. I close my eyes and will it. Before we've even made it to the city centre, I have to ask Greg to pull over. I open the door and empty the contents of my stomach on to the wet tarmac. Then I tuck my embarrassed head back into the car. In silence he hands me a tissue.

We meet Freda on the steps of the High Court. 'Couldn't be more prepared,' she says.

I've never been in the Four Courts before. I've never been in any court before. The place is buzzing. Important-looking people rushing here and there, black capes flapping in their slipstream. Those who aren't tearing around are huddled together in urgent discussion. Some wear wigs; many do not. All look confident, at home. Then there are people like us. All, regardless of status, are reduced to the same level here: at sea, nervous. To the lawyers we're today's business. Just another case. X versus Y. Soon to be replaced by more of the same.

In the courtroom lines and lines of mahogany benches have emptied after the day's business. Ours is the last case. There is nobody in court except the two legal teams. And, of course, us. Where are Ben and Ruth? They have to be here, don't they? I look at their barrister to see if he's concerned. He doesn't seem to be. Maybe they don't have to come. Maybe they're outside. Maybe they'll arrive any minute now. I look back at the door. Nothing. Then at their barrister again. He resembles a well-groomed terrier with pedigree notions. I slip my hand into Greg's. He gives it a quick squeeze. The judge arrives at his elevated mahogany bench and sits towering over us, Peter at the Gates of Heaven. Unlike Peter, though, he is human.

When their barrister stands, he calls for a postponement, pending a Section 47 Report, and all becomes clear. *No wonder they didn't show up. They knew it would be postponed. They knew they were in control. How can they do this? What have we ever done to them?* Tears blur my eyes. That's that. Rachel and Toby won't be coming home. What will we tell them? We said three weeks. We promised. I feel my stomach lurch. I have to leave. And fast. I make it to the toilet in time to retch over a not so clean bowl. Is this *justice*?

When I get back to the courtroom, Greg and Freda are waiting for me at the entrance. It's over.

'I'm sorry,' I say.

'Are you OK?' they ask together.

'Yes. Fine. I'm really sorry. What happened?'

'Jonathan sends his apologies. He had to dash off.'

I nod.

'That went as well as it could have,' she says.

'But they called for a Section 47 Report,' I say. 'Rachel and Toby aren't coming home.'

'That was a given, Lucy,' says Freda.

'I just hoped that maybe –'

'We have to be realistic. What we expected to happen, happened. On the upside, our psychiatrist will be doing the report.'

'Well done on that,' Greg says.

'That's what you're paying me for.'

'And you did well on the access,' he continues. 'Daily access for two hours a day, starting today.'

'Oh, thank God,' I say.

Freda says, 'I wanted to punch the air when the judge scolded them for denying access – you realize that that was, ever so slightly, good for us.'

I try to visualize her punching the air and just can't see it.

The downside, I discover, is that the court case has been postponed for another seven weeks to allow for the completion of the report. *Seven weeks.* How can it possibly take that long? We'll be apart, in total, two and a half months before the court case. Walking out, down the steps of the High Court, my legs are weak, my knees shaking. What will we tell them? How will they ever trust us again?

'Lucy, be realistic,' says Greg, walking back to the car. 'They were always going to ask for that report. We knew that. At least we controlled who does it. At least we have daily access.'

'I know. But seven weeks, Greg. Seven weeks.'

'We'll see them every day. And by God we'll make the most of it.'

'But what if Hilary uses this to tell them we lied, that they can't trust us? God knows what she's already said.'

'We'll have them for two hours every day, away from that environment. We have to make it work for us. If you're negative, they'll pick up on it. We have to be positive. They have to believe it's just a matter of time.'

'But it isn't. We've no guarantee we'll get them back. If that report goes against us, we'll never get them back.'

'Thinking like that won't get us anywhere. Lucy, you have to help me here, back me up, not bring me down.'

That's when I become aware of what I'm doing. I can't be like this. 'I'm sorry. You're right. I'm sorry.'

As we drive home, in a car that smells of vomit, I take stock of our changed situation after five minutes in court. It doesn't look good. Everything seems to hinge on a report by someone we don't know, someone who has access to all Greg's medical records. Who knows what Greg told Betty? Who knows how we will perform under scrutiny? It's all down to one report. If that goes against us, the children are gone.

Visits are to take place at Rob's apartment, with Rob as supervisor. Ben and Ruth are to drive the children there for six o'clock and collect them at eight. We get to the apartment for five. Rob's already there. Bang on six, they arrive. We rush to the door. Open it. They seem to have got bigger. They're wearing new clothes. Toby runs in, straight to his father, hugging him.

'Dad, Dad,' he says into his sweater. Greg lifts him up and hugs him tightly. He looks so happy. 'How's my man?'

'Where's Robert?' asks Ben.

'I'm here,' says Rob behind us, his voice and stance protective.

'Hi, Rob,' shouts Toby.

'Well, I'd better go,' says Ben.

'You do that.' Greg.

'Hi, Rachel,' I say.

'Hi, Lucy.' Her voice is flat.

'Honey,' says Greg. 'Come here, give your old man a hug.'

She walks to him obediently. Lets him hug her.

'How're you doing?' he asks.

'Fine.'

He pulls back, holds her out from him. 'Look at you. You're getting so grown up.'

She looks down.

'Have you eaten? We've just got in pizza and Coke.'

'A Margarita?' asks Toby.

'Of course. Come on, let's go into the kitchen.'

Rob has already begun to dish out the slices. He hands Rachel a plate.

'I'm not hungry,' she says.

Greg looks at me.

'Why don't we all sit down anyway,' I suggest.

At the table Rachel stares into her Coke as if it holds the future.

Greg and I have a slice to keep Toby company. For me it's an effort. I haven't been able to eat anything in three weeks. Rob disappears somewhere.

'Why didn't we go home?' asks Toby matter-of-factly, mouth full. 'Why did we come to Rob's?'

'Ah, well, we thought you'd like to see him too,' says Greg.

'That's not true,' snaps Rachel. 'We're here so Rob can watch you. Hilary told me.'

Greg and I exchange looks.

'What?' asks Toby, confused.

'Gran and Grandad just wanted Rob to be around, that's all.' Greg.

Rachel sighs loudly. Looks out the window.

Silence.

Then she glares at Greg. 'So what's the story? When are we coming home? The three weeks are up.'

'I'm sorry, Rachel, but this is the best we can do for the moment,' says her father.

Toby is eyeing him very carefully now.

'It'll be another few weeks –' Greg starts.

'Seven,' she says.

Toby puts down his triangle of pizza. 'Seven weeks? I thought you said three weeks.'

'Come here, Tobes.' Toby slides off his chair and goes to his father. Greg lifts him up on his lap. 'The three weeks was until we see each other. The three weeks are up, and here we are.'

'For *two hours*,' snaps Rachel.

'I thought we were coming home today,' Toby says, looking bewildered.

Has Hilary told Toby one thing and his sister another? Or maybe she's told Rachel the truth and kept it from him.

'I'm sorry, guys,' says Greg. 'I should have explained better.' He pauses. 'Today the judge was supposed to make his decision. But instead he picked out a doctor to do it, because he thinks the doctor would do a better job. The doctor wants to meet all of us, so he'll take a few weeks to make up his mind. That's why you have to stay where you are for the moment. But we explained to the judge that it would be unfair if you couldn't see Lucy and me until the doctor made his decision. The judge agreed. So every single day until the decision is made, we can all get together for two whole hours, here at Rob's.'

'Two hours isn't much,' says Rachel despondently.

'I know, but, when you think about it, it's pretty good. By the time you come home from school, do your homework and have dinner, it'll be time to come here.'

'I don't want to go back to Gran and Grandad. I don't want to. I want to go home,' says Toby.

'I know, sweetheart,' Greg says, kissing the top of his head, 'and you will soon. And until then we're going to see each other every single day. And then when it's all over, you can come home for good.'

'When?'

'As soon as we can. But we'll see you every day. And you'll still get the surprises in the post. And we're still going to ring you every morning before you go to school and every night before you go to bed.'

'I know how hard this is,' I say. 'But things went well for us in court today. And we're working so hard on this, your father and I. We will get you back. We just have to be patient, make the most of our time together, OK?'

'OK,' they both say.

'And don't always believe everything Hilary says,' adds Greg.

Rachel looks at him. Says nothing.

'Now let's go out and have some fun.'

40

We make a discovery. There isn't a lot you can do with children in the space of two hours, at six in the evening. There isn't enough time for a movie, once you travel there and back. We would take them for something to eat if they didn't arrive just after their dinner. They're too tired to do anything energetic. And anyway, though it's almost May, a chill remains in the air. Staying in brings its own problems. It reminds us of what's happening. Access visits. Conversations. Pressure to talk. We want to have fun for the time we're together, to relax, enjoy ourselves and forget that we'll be separating in two hours.

We find a solution. Rob invites people over. Nobody said he couldn't have guests when the access visits were taking place. First to come are my parents, who are so ecstatic to see the children that they almost suffocate them. Mum brings new stitching things for Rachel and gives her her first tapestry lesson. Dad brings a few bits and pieces that need fixing. Wouldn't surprise me if he broke them deliberately. The children do finally manage to lose themselves for two hours. Grace and the children visit next. So happy is Toby to see Shane and Jason that he calls them his cousins – 'Look, my cousins are here.'

Within a week Freda telephones. She wants to set up a meeting with the psychiatrist responsible for the Section 47 Report. He wants to interview Greg and me separately. We opt for the earliest possible date. Better to get it over with. The psychiatrist, a Dr Webb, also wants to attend one of the access visits. We delay that by a week, hoping that the children will be more comfortable with the visits by then. Rachel still has difficult moments.

For our interviews we attend his offices. On our way there we go through possible questions he might ask and try to come up with suitable answers. We stop when we begin to argue.

There's nothing fancy about Dr Webb's waiting room – straight-back chairs lining the walls, a table with a few outdated magazines, faded curtains. Greg, the chief specimen for analysis, is first up. I'm to follow an hour later. When the psychiatrist sticks his head round the door and calls Greg's name, I see that he bears an uncanny resemblance to Jeremy Irons. Stick-thin and that same tired, almost sad expression.

'Good luck,' I whisper to Greg. They introduce themselves and then the door closes. Alone in the waiting room, I'm restless. I get up, walk to the window, look out. A woman passing with a buggy is trying to control two toddlers. She is shouting. I come away. Switch off my mobile. Pick up a magazine, look at the pictures, nothing registering. I tell the secretary I'm popping out for a while. She asks me to be back ten minutes before my appointment. I walk the length of the street, arms folded, looking down at my feet. Up and down I go.

I'm back in the waiting room, standing by the window again, when the door opens. Greg looks neither shell-shocked nor devastated. Maybe it's not as bad as I thought. He winks. Dr Webb introduces himself, then leads me to his office. I'm surprised by how bright and cheery it is after the waiting room. His chair is pulled out to the side of his antique desk. Another faces it, which he offers to me.

'This must be a difficult time for you,' he says when we've settled.

'Yes.'

'Well,' he says smiling, 'I'll try to make this as painless as possible.'

I force a smile.

'Must have been quite a shock when you realized that the children's grandparents wanted custody?'

'Yes.'

'How did you feel about it?'

I'm obviously not going to get away with monosyllables. 'Well, I suppose, initially, I just couldn't believe it. I thought it must have been a mistake.'

'Why?'

'Greg's an amazing father. He'd never do anything to hurt Rachel or Toby. Never. It seemed incredible that just because he has a medical condition, that gave them the right to take his children from him. I didn't think something like that could happen in this country. Not today.'

'So he didn't drive down the side of a mountain and put your lives in danger?'

'Yes, he did. I'm not denying that. But that happened before Greg was diagnosed, before he was on medication. That was almost two years ago. He takes his lithium. His condition is well-controlled, now. We lead a normal, healthy life. He has never had a relapse. Not once. He is a good father. He is a *great* father.'

'So how do you think he came to be in this situation?'

'Greg wrote a book that he believed would help people. He spoke publicly about his experience to encourage others to get help, and to stress how important it is to stay on lithium. He didn't go on record as saying he was dangerous. He put it in context. He said, "This is what happened to me. And this is what I'm doing about it. And everything's OK now." He was open and honest about having manic depression, and some people just aren't mature enough to try to understand what that means. They're just afraid.' I stop, sorry to have let my anger show.

'Do you think that writing the book was a mistake?'

'No. I don't. It would be easy to blame the book. But that book needed to be written. For Greg. So he could stop hiding. So he could move on and start writing again. Initially, it wasn't meant for publication. It was for me. But I thought it would help other people. I thought it would do something for the stigma of mental illness. Greg's mother, who'd personally gained a lot from it, also urged him to publish it. He did it against his better judgement. *He* regrets it. I don't. Writing that book was good for us, and I'm sure it was good for a lot of people who read it. We just should have explained to Ben and Ruth about Greg's manic depression *before* it was published. That was our mistake.'

'Do you think it would have made a difference?'

I think about that. 'I don't actually know. I always assumed it would have. But maybe it wouldn't. Maybe they'd never have understood.'

'Do you think they're narrow-minded?'

Oh-oh. 'No. Probably not. But they haven't tried to understand. They could have called us up. We could have talked about it. But they didn't. They just came in, all guns blazing.'

'But surely they must have a genuine belief that the children are in danger? What about Greg's suicide plans?'

'Plan, singular. One plan. No attempt. And now just a bad memory of a time before medication. *Not* a good enough reason to take his children from him.'

'Did Greg tell you he was planning suicide?'

'No.'

He writes something.

I'm losing this. What can I say to convince him? 'Greg's never

379

been good enough for them, manic depression or no manic depression.'

'I'm sorry?' He looks up.

'He's never been good enough for Ben. He doesn't have the right background, didn't go to the right school.' I hesitate before saying, 'They blame him for killing their daughter.'

'Could you explain that last comment?'

'Catherine, Greg's wife, died when she was having Toby. They blame Greg for getting her pregnant.'

'They said that?'

'Well, no.' *Shit.* 'But they can't look him in the face.'

I wait for a reaction and get none. Blank.

'Rachel and Toby are their only link to their daughter, and nothing Greg does will ever be good enough for them.'

He raises his eyebrows.

'They have unrealistic expectations, that's all I'm saying.'

'I see.' Does he, though?

I twist my wedding ring. *What can I say to reassure him that Greg's not a danger?* 'Look. Greg would never do anything to hurt Rachel and Toby. If you knew him, you'd know that. If he ever planned suicide again, which I know he wouldn't, he would never expose the children to it. When he was ten, his father committed suicide. Greg found him. Believe me, there is *no way* Greg would do that to his children. No way. You have no idea how much he loves his kids.'

His pen is racing across the page. And I know I've blown it. I've just confirmed that Greg had suicidal tendencies despite witnessing his father's suicide. Suddenly I wish I hadn't been included in that court order. In trying to save Greg, I'm sinking him.

'Look. I know I'm making a mess of this. I don't know what to say. Greg's a great father. Manic depression doesn't change that. He loves his children and they love him. He's a better parent than I'll ever be. You're a psychiatrist. You know. Manic depression is just an illness. Greg takes his medication. He is totally committed to staying healthy. He loves his family. The children mean everything to him. They lost their mother. Please, don't let them lose their father.' *Oh, God, don't make me cry.*

'Would you like to stop for a while?' he asks, offering me a hankie from a box on his desk.

'I'm sorry. I'm no good at this. It's so difficult, so *stressful*. I'm not myself.'

'I understand,' he says, but adds, 'It must be difficult coping with bipolar disorder *and* children from another marriage.'

'They might not be my children, but I love Rachel and Toby as if they were.' I break down. It's official. I've sunk it. I just want to go. 'You know,' I say, my voice high, 'everything was just going so well. Everything had settled. We'd just become a proper family.' I sigh. 'Then this.'

I say nothing about Hilary. I can't see how it would help. It would just sound like some mad conspiracy theory. And talking about her would only make her more important. He might interview her. And who knows what she'd say.

At some point the interview ends. I feel drained, wrung out. I'd a job to do and I failed. No time to recover, though. We have to be at Rob's in forty minutes. If we're late, it'll be a mark against us.

'I blew it,' I say to Greg, in the car. 'I was too honest.'

We go through what I said.

'The only thing I wouldn't have brought up was about their never liking me. Look who you were talking to – a hospital consultant, a member of the establishment – the kind of person who believes in all that stuff about schools, addresses.'

I groan.

'Forget it, Luce. It doesn't matter.'

'No, you're right. I sounded paranoid. When I told him about their blaming you for Catherine's death, he asked me had they said anything. I had to say no.'

'Forget it. No point crucifying yourself.'

'But I brought up about your father's suicide –'

'Lucy, he has access to all my medical records. Whatever isn't in the book or the recording of the radio interview is in the records. He has access to anything he wants. He knows everything anyway. If you wanted to hide anything, you couldn't.'

'It's my fault. If I hadn't encouraged you to write that stupid book, none of this would have happened.'

'No. I've been thinking. We're in this because of fear. Don't blame the book or yourself. You loved me enough to coax me into writing it. And I wrote it out of love for you. It is a pure thing. I've stopped blaming it. We'll get Rachel and Toby back, Lucy. We will. That's all there is to it.'

41

Days pass but it feels like a whole season. Suddenly it's summer. Green everywhere. Daisies, dandelions, buttercups and clover appear among long and lush grass. The horse chestnut tree outside the house bursts into leaf as though someone has waved a magic wand. New ivy leaves on the back of the house are soft and glossy.

This is the time my sister makes a discovery.

She calls one evening and says to my husband, 'I'm taking her out.'

'Good,' Greg says. 'She could do with it.'

'Come on.' She takes my hand and pulls me away from the new Game Boy game I'm stuffing in an envelope for Toby.

'Greg, can you finish this, please?'

'Yep. Go. Go, go, go.'

'What's going on?' I ask, in the car.

'We're going to have a chat. And a walk.'

She drives to Killiney Hill. The evening is stretching out, heralding long summer days ahead.

'Right, let's go,' she says. 'Nothing like a bit of fresh air to clear the cobwebs.'

'Slow down,' I say. 'What's your hurry?'

She stops and waits. 'Sorry.'

We fall into an easy step, in the gentle shade of leafy trees. Sunlight dapples the forest floor where ferns are beginning to appear and unfurl. I love the way they tend this place, nurturing nature, taming it in places but mostly letting it be. I breathe it in, logging the memory for later. I circle my neck and shoulders, stretch my arms. Everything feels so stiff. But it's good to be out.

'You OK?'

'Yeah, just stressed.'

'You should eat, you know.'

'No point. Nothing stays down.'

'Why not?'

'I don't know. Stress, I suppose. The slightest thing has me throwing up. This is killing us, Grace.'

'Lucy, you shouldn't be vomiting. No matter how stressed. Loss of appetite yes, diarrhoea, yes. But not vomiting. How long has this been going on?'

'Since the court case.'

'But that's, what, three weeks ago? You must be exhausted.'

'Tell me about it.'

'You're out of breath. D'you want to sit down?'

'Yeah.' We've reached a bench on the side of the hill where the trees fall away below us, down to the sea. A plaque dedicates it to a couple, Pat and May, regulars probably. The water sparkles and the waves roll on to Killiney Beach.

'When was your last period?' she asks.

'Do you have to be so direct?'

'Yes. So, when?'

'I don't know. It hasn't exactly been top of my agenda.'

'Think back.'

I sigh. Shrug. All I know is that it hasn't yet been another thing to worry about since this all began. Then, I look at her, with sudden realization. It's been over six weeks.

'You're pregnant, Lucy.'

'You can tell by looking at me, can you?' This I don't need. Not now. Not in the middle of a custody battle. 'Stress can make your periods stop, can't it? Weight loss can. I'm about as stressed as a person can be and I've lost tons of weight. I'm not pregnant.'

'What's the big deal if you are?'

'I'll tell you what the big deal *would be* – if I was – which I'm not. It would just be disastrous. That's all there is to it. To announce that a baby's on its way, now of all times when Greg's children have been taken from us. What would they think? That we're replacing them? That we planned it? That we're getting on with life without them? I mean, having a baby at any time would be difficult, given that it'd be our first child together, and Rachel and Toby might feel left out. And it's not just the children. It's Greg. Childbirth killed Catherine. Like he'd really want to hear I was pregnant now. It would be a nightmare. You're wrong, Grace. I'm not pregnant. I'm stressed.'

'Stress doesn't lead to vomiting. And look at you, you're as white as a sheet.'

'I'm tired.'

'You're probably anaemic.'

As usual, Grace is right. After a week of procrastination and denial, I finally take the test she insisted on buying in a late-night pharmacy on the way home from Killiney. I should be happy. I should be ecstatic. A new life. A little person Greg and I have created together. Instead I'm afraid. I can't tell him. Not now. When I place my palm flat against my stomach it feels the same. I'll take another test.

Dr Webb arrives at Rob's before the children. We offer tea, coffee. He politely declines. I'm about to comment on the weather, but who am I fooling? Does anyone think I care? When the psychiatrist asks Greg about where he gets the plots for his Cooper books, I begin to relax. The doorbell rings. We both jump up. I laugh and make to sit back down, but Greg takes my hand and squeezes it. We go to the door together. On his way in, Toby trips, coming down hard on his knees. He starts to cry. In our nervousness, we all rush to comfort him. He wants Rachel. As I'm getting back up, I see that Dr Webb has come into the hall. He is standing quietly, observing the scene. Rob and I go to look for plasters. Good old Rob, making his presence felt, careful to ensure that his role of supervisor can't be questioned.

The incident sets the tone for the visit: Toby sniffling, bad form; Rachel comforting; Greg and I trying too hard to distract Toby. We sound unnatural, on edge. So much depends on this. Everything. We're so used to having people here during the visits – my parents, Grace and the children – that it feels stilted, especially with someone watching.

'Where are Joe and Eileen?' asks Toby. My parents.

'They couldn't come today, Toby, because Dr Webb was coming.'

He looks at Dr Webb. Frowns.

'What about Shane and Jase?'

'Not today, Tobes. Tomorrow, OK?'

'Who is he looking for?' Dr Webb quietly asks Greg.

'Lucy's family. They're close.'

He nods. Says nothing. Then he asks, 'Do you often have people attend the access visits?'

Shit.

'Just Lucy's parents, sister and her kids, occasionally. The distraction helps Rachel and Toby relax and forget that they'll have to go back in two hours.'

Dr Webb makes some notes. I imagine them: 'Parents uncomfortable being alone with children.'

*

Two more weeks crawl by. One to go. I'm in Get Smart one morning, trying to concentrate on work, when Greg rings.

'Freda called,' he says. 'She wants to see us in her office as soon as possible. The Section 47 Report has arrived.'

'Oh, God. Did she say if it was good or bad?'

'No.'

'She gave no hint?'

'No.'

'And you didn't ask?'

'No. I want us to hear it together. Will I pick you up or meet you there?'

'Pick me up.'

This is it. This is what the court will rely on. I shut down the computer, go in to Fint.

He hugs me. 'If that psychiatrist says anything other than that Rachel and Toby should come home, *he's* the one who needs his head examined.'

I circle his office chewing my fingers.

He opens his box of juggling balls. 'Here. Have these.'

'I can't juggle.'

'Learn.'

It takes Greg forty-five minutes to reach me. And that's fast. I'm at the door when he pulls up outside. Five minutes into the drive, he has to stop as, once again, I make my mark on the streets of Dublin.

'Lucy. You need a doctor. This can't go on. You have to get this checked out.'

'I'm fine. It's just nerves. Have we time to stop for mints?'

He smiles. 'The decision's made. Hurrying isn't going to change it.'

Freda's face doesn't give anything away as she hands us each a copy of the report. I look at Greg. Already he's started

387

reading. I'm not sure I can. I look down at the document in my shaking hands. I scan, trying to get an overall picture – a yes or a no. I'm too panicky. I have to start from the beginning.

To Whom It May Concern:

I have been asked to consult on the case of Franklin versus Millar and Arigho. To this effect, I have consulted Mr Greg Millar's medical notes and spoken in detail with his psychiatrist, Professor Con Power. I have interviewed the applicants, the respondents and Rachel Millar, aged twelve, who requested a hearing in a letter I enclose with this report. I have attended an access visit between the children, Rachel and Toby Millar, and their father, Greg Millar, and stepmother, Lucy Arigho. I have witnessed the children interact with their grandparents, Benjamin and Ruth Franklin. I have also spoken to the principal of the children's school. These are my findings.

First, it is clear to me that the children's primary bond is with their father. He has been a guardian to Rachel for twelve years and a sole guardian to both children for seven. It has been suggested that Mr Millar is a danger to his children on the basis of episodes that occurred in the past, relating to dangerous driving and suicidal urges. I have taken this claim very seriously in my examination of this case.

Having gone through Mr Millar's notes and consulted with Professor Power, his treating physician, I am in no doubt that these episodes were the direct result of bipolar disorder, a condition also known as manic depression, with which Mr Millar was diagnosed shortly after the aforementioned events took place. This is important, as it explains his behaviour. The crucial fact, though, in examining this case is not whether or not Mr Millar was a danger two years ago, prior to diagnosis, but whether or not he is a danger to his children now.

Mr Millar has, from the time of diagnosis, responded well to treatment. His improvement has been steady and lasting. He has had no relapses of either mania or depression since diagnosis. He has an excellent understanding of his condition and the need to adhere to medical treatment. When his treatment began to interfere with his work, though tempted, he did not discontinue it, appreciating as he did the importance of adherence. He worked with his physician at securing an alternative solution. This is very encouraging. Mr Millar has never missed a doctor's or outpatient appointment and has regularly attended anxiety management classes. He has a healthy lifestyle, and was happy and fulfilled prior to the removal of his children. He had taken up his career again, writing a book on his experience of bipolar disorder that has proven helpful not only to Mr Millar himself and his family but to many people who suffer from this often stigmatized illness. As Professor Power's report for this court points out, the completion of such a work is indicative of Mr Millar's sound mental health.

Mr Millar has the support of a wife who has helped him through the difficult times pre- and post-diagnosis. She has been and continues to be a solid support both generally and specifically with the children, whom she looked after while Mr Millar was in hospital. The environment from which the children have been removed was a healthy, caring and supportive one.

Given Mr Millar's medical history since diagnosis, in particular his adherence to treatment and his lack of relapse, his outlook is eminently positive. He has done exceptionally well. I am confident that he does not, in any way, pose a threat to his children. The enforced separation of the children from their father, rather, has proven detrimental to their mental health. Rachel and Toby Millar have already experienced traumatic and sudden separation with the death of their mother. To be so suddenly taken from their father, their stepmother, their home and routine has brought about a further unnecessary trauma. Toby, aged seven, began bedwetting as soon as he was removed from the home. At school he has become withdrawn. Rachel, aged twelve, has reacted with anger. Her behaviour has become uncooperative and troublesome at school. It is clear to me that both children are displaying signs of emotional distress.

Greg Millar has an eminently treatable psychiatric condition. It is my view that the very fact that it is psychiatric has worked against him. While the children's grandparents do not appear to bear Mr Millar any direct malice, it is hard to comprehend how they could deny him access to his children for a three-week period. This was most traumatic and unfortunate. I do not believe that the environment the children are currently in is best suited to their welfare. In the company of their grandparents Rachel and Toby are sullen, withdrawn and uncooperative. They are clearly unhappy. It is my view that continued separation would result in ongoing distress and psychological trauma. I strongly recommend that the court return Rachel and Toby Millar to the care of their father and stepmother immediately.

Yours sincerely
Dr Vincent Webb
Encl: photocopy of letter written by Rachel Millar to Dr Webb

I flick over immediately. There is Rachel's neat twelve-year-old handwriting.

Dear Dr Webb

I want to tell you how much Toby and me love our Dad and stepmum, Lucy. We love them so, so much. More than any-

thing. *We want to be together because we belong together.*
Gran and Granddad don't understand. I've told them that Dad
has bipolar disorder and he's fine now because he takes his
tablets. But they won't listen to me. No matter how many
times I tell them. Dad is still a good Dad. No, he's a great Dad.
He's our Dad. And we should be with him. Not over here.
I hate Hilary. It's all her fault. I thought she was my friend.
But she told Granddad lies about Dad. I heard her. She said
Dad was dangerous. She made stuff up about him. She made
Gran and Granddad afraid. I don't know why she did that. But
she did. She said that Lucy lies. But Lucy doesn't. <u>She</u> does. All
the time.

We love our Dad and Lucy and they love us. You're a doctor.
You know about dad's sickness. You know he's better now.
And he's just as good at being a Dad as he always was. And
we are a family. And families should be together especially if
they want to be. Please doctor Webb, make them send us back
to Dad and Lucy.

Some day when you're not too busy maybe you could come
and talk to me because I want to tell you all of this so you'll
believe me. Please Dr Webb. Children should have rights too.

Yours sinserely
Rachel Millar

I look up at Freda.
She's beaming back at me.
'Don't tell me there's a catch.'
She laughs. 'It would be difficult to overcome that evidence.'
When Greg and I eventually let each other go, he asks,
'What happens now?'
'We go to court,' she says. 'Armed and dangerous.' She
smiles again. She's actually quite pretty.

'Can I keep this?' I ask of Rachel's letter.

'Keep the whole thing. I've the original here.'

'Thanks.'

We shake her hand ferociously. 'Thank you. Thank you so much.'

Outside her closed door, I jump up and down, punching the air. Greg's laughing.

'We're going to get them back,' I say. 'I can feel it.'

'Just try and stop us.'

We practically run to the car. I think of Rachel and how she must have felt when she realized that Hilary wasn't her 'friend', alone and separated from us. She is such a strong kid. I'll tell her when I see her later. I open the car window. It seems like centuries since we were in that oppressive, hopeless situation, driving to Freda's preparing for the worst.

As soon as we get home, there's a message from Freda, asking us to call her. My heart stops. Not bad news. Not now. We're almost there.

Greg calls.

Ben and Ruth have been on to her. They want to meet us. Why? What does it mean?

'They want to talk,' she explains.

A bit late for that.

They arrive on their own, an hour and a half later. We show them, in silence, to the living room, without offering a drink.

'We had to talk to you.' Ben clears his throat. 'To apologize.'

Ruth hasn't raised her eyes since she sat down.

'It seems we've made a mistake,' he says.

I feel like shouting, *A mistake? Mistake? Is that what you call it? Have you any idea what you've done?*

'We saw the report this morning. We were very disturbed. We believed, we genuinely believed, the children were in danger.'

'You could have picked up the phone,' Greg says. 'You could have called me to discuss it. That would have been the decent thing to do.'

'I know. I know. And I apologize for that. It's just that you hadn't been entirely straight with us in the past.'

'And why might that be? You'd put anyone on the defensive, Ben – tearing over to France, questioning me as if I were on trial.'

'We were worried.'

'You were aggressive. There's always this underlying threat with you, Ben. You don't exactly get the best out of people.'

'That may be. Still, we took your word over Hilary's. Imagine our shock when we heard you on the radio confirming much of what she'd said. We assumed that there were other things you couldn't speak about publicly, other aspects . . . well, things Hilary relayed to us.'

'Like what, exactly?'

He pauses. 'Well, you never *hurt* the children, did you Greg?'

'What do you mean, *hit* them?'

'Well, yes.'

'No, Ben, I did not.' He is simmering with rage.

'But why would Hilary have lied to us?'

'The fact that we sacked her may have had something to do with it.'

Ben and Ruth look at each other.

Ruth says, 'We're so sorry, Greg, Lucy. We should have come to you. But we were afraid for the children. We felt we should act quickly. We really thought they were in danger. And when they came to stay, they seemed so unhappy; we thought it was because they'd been damaged. Toby wetting his bed, Rachel so rebellious –'

'They had been damaged,' Greg says slowly, angrily, 'by being taken away from their family.'

'I know, now, we were wrong,' says Ben. 'That's why we came to apologize. And to say that our solicitor is talking to yours about sorting all this out.'

'What do you mean?' asks Greg.

'It's clear that the children should be at home. I cannot apologize enough. We should have had more faith.'

That's it? I'm sorry? You can have them back now? After all the damage they've caused. I'm afraid that's not good enough. Before I can consider the consequences, I stand and let Ben have it. 'You say you care about the children. You almost ruined their lives! You put them through hell, snatching them from their home, their father, without warning, as if from a war zone. Rachel and Toby are *people*, with feelings, worries, insecurities. They are not commodities you can help yourself to. What gives you the right to play God over other people's lives? What makes you feel that only *you* can do right? When you heard Greg on the radio, you chose what you wanted to hear. You chose your reaction. And you chose not to pick up the phone. Well, maybe it's time you opened your eyes to the person Greg Millar is: a man who didn't have to rely on yuppie schools and cosy networks to make his way. A man whose wife broke his heart when she gambled with her own life and lost but a man who kept going because of his responsibilities to two children. A writer who is read by millions of people all over the world and who has managed not only to cope with manic depression but to be open about it.' *Where exactly am I going with this?* I think, my anger draining away. 'Anyway, I've said enough,' I finish up, catching Greg's bemused look. I sit down, wondering at myself.

'So when do we get them back?' asks Greg, trying not to smile at his clearly explosive wife.

'Today?' chokes Ben, hardly able to speak. 'Now, if that suits? Our solicitor is talking to yours, but he said we could start packing.'

'The sooner the better,' says Greg, standing.

When they're gone, he hugs me, then calls me an amoeba. I let him live when he says, 'But a lovely amoeba.'

An hour later the phone call comes. No, we'll collect them. Right away. We look at each other. Greg grabs the car keys, and we race to the door. And out. Greg breaks the speed limit. As we pull up in front of the house, they rush out. We leap from the car, leaving the doors open. Everyone's laughing. Except me. I'm crying. Hormones! Toby in his dad's arms. Rachel in mine.

'I'm so proud of you,' I say, over and over. 'I saw your brilliant letter, Rachel. It was so important in getting us all back together again.'

She looks doubtful but hopeful. 'Was it?'

'Ye-es.'

'Even though I'm only a kid?'

'Especially because you're a kid. And a clever one. You helped big time.'

No sign of Hilary. Not even peeping from an upstairs window. Maybe she's already left. I wonder what they said to her. For the first time since this whole thing began, I want to go home. With my family. *All five of us*, I think, resting my hand on my belly. I feel like telling them, right now. But no, I'll wait. For the perfect moment.

42

What I didn't know was that while my imperfect family was falling back into place, a perfect one was falling apart. The week after we've been reunited with the children and begin adoption proceedings, Grace asks to meet me for a drink.

'I'm leaving Kevin,' she announces.

I look at her, think of the boys. 'You *can't*.'

'I knew you'd say that.'

'Grace, things have been difficult between you, I know, but your relationship is so normal, so *stable* –'

'Too normal. Too stable. I can't breathe.'

'But you're the perfect couple –'

'That's the whole point. Nothing's perfect enough for Kevin. Not me. Not the kids. Not the house. I'm suffocating. *Dying*.'

I don't know what to say.

'He's so *controlling*.'

The bar boy comes to take our order. Ballygowan for me. Gin for Grace. Once we're alone again, she continues.

'Lucy, I've spent my life striving for perfection. I'm just so tired.' She looks it, I suddenly see – shoulders slumped, face drawn.

But I can't let her give up on her marriage. 'I thought you liked things perfect.'

'I thought I did too. Until I had kids. I don't want them to be like me, living up to other people's expectations. I want them to be kids, just plain, ordinary kids who're allowed to get grubby, messy, be crabby, noisy. But not Kevin. Oh, no.

He wants them seen, not heard, in bed before he gets home, squeaky clean. He wants performing robots. I want kids with jam on their faces, scuffed shoes, mismatched socks, long hair. I want them to breathe. *I* want to breathe. Do what I want, when I want. Go out at night instead of staying in listening to him give out about everyone else, so he can feel better about himself. I want to work. I want my life back. I'm tired of being held up to the light and checked for smudges. Have you any idea how hard it is to live with someone who always expects more?'

'Yes.' We grew up with the same mother.

The drinks arrive. I pay and tip the guy.

'You know the funny thing?' Grace asks. 'You always envied me, but now I envy you. You've always done your own thing, Lucy. Gone to art college. Married a man you loved despite the challenges, challenges you got through together. You're so *lucky*.'

'That's one way of looking at it.' It's the last thing I've ever felt.

'And what did I do? Married a man who was perfect on paper.'

'A lot of people think I've made a mistake.' All my old friends for starters.

'Well, they're wrong. Look how it's worked out. And d'you know why it has? Because you married for the right reason, the only reason to marry – love.'

'Grace, I'm sure there are millions of people who married for love, and it didn't work out. I'm sure there are millions of people who would advise *against* marrying for love.'

'I'll tell you what I'd advise against – marrying for logic. If I was to do it all again, I'd go for passion, risk, adventure.'

'It's not all it's cracked up to be.'

'If I stay in this marriage I'll die. I will. I'm not going to let it happen. I'm too young. The first time I saw you with Greg, I knew I'd made a mistake. I've never had that passion. There's no way Kevin and I would have got through what you have. We're together, but we're not a couple. He does his thing, and we fit around that. I need to be with a man who notices I'm there – for the right reasons. I need passion in my life. I need a life.'

I'm coming round.

'I've learned so much from what you've been through. When you asked for my help with Greg, I finally admitted to myself how much I miss being a doctor. It's what I've always wanted to do. And I'm not doing it. How could I have given that up? I wanted to be the perfect wife, the perfect mother. But I've only made myself unhappy. I can't hide it any more. I'm too tired. I'm thirty-four but I feel eighty-four. And that won't change unless I change it.' She takes a deep breath. 'I'm going to ask Kevin for a separation.'

'But what about Shane and Jason?'

She looks heartbroken. Her voice wobbles. 'My little men.' Her eyes well and she looks up and blinks fast to try to clear them. 'Shane and Jase are the only reason I've kept going so long. I don't want their mum to be separated from their dad. But their mum is me. And their dad is Kevin. And I can't do that any more. I want to be as fair as I can. I want to sit down and talk it through with Kevin. I want him to see them any time he likes. We can even live close to each other, if he wants that. I'll keep them in the same school, keep as much the same as I can . . .'

She is about to blow her family apart. 'What about counselling?'

She sighs deeply. 'Can counselling make you love a person you never did? Can counselling do anything when you've married the wrong man?'

'I can't believe you're going to do this.'

'I have to.'

I take her hand and squeeze it. 'Well, then, I'm here. Round the clock. You know that.' I smile.

'I know.'

I wait until Saturday, when everyone's sitting down to breakfast. I stand at the head of the table. Clear my throat.

'I've an announcement to make.'

They all look up, stop chewing, cereal bulging in Toby's cheeks.

'Well, I've two.' I pause. 'First, I just want to say how great it is for us all to be back together. We missed you two so much.'

'Hear, hear,' says Greg. I can tell he's wondering what the second announcement is.

'The second announcement is also a family announcement, which is why I'm telling everyone together. Because . . . we're going to have an addition to the family.' I raise my eyebrows and smile.

Greg pales.

Rachel says, 'Oh, my God.'

Toby asks, 'Are we getting a dog?'

Greg is over to me in a flash. 'Are you sure?' he asks.

I nod.

'Shouldn't you be sitting down?'

'What is it? What's going on?' asks Toby.

'Lucy's having a baby,' says Rachel, and I wonder if there's such a thing as a kid reading too much.

Toby's mouth drops open, as if to say, 'How did that happen?'

I smile at him. 'A baby brother or sister for you.'

I wait for someone to qualify that with the word 'half'.

Instead, Toby puts in a request. 'I want a brother.'

'And I want a sister,' says Rachel. A minor battle breaks out.

I turn to Greg. 'Are you OK with this?' I ask quietly.

He slips his arms around my waist. 'More than OK,' he says softly. 'Much, much more than OK.' He kisses my forehead and draws me into a hug. And, as I lean into him and let my body relax, over his shoulder I see, fluttering in through the open window, a bright blue butterfly. It makes its way towards us as though dancing on air, and I smile because it feels like a blessing: I have been given another future.

Acknowledgements

Editor Christie Hickman deserves applause as well as thanks for picking up this book and giving it a good shake. So, both to you.

Thanks to my mum, the wonderful Mary Deegan, who has read every incarnation of this story with the patience of, well, a mother, and whose words of encouragement did wonders for my stamina. Thanks, Mum.

Thank you Patricia Deevy and Michael McLoughlin of Penguin Ireland for your faith in *Love Comes Tumbling* and for striving to make it the best it can be. Grateful thanks to Donna Poppy for eagle-eyed copy editing. And to Stephen Marking – for the wonderful cover. To all at Penguin Ireland for your support, thank you.

Many thanks to my agent, Faith O'Grady, for dealing so gracefully with the business side of things.

In terms of research, this was a busy book. I'd like to thank Hélène Coffey for guidance on matters legal and for her unwavering patience in answering query after query – and then queries on the queries. And thank you Ann Marie Burke for steering me in Hélène's direction. On matters medical, big thank yous to Professor Patricia Casey and Julie Healy. For insight into step-parenting issues, I have many to thank, particularly Eleanor Coughlan. Thank you Diane Gray for sharing with me your experience of losing a parent at a young age and for becoming part of our family, for however short a while. To Quentin Fottrell, many thanks for your help with Fint.

Thank you Reiko Hiruma for correcting my Japanese. And Leslie Williams for culinary advice.

Thanks to all who read and commented on the manuscript – Amanda Byrne, Mary Burnham, Sara Corcoran, Fiona Concannon, Laura Concannon, Amanda Dalton, Laura Egar, Rosemarie Egar, Dee Flynn and Carol Leland. To Rory Hafford, Katherine O'Donnell and my dad, Paddy Deegan, for helping in the search for a title. To Ann Webster Clarke and Gerry Clarke for your encouragement and support.

Thanks to all in the book trade who have got behind me from the word go. It is more than appreciated. To my friends in Sandycove who have been so loyal and lovely in their support, thank you. Thank you, readers, for buying my books. I hope you keep enjoying them.

And a special thank you to my family, Joe, Aimée and Alex, for your faith, humour and inspiration. Love you always.